# DRAWN IN BLOOD

## THE ELLESMERE SAGA
### BOOK TWO

BRITTNEY BREWER

*For Braxton-*

*Because I know you will always find me.*
*I love you.*

To all of the children that left their windows open for
Peter Pan,
Waited for their letter to Hogwarts,
Searched for a closet to Narnia,
And waited for a satyr to take them to Camp Half-Blood…

Welcome back.

# PLAYLIST

Would That I- *Hozier* ♥
Beautiful Things- *Benson Boone* ♥
In The Stars- *Benson Boone* ♥
To Love Someone- *Benson Boone* ♥
Hazel Eyes- *Sabrina Jordan* ♥
The Water Is Fine- *Chloe Ament* ♥
Runaway- *AURORA* ♥
Bones in the Ground - *Alex Roma* ♥
Who's Afraid of Little Old Me?- *Taylor Swift* ♥
The Prophecy- *Taylor Swift* ♥
Invisible String- *Taylor Swift* ♥
In a Week- *Hozier* ♥
Wild Things- *Lø Spirit* ♥
The Bolter- *Taylor Swift* ♥
The Albatross- *Taylor Swift* ♥
No One- *Aly & AJ* ♥

# CONTENTS

CHAPTER 1

# BELIEVE NOTHING THAT YOU HEAR

T he summer breeze whipped through Ember's fiery
red braid as she felt the board under her feet glide
across the air. Maia flanked her to the right, flapping
her wings furiously as she dipped and twirled with the wind,
and Fen was to her left, letting out a barking laugh as he sped
faster. They were quickly approaching Dranganir—a large
rock formation with the center carved out by the wind and
waves. Ember whipped her head to the side and shot a grin
at Fen.

"Meet you at the top," she shouted over the rushing wind.

The little draic, who was now closer to Maeve's Cat Sidhe
Della's size, let out a playful growl and barreled forward,
Ember still hot on her heels. Fen raced forward and let out a
howl as he shot ahead. Instead of slowing to avoid the
monstrous formation, Ember carefully leaned her body
forward, bracing her hands on the edge as she curled her
fingers tightly over the smooth surface. She sped toward the
opening, feeling the salt spray against her cheeks as she dipped
closer to the water.

The sun was still rising ahead of her, bathing the sea in
apricot and violet. After the school year ended, Eira and Otto

had surprised her with an Airwave of her very own. From the moment she got it, she had spent every early summer morning on it, racing Maia across the waves as they licked at her shoes. The days were long and sweet, and she spent every moment that she could on the water.

She always thought she should be afraid of the ocean, that it should've brought back memories of losing her parents, but it didn't. She felt them there, in the way the waves crashed against the rocks and barreled toward the shore. She could feel her mother running her hands through her hair in the wind and could hear her father's laughter in the water that brushed her fingertips. They were there, immortalized. Njord reminded her every chance he got.

The summer solstice had already come and gone, and the start of their second year was quickly approaching. The events of the previous year felt like a distant memory now. She had finally settled into life at the Kitts', spending cozy evenings by the fire playing card games with Maeve or reading a book while Eira patched another hole in the newly seven-year-old's jumper. It felt like home, somewhere familiar and exciting all at once. Her days were spent with Killian and Fen, trying to talk them off the edge of whatever cliff they felt so inclined to throw themselves off that day. She rolled her eyes at their jokes, but secretly loved every moment of it.

Though, she would never let Killian hear her say that.

"Come on, Em!" Fen shouted from the top of the rock formation, waving his arms wildly in the air.

Ember grinned and waved back at him, slowing to a stop midair before looking back toward Maia, who was flying in circles beside her. "One more time?" she whispered, but she didn't wait for a response. She shot straight up into the air, climbing higher and higher as the wind hit her cheeks and sucked the breath out of her lungs. Just when she thought she couldn't get any closer to the clouds, she stopped. Carefully bending over, she unhooked her shoes from her board. She spread her arms out to the side and closed her eyes, listening to the god of the wind and sea whisper in her ear. She sucked in a breath and then fell backwards, plummeting toward the water below.

She fell faster and faster, adrenaline pumping through her veins as she neared the icy water. Just before she hit the waves, she flipped her body around and felt her AirWave firmly beneath her feet. She crouched as it zipped forward, leaning her body back and slowing herself to a stop. She jumped off the board, stumbling for just a moment as her feet sank into the soft grass at the top of Dragnanir.

"That was the smoothest one yet." Fen smiled as they sat on the grass, legs hanging over the edge of the rock.

"Do you really have such little faith in me, Fenrir?" Ember smirked as Maia purred at her side, sage wings folded against her back.

"You're getting faster too. How long was that, like three seconds?" Fen laughed, wiping the sweat from his brow.

"You're so invested in me making the team this year I thought you would have a timer." Ember grinned. She was trying out for Rukr this fall, and Fen had made it a point to train her all summer long.

"You think breakfast is ready yet?" Fen asked, as he leaned back on his elbows and closed his eyes, the sun warming his tan skin. "She was up making all of your favorites when I went out to take care of Arlo—bacon and potato farls with eggs and sausage…"

Ember could've sworn she saw him wipe drool off his chin.

"It's not your birthday, right?"

Ember laughed, her stomach now growling as she realized how hungry she was. To be frank, everything Eira made was her favorite. She couldn't think of a single thing that had ever been placed on the table that she hadn't devoured without a second thought.

3

"Honestly, Fen, do you ever think of anything *other* than food?"

"Sure," he shrugged, "I sleep for like ten hours a night."

Ember shook her head with a laugh. "Well, maybe we should head home and see what the special occasion is?"

THE PAIR KICKED off their shoes as they entered the mudroom, flinging sand all over the floor as they went. The smell of bacon, eggs, and potatoes greeted them as they walked into the kitchen and mugs of hot tea sat waiting on the table to their left.

"If the pair of you track sand into my kitchen again, you'll be mopping the floors for the next week," Eira scolded, but the shadow of a smile played at the corner of her mouth. Ember's heart was fit to burst as she nestled herself in the breakfast nook. It was a morning like every other she had that summer, but she still found herself thinking about how truly grateful she was for the family that she had.

The family that chose her a year ago and had continued to choose her every day since.

Otto's gruff laugh boomed as the front door slammed closed, and he shuffled into the kitchen, Maeve giggling beside him as she clung to his leg.

"Good morning, my loves." Otto smiled as he kissed his wife on the head and pried the giggling seven-year-old off his calf, sticking her in her chair at the table. "What's the occasion?"

"Can't I just love on my family with a filling breakfast?" Eira asked, as she used her spatula to point to the mountains of food piled on the kitchen counter.

"You," Otto smiled as he kissed his wife's cheek, "are a terrible liar, Mrs. Kitt."

Fen groaned as he buried his head in his hands, but Ember couldn't help but smile. The love that lived in their home used to overwhelm her, used to suffocate her and threaten to swallow her whole. But now? Now she couldn't get enough of it.

"So, what are your plans today?" Otto asked, as he sipped his tea.

"We were thinking about going to the Rukr pitch to practice later," Fen said through bites of bacon and eggs. "Professor Bjorn said the wards would be open for students, and Em needs a lot more practice at this point."

Ember kicked his shin under the table, and he proceeded to choke on the too-large bite of eggs he had just stuck in his mouth.

"You're trying out this year?" Eira asked from the kitchen.

"I think so." Ember shrugged with a laugh. "I'm just not sure if I could handle taking orders from Killian if we're being honest."

Killian Vargr had been made Captain of the Rukr team, the first time a second year had ever been given that honor, and it did nothing to help his already inflated ego. He strutted around the orchard with his AirWave tucked under his arm, barking orders to Fen and Ember, and it took all her willpower not to peg him with the apples she was hovering beside at the top of tree.

"I'll run and change and meet you at the door!" Fen almost shouted, as he shoved away from the table and made his way to the stairs.

"Actually," Eira interrupted, as she grabbed him by the shoulder and redirected him back into the kitchen, "we have something we need to talk to you all about, as a family."

Ember furrowed her brow as she chewed the last bite of her breakfast. Otto and Eira looked happy, ecstatic even, but their words coiled around the knot that was quickly forming in her stomach.

Maybe such a heavy breakfast wasn't a good idea.

Fen made his way slowly back to his seat and slumped down, arms crossed over his chest as he tapped his foot impatiently. Eira sat beside Otto, tightly intertwining her small fingers in his.

"Ember," Eira began, voice shaking slightly, "we—"

A bright ball of red flew through the kitchen and hovered ominously over the top of the table. Ember's mouth hung open, and her eyes grew wide as she felt the magic buzz around it, and then a voice echoed through the tiny space.

*"Chief Thorsten has called a town meeting at twelve o'clock this afternoon. Attendance of all residents on Ellesmere Island is mandatory. Please arrive in Sigurvik at town hall promptly. Thank you."*

And then the ball of light, along with the booming voice, disappeared into a cloud of smoke. The table stayed silent only for a moment before Otto chuckled and finished the last sip of his tea.

"I suppose that solidifies our afternoon plans." He smirked as he pushed himself up from the table. "Let's go find you a clean jumper, Maevie."

"We'll talk more when we get home." Eira smiled as she squeezed Ember's hand. "Both of you better go get cleaned up. We'll need to leave in just a few minutes."

Ember nodded as she left the kitchen and climbed the stairs up to her room, the last door on the left. Worry ate away at her as she changed her clothes and re-braided her hair. In the last year she had been on the island, she hadn't so much as seen Chief Thornsten walk down the street, let alone go to a mandatory town meeting. Something told her this wasn't going to be pleasant.

"Honestly, Fen, stop moving your leg so much," Ember scolded, as she elbowed him in the ribs. Fen slowed his leg to a gentle bounce but didn't stop fidgeting completely. The family sat in the drafty room in town hall and waited patiently for Chief Thornsten to come address the restless crowd. Eira, Otto, and Maeve sat near the front, Ember and Fen toward the back.

"Honestly, could he take any longer?" Fen grumbled. "I have better things to do than waste my Saturday in this bloody room. What could be so important?"

Ember shrugged. "How many times have you been to one of these?"

"I can think of exactly zero," a voice about her said. "Howeyah, Starshine?"

Ember rolled her eyes as Killian took the seat to her right and smirked. The sleeves of his white button up were rolled to his elbow and his black slacks looked freshly pressed. He brushed away the white-blond hair that fell in his charcoal eyes and gave her a playful grin.

"Maybe the elves are finally rebelling." Fen shrugged as he pushed his glasses up the bridge of his nose.

"Maybe the British are invading again," Killian joked.

"With their flimsy little wands?" Fen laughed as he leaned across Ember to talk to Killian. "They'd hardly stand a chance."

"You two are insufferable," Ember sighed, as she shoved them apart. "Can't you be serious for five minutes?"

The room quickly grew silent as a tall man with slicked back, onyx hair stepped to the front of the room. He straightened his coat, running his hand along his hair. Killian scoffed under his breath and leaned over to whisper in Ember's ear.

"Some chief. More worried about his hair than his people if you ask me."

Ember rolled her eyes. "You're one to talk, Killian Vargr."

"Thank you all for coming on such short notice," the chief's voice boomed, as he smoothed the sleeves of his ivory shirt. "I imagine you all have things to do this weekend, so I'll make this as brief as possible. We have reason to believe that the children on Ellesmere are in grave danger."

*Bloody hell.*

Whispers carried across the small hall, and Ember felt both the boys that flanked her stiffen. Fen instinctively reached for her hand, and Ember noticed Killian's grip tighten on his knee. His eyes narrowed, and his throat bobbed as he straightened his back.

"We have had three children go missing over the last month," Chief Thornsten continued. "We have it on good authority that they have been taken by the Fae. For what reason, we are still unsure, but rest assured, we are working day and night to bring our children home and make our island safe again."

"Will it be safe for the children to return to Heksheim?" a voice said from the crowd.

"So far, they are only targeting children who are not of age yet, but that doesn't mean everyone shouldn't be aware of their surroundings."

Ember felt Fen's grip tighten around her hand, and his other gripped his knee. Her heart beat steadily in her throat as she squeezed his hand a little tighter.

*Maeve.*

"Travel in groups when possible, and try not to leave children home alone if it isn't absolutely necessary. If they're able, have your older children travel in groups to Heksheim as well. We can't rule anything out quite yet. We are encouraging all parents to keep their young at home," the chief swept his gaze over the crowd, "especially after dark. Wards have been heavily reinforced around Heksheim, as well as across the perimeter of the Dark Forest. We are asking you to do your part to keep our island and our young safe. Does anyone have any questions?"

Quiet murmurs traveled across the room as Chief Thornsten answered each question one by one. The weight of the news settled on the room like a wool blanket, the air heavy.

"It doesn't make sense," Killian mumbled, as he shoved his hands in his pockets, leaning back in his chair.

"What doesn't?" Ember replied.

"The weans goin' missin'," he whispered.

"Children go missing all the time," Ember replied, as she squeezed Fen's hand a final time before dropping it. "It's unfortunate, but not unheard of."

"Not on Ellesmere," Killian said, as he shook his head. "I've never heard of it happening here, not in numbers like this. And they're always found within a day or two uninjured."

Ember chewed her bottom lip. "*Could* it be the Fae?" she asked, wincing as she thought about Asteria.

"The Fae are a proud people," Killian replied. "They would never jeopardize the treaty like this. Not by taking children."

The chief continued to answer questions as people began filing out of the room, soft whispers leaving a trail of worry as they went. The boys followed Ember out the door and into the warm August air, Fen shuffling his feet as blew out a deep breath.

"But Chief Thornsten said—"

"I heard what he said," Killian snapped, "but that doesn't make it the truth."

Ember furrowed her brow. "Are you saying he's lying? If the Fae aren't taking the kids, who is?"

Killian ran his fingers through his hair. "I don't know," he sighed, "but I do know one thing. 'Believe nothing that you hear and only half of what you see.'"

Ember let out a laugh of disbelief. "You're quoting Poe?"

Killian smiled, reaching a hand up as if to brush the back of it against her cheek before quickly pulling it away. "Dark days are ahead, Starshine," he breathed. "Who better to usher them in?"

EMBER GENTLY RUBBED Maia's snout as she laid against her side, feet stretched out in the grass as the sun warmed her face. Small fish splashed in the pond in front of her, birds chirping as Della tried to catch a mid-afternoon snack. Maeve squealed beside her as Della sent water flying through the air.

"Control your cat, Maeve," Fen grumbled, as he polished his AirWave, wiping away the droplets of water splattered across the board. "I'm going to have to start over now!"

Ember blew a stray hair from her face as she rolled her eyes. "Maybe you should do that somewhere that isn't beside a body of water," she laughed, as she sat up and began digging through the picnic basket Eira had packed for them.

"I should be able to enjoy this beautiful weather without being assaulted by my little sister's ridiculous cat," Fen snapped, glaring toward the Cat Sidhe now swishing its tail back and forth as it watched him. Fen stuck out his tongue as he narrowed his eyes further. Maeve sighed as she sank into the grass at the edge of the pond, crossing her arms tightly over her chest.

"This is boring," she whined, as she let her bare feet hang in the water. "Can't I go play with Kady?"

Kady O'Malley, the youngest of the O'Malley children, lived a few miles down the road and was Maeve's best friend. She has spent most of the summer glued to the little girl's side, and they had a tendency to go back and forth between their houses, rarely spending more than a few nights apart.

"No," Fen snapped, as he whipped his head around, chest rising rapidly as he stared his little sister down, "You are not going to Kady's, or into town, or to the beach, or anywhere else unless you're with me and Ember, or Mum and Dad."

"But it's not that far!" Maeve argued, narrowing her eyes toward her brother. "I'll be back before supper, and Mum and Dad will never know— "

"Drop it, Maeve," Fen hissed, as he focused on his board again. "I'll tie you to the tree if I have to, but you aren't going anywhere."

Della seemed to straighten at that, slowly placing herself in front of Maeve. Ember shook her head as she sighed. Fen was scared, and sometimes fear made people do stupid things, like threaten to tie their sister to a tree.

"I can't get this scratch off," Fen mumbled, as tears pooled on his lower lash. He ran the cloth over the same spot over and over again, bottom lip wobbling as he shook his head. "It's ruined. I can't fix it." Tears slipped down his cheeks as he tossed the board in front of him, wringing his hands together as he bit his bottom lip. "I can't fix it," he whispered.

Ember slid beside him, nudging him in the arm as she slid her hand into his and squeezed. The tether at her sternum thrummed, her magic reaching out to his as she sat in silence with him.

"It will be okay," she whispered, as his breathing began to slow. "We will figure this out together."

She wasn't talking about the board.

THE HOUSE SMELLED of warm stew and soda bread when they walked into the kitchen later that evening. The floor was bathed in late summer sun, and Ember felt the warmth of home engulf her once again.

*My home.*

The realization that she had a home didn't hit her the way she expected it to. She always thought it would feel like a storm—something loud and impossible to ignore that left her ears ringing and her pulse racing. A single moment in time that would stand out, forever etched in her memory. The final puzzle piece shifting into place.

But it wasn't like that, not at all. It was slow and steady. It was like going to bed on a cold winter night and waking up to a blanket of snow the next morning. It was like waking up one morning and realizing the shoes you wore the day before were too snug now. Something that happened without notice but happened, nonetheless.

"Em, time for supper!" Fen shouted from the table, pulling out his chair and quickly plopping himself into it.

Ember gave Eira a smile, something she found herself doing more often now than ever before, as she walked past her and into the dining room. Maeve was already talking animatedly about her day while simultaneously inhaling the fresh bread that was waiting in the middle of the table. Eira's smile was turned downward as she entered the room with the stew hovering beside her. She hadn't spoken much since returning home from the town meeting, but Ember could tell with the way her eyes flitted between the three of them that Chief Thornsten's words weighed heavy on her heart.

"Can we still go to Heksheim to practice tonight?" Fen asked, as he shoveled stew into his mouth with a fervor. "The sun shouldn't set for another few hour, and we'll be home before—"

"No," Eira cut in. "Absolutely not."

Fen let out a huff. "But, Mum, you said—"

"I *said* no, Fenrir."

"Don't argue with your mum," Otto said before Fen could argue any further.

"Those poor children," Eira sniffled, as she shook her head and took a shaky breath. "I can't be with you every moment, but I won't let you wander off to find danger on your own."

"Mum, I think we can handle ourselves for the—" Fen began, but quickly snapped his mouth shut as Eira's eyes bore into him.

And that was the end of that.

Supper was quiet for the most part, everyone seeming to be lost in their own thoughts, forgetting the others were there entirely. It wasn't until the last bites of stew were being eaten, that a lightbulb flashed on in Ember's head.

"Wasn't there something you needed to talk to me about?" she asked, as she looked between Eira and Otto. The couple exchanged a knowing glance, and Otto pushed away from the table and quickly left the room. Eira's eyes lit up as they met with Ember's, and she wiped a single tear away that was starting to fall down her cheek. Otto quickly re-entered the dining room and sat back in his seat, laying a sheet of paper on the table in front of him.

"Ember, we love you so much," Eira whispered, as she reached across the table to grab her hand. "We have loved you since the day we met you. You have always been ours."

Ember's heart raced in her chest, and it felt like there was cotton lodged in her throat. She quickly wiped away the tear forming on her bottom lash and gripped her hands together.

*Is this actually happening?*

Something like fear ripped through her chest as every ending with every family she had ever been with tumbled through her mind. Had she become too much? Did they need to focus on protecting Fen and Maeve and not have time for her anymore? Had they finally had enough?

Otto put an arm over his wife's shoulder. "We have a sort of back-to-school gift for you, If you'll have it." He pushed the folded paper across the table and under Ember's tightly clenched fists. She didn't realize just how tight she was holding them until she felt Fen's hands lay on top and give her a gentle squeeze. His smiled calmed her like nothing she had ever felt. Even when everything in her felt turbulent and out of control, he was there to calm the waters. Like a lighthouse in the middle of a hurricane.

Ember unfolded the paper and read it quietly to herself, willing her hands to stop shaking. After a few moments, she looked up at Eira and Otto's expectant eyes and felt her breath hitch in her chest. "What is this," she whispered, as she bit her bottom lip. Her heart beat rapidly in her throat. She knew what it was, but she needed to hear them say it—needed to hear the words out loud.

Eira gave her a smile as tears flowed freely down her cheeks. "We're asking if you would give us the honor of adopting you, Ember Lothbrok."

Ember was certain the world had stopped turning. She had thought about this moment for the last year—the moment she truly became theirs—but it didn't feel like she expected, not really. She expected excitement, insurmountable joy that she could barely contain, but there was something else there, something that she hadn't expected to feel tugging at her chest. Her throat tightened as she tried to swallow. It was a feeling she had pushed away, something she had tried not to feel for months.

It felt like grief.

She shook the thought away quickly, and it wasn't until Maeve squealed and ran around the table, wrapping her in a giant hug, that she remembered to breathe. Eira's face fell, ever so slightly, and Ember tried to put on a smile for her.

"Thank you so much," she replied, as her hands shook, trying not to look at the paper again. "Is it something I can think about?" She didn't know why she needed to think about it. She should be ecstatic. She should be jumping up and down with joy at the thought of having a real family again, a permanent family. It was all she had wanted since she was six years old.

"Of course, Mo Chroí." Otto smiled as he squeezed his wife's hand. "Take all the time you need."

Ember nodded, forcing a smile as she swallowed the lump in her throat. What was wrong with her? What was there to think about? She should just say yes.

But there was that feeling, that tug in her stomach that reminded her that she wasn't a Kitt, no matter how well she might fit into their home. And if she agreed to be adopted, if she agreed to be a part of their family forever, how long would it take for her to forget who she was? Who her parents were? It felt like she was replacing them—betraying them. How could she let them go so permanently?

She plastered on a fake smile as everyone chattered around her, but she couldn't stop the dread pooling in her stomach. Fen gave her a half smile, but she could see the worry playing behind his eyes. No matter what she decided, someone was going to get hurt.

Could she really handle the grief of losing who she was all over again?

# CHAPTER 2
# WELCOME HOME

September was quickly becoming Ember's favorite month of the year. The morning air smelled like lavender and fresh baked bread as she walked the winding path up to Heksheim, and she couldn't help but breathe a deep sigh of relief as she felt the wards bend to accept her on the grounds, the hair on her arms standing on end as the magic brushed against her. There were only a handful of places on the planet that truly felt like home, and Heksheim would always be one of them. But even still, as peaceful as the school grounds felt, something ominous lingered in the air. Everything was the same, but at the same time, everything felt very, very different.

Something was changing.

"Everything alright, Starshine?" Killian whispered, as he walked up beside her and elbowed her in the arm.

"Just thinking about how much has changed." She breathed as she hooked arms with him and the other with Fen.

"All the important stuff is still the same." He shrugged. "Me, you, Fen, as long as we have each other nothing else matters."

"How sentimental," Fen laughed, as he dragged Ember toward the open doors. "Maybe you should prepare a speech for Em's adoption too."

Ember's heart sank, guilt heating her stomach and coiling it into knots.

"Shove off, Kitt," Killian huffed.

The trio made their way into the school, and Ember breathed in the sweet smell of mahogany and oak as they followed the crowd of children into the large hall. Everyone was gathering around the circular tables and chatting animatedly about their summer vacation. They made their way to what had now become their table and took their seats. The chair to Ember's right was empty, just like it had been since Rowan had turned up "missing" the year before. It didn't weigh as heavily on her now, but there were still pangs of grief that flitted through her chest when she thought about the girl who had gotten her through her first year in the magical school.

"Is this seat taken?" a small voice rang out from behind her. Ember turned her head to see bright blue eyes staring just past her head. Platinum hair fell across her bronze shoulders, and bells jingled from her wrists and feet as she moved.

"Oh, hi, Odette." Ember smiled. "Have a seat. How was your summer?"

Odette nodded with a smile as she gently sat at the round table, laying her bag on the ground next to her, "Spent most of it in the garden with my gran. It was very eventful," she chimed with a small smile. "I have a feeling this year will be as well."

"Were your parents on holiday?" Ember asked, as she fiddled with the pen she had pulled out of her bag.

"I lost my da' during the uprising," she whispered, a little softer than normal, "then my mum disappeared when I was a wean. It's just me and my grandparents now."

"Uprising?" Ember replied, furrowing her brow.

"Aye," Fen nodded, "happened when I was just a baby. A few rogue Fae decided they didn't like the rules anymore and took the law into their own hands."

"Da' fought to protect us," Odette nodded. "Perhaps it won't all be in vain."

Killian raised a brow as he elbowed Fen in the ribs, almost making him topple out of his chair. Ember shot them both a glare as they began to whisper amongst themselves, but before she could reach over and smack both over the back of the head, a loud voice rang out from the front of the hall.

"Please take your seats," Professor Moran announced, as she smoothed the sleeves of her blouse. Instead of a slicked back bun this year, tight coils formed a golden-brown halo around her head. Her dark green dress flowed around her ankles as she moved across the stage, and a hush fell over the crowd.

"We are very happy to begin what I'm sure will be another wonderful school year at Heksheim. In front of you, you'll find your syllabus for the year. Please find a safe place to keep it, as replacements will not be able to be made until tomorrow afternoon." Her eyes drifted to Ember's table, where Killian sank in his seat and looked anywhere but the front of the room.

"I told you she would remember!" Fen whispered loudly. "Your sticking charms are worthless mate."

Ember laughed as she rolled her eyes.

Professor Moran cleared her throat as she continued, "Due to the disappearances this summer, the school board and Chief Thornsten have seen fit to heavily reinforce the wards surrounding the forest, as well as the school. While this area is normally off limits to students anyway, I heavily encourage each and every one of you to stay as far from the Dark Forest as possible." Her eyes traveled across the sea of students, and her expression softened to that of a worried parent. "Your safety is of the utmost importance to every adult in this school, but you must meet us halfway by following the rules we have put in place. I assure you, Chief Thornsten only has each of your best interests in mind."

Ember felt her chest grow heavy as she thought back to the end of her first year. She knew all too well what could happen in that forest, but she also knew that sometimes the worst kind of villains hid in plain sight. Her chest tightened as she thought about Rowan, and a lump grew in her throat as she bit the inside of her cheek. Professor Moran's calm voice broke her from her thoughts, and the stern woman folded her hands in front of her with a soft smile.

"For those of you beginning your first year, welcome to Heksheim." Her smile grew as her eyes traveled across the room. "And for those of you returning, welcome home."

The room began to empty as students made their way to class, quietly whispering about what had transpired over the summer. Ember slung her bag over her shoulder and turned to follow her friends out of the room when Professor Moran's voice broke from behind her.

"Miss Lothbrok?" she said, as she walked her way. "I would like to see you in my office this afternoon when you have a moment."

Ember's heart leapt into her throat. "Um, yes, of course, Professor," she replied quietly. "Is everything alright?" Her heartbeat quickened, and her mind began to run a mile a minute as she went through every possible scenario that would require her presence in the dean's office.

Did something happen to the Kitts? Or Maeve? No, of course not, then she would've asked for Fen to come to.

"Perfectly fine," the Dean replied with a warm smile. "We'll discuss more this afternoon, best get to class." And she turned to walk away, checking her watch as she went.

Ember felt dread grow in her stomach as she jogged to catch up with the boys. Killian was leaning lazily against the wall, one foot holding his weight while the other was pressed against the wall, eyes skimming his syllabus. Fen had his hands stuffed in his pockets, forcing a smile as Odette talked to him in her sing-song voice. Killian was the first to notice Ember as she exited the hall and walked quickly in their direction.

"Already getting into trouble, and we haven't even made it to class." He smirked as he pushed himself off the wall. "That must be a new record, Starshine."

Ember rolled her eyes as Fen's head turned to her.

"Everything okay, Em?" he asked, as he furrowed his brow.

Ember smiled softly at her foster brother. His protectiveness of her was endearing, even if they were the same age.

"Professor Moran just needs to see me this afternoon," she shrugged. "I'm sure it's nothing." Though she wanted desperately to believe it, the ball of anxiety that was steadily building in her stomach told her otherwise.

ZOOMANCY HAD QUICKLY BECOME her favorite class during her first year, and Professor Bjorn her favorite teacher. Not only did she find all the fantastical creatures fascinating, but it was a passion she shared with her father. It was something that connected her to him. It was a steady reminder that she wasn't alone, that she came from somewhere and didn't just appear out of thin air. The closer she got with the Kitts, the further she felt she was pulled from her parents, and that thought scared her. So this class, his journal, his ring, it kept her connected to them, to him.

It kept him close. It kept him real.

Ember followed Fen and Killian into the classroom and took their normal seats toward the back, the boys sitting at the table behind her. After sitting in her seat, Odette followed and sat beside her. This had become a more regular occurrence at the end of their first year. At first, it irritated Ember when Odette seemed to be trying to squeeze herself into Rowan's place, like it was a spot that needed to be filled, but after a few days, Ember could tell that wasn't the case. Odette needed a friend just as much as she did.

"Good morning, young Vala!" Professor Bjorn boomed, as he walked down the spiraling staircase at the front of the room, giant paws padding across the lush grass on the floor. "And welcome to the first day of your second year. This year is an important one with your exams, almost as important as fourth year will be, so I expect you all to be prepared to work and study hard."

Ember's heart soared as she pulled out her second year Zoomancy book, her mind already racing about what they were going to learn this year. She was looking forward to a year of nothing but studying in the library, reading in front of the fire at night with the Kitts, and spending her afternoons and weekends flying with Killian and Fen.

A year of peace.

"For the first quarter," the Professor began, "we're going to focus on the magical creatures that live in the forest surrounding the school. Not every creature that lives in the forest is bad, but as you know, there are some that are not what most would deem safe."

"How many evil creatures are there in the forest, do you suppose?" a small girl toward the front asked, hand waving wildly in the air.

Professor Bjorn turned toward the girl and tilted his head while he leaned against the desk. "I don't recall saying anything about 'evil' creatures, Miss Hawthorne."

Lydia Hawthorne dropped her arm quickly while she furrowed her brow.

"But what about the Cu Sidhe?" a boy toward the back asked, as he crossed his arms over his chest.

Professor Bjorn let out a soft laugh as he shook his head. "While very dangerous, they aren't what I would classify as an evil creature."

"But they *eat* people," Lydia gasped, as she flipped through the pages of the textbook, landing on the chapter dedicated to the Cu Sidhe, and grimaced.

"Does anyone know what the job of the Cu Sidhe is?" Professor Bjorn directed at the class, as he began to pace up and down the aisles.

"They're guardians of the gate," Fen replied.

Ember glanced back at him and gave him a soft smile as he straightened his back. No doubt the trio were all reliving the same memory of their own encounter with the Cu Sidhe. Ember grimaced as she remembered how close they had come to losing Killian. She shuddered as memories of his battered body flashed through her mind and turned to give him a small smile. His eyes caught hers, and he gave her a soft nod, sending her a wink that made heat creep up her neck.

"Correct," Professor Bjorn nodded, "it guards the gate to Fae territory. That is it's one purpose, and it takes it very seriously."

"But it's still a killer," Lydia said from the front. "It's still evil. It kills anyone who gets near the gate."

Professor Bjorn made his way back to the front of the room, leaning on his desk and crossing his arms over his burly chest. He furrowed his brow as his eyes met each of the students, then turned his head back to Lydia.

"What would you propose they do then, Miss Hawthorne?" He raised a brow as he waited for her to answer.

"Um…" She hesitated as she fidgeted in her seat. "What would I propose who does?"

"The Fae, of course." He nodded. "How would you propose they protect their land?"

"I… I don't know, Professor."

He turned his attention back to the rest of the class, and his eyes landed on Fen. "Mr. Kitt," he started, "if someone tried to break into your home and threatened your family, what do you think you would do?"

Ember turned around as Fen straightened his back as his eyes met hers. "I would protect them," he replied. "I would do whatever I had to do to protect them if I could."

Professor Bjorn nodded. "Even if that meant using deadly force?"

Ember heard Fen choke on his own breath.

"Yes sir," he replied with an unsteady voice.

Ember's mind briefly drifted back to just a few months before, when he had defended her against Rowan. She shuddered as she remembered his battered body lying lifeless on the floor and her desperate pleas to the gods to take her instead. She fought the lump building in her throat as she bit down on her lip.

"The Cu Sidhe is a guardian," Professor Bjorn directed at the class. "He is a protector. He is only dangerous when he needs to be, when he feels like his people are being threatened. We can't fault a creature for doing what it must do, even if it makes us uncomfortable. Dangerous does not always equate to evil."

Veda Ellingboe scoffed from the back of the class, and Ember rolled her eyes as she turned to look in her direction.

"They're Fae," Veda sneered. "Of course they're evil."

Ember felt Odette stiffen next to her for a moment before she relaxed again.

"That is quite the jump, Miss Ellingboe," Professor Bjorn said, as he furrowed his brow.

"Is it?" Oryn quipped beside her. "They're a lower class at best, and now they're taking the children on the island. I heard my father say so himself. They're evil incarnate, and now they'll finally be dealt with."

Ember stiffened as she turned toward the twins and

narrowed her eyes. The Fae on the island were protective over their home and their history, and after learning what they did about the Merrow, she understood why. She had no way of knowing what was true and what wasn't, and she wasn't about to trust someone like Veda or Oryn Ellingboe to be honest about it.

"They would know about 'evil incarnate,'" Killian whispered under his breath, as he let out a huff. "Truly following in my uncle's footsteps." Fen patted his friend on the shoulder reassuringly.

"There's no proof of anything," Ember spat, as she spun around to look the raven-haired twins in the eyes. "You can't just go throwing around accusations like that with no proof." Her eyes narrowed on the twins as they smirked. Ember was ready to bolt out of her seat and wrap her hands around their petite little necks when she felt a gentle hand on top of hers. She turned to see Odette smiling, calmly shaking her head. Ember felt the heat in her belly simmer to a dull roar as she turned back around.

"If they think it's the Fae," another student said toward the front, "why don't they kick them all out of town? They shouldn't be allowed to run businesses if they're a danger to us."

Murmurs of agreement broke out in a low hush around the room, and Ember felt herself bristle once again as she thought about Asteria.

"Chief Thornsten has had a team of expert ward breakers place reinforced wards around the forest, as well as more around the school," Professor Bjorn said pointedly. "Whether it's the Fae or something else entirely, I can assure you that you are perfectly safe." He smiled gently at the students, but Ember could see the worry clouding his eyes. He didn't believe his words any more than they did.

THE HOURS BLED ON, and before Ember knew it, it was midafternoon, and she was making the trek to Professor Moran's office. She climbed the spiraling staircase that hugged the rounded walls of the school in the tree and held her breath as she stepped off into the fourth floor corridor. The walls were lined with a few offices, but the corridor itself seemed to be completely empty. Ember walked down the empty hall, listening to the sounds of her footsteps and her heavily beating heart echo in her ears. She reached the door at the end of the hall, took a shaky breath, and knocked three times.

"Come in," Professor Moran's voice said from the inside.

Ember reached to open the door, but before she could touch the knob, it swung open on its own. She stepped into the large office, and her eyes went wide. The walls to her left and right were lined with tall bookshelves and directly in front of her was a floor to ceiling window that rounded to meet with the other walls. It looked out over the grounds of Heksheim that were currently bathed in a gorgeous midafternoon glow. Professor Moran was sitting at her desk making notes on a piece of parchment when she looked up with a smile.

"Have a seat, Miss Lothbrok," she said sweetly, as she motioned to the oversized chair in front of her. "How is your first day back going?" She seemed far more relaxed than she did in front of the school that morning. She radiated peacefulness, making Ember's breath slow and heart steady.

"It's going very well," Ember replied, as she sat down. "Thank you, Professor. You needed to see me?"

"Ah, yes, I did." Professor Moran nodded, as she shuffled paper across her desk. "I heard the Kitts had filed paperwork to finalize your adoption, and I wanted to check in with you." A smile lit up her face, and she folded her hands on top of her desk. "You must be feeling a thousand different emotions, which I assure you is completely normal," she continued. "I'm always here if you need to talk or work things out."

Ember shook her head as she tried to smile. "I don't want to bother you with it all."

"It's no bother at all." Professor Moran leaned back in her chair. "It's something I wish I had when I was adopted."

Ember raised her brow. "You were adopted?"

Professor Moran nodded. "I know what you're going through, and I know what emotions must be waging war inside of you," she said, as she shuffled some papers around her desk. "Think of me as a counselor of sorts." Her grin broadened as she winked.

Ember bit the inside of her cheek as she gave her a nod. "I'm doing fine, thank you."

The dean cocked her head as she looked across the desk, and her emerald eyes seemed to stare inside of her. "It would be understandable if you weren't."

"Weren't, Professor?" Ember asked, palms beginning to sweat.

"If you weren't okay," she whispered. "If you were more scared than excited."

Ember's breath hitched in her chest as she reached to her collar, tracing the runes on the pendant that hung at her neck.

"I'm fine, really," she replied, but even she was struggling to believe the lie. "I'm very excited."

"Adoption is a very happy process," the dean nodded, "but it is also riddled with grief. You lost your family. You don't have to put on a show for the benefit of others." Her eyes darkened, as if memories were flitting through her mind.

"It was such a long time ago." Ember shook her head. "I hardly even remember them."

*Lies.*

"Time passed does not equate to healing," Professor Moran replied, folding her hands on top of her desk.

Ember forced down the lump building in her throat as she plastered on a fake smile. "I appreciate the concern, Professor," she took a breath, "but I'll be fine. I'm very excited." The lie tasted foul on her tongue.

"Very well then," Professor Moran replied with a small smile. "You know where to find me if that changes. Now one last thing before I let you go."

Ember held her breath as the Professor skimmed the papers littering her desk.

"I wanted to check and see if you needed the form to submit a name change?"

Ember stiffened, sucking in her breath. "Name change?" she repeated. "I'm sorry?"

Professor Moran nodded. "Yes, will you be going by 'Ember Kitt' after the adoption is finalized?"

Ember felt like cotton was lodged in her throat. Changing her name wasn't something she had even considered when the Kitts brought up the adoption. Of course she would love to be a part of their family, but change her name? Dread filled her chest as she struggled to take in a breath. Her name was the last thing she had left of them. It was the last thing that tethered her to her family—to who she was. Who would she be if she wasn't a Lothbrok?

But if she kept her name, what would that say to the Kitts? They had sacrificed so much, given her so much, what would they think if she didn't take their name? Would they think she was ungrateful? Or that she didn't love them? Dread rolled through her stomach.

Would they change their minds?

"I haven't thought about that yet," she replied quietly, trying to plaster on a fake smile. "I'm not really sure."

Professor Moran gave her a warm smile. "It's not a decision you have to make right now, but I'll give you the form just in case you decide you need it." She waved her hand and a cabinet to her left flew open, and a single piece of paper floated out to land in her outstretched palm. She handed it across the desk to Ember, who quickly stuffed it in her bag.

Professor Moran stood from her seat and waved her hand, allowing the door to open again, "I'm here if you need to talk about anything, Miss Lothbrok," she said sweetly.

Ember nodded stiffly. "Thank you ma'am," was all she could say, and she headed out the door. The hallway was silent, everyone either in class or using their study period to get a head start on homework. Ember's mind ran a mile a minute as she took breath after shaky breath and made her way toward the stairs.

# CHAPTER 3

# THE WOLF & WAIFE

E mber, Fen and Killian made their way through the sea of children and out the front doors of Heksheim. She breathed a sigh of relief as the fresh air hit her lungs and the afternoon sun warmed her face. She took in a deep breath, letting the feeling wash over her as she leaned her head back and smiled.

"Need a minute to recharge?" Killian asked with a smirk.

Ember opened one eye and squinted at him with a smile. "Yeah, just a minute," she sighed.

"While you're over there photosynthesizing," Fen grumbled, "I am currently dying of hunger. Can we go please?"

Ember rolled her eyes as she laughed. "Alright, fine, lets go," she replied, and the trio walked down the path toward the end of the wards.

"I could go for a Moon Cider." Killian shrugged. "We should pop into town before we head home for the day."

"I like how you think." Fen grinned mischievously.

Ember furrowed her brow. "We were specifically told to go straight home," she scolded. "I don't think stopping in town for drinks will go over well."

Fen stopped directly in front of her, putting on a show

complete with puppy dog eyes and a quivering bottom lip. "But, Em," he pouted, "I'm parched. I won't make it home. I need sustenance." His bottom lip stuck out as he grabbed both her hands and tried his hardest to produce tears.

Ember rolled her eyes as she shoved his shoulder with a laugh. "You're worse than Maevie, you know that, right?"

"I'm famished, Em," he continued.

"We don't have a choice, Starshine." Killian grinned, feigning concern as he felt Fen's forehead. "It's a matter of survival at this point."

Ember rolled her eyes as she shoved past the boys and continued down the path. "Fine," she shouted back to them, "but you're paying!"

THE WOLF & Waife sat on the end of Waterware street next to Botánica Mágica. It was a quaint little pub, not run down, but nothing to write home about, either. Standing on their hind legs, front paws stretched on in front of them to create an arch over the front door, were two beautifully carved wooden wolves. Ember ran her hands down the long-dead tree and breathed a sigh as she playfully cut her eyes at Killian.

"Quite realistic if you ask me," she teased. "Though, these are a little scarier than the one I've become acquainted with."

Killian cocked a brow, and he crossed his arms over his chest and leaned against the wolf opposite her. "These are all bark," he said, as he patted the wooden leg, "and I think you'll find that I have a bit more bite, Starshine."

Ember felt a chill run down her spine and the hairs on the back of her neck stood up as he sent her a wink, and the invisible tether connecting her to him seemed to vibrate wildly, like it was a harp string being plucked.

"Ew, gross, that's my sister," Fen said, as he gagged dramatically. "Can we just go inside?"

Killian opened the door, and the trio made their way into the pub, quickly sliding into a booth toward the back. Fen went up to the bar and ordered a round of Moon Cider as Killian and Ember settled in.

"So, do you have the day marked on the calendar yet?" Killian asked, as he leaned back in his seat.

Ember furrowed her brow. "What day?"

"The day you become a Kitt." He grinned, crossing one leg over the other and resting his ankle on his knee.

"Oh… yeah, that day." She nodded. "I mean, I'm being adopted, that doesn't mean I have to change my whole identity." She said it a little meaner than she meant to, evident by the confused look now on Killian's face.

"Who said anything about changing your identity?" Killian asked, as he rested his elbow on the table.

"Everyone just expects me to change my last name and forget who I am and who my parents are. When I do that, if I do that, it'll be like they never existed. Like we never existed." Ember swallowed the lump that was steadily building in her throat as her chest began to rise and fall rapidly.

"Whoa there, Starshine," Killian said, as he laid his hand on hers. "No one said anything about forgetting your parents or changing your last name. You don't have to do anything you aren't comfortable with." He furrowed his brow, and suddenly Ember felt far more dramatic than she meant to be.

"Right, right, of course." She nodded as she shook her head, plastering on a small smile. "I'm just in my head, I'm sorry."

Killian smiled as he leaned forward, his hand still resting on hers. "Nothing to be sorry about, love."

"I come bearing gifts!" Fen announced behind them.

Killian pulled his hand away quickly and leaned back in the booth, which resulted in him smacking his elbow against

31

the back of the seat. Ember yanked her hand into her lap and felt heat creep up her neck as she stared at her nails.

Fen squinted between the two, three bottles of Moon Cider still swinging in his hands. "Stop being weird," was all he said, and then he set the bottles down on the table and took his seat in the booth beside Killian.

"How long till they lock down the whole island, ya reckon?" Killian asked, as he sipped his cider.

Fen shook his head. "I don't think anyone would be able to get onto the docks, let alone on a ferry to the mainland with a missing child in tow. Too many variables. Whoever, or *whatever*, is doing it lives here somewhere. It makes the most sense."

"*Whatever* is doing it?" Ember said, as she furrowed her brow. "Please don't tell me you're buying into this whole 'Fae kidnapping' nonsense too."

"I mean, we have to consider all possibilities here," Fen said, as he tilted his bottle to his lips and took a swig. He sat his bottle on the table and cleared his throat. "Only a handful have businesses in town, and the rest tend to stay in their territory. How much do we really know about them?" He took another sip of his cider and leaned back in the booth. "It could be a rogue Fae, like with Rowan's dad and brother." He chewed on his bottom lip thoughtfully as he tapped his foot. "Or it could be a conspiracy. Maybe they're trying to take back the island slowly, one by one, slowly weakening our forces."

Ember rolled her eyes and kicked him under the table. He let out a grunt, gripping his shin and spilling cider all over his flannel shirt.

"Stop it, Fenrir Kitt," she scolded. "Spreading terrible rumors like that won't help the situation at all. Rumors like that can ruin lives."

Fen had the sense to look properly abashed as he hung his head.

"Well, whoever it is," Killian interjected, as he leaned back in his seat, "they're doing a wonderful job at leaving behind no evidence if Chief Thornsten is this worried. We've never had a town meeting, not over something like this."

Ember chewed on the bottom of her lip as she slowly sipped her cider. She didn't want to believe that the Fae had anything to do with the disappearing children, but she also didn't want to believe there was a Vala running around snatching children and leaving no trace, either. She rubbed the bridge of her nose like she did when she felt a headache coming on. If she was being completely honest, neither felt like wonderful options. She leaned back in her seat and let out a sigh as she crossed her arms over her chest.

Maybe this wouldn't be such a peaceful year after all.

The trio changed the topic of conversation, steering clear of missing children and evil plans, and before they knew it, they had drunk way too many Moon Ciders, and the sun was slowly beginning to drop on the horizon.

"Bloody hell," Fen mumbled, as they stepped outside, "Mum is going to kill us."

Ember rolled her eyes with a laugh. "I don't know what you mean by 'us.' I was very clearly taken here against my will." Fen cut his eyes at her and stuffed his hands in his pockets as they headed toward the Echopoint. Walking through the Yggdrasil Terminal and directly into their house didn't feel like the best plan

"You wouldn't dare," he whispered.

And just like that, a small blue ball of light whizzed in front of the trio, floating in the air ominously. Ember knew who the Helio was from before the message even began.

*"Fenrir Kitt! Ember Lothbrok! Come home this instant!"*

THE SUN WAS QUICKLY SETTING behind the house as Fen and Ember walked up the long drive. Dread pooled in her stomach as she prepared for the firestorm they were about to walk into. They hadn't sent anyone a Helio, didn't let anyone know they would be making a pit stop after school, and she knew they deserved whatever wrath the Kitt matriarch decided to unleash on them. Fen scratched furiously at his arms beside her and pulled the collar of his shirt away from his neck.

"Are these hives?" he asked erratically. "Do these look like hives to you?"

Ember rolled her eyes as she glanced at his arms. "I don't see anything," she replied, "and I don't know why you're the one panicking when going out for drinks was your idea."

Fen let out a sigh as he rubbed the back of his neck. "Felt like a better idea from the safety of school if we're being honest."

The front steps creaked as they slowly made their way to the door, each step feeling like they were inching closer and closer to the guillotine. The door creaked open as they walked into the foyer, both stopping to glance at each other.

"Ready?" Fen whispered.

"As I'll ever be." Ember nodded.

The house was quiet, far too quiet for a September afternoon. Ember listened closely for the sounds of life she had come so accustomed to, but instead, she was met with silence. Maeve couldn't be heard chattering away in the kitchen, and the sounds of pots and pans and dinner plates weren't ringing in her ears. Otto's laugh was absent, as well as Eira's sing-song voice she had grown so used to hearing every night.

The silence was deafening.

"This can't be good," Fen mumbled.

"No, I suppose it can't," a voice said from the dining room.

Fen and Ember spun around to see Eira sitting at the table, both hands folded calmly in front of her.

"Four hours," was all she said as she looked up at the both of them.

"Mum, I can explain—" Fen started, but he was cut off.

"Four. Hours," she repeated, as she closed her eyes.

Ember's breath hitched as she noticed how puffy and red Eira's eyes were. She bit her lip as she dropped her head, the remnants of all of the Moon Cider suddenly tasting sour in her mouth.

"That's how long it's been since school let out," she continued. "That's how long we have been wondering where you were. That's how long I have been beside myself with worry, racking my brain with terrible thoughts of what could have happened." Her voice was shaking as she spoke, and Ember felt like her heart had shattered into a million pieces.

"Mum, we're sorry," Fen tried again. "We stopped by the Wolf & Waife and just lost track of time."

Eira put a hand over her face and took a breath. "I know. Don't you think I deserved the respect of one of you letting me know where you were going?" She dropped her hand and looked between the two teenagers as tears ran down her cheeks. "Children are going missing every day. Your father and I couldn't even get a Helio to go through for several hours because of all the extra wards that have been placed around the island." Her crying grew louder, and soon, her shoulders were shaking. Ember's heart dropped, and she felt bile rise in her throat. "We had no idea what happened to you, and for all we knew you could've been—"

Ember rushed across the room and wrapped her arms around Eira's neck, holding on tightly as if her life depended on it. She buried her face in her foster mother's shoulder as the woman's tears soaked into her shirt. Eira wrapped her arms around Ember's neck, and then Fen's as he came up beside them and embraced them both. They stayed like that, for just a few minutes, before Eira pulled away and ran her hand down each of their cheeks.

"Do not ever do that to me again," she whispered at them both. "I don't know what I would do if something happened to any of you."

Ember straightened up, wiping the stray tears off her cheeks. "We won't do it again." she promised. And she meant it.

"We promise." Fen nodded in agreement, and Ember knew he meant it to. His chest shook briefly as he turned his head and rubbed his hand under his eyes. He furrowed his brow as he turned back to his mother. "Wait, you said you knew where we were. How did you know?"

Eira cocked a brow as she looked between the two teenagers. "After our Helio's failed to find you, I decided a small tracking charm was in order. It's easier for a Helio to make it to you if I know your exact location."

Fen's jaw dropped as he stared at his mother. "You... tracked us?" he whispered. "Honestly, Mum."

Ember rolled her eyes as Eira let out a small laugh. "If you don't want to be tracked, I suggest you not give me a reason to do so next time. Your father will be back with Maeve shortly. I sent them to pick up takeout from Florin's. Go wash up." She kissed both of them on the forehead and shooed them out of the room.

# CHAPTER 4
# A DUEL ON DRANGANIR

T ime seemed to fly by at the speed of sound as Ember threw herself into school, spending the weekends soaking in the last of the summer sun with Fen and Killian in the orchards. Eira made supper every night, and Ember soaked in the familiar feeling of togetherness that she had become so accustomed to.

It was Friday, the last weekend in September, and Thea was supposed to come over soon to talk about the adoption. Ember was a bundle of nerves walking through the halls of Heksheim after the last class. Bells sounded behind her, and Ember felt herself tense up as Odette walked up beside her.

"You're looking a little grey today," Odette said, as she squinted toward Ember, those unseeing eyes piercing her in a way that made the hair on her neck and arms rise. "Or perhaps a tinge of black." She hummed, almost to herself.

"Black?" Ember asked, as she scrunched her brow, adjusting the bag on her shoulder.

Odette nodded as she continued down the spiraling staircase. "Your aura." She shrugged, like it should be common knowledge. "It's normally closer to an indigo, but you seem to be devoid of color all together here lately."

"You can see my aura?" Ember whispered. "But... you can't see anything." Ember mentally berated herself—of course Odette knew that.

"I can see a lot more than many give me credit for," she replied, almost a whisper, face falling.

"And what about Killian?" Ember asked, trying to steer the conversation in any other direction than the dismal destination it was headed.

"Orange," Odette nodded, screwing her face in concentration, "sometimes with a halo of red. Very courageous and protective, but sometimes his ego gets in the way."

Ember chuckled as she nodded—that sounded about right.

"And Fen?" she asked next, feet hitting the last step as she turned and walked toward the towering doors that led out of Heksheim. "What does Fen's aura look like?"

Odette smiled to herself. "Yellow," she replied, her grin growing, "a bright, sunny yellow that lights up every dark crevice in the world around him."

Ember smiled as she nodded, and she could've sworn Odette's cheeks stained crimson. "How long have you been able to see people's aura's?" she asked, as they made their way through the large double doors and out into the sun. She sighed as the light touched her face, like magic caressing her cheeks.

"As long as I can remember," Odette replied. "It's both a gift and a burden, the things I can see." Her face fell, only slightly, like the weight of it had suddenly become too heavy.

"Can you see other things?" Ember asked, kicking a rock by her shoe.

Odette nodded but didn't elaborate.

"Slow down, Em!" Fen said, as he ran up behind the girls, tripping over his feet as he slung his backpack over his shoulder. Ember slowed her gait, turning around with a laugh to help her brother back to his feet.

His cheeks flushed as his eyes landed on Odette, and she gave him a small smile. "Oh, um, hi, Odette," he said, as he cleared his throat, wiping away the bits of dust clinging to his trousers.

"Hello, Fenrir." She smiled with a nod. "I suppose you have to go get ready for the adoption ceremony." She turned to Ember, something like concern washing over her face.

Ember felt her heart begin to rattle against her ribs as she swallowed dryly. "I suppose I do," she replied quietly.

Odette gave her a small smile, and Ember nearly jumped backwards when the girl reached out and took hold of her hand, squeezing it gently. "Be careful," she whispered, barely audible, her white eyes almost glowing as they seemed to see right through her.

Ember swallowed again. "Right, um, have a good weekend, Odette," she replied and then turned and sped away, down the walkway toward the wards surrounding the school.

"Slow down!" Fen yelled again, jogging to catch up.

"Thea will be over in two days," Ember breathed, trying to slow the thumping in her chest.

Fen nodded his head as he scrunched his brow. "Right.... What are we rushing about again?"

Ember huffed as she blew a stray hair out of her eyes and crossed her arms. "I just have stuff to do. I don't know. I have to get ready."

"The only thing you have to do this weekend," Killian said, as he jogged up beside them and threw his arm over her shoulder, "is go flying."

"Flying?" Ember squinted and wriggled her way out of his grasp.

"This weekend we're celebrating." He grinned.

Ember bit her lip. Of course they wanted to celebrate. She turned and walked down the road, both of the boys flanking her left and right, and a wave of guilt washed over her. Fen, she was sure, thought that Thea was just going to give her information about how the adoption worked, and then they would celebrate and everything would be finalized. But if she was being honest, she still wasn't sure if she *wanted* to be adopted. She loved the Kitts so much it hurt, but she couldn't shake the feeling that she was betraying her parents.

This was going to be a long weekend.

"Fenrir, honestly," Ember sighed. She rolled her eyes and let her fingers sink into the sand. "It's not a Rukr game. Do you have to do that?"

Fen was busy stretching on the beach, currently bent over trying to touch his toes, which he was struggling with.

"Your muscles don't care if it's a game or a leisurely ride, Em." He grunted. "They'll pull either way if you don't keep them loose."

Ember rolled her eyes at his theatrics and leaned back on her elbows in the sand, letting the warm sun wash over her skin. Maia curled up beside her, cooing and clicking as she nuzzled her snout into Ember's arm.

"Waiting on me, Starshine?" Killian smirked as he walked up beside her and sat in the sand.

"Couldn't very well start without you, could we?" Ember laughed. "Besides, Fen wouldn't let me even if I wanted to." She shouted the last part in Fen's direction, who shot her a rude gesture over his shoulder.

"I have something for you," Killian said, a little quieter this time. He reached in his pocket and pulled out a small box wrapped in green wrapping paper tied with a gold ribbon.

Ember furrowed her brow as she took it from his hand, twirling it around and admiring the way the ribbon shined in the later afternoon sun. "Were we supposed to exchange gifts?" she asked with a laugh.

Killian shook his head as he smiled. "No nothing like that," he smirked, "Just a little 'I'm sorry Fen will now legally be your brother' gift."

Ember felt her face drop, and Killian gave her a confused look. She forced a smile as she slowly unwrapped the box, wrapping her fingers around the ribbon and pulling it away. Her eyes widened as she took the lid off the box and pulled out a pair of fingerless, leather gloves.

"Killian, these are beautiful," she breathed, though guilt began to coil into a tight knot in her stomach. She averted her eyes, afraid that if she looked into his that he would see right through the already weak facade she was wearing.

Killian's face fell as she bit her lip. "What's wrong?" he asked, as he furrowed his brow.

Ember shook her head as she tried—and failed—to smile. "It's just too much," she replied quietly. "I can't accept these." Not only because she was sure they were wildly expensive, but what if she decided not to go through with the adoption at all?

"You can, and you will," he replied sternly, as a grin played at the corner of his mouth. "Try them on."

Ember hesitated, then finally slipped the gloves over her hands, feeling the leather hug her fingers as she snapped the buttons on the side.

"You're going to mess your hands up with that death grip." Killian shrugged with a smirk. "Just trying to save you some pain in the future."

Ember rolled her eyes and stood to her feet, brushing the sand from her shirt and leggings. "Well," she sighed. "Thank you either way."

"Anytime, Starshine." He winked and then turned to walk toward Fen.

Ember rolled her eyes as she picked up her board and walked over to the boys, Maia a step behind her.

"Ready, Em?" Fen asked enthusiastically.

"I've been ready for ages, dear brother." She grinned as she hopped on her board and snapped the clasps around her shoes, shoving her hands in her pockets. "Shall we?"

Fen barked a laugh as he stepped on his own board, Killian following suit behind him, and the trio sped into the air. Ember closed her eyes as the wind whipped through her hair and bit at her cheeks, falling into a familiarity she never could've imagined was possible. Her body bent and swayed with the board under her feet, and Maia flapped her wings furiously to keep up. Ember gripped the sides of her board and did a nosedive toward the water, pulling up just in time. She hovered just above the waves, stretching out her arm to run her fingers along the crystal water. Maia chirped at her, and she turned her board back up, climbing into the sky.

Killian flew up beside her, flipping the pale hair out of his eyes and nodding toward the rock formation in the distance that was growing closer. "Race ya!" he shouted and then sped off toward Dranganir.

Ember grinned as she looked back toward her brother, who was currently fighting off two seagulls that were pecking at his hair and glasses.

"Fen!" she yelled, as he raised his hand to undoubtedly try and hex them. "They're a protected species—don't hurt them!"

Fen shot her a disgruntled look as he lowered his hand and sped toward her. Ember turned back around and made her way to Dranganir where Killian had already kicked off his board and was lounging in the grass that was spread across the top of the giant rock.

Ember and Fen both hopped off their boards, leaning them against a small rock that sat toward the top of Dranganir, and walked over to Killian.

"You seem to have forgotten what a race is, Starshine," he said smugly, as he laid back in the grass and closed his eyes.

Ember rolled her eyes. "Your mate was being bested by a flock of seagulls, and someone had to rescue him." She quipped as she sat beside him and hung her legs over the edge of the stone formation.

"I was not," Fen scoffed, as he crossed his arm and sat beside her. "I had everything under control, thank you very much."

"You and I have two very different ideas of control."

Killian smiled, eyes still closed as he soaked in the late afternoon sun. Ember shook her head as she laughed.

Fen scoffed as he stood up and wiped his hands on his pants. "Care to test that theory?" he asked, as he backed away from the edge and over to the flat piece of grass at the top of Dranganir. The very top of the formation sat perfectly flat, devoid of any bumps or hills. When one walked to one of the edges, it sloped downward dramatically toward the ocean right before leveling off at the bottom.

Killian pushed himself up on his elbow and stared back at his friend. "Challenge accepted," he said, as he jumped up and ran to the center, directly across from where Fen stood.

"Oh, honestly," Ember sighed, as she rolled her eyes. Their constant 'dueling practice' was getting very old, very quick, and the last thing she wanted to do was watch Fen be bested yet again. Killian didn't have much going for him when it came to his family, but the dueling arena in the manor, complete with targets that hexed back, was something he seemed to not take for granted.

"Hit me with your best shot, Vargr!" Fen yelled, as he got in position, "Don't hold ba—" But before he could finish his thought, Killian fired a stunning spell in his direction, and he fell to the ground.

"Sometimes it's just too easy," Killian laughed, as he jogged to his friend and helped him off the ground. "Less talking might help, Kitt." He grinned.

Fen narrowed his eyes at him as he brushed the dirt off his shirt. "That was a cheap shot, and you know it," he grumbled.

"There's no room for honor in war, my friend." Killian smirked as he dodged Fen's fist.

"Whatever," Fen mumbled. "Ember, your turn!" He waved at his sister and pointed to the spot where Killian had been standing.

"Absolutely not," she replied, as she shook her head, Maia growling along with her. "I do not have a death wish today."

"If you're scared," Killian smirked from above her, "you can just say so."

Ember cut her eyes at him and then back to her brother who was nodding in agreement. She huffed as she rolled her eyes and pushed herself off the ground, making her way to where her brother was standing.

"One round," she said, as she held up a finger, "and none of your silly made up jinxes." Her mind wandered back to the summer before school and how she had spent a full week trying to remove the feathers from her arms. "I will not walk into my meeting with Thea with green hair."

Fen sighed as he nodded his head. "Okay, fine, standard jinxes or hexes only."

Ember nodded and took her place, squaring her shoulder and bending her knees as she prepared to take him down in one shot.

"And... go!" Killian shouted, as he slung his arm down.

The next few seconds seemed to go by in slow motion.

"*Detenair!*" Fen shouted, as he pushed his hand forward and a beam of light shot toward Ember.

Ember quickly flattened her palm. "*Proteger!*" she shouted, as the shielding spell went up. The disarming spell bounced off the wall of light harder than expected, and it sent Ember stumbling backwards. She tried to catch herself, but her foot caught on a rock, and she tumbled backwards. She was too close to the sloped edge of Dranganir, and she realized it far too late.

Her feet slipped out from under her, and then she was rolling down the hill, over sharp rocks that cut into her arms and legs. She righted herself just enough so that she was sliding on her back instead of rolling. She reached out her arms, clawing at the dirt in the hopes that she could grab onto something, anything, to keep her from plummeting into the icy water that lay over the edge of the rock formation. She dug her heels into the dirt to try and slow her down, but it seemed pointless.

Her heart hammered in her chest as her hands continued to search for something to grab. Finally, as she neared the edge, she saw a large boulder right at the edge of the cliff. She used her momentum and threw herself at the rock, wrapping her arms around it in a desperate attempt to keep her body on dry land. Her hands pressed against the cold boulder, and she felt her right ring finger crack as it hit the surface with a little too much force. She cried out in pain as she heaved herself back up from over the edge and laid on the grass as she desperately tried to suck air into her lungs.

"Ember!" Fen shouted, as he flew down the hill toward her, Killian hot on his heels. They had the good sense to ride their AirWaves down instead of running after her, and for that, she was very thankful. Fen jumped off his board and dropped to his knees beside her.

Ember's head spun as she looked up at her brother, tears falling freely down her dirt covered face.

"You alright, Starshine?" Killian said calmly, but his body language betrayed him. His chest was rising and falling rapidly, and his brow was drenched in sweat. He knelt beside her and ran his hand over her hair. It was already matted with blood, no doubt from a rogue rock she hit on her way down.

"I'm okay." She nodded, wincing as she sat herself up. Killian wrapped his arm around her shoulder, gently grabbing her hand to help her stand. She winced and pulled away, looking down to see her right ring finger bent at an odd angle.

And her father's ring was cracked.

She whimpered as she held her hand close to her chest, and tears streamed down her face faster. "I think I broke my hand." She winced as she closed her eyes.

Fen threw back his head and sighed painfully. "Oh gods, Mum is going to kill me."

"FENRIR JAMES, WHAT DID YOU DO!" Eira shouted, as she wrapped her arm around Ember's shoulder and led her into the kitchen. Ember winced as Eira sat her in the chair and inspected her hand, her pale skin already black and blue up to her wrist. Eira handed her a pain tonic that she pulled from the cabinet, and Ember sucked it down as if her life depended on it.

"Why is it always my fault?" Fen replied, as he stomped into the kitchen behind them.

"In her defense, mate," Killian laughed, "it typically is."

"Honestly, it's no one's fault." Ember winced as she waited for the potion to take effect. "We were just dueling on Dran-ganir, and I slipped and—"

"You were what?!," Eira screeched. "Honestly, out of all the idiotic ideas you three have had, this one takes the cake." She cut her eyes at the trio who all looked quickly at the sneakers. "You could've been killed! What were you thinking?" She let out a sigh as she ran a hand through her unruly hair. "Can we please keep the bloodshed to a minimum until after Sunday?"

Killian grinned as he nodded. "Sorry, Mum, it won't happen again."

Eira cut her eyes at the trio and sighed. "Somehow I'm having a very hard time believing that."

Ember spun the ring that was now lying broken on the table beside her. Her chest ached as she fought back tears and grasped it tightly in her left hand.

"What do we have here?" Otto said with a gruff laugh, as he entered the kitchen. His smile immediately fell when he saw Ember in the chair, bloody and bruised. "Now what have you done, Mo Chroí?" he asked in a hushed voice, as he knelt beside her and examined her hand and head.

*My heart.* That's what he called her, and it made Ember tear up every time. For such a gruff, burly man, Otto Kitt had no trouble showing his children affection, Ember included. She crumpled into his chest as he hugged her, tears spilling over her lashes. He smelled like salt water and fish, courtesy of spending his day at the docks and on fishing boats every day, but Ember didn't care. In the moment, she felt safe, and that was all that mattered.

"I broke my ring," she whispered tearfully. "I broke my dad's ring."

Otto gave her a small smile as he rubbed the pad of his calloused thumb across her cheek. "We will go to the blacksmith tomorrow and see what he can do." He smiled. "All that matters is that you're whole, Mo Chroí."

Ember nodded with a half smile as Eira made her way back into the kitchen, shooing Otto out of her way. She rubbed a salve on Ember's hand and then wrapped it a few times in a large bandage.

"That will have to stay on for twenty-four hours," she instructed. "It will give the potion time reset your bone and keep it from moving too much." She pointed at the boys still staring in the doorway. "No carrying on while her hand is healing," she scolded, "and I mean it, Fenrir James. Thea will be beside herself if Ember is in bandages when she arrives Sunday."

Fen threw his hands up in surrender. "No messing around, scouts honor, Mum."

Ember chewed at her bottom lip as she held her bandaged hand to her chest. Thea would be there in two days, and Ember still wasn't any surer now about the adoption than she was when Eira and Otto had brought it up a week ago.

"Go get some rest before supper, love." Eira smiled. "Fen will come get you when it's ready."

Ember nodded as she pushed away from the table, rounded the corner, and headed up the steps, down to the last door on the left. She sat on her four-poster bed and dug through her bag until she found the paper Dean Moran had handed her earlier in the month. It was still blank, the only thing she had managed to write was her name.

Ember Lothbrok.

She stared at the name for a few minutes, trying to imagine herself writing her name any other way. She mumbled, "Ember Kitt," under her breath, rolling the name around in her mouth a few times as she twirled her pen, trying to imagine writing it at the top of her parchments at school.

It didn't feel right—didn't taste right in her mouth. She laid back on her bed, sinking into the pillows, and closed her eyes with a sigh. She would have to tell them she couldn't take their name, couldn't give up that last tangible piece of her parents she was clinging to, if she could even go through with the adoption at all. She took a breath and blew stray hairs from in front of her eyes.

Maybe it wouldn't matter. But no matter how much she tried to convince herself of that, the dread rolling in her stomach did not agree.

CHAPTER 5

# A VISIT FROM THE PAST

Ember fidgeted with her hair at the breakfast table as she tried to put it in a braid, but the bandage on her hand kept getting in her way. Accepting defeat with a huff, she flung the red mess over her shoulders and continued eating her bacon and eggs.

"Would you like some help?" Eira laughed as she walked into the breakfast nook.

Ember nodded sheepishly, handing the hair-tie to her foster mother. Eira made quick work of brushing the tangles out of her hair with her fingers, and then began to hum to herself as she weaved small braids in and out of Ember's hair.

"My mum did this for me every morning before school," she said with a laugh. "Believe it or not, my hair was even wilder than Maeve's." Her magic wrapped around each small braid. Ember saw the glowing light out of the corner of her eye for just a moment before it fizzled out. Ember felt her breath catch as she stiffened.

"What was that?" she asked, as she felt the heat of the magic brush against her scalp.

Eira finished the last braid and then kissed her on the head. "Just a little extra love," she said with a smile.

49

Ember felt her chest tighten as she closed her eyes. She wasn't sure she really deserved the extra love.

"Ready to go, Mo Chroí?" Otto asked, as he kicked the dirt off his shoes at the back door. "The blacksmith should be opening any minute."

Ember finished off her last bite of breakfast, took her plate to the sink, and ran back to her chair to throw her bag over her shoulder.

"Ready!" She nodded as she patted the pocket in her jeans to make sure the ring was still there.

Eira kissed each of them goodbye, and they made their way to the closet door and into Yggdrasil Terminal.

EMBER PICKED up her pace as she followed Otto through town, weaving in and out of the crowds of people. They passed by a small park that sat off the beach, children running around and laughing, wearing party hats as their parents lounged at the picnic tables.

Celestial Steel sat in the middle of the bustling town, and Ember felt her breath catch in her chest as she walked into the open-air shop.

It was clearly mid-morning outside, obvious by the way the sun lit up the dusty cobblestone, but when Ember stepped through the archway and into the shop, all she could see above her were thousands of stars. Constellations twinkled as shooting stars moved across the inky black ceiling, and Ember found herself spinning to take in the view.

"Hello there, Otto," the shopkeeper said, as they walked further inside. "How's the family?"

"Oh they're grand, Cormac," Otto replied. "Keeping busy?"

Cormac laughed as he nodded. "Between carving first year Vegvesirs and fixing broken pendants, I hardly have time to sleep." He leaned against the counter as he rubbed the back of his hand against his brow. "Anything I can help you with today?"

"Aye," Otto nodded, "my daughter seems to have broken her ring. Do you have time for a quick repair today?"

Ember winced as her nails dug into her palms, swallowing dryly at the word.

*Daughter.*

Otto would gladly pluck the moon at out the sky if she asked him to, and she was having a near panic attack about him calling her his daughter. Did she really deserve people as wonderful as the Kitts?

"Of course." Cormac nodded with a smile.

Ember shook away the rising panic and fished the ring out of her pocket, gripping it tightly in her hand as she bit her lip. Otto gave her a gentle nudge and nodded toward the counter with a smile. Ember took a shaky breath and dropped the gold ring in the man's hand, quickly wiping her sweaty palm on her jeans.

"Now let's have a look, shall we," Cormac said, as he slipped a pair of glasses out of a pocket on his shirt and over the bridge of his nose. He turned it over a few times in his blackened fingers, mumbling to himself as he squinted. "Hmm, how interesting," he whispered. "Give me an hour, and I'll have it good as new." He smiled as he slipped his glasses off and put them back in his shirt pocket.

Ember tilted her head and nodded, letting out a breath. Relief washed over her like a tsunami as Otto thanked Cormac, and they made their way back out into the sun.

"How does some fish and chips sound?" Otto said, as they walked down the street.

Ember laughed. "We just had breakfast an hour ago,"

Otto shrugged as he put his arm over her shoulder. "Fish

51

and chips goes to a different part of your stomach," he said. "It's a well-known fact."

Ember laughed at the way he smiled, seeing so much of Fen in him. They made their way toward the docks where a small cart stood on the weathered wood. Otto put in their order, handing the owner a handful of coins while Ember leaned over the railing and kicked pieces of wood into the water. Otto brought over the food wrapped carefully in newspaper, and Ember walked beside him as she stuck salt and vinegar chips in her mouth.

"Are you excited to see Thea tomorrow??" Otto asked, as he stuck a piece of beer battered fish in his mouth.

Ember nodded silently. She loved seeing Thea, the woman would always have a special place in her heart. The way she lit up any room she walked in and never hesitated to check on Ember always made her feel safe. But that wasn't what Otto was asking. The unasked question lingered in the air between them as Ember felt her stomach sour.

*"Have you decided to go ahead with the adoption?"*

He smiled down at her, almost as if he could read her thoughts, and he ruffled her hair. "She's only coming to answer your questions, Mo Chroí," he reassured, as he stole one of her chips. "We meant what we said when we told you to take your time. It's a big decision and not one we want you to make lightly."

Ember swallowed the lump building in her throat as she nodded, unable to think of a reply. They continued and finished their food, stopping to look inside shops as they went.

"Ah, Mr. Kitt," a voice said from behind them.

Ember stopped in her tracks and turned to see Chief Thornsten walking up behind them.

"Good morning, Chief," Otto nodded. Ember noted the way his smile turned serious as he took a small step in front of her, straightening his spine just a hair.

"It is a good morning, isn't it?" Chief Thornsten smiled.

"And this must be Miss Lothbrok." He looked down at Ember. His smile was unnerving and sent a chill up her spine. She couldn't put her finger on why, but she didn't trust him. And from the way Otto was now standing, he didn't seem to, either.

"Aye, this is Ember," Otto replied, as he placed his hand on her shoulder. She felt his grip tighten, and she almost winced.

"I knew you had a foster child in your custody," Chief Thornsten replied, "but I don't believe I realized it was Torin and Aoife's child. How interesting."

Chief Thornsten's gaze raked over Ember, and she was so thankful she still had those green contacts hiding the lavender in her eyes. She hadn't found out any more about herself, no matter how many late nights she spent curled up with ancient books, but she knew better than to reveal her secret to the rest of the island. The chief smiled, and Ember bristled as she stiffened under the weight of Otto's hand. He squeezed her shoulder gently, and she let out a shaky breath.

"We are in the process of adopting her actually." Otto smiled as he looked down at Ember. Ember did her best to force a smile back as she nodded.

"Well, congratulations," Chief Thornsten replied. "I'm sure it will be a delightful day." He turned to Otto, changing the subject, "And your wards? Have you reinforced them?"

"Aye, Chief." He nodded. "Reinforced them yesterday."

"Good, good." Thornsten nodded. "If you need a ward breaker to come by, please Helio the office and let them know. We have several that specialize in warding against Fae and halfbreeds."

Ember choked on her breath as her eyes widened.

"Now, if you'll excuse me," Chief Thornsten continued, as he checked his watch, "I have some business to attend to."

Otto nodded. "Of course, Chief, good to see you."

Chief Thornsten turned to walk away.

"Why would he say that?" Ember asked once he was out of earshot. "They don't know that it's the Fae, do they?"

"No, they don't," Otto replied, as he shook his head, "but prejudice, like Chief Thornsten and many others on the island have, runs deep."

Ember shook her head as she furrowed her brow. They walked past Hidden Moon, and Ember noticed the heavy presence of the Guard around the shop. She couldn't imagine how anyone could be so cruel. Chief Thornsten was submitting these beings to a trial of public opinion, and it wasn't fair.

"Why do they hate them so much?" Ember asked, as she kicked a rock in front of her.

"I don't know that it's so much that they hate them," Otto replied, "but they don't understand them. Their magic is different, and instead of learning about them and trying to understand, they deem them as less than. They feel like their blood makes them superior."

Ember sighed as she crossed her arms. "That's just dumb," she huffed.

Otto let out a gruff laugh. "I agree, Mo Chroí. We can't change how people think, but we can stand up for what we know is right."

THE SKY BURNED ruby as Ember laid on the grass and soaked in the last of the Sunday afternoon. Thea would be by any moment, and Ember was a bundle of nerves. Maia laid on her stomach fast asleep, and Ember absentmindedly ran her hand across her back as she did her best to calm her racing thoughts.

"Em! Thea will be here soon, are you ready?" Fen called from the back door.

Ember turned around and smiled at her foster brother as she pushed herself off the ground. "As I'll ever be I guess," she breathed. "Is that what you're wearing?"

Fen had on his Rukr hoodie and a pair of pajama bottoms, complete with flannel slippers on his feet. He looked down at his outfit and furrowed his brow. "What's wrong with what I'm wearing?" he asked, as he motioned at his shirt.

"A little informal for company, don't you think?" Ember replied with a laugh.

Fen waved his hand as if to dismiss her. "I'm sure it's fine."

The two walked through the back door and into the kitchen where Eira had a pot of tea brewing, the dishes from dinner bobbing to a fro in the sink. Eira walked in from the dining room and narrowed her eyes in Fen's direction.

"Fenrir James, go put on real clothes right now," she scolded.

Fen huffed as he rolled his eyes. "Fine," he mumbled under his breath and headed up the stairs taking them two at a time.

"Ember love," Eira called, "would you set the den up for tea? Thea shouldn't be much longer."

Ember nodded as she grabbed the tray of cups and the pot of tea and carried them into the den, almost getting knocked over by Fen as he came scrambling down the steps.

"Need some help?" he asked eagerly, taking the cups from her hand. They walked into the den, setting everything on the coffee table in the middle of the room. Otto came in with Maeve hanging around his neck, quickly dropping her on the couch beside them. She jumped up on the cushions, twirling in her dress as the sun from the open window lit up her face.

"What do you think, Ember?" she squealed, as she leapt off the couch. "It doesn't have any holes or anything!"

Ember laughed as the girl danced around her. "It's beautiful, Maeve."

Eira walked into the den next, holding a plate of scones. Before she could set them down, a knock sounded at the door.

"Oh, that must be Thea." She smiled, turning back around, and bustling toward the door. She left the room quickly and stepped into the foyer. Ember listened as the door opened, and Eira greeted the woman behind it. She let out a loud gasp, and the sound of glass breaking echoed through the air. Otto's eyes widened as he rushed into the foyer, but his footsteps stopped abruptly, almost as soon as he got through the door. Ember's eyes met Fen's, and he gave her a shrug, but worry clouded his face.

"Ember love," Eira said shakily. "Ember, please come here."

Ember furrowed her brow as she walked toward the door that led to the foyer, chewing on the inside of her cheek.

"What's wrong?" she asked, as she stepped over the threshold. "Who's at the——"

Her eyes went wide as her heart thundered behind her ribs. Suddenly, her knees felt weak, and her legs felt like they might give out at any moment. Her head spun as she gripped the banister behind her, and all of the breath was immediately sucked from her lungs.

Green eyes met hazel, and it felt like cotton was lodged in her throat. She inched forward, moving without even realizing it, until she stood in front of the woman on the other side of the door. Voices echoed around her, but she couldn't hear them——they all sounded a million miles away. She took a shaky breath as she blinked a few times, tears now streaming down her face.

"Mum?" she whispered.

# CHAPTER 6

# A New Adventure

F en walked behind Ember and put his hand on her shoulder, steadying her as she swayed on her feet. Her center of gravity had all but disappeared, and she couldn't figure out which way was up. Her parents were dead, drowned at sea during a storm. She was an orphan.

So, how was it that her mother was now standing in front of her?

Ember shook her head. "I-I don't..." Her voice shook as she gripped the pendant around her neck. "I don't understand."

"Mo Stór," the woman whispered, her eyes glistening with tears, "you're alive."

Ember sucked in a breath and clamped her eyes shut. *My treasure.* That was what her mother had called her every day for six years. Her chest shook as tears slid down her cheeks. She took two steps and collapsed in her mother's arms. Her chest heaved as she sobbed into her shoulder, gripping her shirt with all of her might like she very well might disappear again if she let go.

"You're dead," she whispered again, as she shook her head. "I watched you die."

She had never talked in depth about that day to anyone—not fully. She gave everyone the cliff notes version, but she kept the details to herself. She didn't like reliving the fear on her mother's face as she was washed out to sea, choking on the salty water as waves crashed over her head. She didn't want to remember the way her father looked atop the jagged rocks on the beach—broken and bloody—or how cold he already felt when she curled up next to him and begged the stars to save him.

Her father had been thrown to shore first, salt water already in his lungs and his lips blue. His green eyes were lifeless as Ember beat her tiny hands against his chest, sobbing and retching as she coughed the salt water out of her own lungs. Her mother never washed up on the rocky beach, and Ember always assumed the waves had pulled her under, claiming her as their own.

"For the longest time, I wanted to be," her mother whispered, as she stroked her cheek with the back of her hand. "I'll explain everything, my love."

"Come in, Aoife." Otto motioned toward the living room as Eira nodded her head.

"I'll put on some tea," she mumbled and turned to walk out of the kitchen, wiping the tears off her cheeks. Ember's heart sank as she watched her walk away, ignoring the fact that there was already tea waiting in the den.

"Em, come on," Fen whispered, as he grabbed her hand and led her toward the living room. Ember sank into the couch beside Fen as he held her hand tightly, an anchor in this storm of emotions she wasn't prepared to weather. Aoife's face fell, but Ember couldn't move from her seat—couldn't make herself move to cling to her mother's side.

"I know this must come as a shock to all of you," Aoife said, as she sat in the chair by the fire and crossed her legs. "I was equally as shocked when I found out Ember was alive and on Ellesmere."

"And you're waiting until today to seek her out?" Otto asked, as he crossed his arms over his chest. The seriousness in his voice made the hair on Ember's neck stand on end. There was no laughter in his voice, just grit—ire radiating off his body like a billowing furnace. A fiery determination to protect his family.

And fear.

"If I had known she was here, I would've been here sooner," Aoife said, as she gave a small smile.

Ember squeezed Fen's hand one last time before he let go. It was the way they communicated with each other, something Fen had started doing after their encounter with Rowan the school year before. It was how they silently told each other they were there, no matter what.

Ember furrowed her brow. "I've been here for a year," she replied. "Why did it take you a year to find me? I've been right here." Her voice shook and bottom lip trembled as she squeezed her hands together in her lap.

"After the storm," Aoife breathed, "I woke up on a beach in Scotland. How I managed to get that far and live, I'm not sure, but when I woke up and was tended to by a doctor, they told me you were dead. I phoned the authorities, and they told me you and your father had died. I went back to Galway as fast as I could." She choked on a sob as tears welled in her eyes. "I identified your body and your father's. You were both... *dead*. So, I went back to Scotland to start over, to try to start fresh and forget about..." Her voice trailed off as her throat bobbed, and Ember felt like she had been hit by a truck.

Dead. Her mother thought she had been dead, all these years.

Ember shook her head. "I've been in foster care since I was six." She couldn't think of the right words to say—everything felt wrong on her tongue.

Aoife stood up and walked to the couch, sitting beside

Ember and taking a breath. "Both bodies were so mangled, it was almost impossible to identify, but they said they found you beside your father on the beach." Aoife stroked Ember's hair as she bit her lower lip. "She had your fiery red hair and a million freckles, the same bright green coat and your little pink life jacket." She closed her eyes, like the memory was causing her physical pain. "I am so sorry, my love." She ran her hand down Ember's cheek. "I never stopped praying that you would come back to me."

Tears streamed freely down Ember's face as she allowed herself to fall apart in her mother's arms. She had dreamed for years that she would feel this again, that she would hear her voice and watch the way her hazel eyes twinkled as she smiled. It had been a reoccurring dream she'd had on repeat since she was six years old.

And now it was real.

Eira let out a shaky breath as she walked toward the coffee table. "Tea is ready. I'll get the biscuits in the kitchen," she said gently, giving Ember a sad smile. Her eyes were rimmed red and puffy, and Ember's chest ached as she realized what would probably be one of the happiest days of her life would likely be one of Eira's saddest.

"Thank you, Eira." Aoife smiled. "Let me help."

"No," Eira replied, her smile tight, "no, thank you. I'll just be a moment."

"You okay?" Fen whispered, as he squeezed Ember's hand. He held tight to her, almost like if he let go, she would slip away forever.

"I think so." She nodded.

"I'm sorry to barge in on you this way," Aoife said from the chair by the fire. Her legs were crossed daintily one over the other, one hand in her lap and the other sipping her cup of tea. Her mannerism reminded Ember of Killian—poised and elegant, the perfect example of aristocratic grace. It was jarring. So far from the warm mother she remembered.

But then again, maybe the memory of a six-year-old wasn't one to be trusted.

"I do apologize if I've interrupted anything," she continued.

Fen stiffened, like he wanted to tell her what exactly she had just interrupted, but Ember cut in before he had the chance.

"So, what does this mean?" Ember sniffed as she wiped the moisture off her eyes. "Now that you're here, what happens?"

"If you're alright with it," Aoife smiled, "I would like to take you home."

Ember felt Fen's grip tighten around her fingers as she heard the breath leave his chest. Her own chest simultaneously swelled and ached. This was the only true home she had known in ten years. It was the only place she had ever lived that felt like more than a limbo she was waiting in till it was time for the next place. The Kitts' farm made her feel safe and warm, like she'd always imagined home would feel.

But her parents—her mother... Was this why she felt so stuck? Why the adoption never felt completely right? Because somewhere, in the back of her mind, she knew this story wasn't over?

"Back to Scotland?" she asked quietly. The thought of leaving this island, leaving Heksheim, made her stomach sour.

Aoife shook her head with a light laugh. "Our family home is on the other side of the island. We'll be living there."

Ember blew out a breath of relief. "I would love that, Mum." She smiled, and it was the truth. She had imagined a moment where her parents would walk through the door and take her home since she was six years old, and now, here she was.

"Wonderful." Aoife smiled as she looked around the room. "Would you be at all opposed to coming home with me now?"

*Home.*

Ember bit her lip as she looked toward Fen, then Otto and little Maeve. The latter seemed to be holding back tears as her bottom lip wobbled. Ember chest felt like it might cave in, the sorrow mixed with joy almost unbearable.

"Would it be okay if I finish the school week?" she asked, as she clasped her fingers in her lap, trying to keep from fidgeting. "It would give me time to pack."

*And time to say goodbye.*

"Of course." Aoife nodded, something like sadness flashing through her eyes. "I'll go home and begin preparing your room."

*My room.*

She smiled as she stood up and headed toward the door, Otto following closely behind. Ember gave her a hug as Otto opened the door for her, and Aoife gave her a gentle kiss on the forehead. When the door swung open, Thea was on the other side, shock painted across her perfect face.

"The ferry was late," she said, as her eyes went back and forth between Aoife and Ember. "I seem to have missed a very important development."

"Aoife Lothbrok," Aoife said, as she stuck out a hand to shake Thea's. "It's lovely to make your acquaintance."

Thea's eyes widened as she looked between the mother and daughter. "How lovely to meet you, Mrs. Lothbrok," she replied. "I'm sorry I didn't realize…"

"That I was alive?" Aoife smirked, and Thea's cheeks turned bright red.

"For lack of better words." The social worker nodded. Her eyes trailed to Ember, and they quickly grew misty, though her smile didn't quite reach her eyes.

Aoife turned back to Ember and gave her a kiss on the head, lingering like she didn't truly want to pull away. "I'll be back soon," she promised.

"I'll see you Friday, Mum." Ember smiled. She didn't want

to let go, afraid that if she took her eyes off her she would disappear again.

"I'll be here, Mo Stór," Aoife whispered, "I promise." She gave her one last hug and waved to the Kitts and Thea as she slipped out the door and into the darkness.

"I suppose you won't be needing that meeting tonight," Thea said with an awkward chuckle, but no one else laughed.

"Well," Eira breathed, "I think takeaway is in order tonight. Are you hungry, Thea?"

"Starved." She nodded.

Otto bobbed his head as he took a shaky breath. "I'll run to Florin's," was all he said before walking to the closet and slipping out the door. Eira smiled at Ember and squeezed her hand.

"Go start packing," she whispered to Ember. "We'll eat when your da... when Otto gets back."

Before Ember could turn around, Fen was racing out of the room and up the steps. After a few moments, she heard his door slam closed, and Ember's heart sank.

Eira sighed as she took a breath. "He'll be okay, love."

The faraway look in her eyes told Ember she wasn't only talking about Fen.

Ember took a shaky breath and gave her a half smile. "I'll go talk to him."

She steadied herself against the railing of the stairs as she climbed, counting down from ten to try and slow her breathing. She was excited, thrilled to be going home with her mother, but something deep in her chest ached for the life she had built that she was now leaving behind. She knocked gently on the door as she gripped the pendant swinging around her neck.

"It's open," Fen said quietly from the other side, his voice sounding small and hoarse. The door creaked open, and Ember stepped in, shutting it quietly behind her. Fen was sitting cross legged on his bed, twiddling his thumbs, eyes red and puffy as he sniffed and rubbed his arm across his cheek.

"So, I guess this is it." He sniffed as he pulled his sleeves down over his hands. "You're leaving."

Ember sat on the bed beside Fen and grabbed his hand. "Hey," she whispered, "I'm not moving off the island. We'll still see each other every day."

"But you won't be down the hall anymore." He sniffed as moisture built on his lower lash. "You won't sit across from me at the breakfast table or fly in the orchards with me before supper." He took a shaky breath and shook his head. "Everything is about to change."

Ember squeezed his hand tightly. "This won't change anything other than our sleeping arrangement." She smiled.

"You promise?" He looked up at her expectantly. The grief in his eyes was palpable. Ember was getting her family back; she was gaining something incredible that she had only ever dreamed of...

But Fen was losing his sister, and her heart ached.

"I swear it," she whispered, as she held tight to his hand.

Fen let out a sigh as he ran his fingers through his messy hair. "I don't like change."

Ember shrugged as she dropped his hand and leaned back on her elbows. "Then, we don't let anything change."

THE FAMILY SPENT their evening together around the fire in the living room eating curry chips and reminiscing on the last year. Maeve held tightly to Ember's arm as she snuggled into her shoulder. Ember relaxed into the couch as she laughed along with Fen's retelling of their final Rukr game last season, which ended with Killian in the mud and Fen somehow upside down on his board.

"Ember!" Maeve squeaked, as she bounced on her knees, "this weekend, can we ride in the orchard?"

Ember's heart sank as she looked at the girls' expectant smile. That summer, after receiving her own AirWave, she had been helping Maeve learn to ride. She would hover a foot off the ground, gripping Ember's hands as she squealed. The board didn't move fast, and she didn't go very high, but it was thrilling for the little one, nonetheless, and Ember had come to love spending time with her in the sinking summer sun.

"Maevie," Ember breathed, "I'm leaving Friday. I'm sorry."

The little girl furrowed her brow as she crossed her legs on the couch. "When will you be back?"

Ember sucked in a breath and turned to Eira and Otto, each bearing expressions that she couldn't quite place.

"Maevie, love," Eira said quietly, "Ember is moving home."

Maeve's bottom lip trembled. "But this is Ember's home," she whispered.

Ember closed her eyes as she bit her bottom lip. Tears threatened to spill over as she took slow, steady breaths.

"Mo Chroí," Otto said gently, as he knelt beside the teary-eyed girl, "Ember is going to live with her mum now. She's going back to her home with her family."

Maeve shook her head furiously. "We are her family," she argued, as tears pooled on the bottoms of her lashes. "Ember lives here with us. They can't take her."

Fen rolled his eyes. "No one is taking her, Maevie. How would you like it if someone kept you from Mum and Dad?"

Maeve crossed her arms over her chest. "I wouldn't like it," she mumbled.

"And we would miss you very much," Otto whispered. "That's how Ember's mum feels. She's been searching for her for ten years, longer than you've been alive, and she deserves to have her daughter back with her."

"But why does that mean I have to lose my sister," she whispered.

Ember wrapped her arms around the little girl and held her tight, running her hand down her hair. "You're not losing me, Maevie," she whispered. "Not now, and not ever."

"You'll come back, won't you?" Fen asked, as he twiddled his thumbs on the floor in front of her. "Come fly in the orchard on the weekends?"

Ember grinned as she kicked his knee playfully. "Wild draics couldn't keep me away."

LIGHT FILTERED through Ember's bedroom window, bathing the wood floor in what was left of the slowly setting sun. She was busying herself with packing her suitcase, meticulously checking each drawer in her dresser to make sure she had everything tucked away to take with her. She smiled as she pulled one of Maeve's drawings off the mirror above her dresser, laughing as the stick figure of a curly headed girl came to life and floated across the page, chasing chickens and donkeys through a wind whipped pasture. Ember folded it gently and tucked it inside her messenger bag to hang it in her new room.

Her heart sank, stomach coiling into knots as she walked around the warm room. She perched on the edge of the bed, eying the packed bags sitting by the door, and took a shaky breath. This had been her first true home since she had been placed in the foster system—the first place she had ever felt welcome. These walls had seen more love in the last year than any of the houses she had been in combined since her sixth birthday. She clutched the blankets on her bed, rubbing them between her fingers as she chewed her lip.

"Bittersweet, isn't it?" a voice rang from the doorway.

Ember wiped away the silent tear sliding down her face as Eira walked into the room and sat on the bed beside her. "It is." Ember gave a half smile as she nodded.

"You're allowed to be excited." Eira smiled as she tucked a stray piece of hair behind Ember's ear. "You don't have to keep it tucked away to save our feelings."

"It's so strange," Ember breathed, as tears pooled at the corner of her eyes. "I gave up dreaming of seeing them again before I even turned seven. I never would've imagined she would show up at my front door. It's all so…"

"Overwhelming?" Eira breathed with a laugh.

"Very." Ember shook her head with a smile. "You've all been so kind to me. You treated me like a daughter. I don't know how I'll ever repay you for what you've done for me."

"We did for you what we would've done for any of our children." Eira smiled as her eyes glistened with unshed tears. "No matter where you go, you will always be family, and we will always consider you a daughter. Nothing could change that. We are so thankful for the time we got with you. Now get some rest."

Eira hugged Ember tightly and walked out of the room, quietly closing the door behind her. Ember took a shuddering breath as she changed into her pajamas and slid beneath the sheets, wrapping herself tightly in the heavy quilt.

Her life was about to change forever. This was a moment she hadn't even let herself dream of, let alone think of how it could feel. Joy and grief thrashed in her chest like a tsunami, beating against her ribs and swirling in her stomach. Tomorrow, she would say goodbye to the home she had known for a year, the home that had saved her, and begin a new adventure.

# CHAPTER 7
# LOTHBROK MANOR

"You mean to tell me that in ten years, your mum has never once tried to look for you?" Killian asked, as he leaned against Arlo's stall door, tossing the silver case that his game-winning broja was locked in.

"She thought I was dead, Killian," Ember replied, as she rolled her eyes, quickly gathering all of Maia's things and packing them away in a bag. "Where exactly was she supposed to look? And for the love of Odin, will you stop throwing that? You're going to take someone's eye out."

Killian smirked as he tossed the silver ball into the air, but instead of landing in his hand, it hit the tips of his fingers and flew across the room, smacking right into Fen's face as he lay asleep on a bale of hay. Fen's eye shot open, and with a quick jerk, he tumbled off the bale and wound-up face first in the aisle of the barn.

"I rest my case," Ember mumbled, as she rolled her eyes.

"Sounds a bit odd, doesn't it?" Killian asked, as he helped his friend off the floor. "You've been on the island for a year now, and she had no idea? Ellesmere isn't small by any means, but it's not *that* big."

"She hasn't lived here," Ember replied, as she fed Maia a

handful of berries. "She was in Scotland till a few months ago. You don't know what she went through for the last ten years."

"True." Killian shrugged as he lazily leaned against the stall door. "But I do know I would cross oceans and deserts and otherworldly realms if it meant getting back to someone I loved."

Ember stared daggers at the boy as she grit her teeth. What did he know about losing anyone? His family wasn't perfect, but he had never known anything less than a life of luxury. Pristine floors, sparkling walls, meals fit for a king all inside his giant manor. He didn't know loss, not the kind of loss she had endured. Ember slid Maia's halter over her snout, rubbing the draic between the ears as she stood up and slung the duffel bag over her shoulder.

"Don't make me laugh," she scoffed. "You've never had to work for anything a day in your life."

Fen cleared his throat from the end of the corridor and scuffed his shoe across the paved floor. "Need any help, Em?"

Ember smiled as she shook her head. "No, I think that's about it." She attached the lead rope to Maia's halter and kissed the top of her head right as a Helio shot through the open door and hovered in the middle of the trio.

"Your mum is here, Ember," Eira's voice rang out from the bright blue orb, more meek than normal.

Ember took a breath, patting Maia on top of the head. "Time to see our new home," she whispered, then led the draic down the corridor and toward the house, both boys shuffling along behind her.

Ember rounded the corner of the house to see Eira, Otto, and her mum standing on the front porch. Eira's eyes were rimmed red and puffy, and her cheeks were pink, like she had spent all afternoon rubbing stray tears off them. Otto had her hand in his, and Ember watched his grip tighten around her pale skin every few seconds.

Ember's breath caught in her throat when her eyes landed

69

on her mum. Her long brown hair flowed over her shoulder in waves, and it swayed as she bobbed her head from side to side in conversation. A lump grew in Ember's throat as she tightened her grip on Maia's lead, tugging her along to the porch.

"Mo Chroí," Otto smiled sadly, "do you have everything?"

Ember nodded as she handed off Maia's lead to Killian, whose eyes were narrowed at Aoife. He stood tall, a half step in front of her, acting like she needed protection from her own mother. Fen wasn't much better, standing with his arms crossed tightly over his chest, close enough to her that she could feel that magic dancing like electricity off his skin. The invisible tether between the three tightened, humming as it vibrated. Both boys glanced toward her briefly, but no one else seemed to notice.

She nudged them both and shook her head, just enough for them to lower their guard as they nodded.

"Oh, a draic." Aoife smiled as she turned to pat Maia on the head.

The draic's nostrils flared, lavender eyes widening as she whipped her head back to Ember. Ember shook her head, as if to tell her to *behave*.

"She'll love the barn. I'll have the dryads set her up a stall when we get back to the manor," Aoife continued.

Ember choked on her own spit.

"What?" she breathed, as she furrowed her brow. "You live in a manor?"

"It's been in your father's family for generations. It's sat empty since we left the island, but I've had the dryads and Merrow working all week to get it ready for your return.

"Now who's spoiled," Killian laughed under his breath, as Ember jabbed him in the ribs.

"And who is this?" Aoife asked, as she nodded toward Killian, who was now rubbing between Maia's ears. He straightened himself up, plastered on a cocky grin, and held his hand out to shake Aoife's.

"Killian Vargr, Mrs. Lothbrok." He smiled charismatically. "Pleasure to meet ya."

"Vargr?" Aoife asked, as she tilted her head and squinted. "You wouldn't be kin to Magnus and Asena Vargr, would you?"

Ember glanced to her right as Killian stiffened, the muscle in his jaw tensing as his nostrils flared slightly.

"Aye," he nodded stiffly, "they're my parents."

"Well, do tell them I said hello." Aoife smiled sweetly, seemingly unaware of the way his fists clenched at the sound of his parents' names.

"Are you ready to go, my love?" Aoife turned back to Ember, who nodded her head and took a shaky breath. She gave both Eira and Otto a hug and squeezed Maeve as she leapt into her arms.

"Come back and see me?" the little girl asked through tear filled eyes.

"Of course I will." Ember smiled as she wiped stray tears from her reddened cheeks. "We'll have a flying lesson soon, okay?"

Maeve nodded her head vigorously before giving Ember one last tight hug and slipping back down onto the porch. Ember turned to Fen, who had his arms crossed tightly over his chest and was looking at anything other than her. Her heart sank as she walked toward him, stomach twisting into knots as she bit the inside of her cheek.

Fen was the closest thing she had ever had to a real sibling, him and Maeve both. While she knew this wasn't a forever goodbye, it still stung to see the way his eyes filled with tears every time he looked at her. This would change things, change their dynamic. No matter how much she tried to convince herself otherwise, she knew this was the end of something she had fought for for so long.

"I'll see you at school Monday." Ember smiled as she took a shaky breath. "Save me a seat in Zoomancy?"

"Yeah, of course." He nodded with a half-smile. "Come fly in the orchards soon?"

"Wild draics couldn't keep me away," she whispered back.

EMBER and her mother took the Echopoint outside of the Kitts' home straight to the manor. Hearing Aoife whisper, *"Lothbrok Manor,"* under her breath sent Ember's stomach flipping, but it wasn't from the spin of the Echopoint. She landed with a thud in a patch of bright green grass with yellow daffodils blooming around the trunk of the tree. A smooth cobblestone path stretched past the tree and through a pair of tall iron gates into a courtyard. A fountain sat in the middle of the cobblestone courtyard, the statue of a Kelpie standing in the center, surrounded by bushes of colorful, exotic looking plants and flowers.

Dryads walked amongst the rows of trees outside of the path, trimming low hanging branches while simultaneously sending floating watering cans to gently water the flowers scattered across the grounds. Ember smiled as one particular dryad, vines twisting across his arms and legs and a dark brown tunic with a cape hanging on his shoulders, whispered to one of the lower branches in a language that sounded like wind blowing through the leaves. A bright blue flower grew in his palm where he held the branch before he smiled to himself and turned to tend to the rest of the trees.

"Come, we'll have Maize get Maia situated while he's out here," Aoife said, as she motioned toward the dryad walking their way.

He stood tall, both hands behind his back as he nodded to Aoife, who gave him a kind smile back.

"Good evening, Maize," Aoife said sweetly. "I am very

excited to introduce you to my daughter Ember. Ember, this is Maize, the groundskeeper for the manor."

"Pleasure to meet you, Mr. Maize," Ember whispered.

"And you, Miss Ember." He smiled with a nod.

"Maize, would you be so kind as to take Maia and get her settled in the stables?" Aoife asked, as she motioned to the small draic.

Ember's grip tightened around Maia's lead rope.

"I will take very good care of her, Miss Lothbrok," Maize assured her, as she reluctantly handed over the lead.

Maia whipped her head back, trying to rip the lead from the dryad's hands, and let out a deafening roar like Ember had never heard before. She jumped forward to snatch the lead from his spindly fingers, but before she could get there, Maize was whispering something in Maia's ear, hand running down the draic's snout. Maia immediately settled, purring and clicking as she nuzzled his hand.

"She'll be in the stables waiting for you when you're settled." Maize smiled.

Ember's jaw hung slack as she nodded, her heart beginning to race in her chest before she felt her mother's hand on her shoulder and began to gently guide her toward the manor. Ember followed her mother up the path to the large, oak double doors. She sucked in a breath as they swung open, eyes raking over the mahogany floors bathed in apricot and plum shining through the floor-to-ceiling windows lining the walls. A grand staircase was directly in front of her, spiraling up to the second and third floors, no doubt filled with long halls and cozy rooms. The living room could be seen through a large archway to her right, and Ember's mind reeled with the idea of all the cozy winter nights in front of the fire curled up with a book and a warm cup of tea. Somewhere in the house, a clock chimed eight times, and the door behind her swung shut.

"Your room is up on the second floor, first door on the

right." Aoife smiled as she motioned toward the staircase. "Do you need help getting settled in?"

Ember shook her head with a small smile. "I've got it down to a science at this point," she half laughed. "I'll be okay."

Aoife frowned as she wrapped her in a hug, kissing her gently on the head as she stroked her hair. "I'm so sorry," she whispered, as she pulled away and took a shaky breath. "All of that is over now. Now, you're home."

*Home.*

"Mum?" Ember shouted, as she walked down the stairs the next morning, rounding into the hall toward where she assumed the kitchen was, evident only by the heavenly smell that was wafting toward her. "Mum, are you in here?"

"Good morning, Miss Ember," a voice said from the kitchen. "Breakfast is ready."

Ember walked into the room to see a young Merrow standing at the counter preparing a plate of eggs, bacon, and fried potatoes. A fresh pot of tea was sitting on the stove, and the Merrow summoned it to the teacups sitting on the counter beside her.

"Oh, um, good morning," Ember mumbled, as she entered the room. "I'm sorry, do I know you?" There was something familiar about her that Ember couldn't quite place. The memory was there, buried in the back of her mind, but it was like a shadow lingered over it. She was older than Maren, perhaps a little younger than her mother, and her hair fell in deep mauve waves over her shoulders. Ember's heart broke as she thought about the Clann and what her parents must be going through. How long had she been gone? Had she lived here at the manor her whole life? Did her mum understand what the Merrow went through? Where was her cape?

They would have to talk about that later.

"I don't believe so." The Merrow smiled warmly. "My name is Gaelen. Tea?"

"Oh, yes please." Ember nodded. She walked further into the kitchen but stopped short, her heart jumping into her throat when she peeked into the little breakfast nook in the corner by the large window. There was a little boy with fiery red hair and bright green eyes tucked into the corner eating his breakfast. He didn't so much as flinch when Ember walked into the room, didn't even look up to acknowledge her presence. Gaelen summoned the pot of tea to the center of the small table, charming it to pour the amber liquid into each mug.

"Sit," she said to Ember, as she motioned to the table. "Your mum should be down shortly."

Ember nodded as she slipped into the seat across from the boy, barely acknowledging the plate in front of her as she studied him intently. There was something vaguely familiar about him, but she couldn't place what it was. He bit the edge of his lip as he traced his fingers along the grains of wood. Her breath hitched in her throat with the way his nose scrunched, highlighting the freckles that traveled across the bridge of his nose and over his cheeks.

"Hello there," she whispered, as she tapped her finger against the table. "My name is Ember. What's yours?"

The boy looked up at her for a moment, emerald eyes meeting hers, before he quickly averted them and focused again on his breakfast. Ember furrowed her brow as she waited for a response, but one never came. She let out a sigh as she reached for her tea when another pair of footsteps entered the room.

"Oh, good morning, loves." Aoife smiled as she walked to

the table and kissed Ember gently on the head, then did the same with the boy. "I see you've met Theo."

Ember tilted her head in confusion as she looked at her mother and then back to the boy, who was now staring back at her.

"It's nice to meet you, Theo," she said with a smile. "How old are you?"

Theo looked up at Aoife and then back to Ember.

"He can't answer you, I'm afraid," Aoife said, as she smiled down at the boy, patting his head. "He's mute."

Ember's chest tightened as she sucked in a breath. " Mute?" she whispered. "He can't speak at all?"

"Not at all," Aoife replied, a sad smile tugging at her lips. "I assumed it would happen eventually, but it never did." Something like regret washed over her face—a shadow of blame, like it was somehow her fault.

"How old is he?" Ember asked, as she tilted her head.

"Ten." Aoife smoothed the boy's hair. "We just celebrated his birthday a month ago."

Ember stiffened, her chest tightening as she looked the little boy over again, trying to place where she knew him, where she had seen him before. His green eyes sparkled as he looked toward her, and something vaguely familiar stared back that made Ember's stomach coil into tight knots.

"Does he live here?" Ember asked, as she furrowed her brow.

"Oh, love, yes, I'm sorry." Aoife smiled as she shook her head. "Theo is your little brother."

Ember's head began to spin as she sucked in a breath, and the realization of where she knew him from, where she recognized those eyes and freckles from, hit her like a freight train barreling down a mountain.

She was staring into her father's eyes.

"My brother?" she whispered, struggling to catch her breath. "But that means you were—"

"Yes," Aoife nodded, "I was pregnant before the storm. Just barely, though. I didn't find out until a few months after."

"Why didn't you tell me?" Ember asked, suddenly at a loss for what she really wanted to say.

*Why did you lie?*

"It felt like something you needed to see in person first," Aoife replied with a placating smile.

Ember nodded, suddenly unable to form any actual thoughts, let alone sentences. The little boy looked up at her, green eyes twinkling as he gave her a small smile, and Ember could've sworn she was back in their cottage in Galway, staring at those same green eyes and freckled face as her father told her stories about the witches in the stars.

"Gaelen," Aoife said over her shoulder, "would you mind getting Theo ready for the day? He has riding lessons this afternoon." She kissed Theo on the head as Gaelen motioned for him and led him out of the room.

"I had Gaelen plan a special supper tonight in honor of your return," Aoife said., "How does corned beef and cabbage with potatoes sound? I even had Maize pick some fresh peas from the garden to go on the side."

Ember gritted her teeth. "Oh, um, I don't like peas, Mum," She forced a smile. "But I'm sure it will be lovely."

"Oh," Aoife gave an apologetic smile, "I'm sorry, love, I must've forgotten. I could've sworn you loved them."

There had never been a day in her life Ember had liked peas, or corned beef for the matter. Since she was old enough to sit at a table on her own, she had done everything in her power to keep them off her plate. But it had been years since her mother had made her food, let alone sat at a table with her, so of course she wouldn't remember something as insignificant as her hatred of peas.

Ember's face fell, and Aoife squeezed her hand.

"You'll have to forgive me," she said, as she loosed a breath. "It's been so long, it's going to take some time to find our new normal. For *me* to find my new normal." She bit her lip as she tapped a finger on the table. "How would you like to go into town with me tomorrow?" Aoife continued, as she sat at the table opposite her daughter. "Maybe see if there are any new releases at the Bookwyrm?"

Ember could feel her face light up as she nodded vigorously, the tea in her mug sloshing around as she moved. She felt something warm in her chest, like small puzzle pieces shifting back into place. She took a sip of her tea when a knock sounded on the front door.

"Hm," Aoife said, as she furrowed her brow, "I don't think we're expecting anyone."

"I'll get it." Ember smiled as she walked away from the table into the foyer. The door swung open, and her heart leapt into her throat. "Killian! Fen!" She nearly screamed with excitement. "What are you doing here?"

"You forgot your AirWave." Fen smiled as he handed her the board that was tucked under his arm. "And Da' picked up your ring, had to bring them over. Can't have you getting rusty laid up in this big house with all your books."

"Plus I had to see if your new house was bigger than mine." Killian smirked as he waltzed into the foyer, hands stuffed lazily in his pockets as he let out a low whistle. "Very nice, Starshine."

Ember rolled her eyes as she shut the door and watched both boys inspect the rich mahogany on the banister. "It's quite big," she breathed a small laugh. "Haven't had much of a chance to explore yet, though. I've been a bit... preoccupied this morning." Her breath caught as she remembered Theo, his bright green eyes staring at her from across the breakfast table. "I have something to tell you, but not here. Let's go outside."

Both boys exchanged a worried look and nodded wordlessly, following Ember out the door and into the garden. She sat on the edge of the fountain, feeling the sun beat down on her face as both boys looked at each other in worried silence.

"Find a body in the basement or something?" Fen laughed as he sat beside her.

Ember shook her head with a smile that didn't quite reach her eyes.

Killian furrowed his brow, arms crossed tightly over his chest as he cocked his head. "What's going on, Starshine?" he whispered.

Ember took a shaky breath. "I have a little brother," she whispered, as she bit her lip. "I met him just a little while ago."

Fen's jaw hung slack as his eyebrows shot up his forehead.

"How is that even possible?" Killian asked, as he furrowed his brow.

"Well, Vargr," Fen quipped, "when a mummy witch and a daddy witch love each other very much—"

"Now is not the time, Fenrir James," Ember scolded, as she rolled her eyes and turned toward Killian. "She was pregnant before the storm. He's ten, and he's mute."

"He can't talk at all?" Fen asked, as he leaned back on the fountain, dipping his hands in the water to play with the fish.

Ember shrugged. "Mum says he never has."

"Can't talk? Or *won't* talk?" Killian asked, as he arched a brow.

Ember shot him a glare.

"Does he know sign language? Or any other way to communicate?" Killian continued, as he crossed his arms.

Ember shrugged again.

"Maybe telepathy?" Fen tapped his chin. Ember cut her eyes at him, and he threw his hands up in front of him. "Just a thought."

Killian scoffed as he looked back up to the house. "Your mum has plenty of money to figure something out."

Ember furrowed her brow angrily. "Are you saying she did

this intentionally? That she has willingly neglected her son? Honestly, Killian, don't be stupid."

Killian's eyes narrowed. "I'm saying there are alternatives to letting a child suffer in silence and not be able to communicate with his own mother, that's all."

Ember crossed her arms tightly over her chest. "She's doing the best she can," she argued. "She lost her husband and daughter and had to raise him on her own. Not everyone has it as easy as you do, Vargr."

His face fell, and Ember immediately regretted her words. Killian had anything but an easy life, at least when it came to his family. His past was bloody and bruised, littered with hidden scars and terrible secrets. Ember closed her eyes as she bit her lip.

"I'm sorry," she whispered. "I didn't mean that."

Killian shrugged with a half smile. "I won't lie and say I didn't have it better than most in some ways."

Ember caught Fen turning around out of the corner of her eye, and she whipped around to see him ogling at Maize pruning the trees around the yard.

"You have a dryad?" he whispered, as his jaw hung slack. "You *must* be loaded."

Ember rolled her eyes. "I don't *have* a dryad," she quipped. "He's not a potted plant. He works here."

"That's not how that works with these types of families." Killian laughed. "He might not be a Merrow, but he most certainly doesn't do this because he wants to."

Ember huffed. "Can we talk about anything other than my mother's money please?" she groaned.

"Alright." Killian smirked. "Are you ready for tryouts?"

"Ugh." Ember rubbed the bridge of her nose. "Anything other than that too."

"Scared, Lothbrok?" Killian smirked. Ember cut her eyes at him before letting out a long sigh.

"Scared or not," Fen said loudly, as he pulled an apple off

one of the low hanging branches, prompting Maize to give him a stare that forced him to back away slowly, "they're coming up quickly. We should probably practice this weekend. Maybe at the orchards?"

Ember chewed her lip as she shook her head. "I have plans with my mum actually." She tried not to smile too widely at the thought of shopping with her mum, something she never dreamed she would get to do. "I should probably stay close to home for now, until I'm settled anyway. I wouldn't want her to think I'm not happy."

Fen's face fell, and Ember felt her chest tighten. She didn't want to lose Fen, but she had to focus on rebuilding her relationship with her mother. That was what was important right now. She shook the thought away—she would find her new normal with Fen eventually, but right now, this is what mattered.

Fen nodded with a shrug, forcing a smile. "Maybe some other time."

Ember nodded in reply. "Yeah, maybe. I should head back inside, but see you at school?"

"See you then, Starshine." Killian winked and quickly pulled Fen down the long drive toward the Echopoint.

Ember wandered back in the house, slowly making her way up the steps to her room. She winced as she stood in front of the oak door. It didn't feel like her room, not the way she thought it would, not the way her room at the Kitts' had felt. She shook her head and turned the knob, insistent that the feeling of all the newness would pass and she would feel just as comfortable in this manor as she had at the farm. It would just take time.

Her room was filled with deep greens, her favorite color for as long as she could remember. Her four-poster bed was pushed up against the center of the wall, and large picture windows were scattered throughout. All of her favorite books from her childhood filled the small bookshelf on the far wall, some even still had the bookmarks in them where her father had stopped reading for the night. Her chest clenched as she climbed onto bed and hugged the stuffed dragon her mother had given her for her second birthday, something she always imagined had been lost forever.

The entire room was curated just for her, to make her feel as at home as possible after ten years of longing for this feeling. It was filled with love and comfort and nostalgia for a home that she never imagined she would even glimpse again. Her breathing eased as she looked out the window to the gardens beyond. Yes, it would just take time.

Time was something she was very good at.

## CHAPTER 8
# NOBLE BLOOD AND BRUISES

**K**illian's shoes echoed off the tile as he walked through the foyer and toward the kitchen. Isra, their new Merrow, was preparing food at the stove when he walked in and slid himself into a seat at the bar. Isra had been brought to the house almost immediately after Maren had gone "missing," much to the trio's dismay. She looked to be no older than eighteen or nineteen, and for her first month in the manor, she could barely hold a spoon with how bad her hands shook. Killian, Ember, and Fen searched the cold house up and down, looking for her cape to send her back home, but they never found it. Apparently, his father had found a *much* better hiding place this time.

So much for freeing an enslaved race.

Leif was already at the bar, jabbering away about nothing and everything, snacking on a plate of apples and cheese. Killian snatched a slice, quickly popping it in his mouth. Leif narrowed his eyes at his older brother, grabbing the plate and wrapping his arms around it, acting like a human shield.

"Get your own food," he mumbled through bites of cheddar and swiss.

Killian laughed as he drummed his fingers on the kitchen

counter. "Isra," he said, as he turned to the Merrow, "do we have any books on sign language?" He felt bad for Ember, that she couldn't talk to her little brother, but he felt even worse for Theo. He knew all too well how it felt to live with a parent who didn't take the time to see to even their most basic needs.

Isra smiled as she nodded. "I believe your mother has a few in her study," she said, as she stirred the stew on the stove, "so you might ask her if you can borrow them."

Killian groaned as he laid his head on his arms—that was quite literally the last thing he wanted to do. Their education on any subject had never been their mother's responsibility. Their father saw to it that they knew what they needed to be upstanding members of society, hiring tutors and teachers until they were of age to go to Heksheim. Killian could see the way it hurt his mother not to be a bigger part of their life, but that wasn't the way for Vala like them, and no number of tears from a broken little boy would change that—would change *her*.

"Go talk to her," Isra whispered and then turned away, ignoring him completely.

Killian walked slowly down the hall, knocking quietly when he got to the study door. It opened gently, and his mother sat on the other side, reading a book in her chair, polite and poised in front of the fire. Righteous anger bubbled in his chest—his father was on the other side of the manor in his own study. Why couldn't he spend time with her? He thought about the Kitts and how Eira and Otto never seemed to leave each other's sides, and he couldn't help but feel pity for his parents, for the love they would never truly feel.

"Mother," he said, as he walked into the room and cleared his throat, "I was wondering if I could borrow a book."

Asena tilted her head as she narrowed her eyes. "A book?" she asked. "What kind of book?"

Killian walked into the room, stuffing his hands in his pockets. "A book of sign language," he said, as he looked

84

toward the shelves, scanning the spines, "to help a friend." She didn't need all the details, and he wasn't about to offer any.

"Ember Lothbrok?" Asena asked quietly, eyes twinkling as she closed the book in her hands.

Killian's chest tightened as he gave a quick nod.

"I see," Asena replied. "Want to brush up on everything your tutors taught you?"

Killian nodded as he walked toward the shelves. His tutors had tried to teach him sign language when he was Leif's age, but the truth was, he didn't remember much. He spent most of his time doodling or staring out the window, failing almost every single test they gave him. The only reason they gave him a passing grade, his brother said, is because their father had made some very pointed threats toward their families.

"I didn't know the Lothbrok girl's mother had turned up," a voice boomed from the entryway to the room. "What a surprising turn of events."

Killian tried not to jump as his father walked through the door, snatching a piece of paper from the desk in the far corner and stuffing it in his pocket.

"Good thing if you ask me," he laughed gruffly, pouring himself a glass of whiskey from the decanter by the window. "She needs to be with her own kind."

"What is that supposed to mean?" Killian asked, as he narrowed his eyes.

"The Kitts aren't exactly of *noble* blood," Magnus said, as he tilted the glass to his lips, whiskey dripping down his beard. "They don't need to be in charge of raising any more of the next generation if you ask me."

Asena seemed to nod just to placate him, and Killian grit his teeth.

"They are some of the best people on this island," Killian hissed. "Just because they don't have as much money as you do doesn't make them any less than."

"That's exactly what it makes them." Magnus grinned.

"No child of mine would be raised by people like them. Good on Aoife for finally finding her and bringing her back where she belongs."

Killian flexed his fingers. His father hadn't raised any of them, so what did he know about parenting to begin with? He grabbed a few books from the shelf and then strode to the door, slamming it as he walked away. He stomped up the steps, locking himself in his room.

The truth was, he would give anything to have a mother like Eira, even if she did have a temper. He loved his mother, but she would never stand up for him or his brothers the way they deserved. She would always let his father have the final word. Something inside her broke long before Killian was born, and she had never gathered the strength to try to mend it.

Some days, Killian wanted to hate her for it, wanted to grab her by the shoulders and shake her as hard as he could. He couldn't stand the way his father walked all over her and the way she just let him. Righteous anger burned in his chest when he saw the bruises, saw the welts and the black eyes that couldn't be hidden by powder and blush. She wore them with her head held high, but Killian could see the brokenness underneath.

He sighed and shook his head, throwing the books onto his bed and kicking off his shoes. There wasn't much he could do about his home life, but he could work to make Ember and Theo's a little easier. He dug into the books, committing every word to memory, practicing the signs until his fingers went numb. Things he had been taught as a child came flooding back, like he had unlocked a dam, rushing to flood his memories. His eyes burned as he flipped the pages over and over, and just as his stomach began to rumble, demanding food, his door creaked open.

"You missed supper," Leif said, as he peeked his head in.

"Isra saved you some leftovers." The little boy tiptoed into the room, a bowl of stew and bread in his hands.

"Gods, I didn't even realize how late it was," Killian said, as he rubbed his eyes, flipping the book in front of him closed. Leif gave him the bowl, and then climbed on the bed to sit with him as he ate.

"What are you reading?" he asked, as he peered at the titles. He was seven, the same age as Maeve, sharing Killian's blond hair and grey eyes, but the two boys couldn't have been more different. He was their mother's perfect angel and could do no wrong in her eyes. And while he might not be the heir that Rafe was, his father still showed him a love—or something akin to it—that Killian had never experienced.

But despite it all, for reasons Killian didn't fully understand, Leif looked up to him. He followed him around, often ending up in his room asking questions he could've easily gotten the answer for from Isra or Rafe. It annoyed Killian at first, the way he seemed to follow him around like a lost puppy, but as he got older, he began not to mind. Sometimes he even enjoyed it. Because despite how their mother fawned over him, no matter how kind their father pretended to be, there till seemed to be a lost little boy underneath it all, begging for some form of warmth in this cold house.

Killian could see a fire flickering behind the little boy's eyes. A fire, that if fanned just right, could burn forests to the ground.

"I'm learning sign language," Killian said in between bites of stew, "to help a friend be able to talk to her little brother."

"Your friend Ember?" Leif asked. He had no doubt heard him talking to Isra about her before.

Killian nodded his head as he chewed.

"Da' says you should be careful around her," he said nonchalantly, "her and the Kitts. I heard him talking to Mummy about it."

Killian narrowed his eyes. "I wouldn't worry too much

about what Da' says," he huffed, as he took another bite. "Ember and the Kitts are some of the best people I know. Better than the lot he brings around. Better than most of the people that live in this house."

Leif's face sank, and Killian winced.

"Wanna help me practice?" he asked the little boy, as he set the bowl aside. "Maybe you and Theo could be friends. I bet he could use a friend as great as you."

Leif's face lit up as he nodded and scrambled to sit beside Killian, who opened the book and began.

# CHAPTER 9

# SIGN LANGUAGE AND OTHER SECRETS

E mber walked into the kitchen after school, her stomach growling, and legs aching. Fen had made her stay to get in some flying practice after classes concluded, and she was ready to eat and collapse in her warm bed for the rest of the evening. She made her way into the kitchen but stopped when she saw Theo and Gaelen at the table.

Theo's hands moved rapidly in front of him as he grinned in between taking bites of the sliced apple on his plate. Gaelen laughed at something and then began moving her fingers as she shook her head.

"Why does he know sign language?" Ember asked, as she stepped into the room.

Theo's eyes widened as he shrunk into himself, snapping his head toward Gaelen.

"It's how he communicates," Gaelen replied, "and how I communicate with him."

"He can't hear you?" Ember furrowed her brow.

Gaelen shook her head. "Theo is deaf." She gave a half smile. "he can't hear anything."

The little boy twiddled his thumbs beside her, and Ember felt her heart sink.

"Does Mum not know?" she asked. "Did no one think to tell her?"

"She knows," Gaelen replied with a sad smile. "I think It's been hard for her to come to terms with, and often times, she denies it altogether. She blames herself for it."

"Why?" Ember asked, as she furrowed her brow.

"Theo was raised by me, just like most Vala children and the Merrow that work in their homes," Gaelen replied. "It happened after he suffered a very high fever for a prolonged amount of time when he was little. He didn't speak before that, that much is true, but the loss of his hearing made it almost impossible for him to speak after the fact."

"And there's nothing the healers could do?" Ember asked, as rage burned in her stomach. "No spell or potion or ritual that could bring his hearing back? They just sat back an allowed it?"

"*I* am his healer." Gaelen straightened, cocking a brow. "His magical core was damaged along with the fever. There was nothing any of us could do."

"Why didn't my mum tell me he was deaf?" Ember asked, as she looked over toward Theo. "Why didn't *you* tell me?" He was her little brother after all, even if they had only known each other for a few days.

"Theo didn't want anyone to know. It wasn't my secret to tell." She peered at Ember, as if to say *you of all people should understand that.*

Ember nodded, biting her lip as she gripped the strap of her bag, and then turned to walk out of the room. She crossed the foyer, making her way into the den and immediately began rifling through the books on the shelves lining the walls.

"Looking for something in particular?" Aoife asked, as she walked into the room.

Ember jumped, knocking a book off the shelf as she

turned. She frowned as she bent to pick up the copy of *A Vala's Guide to Magical Maladies* and gently placed it back on the shelf. "Sorry," she mumbled, as she averted her eyes. "Do we have any books about sign language?" She didn't mention what it was for, but Aoife didn't seem inclined to ask.

Aoife tapped her chin as she seemed to rack her brain. "I'm afraid I have no idea," she sighed. "Books were always your father's favorite pastime, something I see you've inherited from him. We do have a very well stocked library upstairs that has been collecting dust for some time now. You could take a look in there. I'm sure he had something."

Ember's heart leapt into her throat as she grinned. The idea that her father might have things here that he had left had never even crossed her mind. She had gone her entire childhood with just a journal and a ring to remind her of her parents, and now she had an entire manor full of things that whispered of him. She quickly threw her bag back over her shoulder and rushed across the room in two strides to wrap Aoife in a hug.

"Thanks, Mum," she whispered with a smile.

"Of course, Mo Stor," Aoife replied, as she brushed a stray hair off her cheek. "I'll be in the kitchen if you need anything."

Ember nodded with a smile as her mother left the room, and then all but sprinted toward the stairs in the foyer. After running up two sets of spiral stairs and getting lost down several halls that felt never ending, Ember finally spotted a set of double doors at the end of a long corridor and quickly walked up and pushed them open.

The sight that greeted her was one she had only ever dreamed of. Sunlight beamed through the large window, soaking the floor in peach and lilac. The window reached all the way to the top of the vaulted ceiling that was supported by large beams running from wall to wall. Shelves lined the walls, accompanied by stairs on each side and led to the second floor of books. Ember felt her stomach flip, positive she was dreaming.

Oh, but what a wonderful dream it was.

She quickly dropped her father's journal in a comfy chair tucked away in a corner and Helio'd Killian to ask for a book recommendation. He had mentioned something earlier that day about a book on sign language he had found, and she was willing to bet her father had a copy somewhere too. She walked along the shelves, pulling out old tomes and searching for anything that had to do with sign language, when she heard the double doors swing open and then close again. Ember poked her head around a shelf, only to see a tall blond with campfire eyes leaning against the wall.

Instead of replying to her Helio, Killian had decided it was best to just show up.

"How did you get in here?" were the only words she could think of as she furrowed her brow and struggled under the weight of the books in her arms.

Killian glided across the room, snatching them away, and carried them to the chair she had set her father's journal in.

"Your Merrow let me in, erm…" He stared at the ceiling for a moment. "Gaelen, I think? She told me I could find you in the library."

"It took me a solid twenty-five minutes to find this room," she scoffed. "How did you get here so quickly?"

Killian barked a laugh as he sank into the chair. "I've been navigating manors since I could walk, Starhshine," He smirked. "They're all grand, but all laid out in the same fashion. The library is always on the third or fourth floor, at the end of a wide corridor with giant, double doors. It took me five minutes."

Ember furrowed her brow as she pressed her arms tightly across her chest. She had been thrown into this life, and she stuck out like a sore thumb. But he had been raised this way, and it was almost infuriating how easy it all was for him.

"Gaelen also told me where the library was." He smirked, laughing as he dodged the book Ember had hurtled at his head.

"Well, as long as you're here, you might as well help," she replied, quickly summoning the book back to her and shoving it into Killian's chest. "What do you know about sign language?"

"I know a bit." He shrugged. "Why do you ask?"

"Because Theo isn't mute," she replied, as she shuffled through books. "He's deaf. If I learn, then I can talk to him without Gaelen needing to interpret."

"Your mum doesn't know he's deaf?" Killian narrowed his eyes, and Ember averted hers—she wasn't interested in hearing what he thought about her mother again.

"She does. She just didn't tell me." Ember tried to ignore the sting at that realization, the way the words sighed heavy on her chest. "Theo didn't want anyone to know, so Gaelen didn't say anything." She blew a stray piece of hair out of her eyes as she leaned on the table. "But that is irrelevant," she continued. "I want to be able to communicate with my brother, even if he didn't want anyone to know." She knew how lonely it was to be in a house full of people that couldn't understand a word you were saying—or didn't bother to try.

"Right," Killian nodded. "Well, I suppose let's start with the basics." He pushed himself out of the chair and took a step forward, directly in front of Ember. He undid the top button of his shirt, revealing the skin beneath, and rolled both sleeves up to his elbows. Something about it felt strangely intimate, and Ember found herself searching for something else to look at, squeezing the book she was holding tightly against her chest. He placed his hand on the book and tugged it out of her arms.

"First step is to put away the book, Starshine." He smirked and tossed it into the chair behind him.

Ember nodded as she swallowed dryly. "Right, of course." She dropped her hands and flexed them at her sides.

"Assuming he probably has no idea who you are," he huffed, almost angrily, "it's best start with the introduction." He placed his fist in the center of his chest and nodded at Ember to do the same.

"My…" he said, moving his hand out and back to his chest. "…name…" He held his right hand in front of his face, holding up just his pointer and thumb in front of his mouth before he pinched them together and pulled his arm to the right. "…is Ember," he whispered, as he signed each letter of her name.

She could hardly pay attention to what he was doing. The way he breathed her name made her chest tighten, goose bumps running down her arms, heat creeping up her neck.

"Starshine?" he asked, as he waved his hand in front of her face, snapping her out of her trance.

"What?" she whispered.

"You try." He laughed as he nodded in her direction with a smile.

"Oh, right," she sighed, as she shook her head. "My… name… is… Ember," she said, as she concentrated on mirroring the movements Killian had done before. She looked up at him smiling with his hand over his mouth shaking his head. "This is too complicated."

"It's not," he chuckled. "You're just making it complicated. Here, it's like this." He stepped closer and gently grabbed her right wrist, put his hand over her fingers, curled them into a fist, and then placed it over the center of her chest. "My…" he whispered, as he stepped closer.

Ember's breath hitched in her chest as she swallowed dryly and nodded, green eyes locked with charcoal. He took her hand again, moving her fingers to make a backwards 'L.' His fingers brushed against her cheek, and he gently pulled her wrist to the right of her face, making her skin tingle and heart flutter.

"Name…" he whispered with a grin, stepping closer, hand still wrapped around her tiny wrist. He slowly moved her hand to form the different letters of her name as she took a shaky breath. "Is Ember," he said huskily, his fingers gently brushing against the back of her hand.

Ember's breath stuttered as her heartbeat wildly in her chest. She nodded that she understood, but before either of them could say anything, or acknowledge the heaviness that had settled in the room, a Helio zipped under the closed door of the library and stopped right in the middle of them, hovering at their chests. Ember took a step back as Fen's panicked voice rang through the room around them.

*"Come quick,"* was all he said before the blue light vanished in a puff of mist.

EMBER RAN down the steps to tell her mother where she was going and caught the tail end of a Helio she was sending out.

"She's safe with me," Aoife snapped on the other side of the study door, "She's with me now."

Ember shook away the questions as Killian grabbed her hand and sped out the front door and to the Echopoint at the end of the front path. They grabbed the lowest branch, and Ember barely registered that Killian had grabbed her free hand and muttered, *"Kitt,"* under his breath. They spun through the air, landing with a thud outside the familiar gate, pushing through it and running quickly up the long drive. When they finally reached the house, Ember's heart dropped to her stomach. She sucked in a breath, instinctively squeezing Killian's hand that she still hadn't let go of.

The porch was covered in officers of the Guard. Wardens. Men clad in black and brown leather, like warriors from one of her fantasy books, walking in and out of the house and around the back and sides. Ember noticed the leather bracelets that each of them had on their wrists, and the runes tattooed on their right arms. One of them narrowed his eyes at Ember as they made their way across the front lawn, jaw tensing as he watched her walk. Ember swallowed dryly as she averted her eyes. Even Chief Thornsten was there, standing in the yard, talking to Otto and Eira as Killian and Ember made their way toward them.

"Ember!" Maeve yelled, but not in the joyful squeal she had become accustomed to hearing from the little girl. Her freckled cheeks were bright red and coated in dried tears, and she sniffled as she wrapped her arms tightly around Ember's waist.

"Maeve, what's wrong?" Ember asked quietly, as she knelt to hug the little girl, who then collapsed into her arms.

"It was so scary," was all she whispered, as she buried her head into Ember's neck.

Ember stood up and walked toward the family standing by the porch, Maeve's arms still wrapped tightly around her waist.

"Mo Chroi, you're okay," Otto breathed, as he broke away from the chief and wrapped Ember in a hug, kissing her lovingly on the head before scooping Maeve into his arms.

Ember furrowed her brow in confusion as she nodded. Of course she was fine. Her house wasn't the one covered in Wardens.

"You made it," Fen said, as he rushed toward them, stopping abruptly as he narrowed his eyes. "At the same time," he said, as he looked between the two. "Were you together?"

"Killian came over to help me learn some sign language," Ember said quickly before Killian could chime in. "We got your Helio and came over together."

She wasn't sure why she was nervous, or why she felt like she was lying to Fen. All they had done was learn sign language. She was choosing to ignore the butterflies and the way her veins felt like they had molten lava running through them when Killian's hand touched hers.

"I can't believe you hung out without me," Fen grumbled, as they walked toward the house.

Ember rolled her eyes. "Are you going to fill us in or complain about how we spent the afternoon?"

Fen huffed as he took a few steps away from his parents, motioning for the other two to follow him. "Mum had to go to the market, and she didn't want us staying home alone."

Killian snickered, and Fen shot him a glare, prompting the blond to quickly close his mouth.

"When we came home, everything seemed normal enough until Maeve went upstairs and started screaming."

Ember winced at the thought of the terrified little girl, the little one who she considered her sister for the last year, and her heart ached. She remembered all too vividly how it felt to be a terrified seven-year-old.

"Her room was a disaster," he continued. "Sheets ripped off the bed, window broken, door ripped damn near off it's hinges." He shuddered as he crossed his arms.

Ember furrowed her brow as her heart sank. "They only went in Maevie's room?"

Fen sighed as he stuffed his hands in his pockets. "And yours."

Ember's heart sank. She didn't even live here anymore, so why would anyone be in her room? She shook her head.

*My old room.*

"Mum and Dad were worried they had gone to your house when they realized you were gone," Fen continued. "That's why I sent the Helio."

Ember shook her head. "No I'm fine. Mum has some pretty strong wards." She furrowed her brow as her eyes

97

narrowed at Killian. "How did you get through them actually?"

Killian smirked as he cocked his brow. "Mothers love me, what can I say." He shrugged.

Ember rolled her eyes before turning back to Fen. "Don't your parents have wards up?"

Fen sighed as he nodded. "Da' took them down to rework something. He didn't feel like the 'standard' wards the chief suggested were strong enough. He had planned to reinforce them when he got off work."

"Did they take anything?" Ember knew the answer before she asked the question, but she didn't want to believe it. Out of all the break ins and kidnappings that had happened over the summer, the only thing that ever turned up missing were the children. Pearls and priceless family heirlooms were always left untouched, but they still took the most valuable thing from these families. The thought that they had gone into the Kitts' home, with only the intention of taking Maeve, made her sick to her stomach.

"Nothing," Fen confirmed, as he shook his head, though it looked like that thought had settled him just as much as it had her. "It was odd, though. Your room looked like a war zone, like a bomb had been dropped in the center of it. Maeve's wasn't as bad, almost like it was an afterthought."

Ember shuddered as she shook her head. "Maybe they thought it was Maeve's room. Maybe it was a mistake."

"Maybe," Killian shrugged as he ran his hand through his hair, "but these people don't strike me as the type to make mistakes."

"There's another problem, though," Fen whispered, as he checked over his shoulder. "You remember the O'Malley's down the road?"

Ember nodded as she furrowed her brow. They had spent many days last summer helping Mrs. O'Malley with things around their farm while her husband was away visiting family in Scotland. She had her hands full with three young children, and another on the way, and didn't have the time or energy to take care of the garden or livestock the way she normally could. Ember spent many mornings pulling weeds and harvesting vegetables while Mrs. O'Malley chatted her ear off and brought her honey sandwiches and moon cider for lunch.

"Kady went missing last night," he whispered. "Plucked straight out of her bed without a sound. All of this is getting far too close to home for my liking."

Ember's breath caught in her chest. Fen was right, this was becoming very real very fast.

"Oh, my love," Ember heard Eira say, as she walked up to the group of teenagers, wrapping her in a hug that felt like warmth and home and adventure all at once. "Are you alright? You're not hurt, are you?" Eira cupped Ember's face gently in her hands, checking her over once, twice, three times for any obvious injuries. After a moment, she wrapped her in another hug, and Ember felt herself relax in the embrace.

"Ah, Miss Lothbrok," Chief Thornsten's voice rang, as he walked toward the group, "I didn't see you when we arrived."

Ember squared her shoulders as he walked closer—something about him made her skin crawl.

"I only just arrived, sir," she replied quietly.

A Warden walked up to the small group, both hands behind his back as he stood tall beside Chief Thornsten. He squared his broad shoulders, his back stiff as a board, green eyes boring holes into the three teenagers. His red, wavy hair was cut short around his ears, left longer at the top, and freckles traveled across his tan face.

"Ah, Captain," the chief said to the man with a nod, turning back to Otto. "Otto, this is Captain Eoghan Balor."

Captain Balor nodded, shaking Otto's hand. "My men have finished searching the premises, and everything seems to be clear, no sign of the intruders wandering about or hiding in the barn." He gave a nod in the direction of the barn and house. "You are free to go inside and get your room back in order, Miss Lothbrok." He looked straight at her, like they had already been introduced and had known each other for years. A chill ran down her spine.

Ember furrowed her brow. "Oh, no. I don't live here anymore," she said, as she shook her head. "I'm with my mother now."

Chief Thornsten's eyebrows shot up. "Well then," he muttered, as he cleared his throat and adjusted the onyx tie around his neck. "I wasn't aware that she was… here." *Not dead* were the words that hung in the air between them. "Congratulations, Miss Lothbrok." He cleared his throat, turning back to Otto and Eira. "Otto, I expect I'll be seeing you at the meeting on Sunday?"

Otto stiffened, and Ember watched as his jaw tensed. "Of course, Chief Thornsten," he nodded. "I'll be there."

"Perfect." The chief beamed as he picked an invisible piece of lint off his jacket sleeve. "Have a lovely afternoon, Otto, Eira." He nodded at the couple and then turned with Captain Balor to gather what was left of the officers milling about the front yard before disappearing down the drive and outside of the wards. Ember expected them to turn toward the Echopoint, but instead, each of them disappeared into a cloud of mist without a sound.

Ember's heart lurched as she watched them vanish, turning to Killian and Fen to make sure she wasn't seeing things. "How did they do that?" she asked, wide eyed as the boys chuckled under their breath.

"When you become a Warden," Fen replied, "you get a bracelet that gives you the ability to Echo. They can travel anywhere on island without the use of Echopoints or the Yggdrasil Terminal. It's a pretty great selling point for the kids who want to join the academy honestly."

Ember shook her head as the boys began to talk amongst themselves about how grueling they thought the academy might be, but her heart sank as she watched Maeve run carefree through the front yard, Della sticking very close by.

This was all becoming very real very fast, and Ember was scared.

THE SUN WAS SLOWLY SLIPPING over the horizon when Ember finally made her way back home and through the large double doors into the foyer. She kept waiting for it to hit her, that feeling of coming 'home' when she walked inside. She waited for the comforting warmth like she felt sitting in front of the Kitts' fireplace after school or the way every worry she had seemed to fade away at the breakfast table while she watched Eira float around the kitchen.

She shook her head as she shut the door behind her, taking a breath as she stopped to listen to any signs of the people that occupied her new home. The sound of humming filled her ears, and she was instantly transported back to that small cottage in Galway filled with her mother's warmth. A smile overtook her as she wandered through the foyer and into the kitchen, where Gaelen was busy plating dinner and putting it on the table, and Aoife was pulling a fresh loaf of bread out of the oven.

"You're just in time for supper," Aoife said sweetly, as Ember slipped into the room. "I hope you don't mind stew and soda bread. I haven't had a moment to go to the market this week. Sit, sit." She motioned to the beautifully set table in the dining room where Theo was quietly sitting with his hands in his lap.

"That sounds lovely, Mum." Ember smiled as she slipped into the chair across from the little boy. Gaelen gently wiped her hands on the apron tied around her waist as Ember's mouth began to water.

"Is everything alright with the Kitts?" Aoife asked, as she sat at the table and began to cut the piping hot loaf of bread.

"They're fine." Ember nodded, watching as plumes of steam spiral through the air from her bowl of stew. "Someone broke into their house, but luckily, no one was home." She left out the part about what rooms were ransacked. She didn't want to worry her mother more than she probably already was.

"Oh, how awful," Aoife replied, as she shook her head. "I can only imagine how terrifying that must've been. I'm so glad you were safe at home."

"Me too, Mum." Ember smiled, and she meant it. She was scared, and some days felt completely out of place, but she was so happy to be home. Ember's eyes widened as a red ball of light buzzed through the kitchen, blinking rapidly as it hovered over the table.

Aoife sighed as she rolled her eyes. "I have to take the Helio right quick," she said, as she pushed away from the table. "I'll be back in two shakes." And then she strode off toward her study on the other side of the manor.

Ember breathed a laugh and turned back to the stew sitting in front of her. She took a few bites, savoring the warmth of the potatoes and carrots before setting her spoon down and looking over at Theo. She smiled as she waved at him, trying to catch his attention. His head popped up and eyes widened, and he looked like he was ready to run away and hide when Ember started signing.

*"My name is Ember,"* she signed, remembering what she and Killian had practiced in the library earlier that afternoon.

Theo grinned brightly, eyes widening as they lit up, and he gave her a gentle nod. *"My name is Theo."*

His smile was so bright Ember was certain it could light the entire manor, floor to ceiling.

Her smile widened as she signed, *"I'm your sister."*

# CHAPTER 10
# ELEMENTAL MAGIC AND LESSONS IN BRAILLE

"How long are we supposed to sit here," Fen whispered, as he shifted on the pillow underneath him.

Ember sat cross legged next to him, laying her bag quietly on the floor beside her as she rolled her eyes. "I suppose until Professor Eid tells us otherwise?" she whispered in reply with a smirk.

Said Professor was in the middle of the round room, floating a foot off the floor with her legs crossed and both hands on her knees. Her eyes were closed in deep concentration. Rows of large, ornate pillows surrounded her on all sides, each with a student sitting quietly on top. The room was broken into four quadrants, each pillow representing one of the four elements in color and style. Tan and sage, sea green mixed with turquoise, white and silver, and red with orange. Incense burned in the center of the room on a small table beside the professor, and the whole room gave off a relaxing feeling that instantly settled any anxiety Ember might have had before she walked in.

"Might as well get a quick nap in," Killian chimed, as he

tossed his backpack to the ground and laid on the pillow, both hands behind his head.

"I believe you're supposed to be meditating, Mr. Vargr," Professor Eid said, her eyes still closed. "Sitting up please."

"How do they do that?" Fen whispered, as he crossed his legs underneath one another. "It's like having Mum at school. They can all see out of the back of their heads."

Ember laughed as she shook her head, closing her eyes and sitting crisscross on the plush pillow underneath her. She took slow breaths, focusing on her breathing and the way the air filled her lungs slowly, inch by inch. She felt her magic sway and pull in her veins as she breathed, like the tide rippling under her skin. She centered her thoughts on class, focusing on the lesson Professor Eid had them prepare for the week before.

"I wonder why Elemental Magic doesn't start until second year," Killian whispered, as he tapped a finger on his bent knee.

"Do you remember what you were like last year?" Ember laughed quietly. "I can't imagine any class involving controlling the elements would be good for a first year. I have doubts about the second years if we're being honest."

Killian huffed in reply but didn't respond.

After five more minutes of quiet meditation, Professor Eid gracefully placed both feet on the ground and stood up. "Welcome, young ones," she said softly, brushing her hijab off her shoulder. The deep purple of her robes matched with the silk draped intricately around her head, accented by the lavender details swirling down her sleeves. Her honey eyes sparkled in the dim candlelight shining from the sconces scattered across the circular wall, and a gentle smile played at the corners of her mouth. "We are focusing on one element per quarter," Professor Eid said, as she began to pace up and down the room. "This quarter will be water."

Fen's hand quickly shot into the air. "Why water?" he asked. "Why not fire? Start the year out with a bang!"

Giggles erupted around the room, and Ember rolled her eyes.

"That's a very good question, Mr. Kitt," Professor Eid smiled. "Now tell me, when you go home this week and practice what you learned today, what are you going to do when you accidentally catch a curtain on fire? Or the garden? Or your little sister's pigtails?"

Killian smirked. "I would grab the water hose." He shrugged.

Professor Eid nodded thoughtfully as she held up her hand and produced a small flame that danced against her fingertips. She walked to Killian's desk, and gently laid it against his paper.

It danced across the page, engulfing the parchment and turning it to ash in front of him. His eyes widened as the fire crept slowly in front of him, getting dangerously close to his freshly pressed white button down.

"And what would you do when you find that you *can't* put the flame out with the hose or a glass of water?" She nodded to the cup sitting beside him and motioned for him to pour.

He dumped the water onto the flame, but it seemed to have an invisible barrier around it, and it didn't so much as sizzle. His eyes widened as he visibly swallowed and sank further into the pillow beneath him.

"Magically conjured fire can *only* be put out by magically conjured *water.* It is the first rule of elemental magic, and one of the most important." She cocked an eyebrow at both boys, who had averted their eyes to their laps. "It is also the reason fire will be the *final* elemental we will be studying this year." At that moment, a small bead of water formed in the palm of the professor's hand, and she let it fall onto the flame. No sooner than Ember could blink, it was gone, not even ash left where it was floating.

Ember shook her head with a small laugh as she leaned back on her pillow; the very last thing either of those boys needed was the ability to conjure fire, and she was very thankful they wouldn't possess the knowledge to do so for quite a long time.

"But this year, you will not be conjuring anything," Professor Eid said to the class. There was a collective grumble that sounded through the room, accompanied by some pouting from the boys. "Creating things without having the ability to control them is a dangerous game to play. It's how wildfires and floods and dead gardens happen," she eyed the boys who each let out a huff at the same time. "This year, you will learn to control each element, and only after you have complete control will you learn to conjure. Your magic is like building a house. You must have a strong foundation before you add the walls, or windows, or doors."

Professor Eid walked back to the center of the room where she picked up a clay bowl filled with water and motioned for the class to come closer.

"Gather round up here," she said whimsically.

The students all hurried to the middle of the room, standing on their tiptoes to get a decent view of what the professor was doing.

"Today, you will learn to control just some small waves," she smiled. "You will break into pairs, and each group will have a bowl charmed with continuous waves. You will practice slowing the waves at first, then work on stopping them fully."

Right on cue the water in the bowl began churning, like a small ocean contained inside the clay basin. Waves rose and fell, and Ember could've sworn she saw the tiny shadows of fish flitting beneath the surface.

"To slow the wave," she said calmly, "you will hold your hand gently over the water and say *mal*."

Ember's eyes widened as the waves slowed, calming to a

soft ripple on the top of the water. They pushed and pulled until finally slowing to a light ripple and stopping all together.

"That's it?" Fen asked under his breath. "We just have to slow the water down? How hard can that be?"

Professor Eid smirked as she tilted her head. "It's harder than you might think, Mr. Kitt," she replied. "There is a basin at each of your pillows. Take a seat with your partner, and please begin."

Ember walked back to her seat, Odette sitting quietly beside her, and watched as each water-filled basin around the room began to churn, waves slapping against the edge of the clay.

"Would you like to begin, or would you like me to?" she asked Odette.

"Why don't you try, and I'll follow your lead," she replied sweetly, eyes trained just above Ember's head. She ran one hand around the diameter of the bowl and nodded with a smile. "Not too big, so it should only take a few tries."

Ember breathed a laugh as she nodded. She shook out her shoulders and took a breath, before resting her palm just above the churning waves.

"*Mal,*" she whispered, but the waves only calmed to a dull roar. She furrowed her brow and huffed.

"Let me try." Odette smiled. Her hand hovered above the basin, and like it was second nature, she confidently said the incantation, and the water stilled.

"You're so skilled at incantation," Ember said, as the water began to bubble and churn again. "Where did you learn to do it all so seamlessly?"

Odette laid her hands in her lap. "My mum immigrated here when she was a little girl. She's from Honduras. All magical language originated from her tribe in Ocotepeque. They're one of the oldest known users in the world. We grew up speaking Spanish in the home, so it makes pronouncing incantations a little easier."

Ember's brow rose. "Spanish? Our spells are Spanish?"

"Aye." Odette nodded with a smug grin. "Most spells are of Spanish origin. Some societies use Latin, but most are the original dialect."

"Huh," Ember breathed, as she leaned back on one arm. Before she could reply, a yelp sounded from the set of pillows beside her. She looked over her shoulder to see Killian with his jaw on the floor and staring at the other side of the basin. Ember followed his line of sight to where Fen was sitting on his pillow, completely drenched from head to toe.

"Not as easy as it looks, is it, Mr. Kitt?" Professor Eid said from the center of the room, eyes closed as she hovered above her pillow. She held her hand out and mumbled something under her breath, and Fen was hit with a quick gust of wind that immediately dried him off. His cheeks were stained crimson, and he dropped his head as Killian barked a laugh.

Ember laughed as she rolled her eyes and turned back around, trying the charm a few more times before she felt like she had it. Professor Eid walked around to each pair, having them demonstrate for her, and then walked back to the center of the room.

"Please practice your incantation at home and read chapter thirteen before Thursday. You are dismissed." She waved her hand, and the doors at the back of the class were flung open, light pouring in from the windows in the corridor. The classroom erupted in conversation as everyone gathered their things and began to walk to their next class.

Ember threw her bag over her shoulder and headed toward the door when she felt a hand wrap gently around her wrist.

"Off in a hurry there, Starshine?" Killian smiled beside her.

Ember rolled her eyes as she slowed down, and Fen came running up behind them. He furrowed his brow as he looked between the two, and Killian quickly dropped his hand from where it was still gripping Ember's wrist.

"Why are you acting weird," Fen prodded. "Where are you two going?"

"The only weird one here is you, Fenrir," Ember hissed jokingly. "I have a free period and thought I'd spend it outside. You're both more than welcome to join me." She turned on her heels and walked out the door, turning toward the steps that hugged the edge of the large tree and led out the double doors.

"Outside? You mean to relax?" Killian asked, as he quirked his brow. "Are you feeling alright? Coming down with something?" He held the back of his hand up to her forehead, and she quickly swatted it away.

"Of course I am," Ember huffed. "I just want to spend some time outdoors before it starts getting cold again."

"You mean you don't intend to study yourself to death this year?" Fen asked jokingly.

Ember rolled her eyes as she shoved the doors open, taking in a deep breath as she walked into the sun. She walked through the grass and up to the creek that ran through the grounds, Odette already sitting under the large oak tree that was nestled on the bank.

"Mind if I sit?" she asked quietly.

Odette smiled as she nodded. "Of course not," she replied. "I'm just studying."

"Oh great," Fen mumbled. "That's exactly what she needs, a study buddy to make her even less fun."

Ember ignored him and charmed the napkin in her bag into a blanket. After she sat down, settling herself onto the blanket, she quickly pulled a book out of her bag.

"Ah, yes, that makes more sense," Killian chided. "Less relaxing, more reading."

Ember glared at him but chose not to respond. These boys were not going to ruin her relaxing afternoon. She glanced over at Odette, who was reading very intently out of her Galdr textbook, when she noticed the raised bumps on the pages that her fingers were moving briskly over.

"Your book is in braille," Ember noted, as she tilted her head. "I've never seen a braille textbook."

Odette nodded. "It makes studying much easier," she replied, as she flipped a page. "Otherwise, I would have to rely on recorded lectures and notes. I prefer to just read from the text."

"How would you read notes?" Ember asked, flipping her book closed and leaning back against the tree.

"A conversion spell of sorts," Odette replied. "My mum actually created it before she..." Her voice trailed off as she chewed on her bottom lip, and Ember felt her heart sink.

"Can you show me?" she asked, as she pulled out a notebook and pen and handed it to the girl.

Odette smiled as she nodded, taking the pen, and scribbling a few words onto the paper. She mumbled under her breath, a spell Ember didn't catch, and then the words scribbled in ink suddenly turned to raised bumps littered across the pages. Ember trailed her finger over them and grinned.

"Wicked." Fen grinned, and Odette's cheeks turned a brilliant shade of crimson. Ember opened her book again and settled against the tree, content to study in silence with Odette for the rest of the afternoon.

They all sat for a few minutes, and Ember thought maybe this could work—maybe the boys would let her relax and read her book in peace. Killian and Fen were skipping stones in the creek, having a quiet competition to see whose could reach the other side first, when Fen accidentally splashed Killian in the face, and before she knew it, both boys were shouting and wrestling and covered in muck and water.

"Oh, honestly," Ember mumbled, as she closed her book and laid it beside her. "I should just leave you like that," she shouted to them, "and let you explain to Professor Walsh why you're walking into her classroom sopping wet and getting mud all over the corridors."

Both boys paled at the mention of their teacher and quickly hopped out of the stream and over to the blanket, spraying water all over Ember and Odette as they shook the water out of their hair.

Ember rolled her eyes and cast a quick drying charm in their directions. Both boys gave her a sheepish smile before sitting down. It wasn't a charm they had learned in class yet, but Ember had taken the time to learn it over the summer after the tenth time that Maeve had fallen into the pond while playing with Della. It seemed to come in handy.

"Thanks, Starshine," Killian mumbled, as he laid on his back, both hands behind his head.

Fen leaned back on both elbows and tilted his head toward the cloudless sky, eyes closed as he smiled. "I'm not ready for the days to start getting shorter again," he sighed. "Sunsets at five in the evening are my personal hell."

Ember chuckled and shook her head as Killian shifted to prop himself up on one elbow.

"You think that's bad?" he asked, as he quirked a brow. "In some countries during the winter, you don't see the sun for the entire season. It goes down and doesn't come back up until the spring."

Fen gasped, and Ember almost choked on a laugh.

"That sounds bleeding awful," Fen whispered, as he shook his head. "I don't think I would make it."

"A little dramatic, aren't we?" Ember grinned as she put her book back in her bag, confident that she would not be getting any more reading done that afternoon.

"It's actually quite nice," Odette smiled whimsically. "You can even see the northern lights if the weather is just right in some places."

"At this rate, I'll never get to see anything like that," Fen replied, as he rolled his eyes. "I'm lucky I even get to come to school to be honest. Mum and Dad are losing their minds over these kidnappings."

Ember bit her lip as she thought back to Maeve and the close call the other night. She shivered as she thought about what could've happened if Maevie had been there.

Or if Ember had.

EMBER QUICKLY PUT on sweatpants and her favorite jumper. She walked out her door and down the steps, making her way into the kitchen where Theo was coloring at the table. Gaelen hummed at the stove where she was cooking supper, and Ember furrowed her brow when she couldn't find who she was looking for.

"Is Mum not home?" she asked the Merrow, as she walked to the island in the middle of the room.

"She's in her study," Gaelen said. "I believe she had to send someone a quick Helio." She looked Ember up and down, eyes landing on her sneakers and bag before she tilted her head. "Will you be joining us for supper?"

"Oh, no." Ember smiled sheepishly. "I have a lot of home-work to do. But I'd love to have some later."

Gaelen smiled with a nod and continued chopping vegetables as Ember wandered to the table where her brother was sitting. She tapped lightly on the wood to get his attention, and he gave her a shy smile when he looked up. She quickly pulled a small notebook out of her back pocket, along with a pen, and scribbled, *"Hello, Theo,"* on it before sliding it across the table. He scrunched his nose as his eyes traveled across the page, like he was struggling to make out the letters before he picked up the pen and began to write. He slid the notebook back to Ember with a small smile and quickly looked down at his hands as he twiddled his thumbs.

*"Hello, Ember."*

Ember smiled as she nodded and stuffed the notebook back in her pocket. She waved goodbye to Theo and Gaelen and quickly made her way back up the steps to her room.

She threw her bag on her bed, pulling out her books and ready to begin her late-night study session. It was only the beginning of the year, but she refused to get behind like she almost had last year.

As hard as she tried to concentrate, her mind kept drifting to the Kitts and how much she missed studying in the small library with Fen and Killian. She was trying to feel at home here, but something still felt like it was missing.

Maybe this was just how it would be now. Maybe she would never feel truly at home anywhere ever again.

After studying for an hour, she was just about to grab another book when a Helio zipped under her door, hovering right in front of her on her desk. She furrowed her brow as Asteria's voice came out of it.

*"Meet me at the Wolf and Waife tomorrow afternoon. It cannot wait."*

# CHAPTER II

# A GATE TO ARCELIA

"**M**y parents are going to kill me," Fen grumbled, as the trio trudged through Sigurvik toward the Wolf and Waife. Ember absentmindedly kicked rocks into shallow puddles as rogue raindrops wet her cheeks. He and Killian had received the same Helio the night before, and the three of them met at the terminal to walk into town together.

"She's got courage, I'll give her that." Killian half laughed.

Ember furrowed her brow as she looked up at him. "Courage?" Sshe asked, as she shifted her bag to her other shoulder.

Killian nodded. "If I were Fae, I wouldn't be showing myself anywhere in town right now, especially with young Vala. Odin knows what she's been dealing with in all of this."

Ember nodded silently. Honestly, she hadn't thought about what Asteria, or any of the other Fae, might be dealing with. She shook her head as she mentally berated herself; she had been so wrapped up in her new home that she hadn't even thought about her friends. If it wasn't for Asteria, she never would've gotten through the last year. She owed the Fae a life debt.

"Not too late to turn back," Fen mumbled under his breath, as they stood in front of the giant door that led into the pub.

Ember laughed as Killian cocked a brow and shoved his hands in his pockets.

"Scared, Kitt?" He grinned.

Fen crossed his arms over his chest as he narrowed his eyes. "Of course not," he huffed. "Not of Asteria. Mostly of my mum."

Ember laughed as she rolled her eyes and shoved both doors open. They wandered through the dimly lit pub toward a booth in the back where Asteria sat with her head down, looking like she was doing her best not to be seen. Ember's breath hitched in her chest—this was not the lighthearted Fae that had helped her the year before. This woman was broken, like something inside of her had been trampled on and left to fester. The light in her eyes was dim, even behind the weak smile she tried to give the trio.

"Asteria, what's wrong?" Ember asked, as she slid into the booth. "What was so urgent that you needed to see us today?"

Asteria shook her head as she looked warily around the bar, silently threw her hand up in front of her, and mumbled something under her breath. "No one must know I was here," she said quietly. "Technically speaking, I'm not supposed to be anywhere other than home and Hidden Moon, but with the Wardens that have been placed outside of my shop, I didn't feel like it was safe to meet there."

"Wardens?" Ember asked, as she furrowed her brow. "Why are there still Wardens in front of your shop?"

Asteria shrugged as she leaned back. "They don't trust any of us. We're all being closely watched, especially those of us that work in town."

Fen huffed as he impatiently tapped the top of the table.

"That's bloody stupid," he replied, as he rolled his eyes. "What do they think you're going to do? Snatch a baby while its mum is buying tea?"

"They're not thinking," Asteria sighed. "That's the problem. They're acting out of fear, so nothing they're doing is rational."

"What did you call us here for?" Killian asked warily. "None of us have any pull with the Chief of the Guard. I don't think we'll be much help on that front."

Asteria shook her head as she waved her hand. "That's not it. I can handle that on my own. But I've been sent a message from Lord Erevan, and he wants to see you."

"Who?" Ember asked, as she furrowed her brow.

"He's the Fae king of sorts," Fen replied, as his eyes narrowed toward Asteria. "What does he want with us?"

"He didn't tell me that," Asteria replied, as she shook her head. "Just that he needs to see you, and that it's an urgent matter. It cannot wait. It must be tonight."

"Tonight?" Fen asked, as he stiffened. "Mum will never let me go out tonight, not without them."

"Since when did we start asking permission?" Killian asked with a grin.

Fen narrowed his eyes toward his friend and crossed his arms tightly over his chest.

"How do we get there?" Ember asked, as she focused on Asteria. "We've never even been to the Fae territory."

"Meet me at the Echopoint going toward Heksheim," Asteria replied. "I'll lead you to the gate and get you in. He was very adamant that it must be you three, no exceptions."

Ember nodded as she chewed on the inside of her cheek. "Tonight then."

Fen sighed as he ran a hand through his hair. "Mum is going to kill me."

. . .

———————

RAIN PELTED the side of Ember's face as she sneaked down the long drive and toward the Echopoint on the other side of the front gate. With a house as big as Lothbrok Manor, it had been easy enough to sneak out without being noticed and make her way to the barn to grab Maia. Ember thought she should feel relieved that she didn't have such a watchful eye on her, but something about it made her chest ache. She missed the coziness of the Kitts', something she didn't quite feel here.

Not yet anyway.

Maia nuzzled her hand as she held her breath and grabbed the low hanging branch on the Echopoint, the familiar pull in her stomach before she dropped to the ground on the side of the road leading to Heksheim. She brushed the dust off her jeans and quickly adjusted the strap of her bag while she looked down the road. Just as she turned her head, she heard two thuds back-to-back and turned to see Fen and Killian in a tangled mess at the trunk of the tree. Maia clicked her disapproval and let out a low growl.

"Honestly," Ember breathed, as she rolled her eyes with a grin, "I don't know how the pair of you ever get anything productive done."

Killian brushed the dirt off his shirt as he cut his eyes toward Fen. "I told you to wait till five minutes after twelve so *this,*" he motioned toward the spot they had fallen, "wouldn't happen."

"I *did* wait," Fen replied, as he shot him a dirty look. "You were just five minutes too late."

"Maybe you can continue this argument later," a voice echoed from behind them.

Ember whipped her head around to see Asteria standing just a few steps down the road. When had she gotten there?

Ember hadn't even heard anyone walk up, and she hadn't used the Echopoint.

"We must hurry," Asteria said, as she nodded toward the looming tree line. "We don't have any time to waste."

Ember nodded and tugged both bickering boys down the road, placing herself between them to try and keep the peace for the remainder of their walk. As they reached the ward surrounding the school, Ember sucked in a breath as they veered left, toward the entrance to the forest.

"Into the bloody forest we go again," Fen grumbled, as he shoved both hands in the pocket of his hoodie. "I was hoping we were done with this place."

"Sometimes the place we least want to go," Asteria replied, "is the place we are most needed."

Ember felt a chill run down her spine as she wrapped her arms around her waist.

"Cold, Starshine?" Killian whispered, a little too close for comfort.

Ember felt another chill run down her spine as she shook her head. "I'm fine, it's just the rain," she replied softly, as heat crept up her neck.

Killian nodded and pulled something out of his pocket, a small piece of cloth. He mumbled something under his breath that Ember didn't quite catch, and then the piece of cloth suddenly turned into a full-sized jacket with a hood. He smirked as he draped it over Ember's shoulders. "Packed it just in case." He shrugged, as if he was answering a question Ember hadn't asked out loud.

"How did you do that," she whispered, as she rubbed the fabric between her fingers, inspecting the zipper and the stitching. "We haven't learned that spell."

Killian shrugged again and shoved his hands in his pockets. "When you live with the family that I do, you get good at hiding things."

Ember nodded as she averted her eyes. "Thank you," she said under her breath.

"Don't mention it, Starshine," he said, as a smile tugged at the corner of his mouth.

Killian shifted into his wolf form, keeping close by Ember's side as they walked in silence for another hour.

Just when Ember was starting to doubt her trust in the Fae, she stopped abruptly in front of them.

In the deafening silence of the forest around them, Ember almost jumped out of her skin when the faint sound of tiny bells erupted behind her. Killian let out a low growl, the white fur on his neck standing straight up as he bared his teeth. Maia didn't seem to notice, or maybe she knew something the rest of them didn't.

White flashed between the trees, and Ember felt her magic thrum wildly in her veins, preparing to defend herself and her friends from whatever lurked in the trees. Fen's face had gone pale, his eyes wide, but Asteria just had a small smirk painted on her mouth.

Ember let out a breath and heard Killian do the same beside her, watching as Odette Quinn waltzed out of the tree line and onto the trail.

"You've got to be feckin' kidding me," Fen mumbled, as he loosed a breath.

"It's such a lovely night for a stroll," Odette said as she walked up to Ember, petting Maia's snout and between her eyes.

Maia closed her eyes, clicking and cooing into her touch as her tail thumped against the dirt.

"Odette, what are you doing here?" Ember asked, eyes wide as she scanned the tree line beyond.

Odette shrugged nonchalantly as she patted Killian's head. The wolf let out a low growl as he huffed.

"Sometimes I come out here at night to think," she

replied. "Sometimes I just enjoy hearing the trees whisper. They have quite a lot to say if you know how to listen."

"Right, of course," Fen mumbled. "Let's traipse into the forest to converse with the trees."

Ember jabbed him in the ribs as she shot him a pointed glare. She thought back to the year before, how all three of them together hadn't even been able to control the Cu Sidhe, and she winced as she thought about Odette alone out here at night with no protection. "Why don't you come with us?" Ember said with a smile.

Fen let out a groan, but Asteria only tilted her head, studying the white-haired girl like she was some sort of a puzzle.

"I think Erevan said—" Fen began, but Asteria cut him off.

"That sounds like a lovely idea." She smiled.

Fen gaped at her, but wisely said nothing else. "How much further?" he asked instead.

"We're here," she whispered. In front of them was a large arch made entirely of trees. Had they been taking a stroll through the woods, they probably would've missed it if they didn't know it was there. Ember squinted as she looked through it and turned her head to the left and the right.

"Where?" Fen asked, a little too loudly. "Is it a door or something?"

Asteria smirked as she walked up to the arch. "Or something," she replied cryptically. She laid her hand against the bark and began mumbling under her breath. She traced the tips of her fingers against the grains of wood, and glowing runes appeared as if she had written them with ink. Ember furrowed her brow as she watched small wisps of magic fly off the runes and into the wind, clinging to the leaves and bark on the arch in front of them.

"What was that," Ember whispered, as her eyes widened.

The whole tree was glowing now, engulfed in the small wisps of magic that had come off the runes.

Fen furrowed his brow as he looked around. "What was what?" he asked hesitantly, as if something was going to leap out from behind a tree and carry him off into the darkness.

"The glowing," Ember said, as she pointed toward the arch. "You didn't see that?" She looked at Killian and Fen, who both shook their heads, staring at her as if she had spontaneously grown antlers and a tail. Odette only smirked, unseeing eyes staring toward the arch.

Asteria whipped her head around, and for a moment, Ember saw the spark in her eyes again. "What did you say?" she asked.

"The glowing from the runes you wrote on the tree," Ember said, as she pointed toward where Asteria's fingers had just been.

Killian was standing beside her again, back in his human form, and gently placed a hand on her shoulder and squeezed. "What runes, Starshine?" he asked.

Ember pulled her shoulder out of his grasp and crossed her arms.

"You can see the runes?" Asteria asked, as she pointed to the tree behind her.

Ember nodded as she shifted her weight.

"Interesting." The Fae smirked and seemed to glance toward Odette, then turned back toward the arch. "Follow me, we're late."

Ember chewed on her lip as she walked forward, hesitating with each step. Asteria disappeared through the archway in front of them, and Fen and Killian walked behind Odette and Ember. Odette seemed to take in a shuddering breath, like she was holding back tears as they made their way forward. Ember held her own breath, feeling the magic of the ward they traveled through wash over her like cold water, leaving her skin feeling like it had satin rubbing against it. Small wisps of bright blue clung to the fabric of her coat before disappearing in the breeze.

Ember decided to keep that to herself.

As they stepped through the ward, Ember gasped. She spun around and rubbed her eyes, certain that this had to be a dream. They weren't in the forest anymore, not really. They had been transported to another land entirely.

"The first time is always a shock." Asteria smirked as she tilted her head. "Welcome to Arcelia. Come now, Lord Erevan is waiting for us."

Ember nodded as she swallowed, feeling like her eyes might bulge completely out of her head. Mrs. Kitt was going to kill all four of them if she ever found out about this.

They walked down a hill and into a city that resembled Aztec ruins. The entire city sat at the top of three towering waterfalls, and Ember was mesmerized as she watched the blue crash into the jagged rocks at the bottom. Maia took off into the sky, and Ember gasped as the draic flew away, spinning and diving through the air as she let out a loud roar that shook the trees around them.

"She'll find her way back," Odette whispered. How the girl saw Maia fly away, she was unsure.

They walked over a bridge and through a gate, presumably the entrance to the city, and picked up their pace as they followed Asteria down the glittering roads. The streets were near silent, everyone presumably winding down for the evening while they spent time with their family and friends. Young Fae played on the front stoops of their homes as their mothers tended to the gardens, something Ember had never seen anyone do at night. The plants at their fingertips glowed, and small wisps of blue glowed around them. Ember averted her eyes and focused on the road. The moon lit the ground in front of them, and Ember thought it felt closer than it had before. The wind pulled them down the path, toward a temple at the center of the city.

"This is eerie," Fen whispered from Ember's left, as he rubbed his arm. The teenagers looked at each other, and Ember shuddered, taking a step closer to Killian without even realizing it. They traveled up the gold steps of the temple, and Ember took slow breaths as she listened to her footsteps echoing through the trees surrounding the city.

Asteria shoved open a large set of wooden doors and ushered the group inside. "Quickly this way," she ordered in a hushed tone.

They followed her through the temple, and Ember felt very small under the arches of the grand ceilings. Asteria quickly ushered them through another set of doors and closed them behind her. Ember wasn't sure what she was expecting, but it certainly wasn't two beautiful Fae sitting on a couch in front of a fire.

The whole room emitted a warmth that Ember hadn't felt in months, and she wanted nothing more than to curl up with a book in one of the plush chairs and read the rest of the night away. She was quickly jolted back to reality when Asteria place a firm hand on her shoulder and pulled her further into the room.

"My Lord," she said firmly, as she cleared her throat, "I've brought Ember Lothbrok and her—erm—friends as you requested."

Lord Erevan turned toward the group and gracefully stood from the couch. His dark green robe hung just above the ground, and Ember drew in a breath as he stood at his full height. He was close to seven feet tall and all lean muscle. His chiseled jaw twitched as he watched them all gape, the bronze in his skin almost glowing in the moonlight, and Ember could just make out the pointed ears poking out from his perfectly groomed brunette hair.

There was a woman to his right, who stood with him, her violet gown brushing the tops of her bare feet. Her golden hair hung in waves as she smiled warmly, and Ember couldn't help but feel like she recognized that smile. Not just in Asteria, but from somewhere else.

The royals were both barefoot, casual in dress and in the way they greeted their visitors. Ember furrowed her brow. This was not what she expected from royalty, but she didn't have much to go off, either.

Ember looked to her left, just in time to see Odette's face pale and throat bob as the royals came into view. What she was seeing—or feeling—Ember wasn't sure.

"Good evening, Your Majesties," Odette said, as she curtsied.

Lord Erevan furrowed his brow but quickly blinked away the confusion written on his face "Welcome, Ember and friends," he said, as he motioned for them to sit.

The group sat as close together as they could without being on top of each other, and Ember notice both Killian and Fen were sitting straight as boards, hands clenched tightly on their knees. Odette flowed across the room, settling on a pillow on the floor as she crossed her legs over one another. She relaxed her back on the front of the couch, leaning against Fen's legs. He grimaced as he visibly tried not to squirm away from the contact.

"You wanted to see us?" Ember asked quietly, as she looked back and forth from the royals to Asteria.

"We did," he replied, gently patting the woman's hand to his right as he smiled. "My name is Lord Erevan, and this is my wife, Lady Adalaena. I'm terribly sorry we haven't made your acquaintance until now, and I do wish it were under better circumstances."

Ember nodded as her stomach dropped, and the hairs on the back of her neck stood straight up.

"It's lovely to meet you," Odette chimed in, like this midnight rendezvous in the Fae territory wasn't abnormal in the slightest.

"I understand there have been children going missing on Ellesmere this summer," Lord Erevan continued.

Ember nodded slowly and felt both boys stiffen beside her. Killian's jaw twitched, and she could've sworn she heard him growl. She gently squeezed his knee and listened as he let out a breath.

"Yes," Ember replied warily, glancing briefly back toward Asteria who currently had her feet propped up on the couch, catching grapes in her mouth as she threw them up into the air. She wouldn't willingly walk them into a trap. She wouldn't knowingly put them in danger. Not the Fae that helped her last year, not the woman that made her tea on the weekends and listened to her go on about her class schedule. She couldn't.

Right?

"And if I'm understanding correctly," Lord Erevan continued, as he crossed one leg over his knee, "there are a few suspects, yes?"

Ember swallowed and bit her lip. "Um, yes, sir. They suspect it might be Fae kidnappings." She cleared her throat and fidgeted in her seat, glancing around them room and hoping that *someone* would help her out.

"We of course don't believe that," Odette chimed in with a smile, "but you seem to know that already."

Ember's eyes widened at the frankness in her voice. This was the most she had ever heard Odette say. Her white hair swayed past her shoulders, and she could've sworn she heard Fen choke beside her on the couch.

Lord Erevan cocked a brow as he looked at the girl, eying her carefully. "Of course." He nodded seriously, uncrossing his legs, and leaning both elbow on his knees. "We seem to be in the same predicament."

Ember scrunched her brow as she slumped in her seat. "I'm sorry I don't think I follow," she replied hesitantly.

"Come with me." Lord Erevan waved for them to follow as he stood from his seat toward the window that overlooked the city and leaned against the wall as they soaked in the view.

The moon reflected off the crystal-clear water below them, and the entire city looked like it could've been floating on the fog that had settled on the surface. A few lights dotted the windows on the houses, and Ember smiled. It was probably a child reading past their bedtime. The entire town square was visible from where they stood, shops and carts and stalls in a shape that looked like the sun. Ember closed her eyes as she imagined what it looked like during the day, what kind of food and drink and trinkets the shopkeepers might sell. Were there books she had never read before? All of a sudden, she had the urge to hunker down and never leave until she had explored every inch of this beautiful city.

"Am I correct in assuming this is your first visit to Arcelia?" Lord Erevan smirked.

Ember snapped her jaw closed and nodded.

"I've heard stories," Fen almost whispered, "but I never imagined it would look like this."

Ember looked over to Odette, and to her surprise, the girl had silent tears pooling on her lower lash. She didn't blink, hardly seemed to breath as she looked out toward the ancient city, and Ember couldn't help but wonder if she was seeing something the others couldn't.

"Why do you bother coming to work in a tea shop?" Killian asked over his shoulder to Asteria, who was still lounging on the couch in front of the fire. "You could open a shop here, so what's the point?"

Asteria shrugged as she sat up. "You get a bit stir crazy staying in one place your whole life." She gracefully stood from the couch and waltzed over to where they stood. "Gives me something to do other than stare at the same things every day."

"Our Asteria has always been a wanderer at heart." Lady Adalaena smiled as she walked toward them, gently kissing Asteria on the temple. Asteria grimaced as she rolled her eyes.

"These are your parents?" Ember asked, as her eyes widened. "You grew up here?"

Asteria nodded shyly, an emotion Ember wasn't ever aware she could convey. "With my brother." She almost whispered it, like it was a secret she kept close to her chest.

"Wicked." Fen grinned, suddenly emboldened by the fact that they weren't in imminent danger. "So, you're rich?"

Ember jabbed him in the ribs with her elbow, and he let out a yelp as he jumped away.

"What?" he asked, as he rubbed the bruise Ember was sure was forming under his shirt.

"You have a brother?" Ember asked, as she scrunched her brow, and she didn't miss the way Lady Adalaena's eyes grew misty.

Asteria nodded. "He died, during the uprising—the war." She spat the words like they left an awful taste in her mouth. "I don't like to remain here for longer than necessary."

Ember nodded. No other explanation was needed, she understood that feeling all too well.

"Your city is beautiful," Odette said quietly.

"I'm still not sure why you've brought us here, I'm afraid," Ember continued.

"Don't ask questions," Fen mumbled, as he stuffed chocolate in his pockets and mouth from a jar on a table by the window. Killian jabbed him in the ribs, and Fen yelped, quickly wiping his mouth with the back of his hand.

"You're both so violent," he mumbled and stuffed his hands in his now full pockets.

"It's Fae food," Killian hissed under his breath.

"Those are silly bedtime stories meant to make young Vala fear us." Lady Adalaena smiled. "Take as much as you like."

"I wanted to give you the opportunity to look around the town," Lord Erevan continued. "You're free to go wherever you wish, inside the temple and out." He held both arms behind his back and looked out the window.

"I'm afraid I don't follow," Ember said slowly, looking at both Killian and Fen and then to Odette to see if they caught something she might've missed. Killian shrugged, and Fen shook his head.

"They want to show you," Asteria interjected, "that they have nothing to hide. *We* have nothing to hide."

"You see," Lady Adalaena said, as she crossed the room to the open window, "our young are going missing too. Every few days, we have reports of a little one not returning home from school or from playing with friends. It's concerning. Our territory is supposed to be protected from outsiders, from anyone who isn't of Fae descent, but it seems we've let our guard down for too long."

Ember's heart sank, and by the looks on their faces, she could tell Fen and Killian were feeling the same way. If the Fae were truly innocent, and victims themselves, where did that leave them? Ember brushed the moisture from her lower lash as she leaned on the open window. People below them were leaving their homes, one by one, and walking out into their gardens. A distant hum started ringing in Ember's ears as she watched, like a very soft whisper.

"What about someone that's Faekin?" Fen said, as he peered out the window.

"Fae what?" Ember furrowed her brow.

"Someone half Fae," Odette replied quietly. "Not as common these days, and most of the time, they don't even know what they are. But if they do know, they can get past the wards."

"We've considered the possibility," Lord Erevan replied,

"but unfortunately, it's hard to confirm. Faekin don't live in Arcelia, but that doesn't mean they haven't figured out how to get past the wards on their own."

"I don't know what you expect me to do," Ember mumbled. "I'm not even sixteen yet. I can't change anything. I can't bring them back."

"We do not expect change from you three," Lord Erevan replied, "but we're hoping you can be the beginnings of a bridge. We will not be able to bring our children home until we stop blaming those who aren't responsible and start looking for other possibilities."

"I think Chief Thornsten is fairly set on placing all of the blame on you," Killian huffed, as he crossed his arms tightly over his chest. "A few teenagers with a penchant for endangering themselves won't change his mind."

"Perhaps not," Adalaena replied with a nod, "but planting the seed with someone he'll listen to won't hurt."

Ember squinted her eyes as she watched the women tending to the glowing flowers and the children run through the moonlit gardens.

"It's the middle of the night," she mumbled. "What are they doing out in the middle of the night?"

"It's the best time to harvest from the Flor de Luna." Asteria smiled. "They're incredibly valuable ingredients in lots of potions, worth a small fortune."

"Can I go see them?" Ember asked before she could stop herself. There was something pulling her to them, almost like the tug she felt between Killian and Fen—something otherworldly and mildly unsettling.

"What, the flowers?" Fen asked, as he scrunched his nose.

"The city, Fenrir," she huffed.

"Of course." Asteria grinned as she grabbed Ember's hand. "Come with me."

Asteria led the teenagers through the temple and down the steps into the town once again. The energy filling the streets was palpable. Everyone had seemed to be asleep when they arrived, nestled in their homes, but now giggles filled the air as young Fae ran amuck, and parents sat on the front porches and milled about in the gardens like it was mid-day, not the middle of the night.

"Our sleep schedule differs a little from yours," Asteria chimed in. "For those that live in town, most wake during the middle of the night to spend time together as a family outdoors when the weather permits. Shops aren't open, but there's something about a few hours in the midnight air that is good for the soul."

Ember grinned as she watched a group of children ahead of them playing in the street, hitting a ball back and forth with little wooden sticks. A woman, who Ember assumed was their mother, carried out a tray of snacks and drinks on the porch and called them all over. They weren't all that different from the Vala, not really.

Out of nowhere, a faint trail of glowing blue light appeared in front of Ember. Her heart leapt into her throat as the little blue wisps flew around the ground, creating a trail toward a small flower behind the wall of a beautiful garden.

"Everything alright, Starshine?" Killian asked, as he furrowed his brow.

Ember swallowed as she inched closer to the flower, the humming in her ear now growing louder. "Do you hear that," she whispered, as she inched closer.

"Hear… what?" Fen asked, worry clouding his face.

"That buzzing," Ember replied, pointing at her ear, "and those little wisps, you don't see them?"

Killian and Fen looked between each other and shrugged, but Odette just smiled, cocking her head as if waiting for something.

"There's nothing there, Starshine," Killian said gently, as he put his hand on her arm. "It's late. Maybe we should head back home."

"No, not yet," Ember replied, as she shook her head. "Give me just a second." Without hesitating, she swung open the garden gate, following the wisps to the glowing flower.

"Em, I don't think that's a good idea," Fen whispered, but Ember ignored him. Before she even realized what she was doing, she was in the dirt on her knees reaching toward the flower. Her fingers made contact, and the world went black.

CHAPTER 12

# WILL O' THE WISP

W aves rocked violently back and forth as the girl lay in the bottom of the boat, trying to protect her head from the falling water filling the bottom of the vessel. She paddled harder, following the light of a shooting star in the only direction she knew to go. Though the wind and waves were relentless, she sang a song she had become so familiar with.

TRÍ STOIRME agus farraige caillimid cé muid féin,
    Ach amháin le fáil ag réalta tar éis titim.
    Snámh i dtreo an chladaigh i bhfad i gcéin,
    óir níl aon áit caillte againn níos mó.

TRÍ FEAR TAR eis fás agus foraoisí cosc,
    Sin an ait a bhfaighidh tú na daoine óga, goidte agus i bhfolach.
    Thar na gcnoc is na gcloch liath,
    Sin an ait a rachaidh sibh go léir isteach sa chraic.

. . .

*THE WOOD from the boat let out a deafening crash, and water rushed in, pulling the vessel and its occupant under the waves and into the inky water. The girl thrashed in the water, clawing her way to the surface, grasping desperately for something to grab onto to pull herself up. Salt-water burned her lungs, but still, she fought. Suddenly, she was hurled onto a sandy beach, desperately coughing up the water that had tried to take her life. She laid her head on the sand, lips chapped and lungs heavy, and continued to sing.*

*TRÍ STOIRME agus farraige caillimid cé muid féin,*
   *Ach amháin le fáil ag réalta tar éis titim.*

EMBER GASPED as her eyes opened, and she quickly realized she was lying on her back in the grass, stars dancing above her, and Maia leaning on her chest. Everything began to rapidly come back to her as she moved the draic off her ribs, and she was suddenly aware of the hand gripping hers, fear pulsating through his fingertips like their veins were connected.

"Starshine, are you alright?" Killian asked through a furrowed brow. His breathing was steady, but Ember could feel his grip tighten, like if he were to let go, she might slip away again.

"Yeah, I'm fine," she replied, pushing herself up with her free hand as Killian helped her into a sitting position.

"Well, I'm bloody happy someone is because I'm sure not," Fen replied, wiping sweat off his brow. "Honestly, Em, don't ever do that again."

"You fainted after you touched that flower," Killian

replied, pointing at the Flor de Lune that swayed gently in the breeze. "You barely touched it and then you just collapsed."

"You saw the wisps, didn't you?" Odette asked, sitting cross legged in front of Ember with a smile that looked far too happy for their current situation.

Asteria shot her a shocked glance as she scrunched her brow.

"The what?" Ember asked, rubbing the back of her head.

"The wisps," Asteria replied, eyes lingering on Odette for a moment. She twisted her fingers in the air in front of her, and a picture appeared before her, like something you would see on the tv or a computer screen. Ember sucked in a breath as she saw the picture that floated in front of her, the small blue wisps of light that glowed around the runes at the gate and then again on the path before she collapsed.

"What are those," Killian asked, still gripping Ember's hand tightly. Her fingers started to ache, but she couldn't bring herself to pull away.

"We've always just called them wisps, or Will o' the Wisp," Asteria replied. "They're small traces of ancient magic not visible to the naked eye. Some Fae can see them, but only through years of very intense training. I only know of a handful that can, and it took them longer than I've been alive to learn."

Ember swallowed dryly and took a shuddering breath. "So, why can I see them," she whispered.

"Now that," Asteria replied, waving away the image from the air, and glancing back at Odette briefly, "I'm not sure. There are legends about beings that can see traces of ancient magic, beings that are something... different."

"Like a Wildling," Ember whispered, eyes closed as she gripped Killian's hand like it was a life preserver. Fen's hand gripped her shoulder, and she was certain she might pass out again if it wasn't for the boys. She barely registered that

Odette didn't so much as raise her brow at the name or balk at the events that were unfolding.

That was something she would unpack later.

"I've heard that name be used before," Asteria smirked, plucking a blade of grass from in front of her to twirl through her fingers, "but only whispers. I'm afraid that's all I know."

Ember nodded as she took a shaky breath. It seemed no matter what she did, her life would always be more questions than answers. There would always be a secret to unravel, always a shadow playing out the corner of her eye.

"I think it's time we get you home," Killian interjected. "Seems to be enough adventure for one night."

"Thank you for coming," Asteria said, as they stood, gratitude filling her voice as she smiled. "It meant the world to my parents to feel like at least some Vala are on our side. It is beautiful here, but it can be lonely when you feel like a whole island is waiting for your kingdom to fall."

Ember swallowed dryly, and Odette gave a small nod beside her, like she understood what it meant to feel like she was heard, like maybe this night had shifted something forever inside of her too.

"We're always happy to help." Ember smiled as she brushed off her pants, patting Maia on the snout as she nuzzled into her arm. "I'm sorry there isn't more we can do."

"You did enough." She nodded. "I have a feeling you'll be able to help with a lot more than you think."

Ember gave her a small nod, and they said their goodbyes, heading back up through the now quiet town and through the gate, into the Dark Forest.

Ember furrowed her brow as they walked. "How can they do that?" she asked no one and everyone. "How can anyone just take children?"

"Who knows." Killian shrugged, quickly shifting back into the great white wolf as they made their way down the trail. Odette hummed quietly beside them, lost in her own thoughts as the bells at her ankles and wrists jingled while she walked.

"Anything you would like to add, Quinn?" Fen said with a mocking smile.

Ember frowned at him as she shook her head.

Odette simply shrugged; her unseeing eyes locked in front of them. "There are secrets buried so deep in this island that it would take a truly magnificent person to uncover them."

"Secrets?" Fen snorted. "What sort of secrets could be hidden under the pristine cobblestone in Sigurvik? Or perhaps they're scribbled under the paint on the side of the Bookwyrm or buried in the walls of all the gods forsaken manors?" He laughed to himself, but Odette simply cocked her head, face serious in a way that made Ember's stomach coil into tight knots.

"The secrets of this island are all drawn in blood."

"Are you sure you don't need us to take you home?" Fen asked, as they neared the Echopoint by the school. The walk back through the Forest had been surprisingly uneventful, and Ember wanted nothing more than to climb into her warm bed and sleep until she had to be up for school the next day.

"I'm sure." She smiled. "You guys need to get home before we all get in trouble."

"Well, I'm off then," Fen replied with a salute. "Someone save me a seat in Zoomancy tomorrow." And with a pop, he was gone, Odette following quickly after him, leaving Ember and Killian under the stars alone.

"Ladies first." Killian grinned as he motioned toward the low hanging branch on the Echopoint. Ember nodded and grabbed the tree as Maia leaned against her leg, and just as she whispered, "Lothbrok Manor," under her breath, Killian was beside her, holding tight to the tree and her hand. They landed with a thud on the ground outside the gate, and Ember quickly brushed the dust off her jeans.

"What on earth are you doing?" she whispered hoarsely. "You need to go home before we're caught."

"Starshine, if you know anything by now, it's that I don't do what I'm told." He flashed his teeth at her with a wink as he held out his arm to escort her up the long drive, whispering into her ear, "And I don't get caught."

Ember felt heat creep up her neck as she smacked his arm away, but she couldn't hide the smile that played at the corner of her mouth.

"I'm walking you to the door," he continued, matching her stride. "What kind of man do you take me for?"

"*Man* would be a stretch," Ember smirked, "but thank you. I appreciate the chivalry."

"Always, Starshine." He winked as they quietly walked toward the front door. Maia trotted through the yard toward the barn at the back of the house, and Ember quietly made her way up the steps.

Ember grabbed the handle to the large door and hesitated, looking back at the tall blond with smoky eyes. His face was leaner than last year, more chiseled. As much as she liked to joke with them about still being boys, they seemed to have turned into men overnight. A chill ran down Ember's spine as she took a breath and gave him a quick nod.

"Well, goodnight," she whispered.

Killian gave her hand a squeeze, lingering for a few seconds longer than Ember expected. "Sleep tight, Starshine." He grinned and then turned to walk back down the dark drive.

Ember slipped through the door and leaned against it as it quietly shut behind her. She wasn't sure why she was struggling to breathe or why her heart suddenly felt like it was going to leap out of her chest and dance around the hardwood floor in front of her. Since when did Killian Vargr make her feel like she couldn't breathe, like she might melt into a puddle from his smile alone?

Ember shook her head and pushed herself off the door, creeping through the darkness toward the steps to head to her room.

"Bit late to be out on a walk, don't you think?" a voice cut from the sitting room to her right.

Ember froze and sucked in a breath before turning and walking into the other room. "How long have you been waiting for me?" she asked sheepishly, scuffing her foot on the floor as she stood behind the sofa.

"Since I came out of my office to check on you before bed and you weren't anywhere to be found," her mother replied without turning around, not even bothering to put the book down that was in her hands. "Gaelen said she might have seen you sneak out, so I decided it was best to wait up and make sure you got home safe."

"I didn't mean to worry you," Ember replied.

"Worry me?" Aoife scolded, as she closed the book and turned around. "I was terrified, Ember. You can't just run off without a word of where you're going. I just got you back. I can't lose you again."

Ember felt the guilt crack open her chest and burrow itself inside of her.

"I was just with Killian, Fen, and Odette," Ember replied, but the excuse didn't sound convincing, and by the look Aoife was giving her, it certainly wasn't enough.

"I know exactly who you were with, my tracking charm finally located you near the school earlier." Aoife patted the couch, motioning for Ember to sit beside her. "If you want to see your friends, all you have to do is ask. You don't have to sneak around."

"I know, Mum." Ember nodded. "I'm sorry."

"I know what happened with that girl last year," Aoife continued, as she conjured a kettle and two cups. Ember sucked in a breath as she closed her eyes. "I couldn't bear it if something happened to you. I need you to be honest with me, even if you think I might hate what you have to say."

Ember closed her eyes as she took a shaky breath. The last thing she wanted was to make her mum feel like she was sneaking around and lying and couldn't trust her. Suddenly, her heart was heavy for a fireplace and kitchen table and warm bed that weren't hers anymore.

"I think I'm just having trouble... adjusting," Ember sighed, as she sipped the tea from her mug.

"That's understandable." Aoife nodded. "You had a home and a family. Any change, even a happy change, is scary."

Ember swallowed the lump in her throat as she nodded, unable to come up with words to reply. She missed the boys terribly—missed the Kitts so bad it hurt some days. But they couldn't come first, not anymore. She had to rebuild this relationship with her mother, even when the loss ached.

"Can I tell you a secret?" Aoife asked, as she gave her a soft smile.

Ember nodded as she laid her head on her mother's shoulder, eyes growing heavy.

"I'm having a hard time adjusting too."

Ember furrowed her brow as she looked up at her mother, and something like relief flooded through her.

"I never thought I would get this with you, and sometimes I don't know if I'm doing it right."

"You're doing just fine, Mum," Ember whispered, and she meant it. With her entire being, she meant it.

"It will get easier, Mo Stor," Aoife said, as she kissed the top of her head. "We will find our way together, you have my word."

# CHAPTER 13
# NO SUCH THING AS A PERFECT CRIME

Ember raced down the steps, wringing water out of her hair as she went. She had slept through both of her alarms, still wildly exhausted from her midnight romp in the forest the night before. She had slept through any chance of a slow, quiet breakfast, but with any luck, there would be a breakfast roll in the kitchen waiting for her.

"Running behind, are we?" Aoife said from the table, pushing a plate of breakfast rolls toward Ember as she laughed. "Best get to bed early tonight."

Ember had the sense to look properly abashed but smiled as she quickly grabbed a roll and took a too-large bite. "Sorry, Mum." She grinned, mouth still full of food like a six-year-old with no table manners.

Aoife laughed as she continued to sip her tea, humming to herself as she began cleaning up the kitchen. Ember slipped a piece of paper out of her pocket and onto the table, Theo's name written in pen on the top of the folded parchment. Gaelen came into the kitchen moments later, just as Aoife sent her mug to the sink.

"I have to head to a meeting," Aoife said, as she kissed Ember on the head and plucked a few invisible pieces of lint from her jumper. "Can you get to school on your own? I can be a little late if I need to walk with you."

Ember rolled her eyes with a sheepish grin. "Yes, Mum, I'll be fine," she replied.

Aoife nodded with a smile before leaving the room. Ember turned to Gaelen with a warm smile and pointed to the note on the kitchen table.

"Will you make sure Theo gets that?" she asked, as she slung her bag over her shoulder and took another bite of her breakfast roll.

"Of course, miss," Gaelen nodded and then turned to busy herself with cleaning the kitchen.

Ember spun around and bolted out the door- with no time to argue that Gaelen did *not* have to call her miss- and headed for the Echopoint at the end of the drive.

"IF YOU SO MUCH AS whisper during this class, I will feed you both to the Cu Sidhe," Ember said, as she plopped down in her seat for Galdr, Odette already in the chair beside her looking chipper as ever. Fen and Killian had been mostly quiet during Zoomancy that morning, no doubt both still exhausted from their adventure the night before, but they seemed to have found their normal amount of energy in the corridor during their walk to Galdr, and Ember wasn't prepared to deal with their antics that afternoon.

"Whoa there, Starshine." Killian grinned as he dropped his bag and leaned on the table. "Not get enough sleep last night?"

Ember cut her eyes at both the boys and quickly turned to face the front of the room.

"Someone is moody this morning," Fen poked, as he sat

beside Killian. "Sounds like she woke up on the wrong side of her very expensive bed." Both the boys giggled, and Ember whipped around to glare at them.

"If you do not both act like proper gentlemen and leave your childish games at the door for the rest of the day, I won't even bother talking to Eira," she hissed. "I'll drag you both by the ears to the edge of the Forest and cut off your—"

"Good morning, class," Professor Walsh said, as she waltzed to the center of the room onto the round stage. "Today will be a practical lesson. Up, up." The professor motioned for everyone to stand, and when they did, their desk and chairs slid gracefully to the walls, opening the whole floor up. The spells they were learning during Galdr were becoming increasingly more difficult this year, but Ember loved every second of it. Something about mastering a truly difficult piece of magic after struggling with it for so long made her feel accomplished, like she could walk on water.

"I was really hoping for a wee nap today." Fen yawned as he stretched his arms above his head. "Maybe we could sneak out for a little siesta on the lawn."

"I think not, Mr. Kitt," Professor Walsh replied from the center of the room, as she shuffled papers.

Killian snickered as Fen sank into himself and scuffed the toe of his sneaker on the wood floor.

"Please make one line across the room, side by side," Professor Walsh continued, as she flipped her wrist. A red line appeared on the floor, and each student quickly found a place behind it. "Today, we are learning the blasting curse," she continued. "This will not be a spell you work on independently or at home. You will not be permitted to use this spell outside of the classroom until after your final exam at the end of the school year. Doing so before then will result in a failing grade for the spell, as well as a letter of reprimand in your permanent file."

"We'll just practice in the orchards," Fen whispered. "Who's going to find out?"

"I will, Mr. Kitt," Professor Walsh said, as she cut her eye toward him. "Chief Thornsten gives special permission every year to place small tracking spells on each second-year student for this spell specifically. If you so much as whisper the incantation, the Guard will be notified, as will I. It would be in your best interest to do as you're told."

Fen's eyes widened as he nodded, audibly swallowing as he took the smallest step back.

"Now that we have that out of the way," she continued, "I will be demonstrating one time for you. I trust that you all read ahead and should have a basic knowledge of the incantation at this point?"

Fen's eyes shot to the ceiling, and Killian looked at the floor. Ember rolled her eyes—of course they hadn't read ahead. She was lucky if she could get them to read at all most days. They would much rather be in the orchards flying than have their nose in a book. Eira had to all but glue them to their seats to get them to actually study for their final exams the year before.

Ember was quickly pulled from her thoughts as several solid brick walls rose from the ground across the room. An almost clear, shimmery dome appeared next, covering the room around the students and walls.

"I know it, Professor Walsh," Veda Ellingboe's voice cut through the air, sickly sweet. "Shall I demonstrate?"

Professor Walsh gave a nod and motioned toward the center of the room, and Veda glided forward. Her eyes narrowed at the solid brick wall, her head tilting just slightly as she drew in a small breath. Her arm rose in front of her, parallel to the ground, and she rotated her palm toward the ceiling, fist closed. She drew in a breath, eyes close, before quickly flipping her open palm up to face the brick wall and quietly saying, *"Destra."*

The room was filled with gasps as students instinctively covered their heads. The wall exploded in a thousand tiny pieces, small pieces of brick and mortar flying through the air and bouncing off the shimmering shield.

"Thank you, Miss Ellingboe. You may step back," Professor Walsh said, as she nodded.

Veda smiled and gave a small curtsy as stepped back, flipping her raven hair over her shoulder. Ember stifled a laugh as she rolled her eyes, and Veda quickly narrowed her toward her.

"Something funny, worm?" she hissed.

Ember rolled her eyes as she crossed her arms tightly over her chest, not bothering to give Veda the satisfaction of a reply.

"I'd be happy to show you some other spells I have in my arsenal," she whispered with a wry smile. "Though, I'm sure Mummy could show you a few that would make even my father wince."

Ember narrowed her eyes as she flipped her head around, clenching her hands into tight fists. Odette didn't say anything, but Ember could feel a strange magic rippling off the girl, something soothing that made the tightness in her chest ease, just slightly. She felt her small hand on her balled fist, but her anger was already reaching a breaking point.

"What?" Veda continued, her smile growing as she whispered sweetly. "Has your mummy not told you what she's been up to? What she knows?"

Ember's chest tightened as she took the smallest step forward.

"Oh, I'm sure she has some stories to tell you. She's quite powerful," Veda continued, nonchalantly flipping her hair over her shoulder. "It's too bad you're just a stupid little—"

"Watch it," Killian hissed, as he grabbed Ember's other fist, stopping her abruptly from wrapping her hand's around the girl's petite neck. "You've had your fun, now stop."

"Oh, cousin," Veda smiled, "the fun hasn't even begun."

Professor Walsh waltzed to the center of the room after repairing the wall and cleared her throat to gather the class's attention once again.

"As you saw Miss Ellingboe demonstrate," she began, "the blasting curse is a simple one. You will begin with holding your arm parallel to the ground, palm toward the ceiling, and closing your hand into a fist." She demonstrated the correction position and waited as the class mirrored her. "Next, you will quickly rotate your arm 180 degrees, flicking your wrist upward, and open your palm in one swift motion so it is facing the wall." Professor Walsh waited as the students practiced the motion, correcting several as she glided around the room. After a few minutes of practice, the professor waltzed back to the center of the room. "After completing the motion, you will firmly say '*destra*' as your palm opens. This particular bit of magic should be felt traveling from your sternum and through your arm, if done correctly. It is a powerful spell that requires control and a steady hand, so don't be surprised if it takes you a while longer than most spells to master."

The room erupted in a cacophony of lights and voices bouncing off the protective dome, and the sudden noise made Ember's chest tighten, reminding her briefly of a crumbling mansion at the top of a hill, bits of stained glass flying through the air and cutting into her skin. She closed her eyes as she drew in a breath, chest shaking as she tried to forget, to erase the nightmare that replayed in her mind on an almost nightly basis.

"You okay, Starshine?" Killian asked, as he gently squeezed her arm, his fingers lingering on her skin, leaving a trail of goosebumps.

"Of course." She nodded, shaking her shoulders loose as she looked toward the brick wall. "Just trying to focus."

Killian nodded, a nod that told her he didn't quite believe her but knew better than to pry. Ember narrowed her eyes at the wall, holding her arm steady in front of her. She took in a slow breath before quickly rotating her arm, flipping her wrist and flinging her palm open. Ember's chest shook as visions of a friend with brown curls and a glowing smile flitted through her mind. Studying in the grass outside of Heksheim, laughing in the orchard at the Kitts' farm, morning meetings at Hidden Moon. Grief and anger moved through her veins like fire, igniting her skin as tears pricked the corner of her eyes.

*"Destra!"* she almost shouted, anger bubbling in her chest she wasn't fully aware was there. The wall in front of her crumbled, blasting into a thousand tiny pieces that flew through the air. The room quieted as everyone whipped their heads around. Ember dropped her arm, taking a step back and curling into herself as she folded her arms tightly over her chest.

"Very impressive, Miss Lothbrok," Professor Walsh almost smiled. "Perhaps we will learn the repairing charm next." She silently flipped her wrist, and the wall quickly shifted back into place, not even dust left on the pristine floor. "The trick with destra is to give enough power to the spell, but not so much that those around you are injured as well. It is a tricky thing to control this sort of raw power. Tricky, but not impossible."

Fen gave Ember a smile, and the class continued, her chest feeling lighter as she practiced the spell repeatedly, focusing on not letting her anger give the spell more power than it required. As quickly as the class began, it ended, and soon everyone was packing their bags and chattering away as they headed out the large wooden doors.

"I don't know about you lot," Fen announced, as he slung his bag over his shoulder, "but I could really go for a snack."

Ember rolled her eyes as Killian nodded vigorously, and the trio set off out the door and toward the little cafe on the ground floor. She stopped and turned around, watching Odette quietly pack her things. Ember didn't miss the fact that the girl was always alone—how people tended to walk in the other direction when she came down the hall. Odette Quinn was odd, even by Vala standards, and Ember knew all too well how that felt.

After all, she was the one people whispered about in the hall for most of her childhood.

"Odette!" Ember smiled as the girl began to walk toward the large double doors. "Fancy some tea?"

Odette's smile grew as she nodded. "That sounds lovely," she replied quietly.

After quickly making their way down the moving steps, laughing as Killian tried—and failed—to slide down the banister, they slipped into the small cafe and found an empty table at the back of the room. Killian made his way to the empty counter where tea kettles and coffee pots were charmed to pour themselves into waiting mugs.

Ember sighed happily as she slipped her bag off her shoulder and breathed in the aroma of freshly brewed coffee and tea with scones and jam. Her mouth began to water as she pulled her Elemental Magic textbook out of her bag, flipping to the chapter she had been reading the day before. Killian returned and placed a teacup in front of her before taking his seat beside her.

"One sugar and a dash of Invigorating draught." He smiled as he pulled out his textbook and plopped it on the table in front of him.

Ember's face flushed—did she really look that tired? And when had Killian memorized how she took her tea? She shook her head as she focused on the text in front of her.

"So, are we going to talk about last night?" Fen asked, bits of scones falling onto the table as he talked. Ember wrinkled her nose as she shoved a napkin in his direction and brushed the crumbs from the pages of her book.

"What's there to talk about?" Killian asked, as he tore a

piece of paper from a notebook and began folding it. "It's not like we can change anything."

"Maybe not," Fen said, as he chewed thoughtfully, "but we can't very well sit around doing nothing, either."

"And what do you propose we do?" Killian replied. "Go knock on doors across the island and demand we check their property for abducted children?"

Fen shrugged as he tapped on the table thoughtfully. Killian folded his paper a few more times before laying an origami on the table in front of him. He mumbled under his breath, and the bird began to flutter its wings, floating up from the table and flying around Fen's head, pecking lightly at his glasses. Fen fought the paper bird as Killian laughed, and Ember sighed as she laid down her pen.

"I don't think it's the citizens around the island we have to worry about," she said, as she took a sip of her tea and silently summoned the bird toward her, laying it gently in the middle of the table.

"Oh?" Killian said, as he leaned back in his chair. "Care to share your thoughts with the class, Starshine?"

"I mean, think about it," she said, as she closed her book. "The Guard has been all over the island placing and reinforcing wards. Chief Thornsten himself has been overseeing it. Even a more experienced ward breaker would struggle to get through them."

"So, what are you saying?" Fen asked, as he scrunched his brow. Killian levitated the paper bird in the middle of the table, and it fluttered gently over to Ember, nuzzling its beak against her hand. Ember smiled as her cheeks flushed, and Killian shot her wink.

"I think what she's saying," he said, as he slowly turned his eyes from her to Fen, "is that the call is coming from inside the house."

"What?" Fen said, as he pushed her glasses up the bridge of his nose.

"Think about it," Ember continued, as she took another sip of her tea. "The only way the kidnappings make any sense is if someone in the Guard had something to do with it. The wards are not only keyed to the people in the homes, but to certain Wardens as well. They have full access to take them down or reconfigure them whenever they want." She tapped her finger on the table thoughtfully as she lowered her voice. "The only thing that makes any sense is that it's an inside job."

"You think Chief Thornsten is behind this?" Odette asked, as she summoned a cup of tea and took a sip. Fen jumped, almost like he forgot she was there. She was so quiet it was easy to miss her if you weren't looking.

"Not necessarily him," Ember said, as she shook her head. "I can't imagine he would get his hands dirty like this. But someone underneath him? Absolutely."

The table grew silent as they each lost themselves in their own thoughts. If this wasn't a random thing, if there were government officials behind this, what did that mean for them? For the island? This felt like too much for any one person to tackle alone, let alone a group of sixteen-year-old kids.

"You saw something last night, didn't you?" Odette asked quietly. "When you touched the wisps, you saw something."

Ember swallowed dryly, palms beginning to sweat. She had tried not to think about the vision she had, about the woman sinking beneath the waves—about the unearthly song that came from her lips.

"It was just a strange dream." She tried to sound as nonchalant as possible, but the tremor in her voice was evident. "There was a woman in a boat during a storm. I think she was drowning. I thought it was my mum at first, like a memory of sorts, but now I'm not sure."

Odette just nodded her head as she furrowed her brow. "How interesting," was all she mumbled.

"So, what do we do now?" Fen asked quietly, as he looked around them.

"Not hatching any evil plans, are we?" a voice said from behind them.

Fen stiffened, and Killian instinctively grabbed Ember's hand under the table as the Ellingboe twins waltzed up next to them. Ember felt Killian's grip tighten as Oryn placed his hand on his shoulder.

"What do you want, Oryn?" Killian said through gritted teeth.

"Now, now, cousin, why the hostility? That's not how you treat family." Oryn grinned, flashing his teeth at the boy beside him.

Ember gently squeezed Killian's hand—partly for support, and partly because he was cutting off the circulation to her fingers—and she felt him relax beside her.

"We were just coming to see if you would be coming by the manor this weekend," Veda said, as she adjusted the sleeve of her sweater. "Daddy seems to think a family meeting is in order. He and Uncle Magnus asked us to relay the message."

Killian rolled his eyes as he drummed his fingers on the table. "If my father needs me, he can ask me himself. I don't need to hear it from the two of you."

"Feisty today, aren't we, cousins?" Oryn asked with a smile, as his eyes drifted to Ember, looking her up and down. "Lothbrok seems to be rubbing off on you."

Ember instinctively used her free hand to wrap her sweater tighter around her torso as she shifted in her seat. Oryn leaned on the table in front of Killian, bracing himself with one arm as his other hand went to Ember's hair. She held her breath, too afraid to move as his cold fingers traced a line down her cheek,

"Maybe we'll get to see that famous Lothbrok fire Father always talks about." He grinned.

Before Ember could move, much less form a sentence,

Killian shot up from his seat, grabbing Oryn by his biceps and shoving him into the wall beside them.

"Watch it," Killian hissed, as his grip tightened. "Whatever you're up to, leave her out of it."

"Or what?" Oryn asked, gritting his teeth. "Her little puppy will come after me?"

"I think you and I both know what I'm capable of," Killian almost growled, and Ember felt her heart leap into her throat. "Stay away from her."

"Is that a threat, cousin?" Oryn grinned manically, as his eyes cut toward Ember again. "There are so many fun games we could play with her, it might just be worth it." He licked his lips as his eyes connected with Ember's, and she felt bile rise in her throat. Before she could voice her disgust, Fen was launching himself across the table, right as Killian's fist connected with Oryn's jaw. Fen was on top of him next as Veda's screech pierced the air, and Ember finally jumped up and ran around the table, grabbing Fen by the shoulders and trying to pry both him and Killian off the boy, who was also throwing punches as best he could from the ground.

With Odette's help, Ember finally pulled the boys apart, blood dripping from their faces, and she felt heat rise in her chest. Veda narrowed her eyes at Ember and the boys as she helped her brother off the ground, quickly conjuring a handkerchief to dab the blood dripping from his nose. Both his jaw and eye had already turned a deep shade of purple, and Ember grimaced at the sight of it.

"Keep your attack dogs at bay, worm," Veda spat at Ember, as she supported her brother. "Honestly you'd think the lot of you would have some sort of decorum."

"Watch how you talk about my sister, and there won't be any more problems," Fen spat, blood spraying from his mouth.

Veda scoffed as she turned, leading her brother out the door of the cafe. Ember quickly surveyed the room, noting luckily there were only a handful of students in a far corner who were minding their own business, likely not wanting to get in the middle of anything that the Ellingboe twins were involved in. She sighed as she whipped her head around at the boys, who were now laughing and talking animatedly at the table.

"Are you *trying* to get yourselves expelled?" She almost shouted as she glared at them both, hands on her hips. Odette had conjured two handkerchiefs, handing them to both boys and began to mumble some sort of healing spell under her breath, tendrils of magic leaving her fingertips and lighting up the gash on Fen's brow. His eyes widened, but he didn't say anything, his cheeks turning red as the girl leaned in close.

"Someone had to defend your honor, Starshine." Killian smirked as he titled his head. His grin was playful, but Ember could still feel the heat from the fire behind his eyes.

"Well, you could try to be more discreet," she sighed, as she shook her head at them. "You're no good to me trapped at home. Besides, Eira would kill all of us if you got suspended for fighting."

Fen smiled sheepishly with a nod, and then his eyes widened. "Why don't we meet at the house tomorrow? We can get ready for Rukr tryouts, and I'm sure Mum would love to see you."

Ember's eyes widened as she slipped her bag over her shoulder. She had completely forgotten about Rukr tryouts, and all of a sudden, her stomach was in knots. They had been delayed while Wardens reinforced the wards around the pitch, and with the chaos of moving and school, it had completely slipped her mind.

"Tryouts, right of course." She nodded as she bit her lip. "I'm sure my mum wouldn't mind me leaving for the day. Do you want to come Odette?"

Odette shook her head as she smiled. "I've got plans with Gran."

"Maybe we can make a plan to figure out who is behind the kidnappings while we're at it." Killian grinned as he stuffed his hands in his pockets.

"I think you're severely overestimating our abilities, Vargr," Ember replied, as she rolled her eyes. "I can't imagine Thornsten or his cronies have left behind any evidence that a bunch of teenagers will be able to find."

"You never know till you try." Killian shrugged with a grin. "There's no such thing as a perfect crime."

AFTER DINNER with her mum and Theo, Ember spent the remainder of her evening in the barn with her schoolbooks and Maia, who she felt had been completely neglected since she had moved in. The draic nuzzled her face as she purred, making Ember laugh as she tried to record notes for her Elemental Magic homework. She closed the book, petting Maia's snout as she stood up from the floor.

"How would you like to come in for the evening?" she whispered, quietly slipping a halter and lead over the draic's snout. Maia let out an excited huff as she stomped her front feet. "But you have to be quiet," Ember laughed, and Maia nodded her head. It was still so strange to her how Maia seemed to know exactly what she was thinking. She led her quietly toward the house, slipping in the back door and up the steps to her room, allowing Maia to settle in on her bed. Closing her bedroom door quietly behind her, she made her way down the steps and into the kitchen when she saw Theo in the sitting room out of the corner of her eye.

She rounded the corner and sat on the couch beside him, smiling as she signed, *"How are you?"*

Theo shrugged as he handed her the note she had left for him that morning and looked sheepishly at the ground.

Ember furrowed her brow as she thought back to the sign language book in the library.

*"Can you read?"* she signed and pointed at the piece of paper in her hands.

Theo's cheeks turned red as he shook his head, staring at his fingers as he twiddled his thumbs in his lap.

Ember hummed as she nodded and quickly jumped up from her seat and over to one of the bookshelves lining the wall. She scanned the spines, grinning as her finger ran over a familiar title, and plucked it from its home on the shelf. She sat down beside Theo and showed him the book.

*"The best way to learn to read is by being read to,"* she signed, and then opened the cover. A wave of emotion she wasn't expecting washed over her as she read the title out loud and signed it to Theo. *"The Pegasus and His Boy."*

Theo grinned as he settled in, and Ember felt her chest tighten as she remembered the way she used to snuggle into the couch next to her dad, ready to get lost in whatever magical tale he decided to tell her that night. Her mum had always laughed and told him not to fill her head with fairytales, to save room for practical things like science and arithmetic, but he would just nod and grin. He firmly believed magic and the mundane went together, and now she could see why. Ember felt her heart drop as she realized what all Theo missed not growing up with their dad. He really would have loved him.

Ember crossed her legs underneath one another and laid the book in her lap and began slowly signing as she read. Theo laid his head on her shoulder watching her hands intently as his eyes flitted between her fingers and the book. After a few minutes, Ember looked down and noticed his eyes fluttering closed as he nuzzled his head on her chest. She smiled as she tapped him on the leg.

*"Time for bed?"* she signed. *"You can't hear the story with your eyes closed."*

Theo smiled sleepily as he patted his head and then her chest.

*"Feeling,"* he signed and nuzzled his head back against her collarbone.

Ember grinned as she settled into the couch, reading the story out loud as Theo drifted off to sleep. After his breathing became steady, she gently laid him on the couch, grabbing a blanket from behind her and tucking it around his tiny frame. She smiled as tears pricked at the corners of her eyes. How many times had her father done this for her? Reading her to sleep and then tucking her into bed, oftentimes carrying her into her room from their spot on the couch. A wave of emotion washed over her as she closed her eyes, and for just a moment, she was back in their little cottage, just the three of them without a care in the world. Grief was funny like that— it was sometimes triggered by the most minor, insignificant things. Things that held no weight could become as heavy as bricks, and you had no choice but to carry them.

She took a shaky breath as she brushed Theo's hair out of his eyes and gave him a gentle kiss on the head before tiptoeing out of the room. She couldn't change the past, couldn't get back the years she had lost with her mum and brother, but she could make sure she didn't miss another moment with them as long as she lived.

# CHAPTER 14

# HOMESICK

The wind whipped around Ember as she walked through the woods, the moon lighting the path in front of her. A crow called out above her, high in the branches of the tree, before swooping down in front of her and flying down the moonlit path. Ember didn't know why, but she followed it. Something pulled her through the forest, something deep in her bones. The path widened, and a cottage came into view in the middle of a small clearing. It was an old cottage with a thatch roof and a small well off to the left of the front door. Smoke billowed from the chimney, cutting through the canopy above it. The crow flew fast toward the clearing, and Ember quickened her steps until she was running, trying to catch up with it. She stopped in her tracks when she heard a faint noise coming from the cottage.

A song drifted through the darkness that made her blood run cold.

Trí stoirme agus farraige caillimid cé muid féin,
    Ach amháin le fáil ag réalta tar éis titim.
    Snámh i dtreo an chladaigh i bhfad i gcéin,
    óir níl aon áit caillte againn níos mó.

. . .

*EMBER INCHED FURTHER down the path, and a woman came into view. She had wild, silver curls that fell around her shoulders as she stood hunched over a wash basin. A white hooded cloak blew gently in the breeze as she continued her song, swaying along with her words. She was scrubbing a bloody shirt, something Ember imagined an aristocrat might wear, and continued singing.*

*TRÍ FEAR TAR eis fás agus foraoisí cosc,*
  *Sin an ait a bhfaighidh tú na daoine óga, goidte agus i bhfolach.*
  *Thar na gcnoc is na gcloch liath,*
  *Sin an ait a rachaidh sibh go léir isteach sa chraic.*

*IT SOUNDED LESS like a song and more like a war cry—something Ember imagined troops singing as they marched into battle, flags flying and heads held high. As Ember leaned closer to listen, the crow swooped down in front of her, cutting her arm with its talons as it called out into the night. The woman's head whipped up, looking directly at Ember, and a scream caught in Ember's throat as their eyes met. The woman tilted her head with a smile, and lavender eyes peered back.*

EMBER SUCKED in a breath as she shot up in bed, sweat soaking her sheets and blanket. Maia slowly opened her eyes from where she laid at the foot of the bed and tilted her head. It was the same song she had heard when she touched the flower, the same song now rattling around in her head making her chest shake.

"It was just a dream, girl," Ember said, as she rubbed the draic's muzzle and took a shaky breath. "Just a dream."

She got out of bed, shuffling toward her mirror and

quickly putting her contacts in before heading downstairs with Maia at her heels, unable to fully shake the uneasy feeling in the pit of her stomach. She quietly made her way to the back door where Maize was waiting for her, giving her a stern look. Ember smiled sheepishly as Maize led Maia toward the barn to give her her breakfast, and Ember slipped into the kitchen where Gaelen was making tea. The smell of bacon, eggs, and potato farls filled the room, and Ember smiled as she sat at the table.

"Did Maia sleep well?" Aoife asked as she smirked from behind her mug. Ember's eyes widened as she choked on a bite of bacon, and Aoife laughed as she shook her head.

"How did you know?" Ember asked sheepishly, pushing eggs around her plate.

"A mother always knows." Aoife winked, eyes almost seeming to peer straight through her.

A knock sounded at the door, and Gaelen left the room promptly to answer it. A few moments later, Killian waltzed into the room, hands lazily stuffed in his pockets.

"Well, good morning, Killian." Aoife smiled as she dabbed the corner of her mouth with a napkin.

"Good morning, Mrs. Lothbrok." He grinned as he adjusted the sleeve of his jumper. "*Mornin', Theo,*" he signed, ruffling the little boy's hair.

Theo smiled with a nod and then focused again on the breakfast in front of him.

Killian's eyes landed on her, and she wasn't quite sure why she felt like she needed to run away and hide. The invisible thread at her sternum thrummed as he smirked.

"Ready to go, Starshine?" he asked, as he plucked a piece of bacon off her plate and into his mouth. "You need all the practice you can get."

"Where are you two off to today?" Aoife asked, as she sent her plate toward the sink.

"We're just practicing for Rukr tryouts." Ember smiled as

she got up from the table, taking her plate quickly to the sink. "I'll just be at the Kitts' house. Is that okay?" She realized at that moment she had never actually asked permission.

"Of course, Mo Stór," Aoife replied, as she kissed Ember on the top of the head. "You should take your brother with you. I'm sure he would enjoy getting out of the house."

"Of course, Mum." Ember smiled.

Aoife nodded as she kissed them both on the head one last time and placed her mug in the sink. "Be home in time for supper, and try not to get into any trouble." She cocked a brow as she looked between the two teenagers, and Ember felt her face flush. "It was lovely to see you, Killian."

"I'll have her home in one piece," Killian said with a smirk. "Lovely to see you as well."

Aoife nodded and left the room, and Killian signed something to Theo. He ran out of the room, and moments later, he was back, grinning with shoes and jacket on ready to go. Ember grabbed her AirWave, and then grabbed Maia from the barn, and the four made their way to the Echopoint at the end of the drive.

"You know you didn't have to pick me up," Ember said, as they made their way out the wrought iron gate. "I'm perfectly capable of getting to the Kitts' without a chaperone."

Killian smirked as he grabbed the low hanging branch. "Best not to take any chances." He shrugged, and all four of them were whisked away. After landing at the Echopoint outside of the Kitts' home, they quickly made their way up the drive and to the old farmhouse. Ember felt her heart leap into her throat and couldn't hide her grin. She took the steps on the porch two at a time before stopping abruptly at the door.

"Just gonna stand there all day, Starshine?" Killian asked, as he cocked his brow.

Ember raised her hand as if to knock, unsure if she should just walk in or not, but before she could, the door swung open, and Fen's grin quickly turned to confusion as his eyes bounced back and forth between Killian and Ember.

"Did you come together?" he asked, but before either of them could answer, Eira appeared around the corner.

"Fenrir James, what are you just standing there for? Let them in!" she scolded, as she ushered everyone inside, save for Maia who went straight to the pasture where Arlo was flitting about.

Eira wrapped Ember in a hug, and she immediately felt every worry in the world melt away—nothing else seemed to matter when she was back at the Kitts'. Theo inched closer to Ember and grabbed her hand, and Eira let out a small gasp as she smiled down at the boy.

"Now who is this?" she asked, as she smoothed out her apron.

"This is my brother Theo," Ember replied, as she squeezed his hand.

He gave a small nod and signed, *"Hello,"* before quickly grabbing her hand again.

Eira's eyes went misty as she smiled. "You remind me so much of Siris when he was little," she said to no one in particular. Before Eira could get another word in, Maeve came barreling around the corner and jumped into Ember's arms.

"Ember, Ember!" she all but screamed, clinging to her torso like a life raft.

"Hi, Maevie." Ember smiled, wrapping her in a hug. "This is Theo, my little brother."

Maeve stepped back and tilted her head briefly before sticking her hand out, "I'm Maeve Kitt," she said. "Do you want to meet the chickens?"

Theo looked up expectantly at Ember, slight confusion written on his face. Killian tapped his shoulder gently and signed, *"Chickens,"* and Theo's face lit up. He nodded at Maeve with a huge grin, and the two of them sped off through the back door.

"I'll have lunch ready when you're done," Eira said with a smile and turned to head back into the kitchen. The trio made their way outside to the orchard, Airwaves in hand.

"Okay, so I think we start with a few laps around the perimeter of the orchard," Fen began, as he dropped his board and started to put on his gloves. "Maybe practice a few hairpin turns and then we can work on passing." He took a cloth out of his pocket and began wiping his board down, focusing on the rails before pulling out a roll of grip tape from his pocket as well. "If we feel comfortable at that point," he continued, as he applied the tape, "we can throw in the camans. Have you decided what position you're going for?"

Ember's eyes widened as she slowly pulled on her gloves. "Um, no, not particularly," she stuttered. If she was being honest, she wasn't entirely sure she should even be going out for the team. It seemed more like something Fen and Killian should be doing while she watched from the stands.

"We'll worry about that later." Killian smiled as he squeezed her shoulder. "Just focus on flying for now." Ember's cheeks flushed as she nodded, and Fen narrowed his eyes at the two of them.

"Don't be weird," was all he said, and then he quickly strapped into his board and took off into the air. Ember and Killian followed suit, and then the three of them began flying circles around the orchard. Ember held her breath as she climbed higher in the air, closing her eyes as the wind whipped her braid around her head. In the air, she didn't have to worry about anything—not school or the kidnappings or how hard she was trying to acclimate to her new life. She just had to be, and that was the most freeing feeling in the world. After a few laps, Fen motioned for them to meet in the center of the orchard, hovering just a few feet above the trees.

"Okay, Em, you know how to do hairpin turns, right?" Fen said, as he flipped a Brazul back and forth in his gloved hands.

"Um, maybe?" she replied, not quite as confident as she intended.

Killian smirked as he lazily flew up beside her and squeezed her shoulder. "Here, I'll show you," he replied, and before she could argue, he sped off toward the end of the orchard. He bent forward, hands gripping the edges of his board as he inched closer to the edge of the tree line. One moment, he was flying forward, and the next he had made a complete one hundred and eighty degree turn without slowing or stopping, flying back toward Fen and Ember.

"Well done, mate!" Fen cheered, as he slapped Killian on the shoulder. "Your turn, Em."

Ember swallowed dryly as she gave a nod, flexing her hands at her sides. "Should I maybe watch for a minute more?"

Killian furrowed his brow. "You've done things a lot scarier than a simple hairpin turn this summer," he said. "Don't think about it too much."

Ember felt her ears burn hot as she nodded again. It wasn't the flying that scared her, or even the turn. Killian was right. She had done turns and flips all summer long much higher than this. But at that point, it wasn't training—not to her anyway. It was a fluid feeling, like the breath the swam through her lungs. There was a freedom in being up in the clouds, like everything that weighed her down couldn't reach her up there. She took a shaky breath, rolling her shoulders as she flexed both her hands at her sides.

This felt different, more rigid, and she was having trouble ignoring the tightness in her chest.

She sped off, almost as quickly as Killian had, toward the edge of the trees. Her breathing became rapid as she reached the end of the orchard, and even though she had done it a hundred times before, her board began to wobble underneath her. She crouched low to grab the rails, but it didn't make a difference. She slowed to a steady pace, taking the turn at a speed even Maeve would've laughed at, and then sped back to the other end, face burning from embarrassment.

Fen gave her a sympathetic smile as she approached.

"Should we work drills now?" he said as he tried to change the subject. "Maybe two against one?"

Ember sighed as she rubbed her forehead. "Maybe we can take a break. Get some water and relax?"

"Relax?" Fen said, as he furrowed his brow. "Tryouts are a week away. There's not time to relax!"

"Calm down, mate," Killian said, as he patted his friend on the back. "Fifteen minutes won't set her any further back than she already is."

Ember narrowed her eyes as the boys laughed, making their way down to the ground again and unhooking their feet from their boards. They piled under their favorite tree, and Killian plucked an apple from one of the low hanging branches and took a bite.

"We've got plenty of time to practice," Fen said, as Killian tossed an apple in his direction. "You'll just have to come over a few more times after school and maybe on the weekend after tryouts. We'll get you there."

Ember's heart splintered as he beamed. "Fen, I can't just spend all of my time here," she said quietly, as she shook her head.

"Sure you can," he shrugged. "Mum would love it and so would Maeve. There's plenty of room. You're family after all."

"But I'm not," she snapped. "I *have* a family now—a real family—and I can't spend all of my time away from them just because you miss me. I'm not your sister anymore, Fenrir."

Fen's face fell, and Ember's heart seemed to crack again, guilt filling all of the spaces. She hadn't meant to bite his head off, but he needed to understand.

"I've missed the last decade with them," she said, a little more gently this time. "I have to rebuild my relationship with them. I can't be here as much anymore. I just can't."

Fen's throat bobbed as he nodded. Silence filled the air around them as he averted his eyes, fidgeting with the Brazul he pulled out of his pocket.

"Your mum mentioned Siris earlier," Ember said, trying desperately to change the subject and avoid another moment of awkward silence. "That's your brother, right?"

Fen stiffened beside her, just barely, and dropped the ball on the grass. He quickly picked it back up, stuffing it in the leather case and into his pocket. "Older brother," he mumbled with a nod.

"Where is he?"

"It doesn't matter," he said, as he shook his head.

Killian sighed as he took another bite of his apple. "It's just Ember," he said, as he rolled his eyes. "You can tell her—"

"I said it doesn't matter," Fen spat, more angrily than Ember was expecting. "Talking doesn't bring people back. And besides, she's not *family*, so it doesn't concern her."

Ember flinched as if he had physically punched her in the stomach. She deserved that, she supposed. There was ire in his words, but behind the flame, she could see the hurt—the grief. Whether that was for her or his brother, she wasn't sure.

She sank back against the tree. She knew better than anyone how painful some memories could be, that even talking about them could hurt worse than the original injury —like splitting open a wound and pouring vinegar directly into the vein. She didn't say anything, just reached over to squeeze his hand. They would find some way to navigate all this pain together.

"So, what was that about with Oryn yesterday?" Fen asked, quickly changing the subject, eyes still glued to the grass in front of him.

"Hell if I know." Killian shrugged. "Nothing good, I reckon. That whole lot has been acting *especially* odd here lately."

"Odd?" Ember asked, as she furrowed her brow.

"Aye," Killian nodded, "this isn't the first little meeting I've gotten wind of, just the first I've been invited to."

"You don't think they could have something to do with all of this, could they?" Ember asked, as her eyes widened. The thought that a parent—someone with children of their own— could be the cause of so much grief for other families was almost too hard to believe. But with their connections and the way Veda and Oryn acted even at school, maybe they weren't too far off.

"Anything's possible, Starshine," Killian grimaced. "Maybe I'll pop by my uncle's house this weekend and see what this little meeting is all about." He chewed thoughtfully on his apple.

"Please be careful," she whispered, as she chewed on her bottom lip.

Killian smirked as he shot her a wink. "I always am."

"Ugh, gross," Fen grimaced. "Can you please not do that in front of me?"

Ember laughed, her chest growing lighter as the boys tried to tackle each other, resulting in a tangled mess of limbs flailing about the ground. The invisible tether that connected the three thrummed in her chest, and peace washed over her, a peace she hadn't fully felt since she left the farm. As soon as she felt it, the feeling was immediately replaced by guilt. It was the strangest sensation—like she was homesick for a place she no longer got to call home. Maeve's distant laughter filled the air as the smell of soda bread floated from the house, and Ember's chest tightened as she wrapped her arms around her knees.

This wasn't home anymore, and it never would be again.

# CHAPTER 15

# THE BANSHEE OF ELLESMERE ISLAND

"You *cannot* ask for a Pegasus for your birthday, Fenrir," Ember sighed, as she rolled her eyes, sliding into her seat in Zoomancy. Since the moment she had met the boys at the Echopoint that morning, Fen had been chattering on about a Pegasus he had "bonded" with in Sigurvik that weekend and how it was the only thing he wanted for his birthday now.

"And why not, Em? What's stopping me?" he replied, crossing his arms tightly over his chest like a petulant toddler.

"Eira would never let you, for one," she replied, tapping her pen against her nose as she opened her textbook, "and think of how that would make poor Arlo feel. Replacing him with a flying pony? He would be devastated. Not to mention I'm almost certain they aren't bred as pets."

"She's right, mate," Killian interjected, as he leaned back in his chair. "They're a working breed only. He'd be bloody miserable stuck in your barn all day."

Fen grumbled something unintelligible as he scrunched his nose and leaned on the table, resting his chin in his palm. "Are you coming over for our birthday dinner?" he asked, as he traced the wood grain on the table.

Ember tried not to flinch.

It wasn't *their* birthday, not really. Not anymore. It was her birthday and his birthday, but it wasn't something they would share together again. The sudden realization of that made something inside of her chest crack.

"I think my mom has something planned." She tried to smile. "Maybe we can do something after?"

Fen's face fell as he nodded, and Ember felt something deep inside her crack a bit more.

"Good morning, young Vala," Professor Bjorn's voice boomed, as he descended the spiral staircase. "I trust you all had a weekend full of rest and recuperation? And perhaps some studying?"

Every student seemed to avert their eyes, looking anywhere but the professor towering over them at the front of the classroom. He tapped his giant paw on his tweed vest as he peered at them over his monocle.

"Or perhaps not," he laughed gruffly, as he leaned against his desk. He tapped silently on his chin for a moment before clearing his throat and straightening his vest. "This quarter we are focusing on the creatures that live in the Dark Forest," he continued as he opened the textbook.

A groan sounded out through the room, some students even laying their heads on their desks, and Professor Bjorn rolled his eyes with a small grin.

"Oh, for fecks sake," he mumbled, as he flipped his wrist, promptly closing the book on his desk. "I have an even better idea." With another silent flick of his wrist, his office door opened at the top of the spiraling staircase, and a small book floated toward him, laying gently on his desk. The pages fluttered open quickly, then slowed to a stop somewhere in the middle of the book. Professor Bjorn cleared his throat as he adjusted his monocle, and the class fell silent once more.

"Instead of discussing the creatures in the Dark Forest," he began, "today we are going to discuss Celtic mythological creatures and beings."

The classroom erupted in a cacophony of oohs and aahs as everyone flipped their books closed and began whispering excitedly to the person beside them. Ember smiled as she tapped the desk beside her.

"Do you know many legends about creatures in the forest?" she asked Odette quietly.

"I know stories that even you would have a hard time believing, Ember Lothbrok." Odette grinned as the bells hanging from her ears twinkled lightly.

"Do you ever see anything? When you're out there?" Ember asked in a hushed whisper. She didn't have to specify where the *there* was.

Odette nodded as she smirked. "Sometimes I see things, and sometimes things see me. Sometimes I wake up in my bed, and I'm not sure if I walked back myself or if I was ever there to begin with. Nothing in the forest is truly ever what it seems."

Ember nodded in silent agreement.

"There are many legends about things that lurk about the island," Odette whispered, smiling as she tilted her head toward Ember. "Although, it seems not all legends are steeped completely in lore."

Ember felt her neck burn red as she cut her eyes around the room, but not even Fen and Killian were paying attention to the conversation between her and Odette. "I suppose not," she whispered back.

"Just because we are going off script," Professor Bjorn announced from the front of the room, "does not mean this lesson is not to be taken seriously."

A hush fell over the class as he walked up and down the rows of students.

"It also doesn't mean that this class won't count toward your final grade."

Silence finally fell over the class, and Professor Bjorn smirked as he strode back toward the front of the room.

"Today we will cover the Banshee," he said calmly, sticking small ear plugs into his large ears. "First we will start with the Banshee's song."

Ember's blood ran cold at the sound that came out of the book—the song she had heard in her dreams and the night she had followed the wisps in Arcelia. Her breathing became rapid, the walls threatening to close in on her entirely. She clenched her sweaty palms as her stomach turned, nails digging into the calloused skin. Odette laid a hand on one of her fists, and Ember stiffened in her seat.

The room filled with students grabbing their ears and squeezing their eyes shut, some screaming, "Stop!" as they winced. Ember furrowed her brow as she turned to look at Fen and Killian, who both had their ears covered by their arms. Killian looked up at Ember, his eyes locking quickly with hers, confusion washing over his face. Odette seemed to be the only one other than her who wasn't screaming, but that didn't surprise her in the least.

As everyone continued to cover their ears, Ember couldn't understand why they had a problem with the song the ethereal woman was singing. As her eyes met Professor Bjorn's, he gave her a curious look. After a few more beats, he waved his hand, and the singing stopped, and the rest of the class uncovered their ears.

"Feckin hell," Fen groaned, "what was that?"

Killian narrowed his eyes at Ember and tilted his head, like he was studying her. Ember felt her neck burn hot as she shrank into her seat.

"That, Mr. Kitt," Professor Bjorn, "was the Banshee's song."

"I think *song* is an odd choice of words," Fen mumbled, as he rubbed his temple. "Whoever was in charge of naming that should be fired."

Ember furrowed her brow but kept her eyes forward on Professor Bjorn, who seemed to be trying not to look at her now.

"Can anyone tell me what the Banshee's Song means?" Professor Bjorn asked, as he paced up and down the rows of students.

Odette's hand shot up in the air. "She is said to be a harbinger of death," she said softly. "The Banshee only sings at night, and her song is said to be an omen."

The class went still.

"Very good, Miss Quinn," Professor Bjorn nodded. "As you all heard, her song is more of a wail, and she can only be heard at night. She is said to roam the Dark Forest, and her song brings the death of a loved one or a warrior in battle."

All eyes were on the professor as he walked through the class, so still you could hear a pin drop.

"Some view her as a guide to Valhalla," he continued, "and others just a dark omen. The more likely truth, though, is that she is Fae but was banished from their lands."

Ember furrowed her brow—she had met the king and queen, and they didn't seem like the type to banish one of their own. Perhaps that was part of the legend that had been muddled—a part that had turned more fiction than fact.

"Can anyone tell me what she is said to look like?" Professor Bjorn asked, as he leaned against his desk. Killian's hand shot up in the air, and the professor gave him a small nod.

"That's a trick question," he said with a wry smile. "She looks different to different people."

"Very good." Professor Bjorn nodded. "Care to elaborate?"

Killian cleared his throat and plucked an invisible piece of lint off his pristine white sleeve.

"To some, she looks like a young girl, some say she's the most beautiful Irish noblewoman they've ever seen, and some say she just looks like an old hag." Giggles erupted in the air and Professor Bjorn shot Killian a warning look.

"For the most part, yes," the professor nodded with a chuckle. "Most can't agree on what she looks like, but there are a few things they can agree on. She has long, silver hair that flows past her shoulders and piercing lavender eyes."

Ember closed her eyes and sucked in a breath. She was transported back to the dream she had just a few nights prior, of the cottage in the woods with a woman washing blood-stained clothes in the stream. Has she had a dream about the Banshee? Or was it just a coincidence? She shivered as she wrapped her arms around her chest. Maybe she had read something that made her dream of it. Maybe just a memory of the night in Arcelia.

Whatever the reason, she hoped she never saw the woman again.

Before she realized it, class was over, and Ember was throwing her books in her bag.

"To those it may affect," Professor Bjorn announced, as the class packed their things, "please remember that Rukr tryouts have been moved to this evening. The pitch is heavily warded, and there will be Wardens on watch for your protection."

He cleared his throat as they all settled and looked back at him.

"You have nothing to fear," he continued, "as long as you stay within the grounds and do as the Wardens tell you. They are here to protect you. You're dismissed."

Ember made her way out the door and into the hall when a small memory flitted through her mind. Nothing huge or jarring, but she suddenly remembered a Warden at the Kitts' the day they were broken into. Her heartbeat quickened—he had acted strange, almost standoffish. Wardens were never known to be warm and fuzzy, but he acted different—like he was hiding something. Higher ranking Wardens had access to everyone on the island, the keys to all the wards. It would be simple for someone to slip in and out without raising any alarm. They had the ability to travel at will, without an Echo-point, to anywhere on the island.

Was something bigger happening here than they realized?

Killian and Fen caught up with her as she walked down the corridor, laughing about some joke one of the boys had made. She quickly shook away the impending downward spiral and slowed her gate.

"What did you think about the Banshee song?" Killian asked, as he caught up to Ember.

"It was feckin awful," Fen said, as he scrunched his nose, readjusting the strap on his shoulder.

"It wasn't so bad," Ember replied, as she shrugged. "I thought it was kind of pretty."

Both boys looked at Ember like she had completely lost her mind.

"You have terrible taste in music," Fen mumbled, as he shook his head. "If you can even call it that."

"Have you heard the story about the Banshee in the forest?" Killian asked, as he cocked his brow.

"There's actually one on the island?" Ember asked wide-eyed. She's wrapped her sweater tightly around her waist, the corridor suddenly feeling colder.

"Aye," Killian nodded, "the legend says that hundreds of years ago, a young girl wandered into the forest alone. Some say she was playing a game with friends, and others say she was lured in by something else."

Killian paused for dramatic effect, and Ember rolled her eyes.

"A search party was led through the woods for weeks, but they never found her, dead or alive," he continued. "The legend says that she was taken hostage in the forest after she stumbled onto something she wasn't meant to see."

"Like what?" Ember said, as she breathed a laugh.

"Who knows, the island was so different hundreds of years ago. Could've been a band of Fae, or elves, or any number of dangerous creatures." Killian stuffed his hands in his pockets as they walked down the moving staircase and toward the large greenhouse for Herbal Magic.

"Supposedly, she was cursed," Odette chimed in, as she walked up next to Ember, smiling as she clutched her books to her chest, "and now she wanders the island wailing for her parents. Seeing her is a very bad omen. See her, and you're as good as dead."

Both boys' eyes widened as the girl appeared from nowhere. Ember felt goosebumps run up her arms as she shivered.

"My brother used to tell me stories about her," Fen added. "How she used to drown sailors and ride whales into the sea."

"You both have very overactive imaginations," Ember laughed, as she stepped into the classroom, the sun shining brightly through the glass dome as a bird chirped overhead.

Killian shrugged as they walked down the steps to the wooden tables in the center of the room. "It's just a story to keep the weans out of the forest," he said, as he dropped his bag by the table.

"I think you'll find," Odette said sweetly, "that all legends are steeped in some form of truth, Killian Vargr." She looked toward him as if to say *you of all people should know that.* Killian's eyes widened as he straightened his spine a fraction of an inch.

Ember chewed on her lip as she sighed. She really hoped this one legend didn't have any truth to it at all.

"Come in, come in!" Professor Flora said, as she sauntered to the middle of the room, a yellow canary perched on her shoulder. "Today, we have a very exciting lesson."

Ember pulled out her Herbal Magic Field Guide and quickly flipped to the page she had been working on the week before. When they began a new project, they always started with planting and growing the ingredients themselves. It was monotonous at times, and sometimes a little boring if she was being honest, but Ember couldn't help but love the feeling of the dirt under her fingers while she planted and pruned. Her favorite part, by far, was after the ingredients were grown and harvested and she got to put together whatever draught or tonic they were focusing on.

"Our Ancient Sea Kelp grew beautifully and is ready for pruning in the pond," Professor Flora said, as she fed the canary a small treat. "One person from each group will go prune, and the rest will begin preparing the ingredients on your list. Please be mindful of the jellyfish in the pond, as they have a nasty sting."

Ember scrunched her nose. "Are the jellyfish magic?" she asked, as she scratched some notes in her book.

Professor Flora smiled as she conjured glowing images in the air in front of her. Dozens of jellyfish, big and small, swam through the air leisurely as she made them sway back and forth with the motion of her hand. The class cheered and gasped, and Ember couldn't help but grin.

"Jellyfish are one of the only breeds of creature, on land or sea, that are all of magical origin," she said, as the glowing jellyfish swam through the air around the class. "They are content to wander the ocean, soaking up magic from each full moon. People have been known to use their tentacles for very special potions, but it is a rare ingredient, incredibly hard to come by."

"What makes it so hard?" Flynn Macguire asked from the back of the class, pen twirling in his hand. "Couldn't you just grab one of the buggers and chop it off?"

A few small gasps sounded from girls toward the front of the room, and Ember saw Killian roll his eyes.

"Yes and no," Professor Flora said with a small smile. "You could readily try—and succeed—if that's what you did, but there would be no magic in the tentacles. The only way the tentacles will have magical properties is if they are willingly given. It's a defense mechanism that all breeds of jellyfish have acquired over the span of thousands of years, and it has made using their special magic that much more difficult."

"What makes their magic so special?" Fen asked, as he tapped his fingers on the table.

"Ah, that is the question, isn't it?" Professor Flora said, as she waved her hand in the air. What appeared above their heads was a glowing full moon, tiny jellyfish floating all around it in sync. "Research has been conducted on them," the professor said, as she rubbed the top of the canary's head, "and the only thing that has been gathered is they seem to recharge during the full moon. Their magical core is slowly depleted throughout the month, but after every full moon, it is fully recharged and back to a normal level. We don't know how, or why, they acquire their magic this way. That remains a mystery. There isn't much we know about this type of magic, and no other being has ever been observed to use it."

"Space magic," Fen whispered with a grin that slowly overtook his whole face. "So cool."

Ember rolled her eyes and tried to suppress her grin as the boys began whispering about astronauts with wands and Fae flying around the stars.

"I've never heard of any potions that require something like that," Veda said with a sneer, causing Ember to roll her eyes as she sighed.

"I'm sure there are plenty of tonics and elixirs that you have never heard of, Miss Ellingboe," Professor Flora said with a slight raise of her brow. "There are potions that even I am not familiar with, coming from books long lost to time."

Ember felt her chest lurch, only slightly.

"What kind of books?" a soft voice from the back of the room asked.

"Books filled with ancient spells and potions," the

professor almost whispered, "with ingredients and incantations that haven't been seen or spoken by Vala in hundreds of thousands of years." She walked around the greenhouse. Glowing pictures of runes and strange symbols floated around the students as Professor Flora flitted her wrist, so quiet you could hear a pin drop, the students hanging on her every word.

"Where did these books come from?" Ember asked quietly, Fen's eyes widening as he very subtly shook his head.

"Now that is the mystery, isn't it?" Professor flora replied with a smile, as birds called out above her in the aviary—like they knew a great secret. "Some say they were written by an old king on his deathbed to help preserve the way of life that our ancestors once held." She made her way slowly back to the front of the room as the canary nuzzled against her hand. "Others say they were written by the gods themselves—magic that was too powerful for any one Vala, hidden away to protect us."

"Protect us from what?" Oryn scoffed, as he crossed his arms over his chest.

"From ourselves," Professor Flora said solemnly. She gently removed the canary from her shoulder, placing her on the gold perch beside her. The little bird fluffed her feathers and took a few seeds from the professor's hands, chirping quietly. "Magic like that, something as strong as these potions and spells in these mythical books, could be detrimental in the wrong hands. There are some things that are best hidden away."

Ember felt her heart nearly stop beating as she swallowed dryly. She knew all too well what power like that did to people, even the idea of that power, and what it could destroy. She bit the edge of her lip as she felt Fen nudge her elbow and give her a questioning look.

*Are you okay?*

He didn't say it, not out loud, but she could hear his words rattle around in her head for just a moment. She gave him a small nod and a smile as she took in a shaky breath.

"Now if that is settled," Professor Flora continued, as she flipped her hand, making the glowing pictures still floating around the room vanish, "you may begin making the Breath of the Deep Elixir."

"Shall I run and fetch the kelp?" Odette asked with a whimsical smile. "Perhaps I can convince the jellies to donate a tentacle or two."

Ember laughed as she shook her head. "If anyone could do it, I have no doubt it would be you, Odette."

Ember began chopping ingredients and grinding them to throw in the cauldron while Killian and Fen whispered next to each other like they were sharing a secret.

"Do you plan on helping today," Ember asked, as she scribbled notes in her Field Guide, "or are you hellbent on giving me a terrible grade this term?"

"Lighten up, Starshine." Killian grinned as he leaned on the edge of the long wooden table. "We were just discussing tryouts for tonight, or have you forgotten already?"

Ember felt her stomach lurch as she swallowed. "How could I," she replied, as she began to chop more violently, "with the two of you reminding me multiple times a day for the last two weeks?"

She had received no less than two Helios every day from either Fen or Killian, reminding her of the date, time, and place of Rukr tryouts. Fen also made it a point to send her detailed exercises to do every day after school, and some days, he even tried to follow her back to her house to supervise. As much as she wanted to be annoyed by their insane behavior, she had to admit it was very sweet how invested they were in her success.

"But you have to admit," Fen said, as he pulled a candy bar out of his pocket and began to unwrap it, "you are *signifi-*

*cantly* more prepared now than you would have been without us."

Ember rolled her eyes and tried to hide her grin as she rummaged through the pile of ingredients on the table. "I suppose so," she sighed. "Now can one of you make yourself useful and find me," she squinted, as she read through the list of ingredients in her Field Guide, "one Merrow scale, given willingly," she grimaced as she shook her head, "and three drops of salt water, harvested during the full moon?"

"On it," Fen said with a salute, and then took off to rummage through cabinets at the front of the classroom.

Killian leaned leisurely against the table, tapping his finger on the mortar that sat between them.

"Can you hand me the Pickleweed and Samphire?" Ember asked, as she grabbed a bowl of salt and began to pour it on the gold scale. "It has to marinade in the Celtic sea salt for five minutes."

Killian nodded as he reached across the table, quickly dropping both ingredients into the conch shell and mulling it together with the sea salt. Ember reached across him for another bowl and felt goosebumps run up and down her arms as their hands brushed. She quickly pulled away, heat rising up her neck and into her cheeks as she grabbed a paring knife.

"Let that sit for a few minutes while we chop the mollusk eggs," she tried to say nonchalantly, but the way she stumbled over her words betrayed her.

"You *are* going to be fine," Killian assured her, as he took the knife out of her hand and began thinly slicing the mollusk eggs into even pieces. Ember sat entranced as his fingers moved effortlessly between slicing and tossing them into the bubbling cauldron, focusing on the veins running up his exposed forearm. She shook her head as she ran her fingers through her hair.

"What are you talking about?" she asked, as she checked over the ingredients in the conch.

"Tryouts," he replied, tossing the last piece of mollusk egg into the cauldron. "You're going to do fine. It's not as treacherous as you think it's going to be." He grabbed the towel hanging on the edge of the table and wiped his hands clean.

Ember gave a small nod as she bit the edge of her lip. "I have a tendency to make things harder than they have to be," she half laughed, as she dumped the contents of the conch into the cauldron. "I always seem to find a way to mess a good thing up."

"Self-deprecation does not suit you." He frowned. "Just do your best, that's all anyone can ask for. Your best is good enough."

"I come bearing gifts!" Fen sang, as he waltzed back up to the table, Odette trailing behind him with the kelp in one hand and a triumphant grin painted on her face.

"Finally," Ember sighed, as she took the scale and water from him, quickly dumping both into the smoking cauldron. Odette diced the kelp, slowly and methodically, and then dropped it into the cauldron next, the final ingredient. The group took turns for the next fifteen minutes, carefully stirring before funneling some into a small bottle and taking it up to Professor Flora's desk. One by one, the other groups dropped their bottles off, and everyone fell into a small hush. The professor grabbed a small potted plant off her desk and sat it on a table in the middle of the classroom.

"If brewed correctly," she began, "pouring a drop of the elixir over this plant will create a bubble around it, protecting it from any water poured over top." Without another word, she uncorked one of the bottles and poured one small drop on the flower's petal.

Upon contact, it immediately turned to ash.

Ember's jaw hung slack as Professor Flora uncorked each bottle and watched as each one had the same reaction. Soon, half the plant had turned to ash, and the room was completely silent.

"Well, it seems we are in a wee bit of a pickle," Professor Flora said with a tilt of her head. "All of the elixirs were done incorrectly."

"That doesn't make any sense," Ember said, as she furrowed her brow and shook her head. "I followed the instructions explicitly—to the letter."

"Ah, yes, the instructions." The professor nodded as she tapped her chin, the shadow of a smile playing at the corner of her mouth. "Perhaps I forgot a component." She shrugged as she sauntered to her desk, plucking a piece of paper from the center, and mumbling as she read it over.

Fen furrowed his brow. "Forgot something?" he whispered, as he narrowed his eyes. "You wrote the damn lesson plan."

Professor Flora raised a brow, just for a moment in Fen's direction, and he quickly averted his eyes.

"Ah, yes, here it is," she said aloud. "You seem to all be missing one drop of Kelpie blood." She unlocked the cabinet behind her desk, quickly plucking out a bottle and walking it down to Ember's group. "Would you do the honors, Miss Lothbrok?" she asked, as she handed over the bottle.

Ember nodded, uncorking the vial, and gently pouring one drop into the cauldron. A puff of smoke rose from the liquid, and it immediately turned a beautiful shade of turquoise.

"Lovely." Professor Flora nodded, filling a vial, and walking back over to the plant in the middle of the room.

She poured the elixir over it, and this time instead of turning to ash, a small bubble surrounded it. The professor poured a cup of water over it, and the bubble deflected it with ease, protecting what was left of the flower within it.

"Even being off by one ingredient," the professor said, as she looked down at the plant, "can change a potion in its entirety. This is why it is so important that you read over your instructions carefully and always double check that you have what it calls for. This is one instance where laziness could cost you your life."

The class nodded silently, and Professor Flora gave them a smile as she dismissed them. The friends gathered their things as they made their way to the door, Ember's brow still furrowed in confusion.

"Everything alright, Starshine?" Killian asked, as he held the door open for her.

Ember wrung her hands together as she bit her lip. "Do you think that will count toward my final grade?"

# CHAPTER 16

# A MOTHER ALWAYS KNOWS

E mber wrung her hands as she steadied her breathing, tapping her foot on the plush grass beside the Rukr pitch. As prepared as Killian thought she was for tryouts, she couldn't help but think she would never be as ready as she needed to be. Students milled around in the stadium seating, most there to hang out with friends rather than watch the tryouts no doubt, but that fact did nothing to curb the anxiety pooling in her stomach.

"You made it!" Fen shouted, as he walked over to the bench, leaning his board against it to sit beside Ember. "Are you ready?"

"As I'll ever be," Ember breathed, as she scanned the stadium for the umpteenth time.

Veda and Oryn had just arrived and were currently strapping into the boards to warm up. Veda flew around the pitch effortlessly, like she had been born with wings. Her body bent with ease against the wind, a fluidity that Ember thought had to be a trick of the light. She looked just as graceful in the air as she did walking through the corridors of Heksheim, and something about that made Ember's blood begin to boil. She flew like she knew a secret no one else did, and Ember couldn't help but feel like not knowing was a liability.

Oryn was like a bomb, set to ignite at the slightest wrong move. He barreled around the pitch with speed and stealth like Ember had never seen, shoving past anyone who even seemed to stand in his way. Ember shuddered as she shook her head, focusing on putting her gloves on and not running out of the stadium, back to the safety of her bedroom.

"Don't stress about them," Fen said with a small smile, as he pulled on his gloves. "They're all bark and hardly any bite. You'll blow Veda out of the water."

"Of course she will." Killian smiled as he waltzed over, board slung over his shoulder. "She was trained by yours truly, of course." He shot her a roguish grin and a wink, and Ember felt her cheeks flush as she rolled her eyes.

"Are you forgetting about me?" Fen said, as he scoffed.

Ember laughed as she patted his shoulder, standing up to strap into her board.

"You're going to do great, Starshine," Killian said, pulling on his gloves. "Just focus on what you're doing and don't worry about anyone else. Veda will try to get in your head. Don't let her."

"Easier said than done," Ember sighed, as she shook her head. "She has a tendency to get in my head whether I like it or not."

Killian walked over to her, brushing a stray hair out of her eyes, and straightened her shoulder pad. Ember felt goose-bumps run down her arms as his fingers brushed her skin, her breath catching in her throat as she swallowed dryly.

"Ignore her," he said softly. "You are a lot stronger than you give yourself credit for."

Ember nodded and took a shaky breath when Fen cleared his throat.

"Shall we get in the air, or are you not done making googly eyes at each other?"

Ember felt her cheeks flush as Killian shoved Fen in the shoulder, making him stumble.

"So gross," Fen mumbled, as he rubbed his shoulder and walked toward his board, strapping in and taking off into the air.

"After you, Starshine." Killian smiled as he gestured toward the field.

Ember took a breath and nodded, then took off into the sky. The students in the stand grew smaller as Ember rose higher, and she felt the weight on her chest slowly lighten as the air grew thinner. There was something otherworldly about being in the air—something about the way the magic crackled like electricity around her, humming and buzzing as it brushed against her exposed arms. She closed her eyes and took a deep breath before lowering the nose of her board so she was with the rest of the students trying out and made her way to the center of the pitch.

There were four Rukr teams at Heksheim, and four subsequent team captains helping to run tryouts. Professor Bjorn ran the program, so he oversaw naming the teams, much to the other professors' dismay.

The Kelpies, captained by Flynn Maguire. The Griffins, captained by Kady O'Neill. The Redcaps, captained by Fagan Doyle, and the Wyverns, captained by Killian. Ember wasn't partial to any one team, but she'd be lying if she said she wouldn't be more comfortable with Killian and Fen.

Professor Bjorn waved his arm in an upward motion, and all four captains met in the middle above the field.

"Each captain will run a set of drills they have prepared," Professor Bjorn announced from below, his boisterous voice echoing off the bleacher surrounding the pitch. "You will complete one set of drills in full before moving on. We will go for an hour or two." Professor Bjorn looked at the watch on his burly wrist and nodded to himself. "Captains, you may begin!"

Each student trying out had been given an arm band with team colors on it to split them into groups. Ember's was maroon and silver—the fact that those were the colors Killian and Fen were also wearing did not miss her. She flew to her group, hovering just slightly behind the sea of students, and patiently waited on instructions from the captain—Killian.

She ran the drills as instructed, trying desperately to ignore the way his arms flexed as he gave direction and the way his jersey sleeves hugged his biceps. She couldn't help but notice how much faster everyone seemed. She shook the thought away and adjusted the caman strapped to her back.

*Focus.*

After a few more drills with Killian, and then a handful with the other three captains, Ember slowed to a stop to catch her breath, and Fen flew up next to her, nudging her in the arm.

"Doin' alright?" he asked, as he balanced beside her.

"For now, anyway." She nodded with a sigh. "I don't know how I'm supposed to compete with any of them."

"You're not," he replied with a shrug, "not really anyway. Worry about competing with the best version of yourself, and the rest will work itself out. That's what Da' always says."

Ember smiled. "You're a good friend, Fen."

Fen wrinkled his nose, his face dropping. "Just because you don't live with me anymore doesn't make me any less your brother."

Ember felt her chest clench as she tried to force a smile.

"Lothbrok, let's go!" Flynn shouted from the center of the pitch.

Ember gave Fen a small nod and took off toward the center of the field where the rest of the students were waiting.

"We're going to run a little scrimmage." Flynn grinned, flashing his crooked teeth at the group. "Vargr and Doyle's groups against my and O'neill's. First team to score ten points wins. Any questions?"

Everyone shook their heads, and Flynn gave a quick nod. Ember positioned herself in between the pitch and the center of the field, fiddling with her gloves as she tightened them. To her surprise, Veda flew toward her, hovering just a few feet from her on the right.

"There's still time to give up, you know." She smirked as she brushed her hair over her shoulder. "It would be a shame if there were an accident after you've spent all this time preparing."

Ember rolled her eyes as she shifted her weight on her board. "Shove off, Ellingboe," she hissed, clenching her fists by her side.

"Scared, Lothbrok?" Veda grinned, almost manically.

"You'll find that fear isn't in my vocabulary," Ember replied.

"Perhaps," Veda shrugged, "but it's in your eyes. Not even those pretty contacts can hide that."

Ember felt her stomach drop and mouth go bone dry. Her fingers ached as she clenched her fists, trying to steady her breathing. Her eyes cut through the crowded pitch as she searched for Fen and Killian, just a glance to steady her.

How could Veda know? And if she knew, who else did?

Before she had a chance to think any further, Professor Bjorn blew his whistle, and everyone took off. Ember shook her head, trying to ignore the dread pooling in her stomach, and raced toward the Brazul, caman in hand. The wind whipped her braid back and forth, her breath catching as she sucked cold air into her lungs. She sped through the sea of students, trying desperately to keep her mind off her secret that felt like she was losing control of.

It only took a few seconds of distraction to flip everything upside down.

With her eyes searching the crowd of players for Fen, she missed the Brazul coming straight for her. Instead of using her caman to hit it, she made a sharp left turn, knocking her almost completely off balance, swinging her caman just a hair too late. Instead of hitting the glowing flame buzzing past her head, she hit something solid. A screech sounded through the air, and Ember felt her blood run cold as her eyes widened.

Veda very well could have had steam coming out of her ears, and Ember wouldn't have been surprised. Blood trickled down her chin from her lip, and a bright red imprint from her caman was already beginning to turn purple across her cheek.

*For feck's sake.*

"I...I..." Ember stammered above the howling wind, but she couldn't make the rest of the words come out.

Veda's eyes cut into her like daggers, and Ember was frozen in place, hovering in the air. Professor Bjorn's whistle blew, cutting through the air like a foghorn, and Ember quickly turned and sped down to the safety of the grass. Every eye was on her as she landed, most looking at her in horror, but she caught Fen and Killian grinning out of the corner of her eye. Veda unstrapped from her board across the way by her brother, her eyes never leaving Ember.

"That will conclude tryouts for today," Professor Bjorn said, as he cleared his throat. "I think we've seen all we needed to see for the day. Please leave any camans or gloves you borrowed on the sidelines for collection. The list for teams will be posted at the end of the week. Have great weekend!"

Ember turned to make her way to the changing room, to get out of the vicinity of the Ellingboe twins as fast as possible.

Not fast enough, though, apparently.

Veda shoved past Ember, Oryn hot on her heels.

"You're going to pay for that, worm," she hissed, as she walked by, driving her elbow into Ember's rib. "Mummy can't protect you from everything."

Ember swallowed dryly, narrowing her eyes as her nostrils flared. Veda walked away, and Ember whipped her head around, searching through the sea of students on the pitch.

She turned on her heels, marching directly over to Fen and Killian, and shoved her finger into Killian's chest.

"What did you tell your grimy cousin," She hissed under her breath, shoving her fingers into his sternum several more times.

"Bloody hell, woman." He winced as he caught her by the wrist, holding it tight. "What are you on about?"

Ember wrenched her hand out of his grip and crossed her arms tightly over her chest, narrowing her eyes. "Why does Veda know about my eyes," she asked, lowering her voice. "What did you say?"

It was less a question and more an accusation.

"Your eyes?" Fen asked, bending over to pick camans up off the sideline.

"Yes, my eyes, *Fenrir*," she hissed. "Do I need to spell it out for you?"

"Whoa there, Starshine," Killian said, as he furrowed his brow. "If you're mad at me, that's fine, but don't take it out on, Fen."

Ember ran her tongue along her teeth and sighed. "Fine," she replied, shoving him in the shoulder one more time for good measure. "What did you do, Killian Vargr?"

"I'm sure I have no idea what you're talking about," he replied, cocking a brow as he shoved his hands in his pockets. "What makes you think she knows?"

"Because she bloody well said she did," Ember hissed in reply. "She made some snide remark about my contacts. No one knows about my contacts except for you two."

"Well, someone else must," Killian shrugged, "because I didn't say a word to anyone, least of all my cousins. Now, are you done assaulting me?"

Ember sighed as she ran her hand down her face, biting her lip. "Sorry," she replied quietly, "just shook me up a bit, I guess."

"Can we go now?" Fen asked, shoving his hands in his pockets. "I'm starving."

Ember swallowed as she nodded, anxiety still weighing down her chest, and the trio made their way out of the pitch and up the path toward the front of the grounds. Wardens were positioned throughout the grounds, wandering around stiffly with their hands behind their backs. Ember straightened her spine as they walked through the ward, seeing one Warden standing on the outer edge. He couldn't have been older than twenty-one, too old to be young and hopeful but too young for any true life experience. His long blond hair was tied loosely behind him, braids scattered throughout it. He cut his bright blue eyes at the trio as they stepped past, and Ember felt the hairs on the back of her neck raise.

"Best go straight home," he grunted, nodding in the direction of the Echopoint. "Don't wander."

Ember swallowed dryly, nodding. Fen, on the other hand, stood at full attention and gave the man a salute, shooting him a rude gesture as he turned and trotted away. Killian laughed, and Ember shoved him in the arm.

"Fenrir Kitt, what is *wrong* with you?" she whispered, as they quickly walked toward the Echopoint.

"Relax, Starshine," Killian laughed. "He's just having a bit of fun."

"What's he going to do? Hex me?" Fen asked with a shrug.

"Or talk to the Dean," Ember replied, brow raised.

Fen's eyes widened as he picked up the pace, and Ember laughed as she rolled her eyes, turning back to look at the Warden, now growing smaller behind them.

"Does he look familiar?" she asked.

Fen scrunched his brow as he glanced back and shrugged. "Not particularly, but they all sort of look the same."

"I think he was at your house," she replied, puzzle pieces falling into place. "The day that it was broken into, he was definitely there." Ember remembered the uneasy feeling she had that day, and it felt eerily similar to their encounter moments ago.

"I guess," Fen shrugged again, "but why does it matter?"

Ember furrowed her brow as she sighed. "I guess it doesn't."

THE HOUSE WAS quiet when Ember finally walked up the drive and through the large double doors, but she could hear the distinct sound of humming in the kitchen as the smell of soda bread and roast with potatoes wafted through the entry-way. Cutlery could be heard clinking across pots and pans, and Ember quickened her pace to tell Aoife all about her day.

"Mum, I'm done with tryouts," she called, as she kicked off her shoes. "You'll never believe what happened. I—" She stopped in her tracks when she walked in the kitchen.

Gaelen was standing at the stove, spooning roast into bowls, and Theo was sitting at the table, brow furrowed as he hunched over a large book. Aoife was nowhere to be seen.

"Where's Mum?" she asked, as she sat at the table.

Gaelen set a bowl in front of her, ladling in warm roast as she ruffled Theo's hair. "She's busy tonight," she replied. "Had a meeting she couldn't miss. She'll be 'round later."

Ember bit her lip as she nodded. So many meetings, so many Helios and secret conversations without any explanations. Ember couldn't help but wonder *who* her mother was talking to or what kind of job required so much of her free time. Out of nowhere, she had this desire to fly through the door of the Kitts' with Fen and tell Eira all about her day. All of a sudden she felt pain rising in her chest—a deep ache for a home that was no longer hers, but always would be. A family that filled all the rooms with laughter and hope. A family that shared in each other's joy and grief.

A family that was no longer her family. Not anymore, not really.

Guilt mixed with grief as she listened to the *clink* of her fork against her plate. Her mother had spent a decade thinking she was dead, a decade of grief that Ember understood all too well. So, why wasn't she here every chance she had? She had buried her daughter and husband, and Ember was wishing she was back with a foster family she had only known for a year.

What she had told Fen still stood true—they were not her family, not really. Not anymore. But that hole they had once filled in her chest remained empty. She prayed her mother would fill it one day.

Ember shook the thought away as she took a bite of the roast and tapped lightly on the table. Theo's head popped up, his grimace quickly turning to a smile, and he gave her a small wave.

"*I can help later,*" she signed, as she pointed to the book.

Theo nodded eagerly, closing the book, and quickly stuffing his face with bread and stew. Ember chuckled, ignoring the pain in her chest. Sometimes, in the right setting, Theo reminded her so much of Fen.

The two finished dinner and took their plates to the sink, then raced to the sitting room on the other side of the house, Theo sliding across the floor on his socks and rolling over the carpet as he slipped. His grin lit up his face as it turned bright red. He jumped off the floor, running to one of the large bookshelves and plucking out the book they had been reading together.

"*Do you want to learn,*" she signed, "*or listen?*"

"*Listen,*" he signed back, tapping her collarbone. Ember smiled as she nodded and began where they left off.

After just a chapter, Theo was snoring beside her. Gaelen

walked in, casting a charm on him, and lifting him into her arms. Ember smiled as the Merrow took the boy away, off to his room to tuck him in, and wrapped a blanket around herself, quickly drifting off to sleep too.

After a few minutes, or maybe hours, Ember woke to a gentle nudge on her shoulder.

"I have it on good authority that you have a very comfortable bed upstairs." Aoife smiled as Ember rubbed her eyes, and she picked up the book that had fallen beside the couch. "Your dad always fell asleep reading, used to drive me crazy sharing a bed with a small library." Her smile didn't quite reach her eyes, like she was forcing herself to relive something painful—something she had placed in a box in the back of her mind, intending to forget it altogether.

"Books are good company." Ember smiled. "The only company I had for a while." She laughed, intending it to be a lighthearted joke, but her chest tightened when she saw the pain behind her mother's eyes. Ember bit her lip as she sat up, looking at the floor.

"I'm sorry," she whispered, "I didn't mean—"

"Don't apologize," Aoife replied, smiling as she sat beside her and stroked her hair. "I wasn't there when you needed me, and that is something I will never forgive myself for."

Ember shrugged, forcing a small smile. "I turned out alright," she assured her. "It wasn't all bad."

"You get that from your father," Aoife sighed, the light from the fire dancing across her porcelain skin. "He always knew how to find little pockets of joy where there seemed to be none." She laughed as she shook her head. "Used to drive me mad the way he was always smiling, even when I didn't feel like there was anything worth smiling about."

Ember chewed on her bottom lip. "Can I ask you something, Mum?" Her stomach did a flip as Aoife's brow scrunch.

"Of course, Mo Stór." She nodded.

Ember drew in a breath as she twiddled her thumbs in her

lap. "How did you not know it wasn't me?" She whispered it under her breath, like it was a secret. "When you identified Dad and me," she took a steadying breath, imagining a body so like her own lying on a cold slab in the morgue, "why didn't you realize it wasn't me you were looking at?" She couldn't make sense of it, couldn't understand—because she knew Eira would recognize her. She knew Eira could pick her out in a sea of redheads with freckles in a heartbeat. And that realization terrified her.

Aoife's face fell. "She was identical to you." Aoife shook her head. "Everything I could see looked exactly like you, down to the smattering of freckles across your nose and cheeks. Had I thought, even for a moment, that it wasn't you, I never would have rested till I found you." Her voice was serious, pain and determination warring in her eyes, and Ember knew she meant it. She shook the thoughts away. She should just be grateful they were together now. Picking apart the past wouldn't change anything. It didn't matter now.

Aoife ran her hands through Ember's hair, picking up strands and beginning to cross one over the other as she hummed. "I used to put braids in your hair every morning when you were a wean." She smiled. "You never could sit still long enough for me to do many, but enough to finish the spell."

"The spell?" Ember asked, brow raised.

"Aye," Aoife nodded, "we didn't practice much magic after we left the island, but protection braids were something we never left the house without putting in your hair."

Ember smiled, finally feeling her body relax as her mother hummed to herself, weaving small strands of her hair in and out of each other.

"A spell of safety here I cast, a word of might to hold me fast, a shield before me and behind, to right and left, protection bind. To me may no harm or ill whit come. By power of three, my magic is from. With the sacred light around me, as above, so below, blessed be."

She continued, making several more braids throughout Ember's hair, lovingly kissing her on the head when she was done.

"Your poor father tried so many times to braid your hair, but he never could figure it out. He was a good father. He always made sure you knew you were safe and loved."

"His laugh is what I remember most," Ember grinned, "and the voices he made when he told his stories." She swallowed, her throat tight. Tears pooled at her lower lash as she bit her lip, steadying her breathing.

"He never failed to make sure you had no idea about adult problems," Aoife said. "He loved you very much."

Ember closed her eyes as she nodded, choking back the tears that were threatening to break through.

"It's late, Mo Stór," Aoife said, as she kissed her on the head. "Time for bed."

Ember nodded as she gave her mother a hug and walked toward the stairs.

"And don't forget to take your contacts out," Aoife called out, "or your eyes will dry."

Ember stopped in her tracks, her eyes widening as she turned around.

"You know about my eyes?" she asked, swallowing dryly.

"I'm your mother," Aoife replied. "There are very few things about you that I don't know."

# CHAPTER 17

# A GOLDEN CAGE

"Killian Vargr, is your Vegvisir broken?" Ember huffed, as she carried her breakfast plate to the sink.

Killian leaned against the counter, grabbing an apple from the fruit basket, and took a bite. "Of course not," he replied, as he chewed.

"Then, why on earth," Ember sighed, "would you not Helio before just popping over?"

Killian shrugged as he took another bit from his apple. "We have a lot to do today. No time to waste, Starshine." And with that, he tossed his apple in the bin and made his way toward the stairs in the foyer.

Ember ran a hand down her face. It was going to be a long day.

"You comin'?" Killian grinned, popping his head around the corner again.

Ember sighed with a nod, following him up the steps toward the library. She still hadn't gotten used to the size of her new home—the way the halls wound in and out of each other like a labyrinth, the secret passages that led between rooms, the piles of books that seemed to line each and every wall. She could feel her father here, traces of his magic were intertwined in every ancient fiber and grain of wood. It was home—her home. Her father's home.

So, why did it feel like something was missing?

"Alright, now where were we?" Killian asked, as he waltzed into the library and toward the stack of books Ember had left on the table. Early morning light filtered in through the window, bathing the oak and mahogany shelves in a warm light. She shuffled through the books, grabbing one off the bottom of one of the stacks, and flipped it open to where she had last left off.

"Conversations about food, I think," she replied, as she scanned the pages.

"No, no, we finished that one," Killian said, as he tapped his chin. "Was it the history of Ireland?"

"No, that was last week," Ember replied, as she shook her head. Silence fell over them as they scanned the pages until Killian chimed in.

"So, have you talked to your mum about going to the Kitts' to practice soon?" he asked casually, as he flipped through one of the books. "You'll never get better if you don't practice."

Ember snatched the book from his hand. "I'm doing perfectly well, thank you," she quipped, "and maybe in a few weeks. I don't want to offend my mum."

"Offend her?" Killian scoffed. "What about you spending time with your brother and his best friend is offensive?"

"He's not my brother," Ember whispered, sifting through the pile she had on the table behind her, "not anymore." She could almost feel Killian roll his eyes as she turned around.

"Family is more than who you were born to," he replied, like her statement had personally offended him.

"What about, 'Blood is thicker than water,' and all that?" she asked, stalking to a shelf on the opposite wall.

Killian followed her and yanked her around by her shoulder. "That's not how that quote goes," he replied, "not entirely. It's: 'The blood of the covenant is thicker than the water of the womb.'"

Ember narrowed her eyes at him. "So, am I supposed to just forget about my mum? And Theo? Go running back to the Kitts' and pretend she just doesn't exist?" She was fuming, smoke might as well have been pouring from her ears.

"That's not what I said," Killian replied, as he shook his head. "You can love your mum and Theo and continue to love the Kitts. Family is more than just blood—so much more." He spoke with a conviction that made him almost transparent—a glimpse into what he felt about his own family, no doubt.

"Just because you have awful parents and can't stand to be at home," Ember muttered, "doesn't mean I do too. We are not the same, Killian Vargr."

Killian's eyes widened, and he looked like she had shot an arrow straight through his chest.

Ember squeezed her eyes shut. She hadn't meant for it to come out that harsh, and she immediately regretted it. "Can we talk about it later?"

Killian nodded as he bit his lip, shaking away whatever clouds were momentarily hovering over his head. "Okay, I have an idea. How about a little quiz?"

Ember cocked her brow and shook her head. "I don't know if I'm ready for a quiz."

"Of course you are." He grinned. "Shall we?"

Ember gave a small nod and flexed her hands by her side. Killian began spouting off words and phrases, some that she remembered with ease and some she had to think about longer than she would've cared to admit.

"Did you say, 'Ember the Brave?'" she asked with a laugh.

"Aye," Killian nodded, "the bravest of us all." He stood at attention, giving her a mock salute, and his eyes crinkled at the corners as he smiled.

"I am anything but brave." Ember shook her head, crossing her arms tightly over her chest.

"You are one of the bravest people I have ever met," Killian said, as he leaned against the table. "The way you stood up against Rowan last year? You saved the whole island, and no one even knows it."

"Bravery can look an awful lot like stupidity in the wrong lighting," she replied, laughing dryly as she rolled her eyes.

"Don't do that," Killian said, narrowing his eyes at her.

"Do what?"

"Talk about yourself like you're not worthy of anything you want to achieve."

Ember rolled her eyes as she leaned against the table. "That's easy for you to say," she sighed. "It's easy to be wealthy and successful if you're born into wealth and handed success."

Killian sighed as he shook his head. "Aye," he shrugged, "but a golden cage is still just a cage, Starshine."

Ember wrung her hands as she looked around the library. Tall, arched ceilings and big open windows, gold details swirling across the mahogany and oak bookshelves. There was more money in this one room of her house than many families on the island had put together. She always imagined there would be a certain feeling of freedom that would come with living in a home like this—a feeling of reprieve from the fear and flight she had felt her entire life. But where the fear used to live was now replaced with guilt.

Guilt over the dryads that tended to the grounds at the manor and the payment she knew they didn't receive. Guilt about Gaelen being trapped here, forced to work after being stolen from her family gods knew how long ago. Guilt over her little brother being raised without their father and with a mother who didn't even truly understand her own children—a mother who didn't seem bothered to learn sign language to communicate with him or truly learn anything about who they were and what they loved outside of Ember when she was six years old. Guilt that he wouldn't ever know the mother that raised her because that woman seemed to be lost forever.

Was this her prison now?

"Alright, one more, Starshine," Killian said, as he pushed off the table and clapped his hands together. He made quick motions with his fingers, hands moving like he was born with the knowledge.

Ember wrinkled her nose as she concentrated, trying to keep up. As he finished the phrase, he took a step back and crossed his arms over his chest. "Um," Ember said, as she furrowed her brow, "something about a chair?"

"Aye," Killian grinned, stepping closer, "and?"

"And..." Ember said thoughtfully, "something about a library? The chair in the library?"

Killian's grin grew wider as he nodded. "You're very close, Starshine," he almost whispered, brushing a strand of hair from in front of her eyes. "The chair in the library, by the—"

"Window," Ember whispered, swallowing dryly as she bit her lip. "That's as far as I got."

A quiet knock sounded on the doorframe, and Ember and Killian whipped their heads around to find Theo standing there, a smirk painted across his face. His eyes locked with Killian, and he cocked his brow, and Killian's cheeks turned bright red.

"Right," he said, as he cleared his throat, taking a step back. "Lesson over for the day, I think."

Theo walked further into the room, signing something before ducking his head with a small grin.

"Ice cream?" Ember laughed. "It's freezing outside, and you want to go for ice cream?"

Theo's grin grew, lighting up his entire face as he violently nodded his head, clapping his hands together in front of him like he was pleading.

"That sounds like a brilliant idea." Killian grinned, clapping Theo on the shoulder and walking with him to the door. "You coming, Starshine?"

Ember rolled her eyes, throwing her bag over her shoulder and following them toward the door. They made their way down the many steps, and Ember walked to the front door, but Killian and Theo stayed behind.

*"Terminal,"* Theo signed and nodded back behind him.

"He's right." Killian nodded. "You're bound to have a traveling room. It'll be much quicker than the Echopoint."

Ember nodded, furrowing her brow. She hadn't seen a terminal door since she'd moved in, and she assumed everyone's would be under some steps or in a closet. Theo grabbed her hand, dragging her around the corner, through the sitting room, and toward the back of the house. They entered through a set of double doors, into a small room the size of an office. There was a coat rack to the right, a small chair, and a fireplace to the left, and in the middle of the wall directly in front of her was a beautiful wooden door. A large, ornate tree was carved into the wood, its limbs and roots stretching to the edges of the frame.

Killian walked toward the door, tapping the brass knob a few times, and waited until the tree on the door began to glow. "Shall we?" he said, as he motioned Ember into the room.

She nodded, all of a sudden feeling like that fifteen-year-old girl who had just learned magic was real. She felt Theo gently grab her hand and squeeze. He looked up at her smiling, big green eyes sparkling against the sun shining through the window.

Killian swung the door open, and the trio stepped through into Yggdrasil Terminal and then out onto Waterware Street.

201

ELDEN'S ICE Cream Shoppe sat near the docks a few shops down from the playground on the beach. During the summer, it was swimming with families—children begging their mothers for an ice cream cone, fathers digging through their pockets for extra change. During autumn, on the other hand, it was almost deserted. Anyone walking through Sigurvik was bundled up in coats and gloves to protect from the harsh wind coming in off the bay, and no one so much as glanced at the little ice cream shop. Killian swung the door open, and the bell at the top of the frame jingled.

"Well, good afternoon, youngins," Mr. Elden said from behind the counter. "A bit Baltic out for ice cream, isn't it?"

"We're taking a study break." Ember smiled as she squeezed Theo's hand. "Any specials today?"

Mr. Elden waggled his brow, conjuring three ice cream cones in his hand. "Chocolate is always a fan favorite with the weans," he replied, and as he did, chocolate ice cream floated out of the container in front of him, swirling through the air. "Minotaur tracks is another popular one, and of course, Pint of Many Flavors." Ice cream swirled around in front of him, bending back and forth in the air, just barely missing each other, and Theo's eyes lit up in amusement.

Ember cocked her brow. "Pint of Many Flavors?" she repeated. "What exactly are the many flavors?"

Mr. Elden grinned as he flicked his wrist, making the condiments behind him come to life and dance through the air as well. "Oh, many things," he replied, "chocolate chips, marshmallows, other odds and ends that the Brownies find delightful." He leaned forward, like he was sharing a great secret and whispered, "And the Neverberry, of course."

Ember furrowed her brow. "Neverberry? What's a Neverberry?"

"The sweetest tasting fruit you'll ever have," Mr. Elden replied. "Some say our ancestors brought them over when they landed on the island, others say the Elves have grown them for centuries. But some say they come from somewhere else entirely—another world completely unlike our own, amongst the stars."

"We'll take three." Killian grinned, dropping a handful of coins on the counter. Three cones floated through the air, ice cream landing in each of them before Killian grabbed them, handing them to Ember and Theo.

*"Thank you,"* Theo signed with a bright smile.

Mr. Elden nodded and signed back, *"You're welcome."*

The trio made their way out of the shop and into the biting November wind, Theo licking his ice cream like it might suddenly disappear. Ember led them to the middle of town, and they sat on the edge of the large fountain watching the people mill about as they did their afternoon shopping. Theo watched the kids run around town, yelling and playing games, and Ember couldn't help but notice the hint of sadness in his eyes.

*"Want to go join them?"* she signed after taking her last bite of ice cream.

Theo shook his head, scuffing the toe of his shoe against the cobblestone.

"It's such a beautiful day for ice cream," a voice rang out from across the cobblestone, and Ember found herself smiling as the platinum haired girl walked toward them.

"Hello, Odette," she said, as the girl perched on the fountain beside her. "What are you doing out and about today?" It was so cold that Ember couldn't imagine why anyone else would want to be outside. But then again, this was Odette.

"I had a lovely conversation with the dryads in the park this morning," she mused. "They have some wonderful ideas for the Summer Solstice celebration next year."

Ember grinned as she shook her head. Killian took Theo across the street to hunt for seashells on the beach, and Ember found herself wanting to know more about the odd girl sitting next to her.

"Do you have any plans with friends this weekend?" Ember asked, as she took a bite of her ice cream. After she asked, she realized she never really saw the girl hang out with anyone, and since last spring, Odette had been spending more and more time with her during school hours.

Odette shrugged as she shook her head. "I don't have many friends," she replied. It didn't seem to bother her, but Ember's heart sank.

Ember bit her lip. Perhaps Odette needed a friend just as much as she did. It scared her to make more friends after how terribly Rowan betrayed her, but maybe it was worth it to try again. Not to replace her friendship with Rowan, but to find a way to open her heart to new friendships. New people that would carve a spot in her life simply because they wanted to, not because they wanted something from her.

"You do now." Ember smiled, and she truly meant it.

They sat in silence for a few more minutes, watching the boys across the street dig through the sand and run from the seagulls diving in the air. Ember twiddled her thumb as she looked at Odette.

"Can I ask why you spend so much time in the Dark Forest?" It was something she had wondered since last year, since the first time they had spoken about it. Ember had dreaded every single time she had to walk into those dark woods, but Odette seemed unfazed by it—maybe even enjoyed it—and Ember couldn't understand why.

Odette hummed to herself as she closed her eyes, smiling toward the sky. "Did you know that the Dark Forest isn't its name?"

Ember scrunched her nose. "I've never heard it called anything different." Even the professors all called it that, surely they would know if it had a different name.

Odette nodded. "The Vala gave it their own name when they landed on the island, as they did with everything they touched, claiming it as their own. But this island had a pulse long before our ancestors arrived—long before our ancestors received their magic and decided they deserved more." She spoke with a conviction that made Ember's blood run cold.

She swallowed dryly as she tried to nod. "Do you know its name?"

Odette nodded. "Danann Forest."

Ember furrowed her brow—why did that sound so familiar?

"It is said they arrive on a cloud of mist. The Tuatha Dé Danann are where every being on this island came from," she continued, "either descended from or made entirely. The Tuatha Dé were the beginning of it all. Legends say that the High Danann kings and queens were descended from Anu—the Mother Goddess."

Ember mulled over the words, until it all fell into place.

Tuatha Dé.

*Tribe of Gods.*

Ember sucked in a breath.

"You mean there are more?" she whispered, as if the trees might report back to their creator.

Odette simply shrugged. "More? Perhaps," she replied, "or perhaps they're one in the same. Perhaps the gods that bestowed us our magic are the same ones who bestowed it upon the island—the Fae, Merrow, and dryads. Perhaps we all aren't so different after all."

Ember felt a cold chill run down her spine, but it had nothing to do with the wind whipping through Sigurvik that afternoon.

"I feel him there the most," Odette almost whispered, her voice catching as she spoke. "My Da'. In the trees and the wind and the way the moonlight filters through the canopy if you know where to look. Sometimes I go to talk to him or just to feel him near me. I didn't know him well, not for long. The uprising took him before I was even old enough to learn to read, but sometimes I like to tell him about myself while I'm out there. I like to think he would be proud of me… of everything I've overcome."

Ember didn't even realize she had begun crying until the tears were sliding down her cheeks. Maybe they were more alike than she ever could've imagined. "I think he would be too," she replied quietly.

Ember quickly brushed the tears away as Killian and Theo ran up to them, both covered in sand and laughing so hard their cheeks were red.

"Ready to go, Starshine?" Killian asked, as he brushed the sand off his trousers.

Ember smiled as she nodded. "Can we run into the Bookwyrm first? I need to see if Nessa has that copy of…" But Ember realized Killian wasn't listening anymore.

"Well, what do we have here," he said, as he narrowed his eyes across the street.

"Is that the Warden from Heksheim?" Ember asked, as she squinted toward the end of the street where Killian stared. Blond hair flashed in the sun, and Ember could just make out his gold-plated leather bracelet wrapped tightly around his wrist.

"Aye." Killian nodded; his usual joking manner replaced with a seriousness that gave her chills. "What do you suppose he's up to?"

Ember shrugged as she scrunched her brow. "Completing his weekend errands perhaps?"

The Warden looked over his shoulder several times and quietly slipped away behind a building, hiding him from sight.

Killian cocked his brow, stuffing a hand in his trouser pocket. "I don't know, Starshine," he replied. "Shall we find out?"

Theo looked up at Ember with a grin. *"Follow,"* he signed, nodding in the direction the Warden had snuck away to. Both boys looked at her with pleading eyes, and she couldn't fight the grin that was threatening to take over.

"Oh, alright," she replied, as she rolled her eyes. Theo grabbed her hand and gave it a squeeze, and the four of them made their way down the street, toward the building he had slipped behind.

"We will see what he's doing and then we're leaving," Ember whispered, as she pressed herself up against the brick wall. "I don't have any desire to get roped into whatever he's up to."

"You don't have anything to worry about, Starshine," Killian whispered, his breath hot against the back of her neck. "I'll protect you."

Ember felt her cheeks burn as she swallowed dryly, inching closer to the edge of the building. She could hear two voices mumbling back and forth to each other but still couldn't make out what they were saying.

"He's talking to someone," Ember whispered. "What's he up to?"

The voice grew louder as they reached the end of the building, and Ember could see the two men standing just a few feet away from them now. Theo's grip on her hand tightened as they stopped, and she put a finger to her lips.

"Either, you have something, or you don't," a gruff voice said, coming from the man standing opposite the Warden. "He won't wait much longer, Collum."

"Aye, I know," the Warden—Collum—replied. "I'll have it soon. I just need a few more days."

"Well, I'll be damned," Killian whispered. "Uncle Malcom is having shady business meetings in dark alleys now it seems."

"That's your uncle?" Ember asked, wide-eyed.

"Aye," Killian nodded, "and if Collum has anything to do with my kin, he can't have good intentions."

"He's red," Odette whispered.

"Red?" Killian scrunched his brow as he stared at the girl. Odette nodded.

"Collum. His aura."

"And my uncle?" he asked almost sarcastically.

"Black." She whispered in reply, and Ember felt her blood run cold.

"You will bring her to him immediately," Malcom replied. "No more excuses."

"Of course," Collum nodded. "I just need a few more days."

Theo shifted his weight from one foot to another and leaned too hard on one of the loose bricks in the walls. The scrape, however brief, ricocheted between the buildings and through the alley, like thunder echoing through a cavern. Ember, Killian, and Odette winced simultaneously, and Theo gave them a confused look until it dawned on him.

"*Loud?*" he signed, guilt almost audible in the way his fingers trembled.

"*A little,*" Ember replied, trying not to make him feel any worse than he seemed to.

"Who's there?" Malcom asked, peering through the darkness in their direction.

Ember's heart thumped in her throat as she grabbed Theo's hand and felt Killian's hand wrap around her other.

"We need to go *now,*" he whispered and tugged her down the back of the alley, Odette following close behind.

Killian slowed down as they reached the busy street once again, but Ember could still feel her stomach coiling into tight knots. Killian was right—whatever Collum was up to, it couldn't be anything good, not if Malcom Ellingboe was involved.

"Becareful," Odette said quietly, and then disappeared down the street. Theo's face brightened to a smile again as they made their way toward the terminal. Ember could feel the familiar tug in her sternum that stretched toward Killian and Fen, even though Fen wasn't there. She was beginning to find her rhythm in this new life, a comfort she wasn't sure would ever replace her time at the Kitts'. She didn't need to tangle herself in yet another mystery that could upend everything. She didn't need to put these people that she loved so deeply in danger again.

Right?

# CHAPTER 18

# TOGETHER

"You mean to tell me," Fen quipped, as he tossed his bag next to the pillow on the ground, "you went to get *ice cream* together—my favorite dessert—and then stumbled upon a possible mole in the Guard? *And* with Odette? *Without* me?" He crossed his arms tightly over his chest, sitting on his pillow and pouting like a toddler. As if on cue, Odette waltzed over to the trio, sitting down beside Ember. Fen's cheeks burned scarlet as he huffed.

"That's your takeaway from this whole story?" Killian replied. "Not my crazy uncle and the possible mole in the Guard, but the ice cream?"

"Honestly, Fenrir, it was for Theo," Ember replied, as she rolled her eyes. "It's not like we went on a secret date without telling you." Ember closed her eyes tightly, realizing what she had just said.

Killian let out a slight snicker behind her, and she wished the floor would swallow her up.

"It would be lovely if you could come next time." Odette said with a small smile.

Fen cut his eyes, looking back and forth between Killian and Ember before averting his eyes back to the front. "I don't appreciate all this time you're spending without me," he mumbled.

"You could come more often if Mummy would let you leave the house," Killian laughed, as he sat on the other side of Ember, leaning back against the pillow on his elbow.

"She wants someone to have eyes on Maeve at all times," Fen replied, as he rolled his eyes. "Honestly, she acts like someone's just going to pluck her out of her bedroom in the middle of the day. And what am I supposed to do about it?" He shoved his glasses up the bridge of his nose, the tip of his nose turning bright red, the way it always did when he was getting angry. "Am I supposed to just go after a rogue Vala?" he continued, nostrils flaring. "With what? A blasting curse? I can't even properly hit a wall during Galdr, so how am I supposed to hit a person?"

His breathing was growing heavier, and Ember quickly grabbed his hand and steadied her own breathing. It was something they had started doing over the summer—when one of them got worked up, or anxious or just couldn't seem to settle, the other would grab their hand and not let go until their breathing matched exactly. It wasn't something Ember had intended to start doing, but it happened, nonetheless. They were connected in a soul-defining kind of way—the way only siblings could be.

Fen locked eyes with her, his breathing beginning to steady, and she could just barely see the shine of tears pricking the corner of his eyes. He wasn't angry at Maeve or frustrated with Eira and Otto.

He was scared.

"So, what are we going to do about it?" Killian asked.

"About what?" Odette replied as she began digging in her bag.

"Collum and my uncle and the way no one feels safe enough to leave their homes anymore." Killian replied with a sigh.

"And what," Ember asked, "do you propose a group of sixteen-year-olds is *supposed* to do about it?"

"We could tell my parents about Collum and Malcolm," Fen shrugged, "or Aoife. Maybe one of them would know what to do."

"We could talk to Professor Bjorn," Odette added, and Fen nodded in agreement.

"No, no adults." Ember shook her head. "It'll just put them in danger, and possibly Maeve or Theo. We don't need to make them targets."

"Going off on our own didn't bode so well last time," Fen replied. "I don't think we can do this on our own."

"There's too much at stake," she whispered, shaking her head.

Too many people she loved. Too much to lose. Too much.

"Good afternoon, students!" Professor Eid said, as she walked to the center of the room. "I trust you all had a restful weekend?" Murmurs of agreement—and exhaustion—sounded through the room, and Professor Eid nodded her head with a smile. "Good then! As a reward for all your hard work this term, I thought I would give you a little treat today." She conjured a large bowl in the middle of the room and flicked her hand in its direction.

It erupted into flames, and Ember could feel the heat licking at the tip of her nose.

"I told you at the beginning of the year that you would not learn to conjure fire yet, and I stand by that." Groans sounded throughout the room, and Professor Eid gave them a very pointed look before she continued. "Instead of waiting until the end of the year, I thought we would get a small sneak peek at what our lessons on fire will look like."

Ember groaned as Killian and Fen began to whisper amongst themselves.

"We will work on the first steps—control. As I said before, you cannot hope to successfully conjure even a spark if you don't have the ability to control it when it roars to life."

Small bowls appeared in front of the pillows, one for every two students, and the basins filled with onyx rocks that shone against the light filtering in from the windows. Professor Eid walked around the circle of students, lighting each bowl with a flick of her wrist as she went. Light from the small flames danced across Fen's rosy cheeks as his bowl came to life, and the grin on his face was only mildly unsettling—something about these boys and fire just didn't sit right with her. She laughed as Fen reached out to touch it and quickly snapped his hand back, clutching it tightly to his chest.

"It's fire, Fenrir," Odette whispered. "Magic or not, you probably shouldn't touch it."

Ember giggled as Fen made a mocking face and crossed his arms, his cheeks turning red from embarrassment. Professor Eid made her way back to the center of the room, folding her hands gently in front of her as she looked around at each student.

"All I want you to do for now is focus on making the flame grow," she said, as she nodded to the flames dancing in the small bowls. They were small, barely the size of a lit match, and they seemed to stay lit by sheer willpower. "Keep the fire inside the basin, but make it larger if you're able."

"Is there a spell we should say? Or some sort of incantation?" Flynn Macguire asked from the other side of the room.

Professor Eid smiled as she shook her head. "Elemental magic is a wee bit different than Galdr," she replied. "There are no magic words or incantations that can control flame or conjure waves or crack the earth open at its seams." The room quieted, all the students hanging on her every word. "It's something you have to feel—something that vibrates your bones. You have to open yourself up to the power that is already inside of you."

Killian and Fen snickered, and Ember had to use all of

her self-control not to channel Eira and smack them both upside the head.

"So…" Fen said, drumming his fingers on his knee, "what exactly are we supposed to do?"

Professor Eid gave him a gentle smile in a way that reminded Ember so much of Odette.

"Your magic will tell you what to do," was all she said.

Fen groaned, sweat already beading on his forehead.

"I will check in periodically. You may begin." Professor Eid floated back to the center of the room, sitting on the pillow, and began to meditate.

Ember focused on the flame in front of her, willing her magic to connect, but nothing seemed to happen. After several minutes of flicking her wrist and cursing under her breath, she let out a sigh and blew a stray hair from in front of her eyes.

"Would you like a go?" she asked Odette, the blonde sitting silently beside her. Her bronze skin seemed to glow against the flame, giving her an otherworldly aura that gave Ember goosebumps.

Odette shook her head. "I don't think my magic is quite ready yet." She closed her eyes and began to meditate on the pillow, mimicking the way Professor Eid was sitting, and Ember wondered if maybe she should take a page out of Odette's book for this lesson.

"This is hopeless," Fen mumbled beside her, rubbing his temple as he squinted. "How are we supposed to figure out how to control fire with no guidance? Absolute shite."

Professor Eid cleared her throat, briefly opening one eye and peering toward Fen. Ember chuckled as she rolled her eyes, focusing back on her own bowl. She wouldn't say it out loud, but she agreed with Fen—it did feel hopeless. She felt the invisible chord tug at her sternum, the boy's magic playing off her own, trying to draw some sort of extra strength, but it didn't do anything. Ember sighed again, leaning back on her elbows as she tapped her hand against the ground. She was about to give up and possibly spend the rest of the class period reading until she saw something glimmer out of the corner of her eye.

Little glowing wisps of light bounced around the center of the room, a few feet from Professor Eid, just out of Ember's grasp. She bolted upright, her back stiff as a board as she held her breath. It was the same blue wisps she had seen in the Fae garden and on the runes glowing around the portal to Arcelia. No one else seemed to notice them, just like before.

They began floating toward her, and Ember's felt her chest tighten as they neared the edge of her pillow. She laid her hand flat, like she was coaxing a shy rabbit to eat some berries out of her palm, and felt electricity travel along her skin as they rubbed up against her fingers. She scooped them up into her hand, the wisps danced across her freckled skin like droplets of water beading on a windshield. She felt the buzz of their magic, something strange and familiar all at once, and she felt her own magic begin to thrum in her veins. She focused her energy on the little balls of light as their glow intensified, and they danced in her hands. The magic tasted like copper and salt on her tongue, and she felt her heart beating faster.

She laid the wisps back down on the floor in front of her and focused her energy back on the flame in the bowl, still barely flickering against the stones beneath it. As she focused, the flame intensified, growing brighter and brighter as her hand began to tremble. As it grew brighter, Ember could feel Killian and Fen's eyes on her.

"How did you do that," Fen whispered, eyes wide.

"I don't know." She shrugged. "It just happened." She didn't mention the wisps or the way it felt like their strange magic had melded with her own—strengthened it. Something about the way their light seemed to whisper told her this was their secret.

"Easy there, Starshine," Killian whispered, placing his hand gently on her arm. "Don't do more than you can control."

Ember ignored him as the flame grew bigger fast, and before she knew it, it was billowing above her head, threatening to spill from the bowl and onto the marble floor. Odette laid a hand on her shoulder, trying to coax her out of whatever well she had fallen into, but she was falling too fast

Professor Eid shot up from the center of the room, racing to Ember and the flame that threatened to engulf the rest of the class. "That's very good, Miss Lothbrok," she said cautiously. "Now try to make it smaller. Power is easy to gain, but learning to control it is another thing entirely."

Ember nodded, squinting her eyes in concentration as she willed the flame to grow smaller.

But it wouldn't.

Ember's heart raced as the flame grew higher, and she could feel sweat trickling down her forehead—more from the fear than the heat. The little wisps of light danced around the floor, floating through the air and wrapping themselves tightly around her wrist and hand like a glove, traveling up her arm to her shoulder. She felt her magic pulse stronger, running like molten lava through her veins. The flame didn't falter, not until Fen and Killian grabbed both of her wrists, squeezing tightly, and Professor Eid sent water spraying into the basin in front of her.

Ember sank back into the pillow, closing her eyes tightly as whispers circulated around the room. Tears pricked the corner of her eyes as memories from her childhood hurtled back to her like a train, knocking her down and sucking the breath from her lungs.

*"Did you see what she did? What a freak!"*

*"She's so odd."*

*"You can't play with us. You're far too weird."*

216

Fen squeezed her hand, bringing her back to the present, and gave her a comforting smile.

*You are not alone this time.*

"That was very good, Miss Lothbrok," Professor Eid said gently. "Let's just work on our control a little more."

Ember gave a half smile with a nod, and the professor made her way around the room, pulling the students' focus back to their own work. Ember stared down at her arms, the little blue wisps vanished, and her skin was left completely unblemished, like they had never existed.

*Maybe they didn't. Maybe I'm finally losing it.*

Class ended shortly after, and Ember quickly threw her bag over her shoulder and made her way toward the double doors. She didn't bother to look, but she knew Fen and Killian weren't very far behind. She made her way to the cafe, throwing her bag on the ground beside her, and buried her head in her arms on the table. Killian set a cup of tea beside her and took his seat across the table without saying a word.

Fen was not so quiet.

"What the bloody hell was that?" he asked, as he sat down across from her, stuffing a biscuit in his mouth. "Are you some sort of Elemental Magic Mage now?"

Ember cut her eyes at Fen. "No," she sneered, sighing as she ran a hand down her face. "I don't know what happened. I just know I couldn't make it stop. I haven't felt my magic that out of control since I lived in Galway." Ember felt her throat constrict as memories from her childhood came flooding back, memories she was sure she had buried deep enough that they would never resurface.

"How about a change of subject?" Killian asked, as he began rummaging around in his bag.

"Oh, I almost forgot!" Fen said, as he also began rummaging through his bag.

Ember cocked a brow as she watched both the boys pull

small boxes out of their backpacks, both wrapped in some form of green wrapping paper—her favorite color.

"We missed your birthday—our birthday—with all the madness going on," Fen said, as he slid the box across the table. "Felt like now was as good a time as ever to go ahead and give you your present. It's from Mum and Dad and Maeve too."

"Fen, you didn't have to do that," she replied with a grin, reaching down to dig in her own bag, "but I brought yours too." She smiled as she pushed it toward him, taking his gift in her hands and shaking it lightly.

"Go ahead." Killian smiled. "Don't make the poor lad wait any longer, or he might crawl out of his skin."

Ember laughed as she gingerly started to pull back the wrapping paper, exposing a light brown box. She pulled the lid off, pulling out a few pieces of paper inside, and her eyes went wide.

"Fenrir James," she whispered, "did you get me a phone?" It looked a lot like his. A glass touch screen with a camera on the front and back, and a picture of the three of them on the home screen. It was in a forest green case with a little fox running to and fro on the back.

"Like I said," he shrugged, cheeks tinged pink, "it's from all of us. But I put my own personal touches on it." He laid out his hand, and she set the phone gently in his palm. He quickly got to work swiping on the screen. "I downloaded a few of my apps, though, just to personalize it a bit." He swiped a few more times and then smiled, clicking a few buttons. "Ah, right here we go."

He turned the phone in her direction and began swiping through pages filled with tiny squares.

"This is a tracking app. It acts sort of like the spell, but it leaves no trace—quite dangerous if you're on the other end." Fen grinned mischievously as he swiped again. "This one is a database I've been putting together for different plants and herbs and where they're located. It's also got a spot to record any potions or elixirs you come up with and preloaded standard recipes."

"Are books going to become obsolete?" Ember laughed as she shook her head, thinking about the piles of Herbal Magic and magical plant books she had in the library at home.

"Of course not," he replied, a little more serious than she expected, "but you can't very well stick twenty books in your pocket, can you? This just makes it a little easier to store information."

Ember nodded—he was right, this did seem very convenient.

"This is one of my personal favorites," he said quietly, clicking on a glowing blue app on the home screen. "Helios are notorious for not being received when you're off the island —something about the wards around the island and the disconnect between here and the mainland make it nearly impossible to get through. This will send Helios outside of the island, even completely overseas, as easy as if you were sitting next door." He beamed as he handed her the phone and let her scroll through it, very proud of the hard work he had put into her gift.

"It's lovely, Fen." She smiled, clicking on a small app at the bottom of the screen. "What's this one do?"

"Oh, that," he grinned, "that's for texting. I've got my number programmed in already."

"Mine too." Killian smiled, pulling his phone out of his pocket and waving it in front of him. "Thought it would be best if we all had a more discreet way to communicate. Buzzing balls of blue light tend to catch the eye."

"It's perfect." She smiled. "Okay, now your turn." She laid the phone down on the table, bouncing eagerly on her chair as Fen opened his gift.

"Oh wow!" he beamed. "Em, I love it!" He pulled a sweatshirt out of the box, sporting his favorite Rukr team on the front. A majestic grey horse with backwards hooves danced across the fabric, the stitching from the embroidered animal moving back and forth like water. "The Ykur's are going to dominate Worlds this year."

"So you've said." Ember smiled, rolling her eyes as she shook her head. "Now you can properly support them."

"Thank, Em." He grinned. "It's perfect."

"Speaking of Rukr," Killian said, as he leaned back in his chair, crossing his arms over his chest, "I have a bit of a birthday surprise of my own." His grin sent goosebumps trailing down her arms as he tilted his head. "Are you ready for your first game this week, Starshine?"

Ember's stomach did a flip as she swallowed dryly. "I made the team?" she asked with a smile.

"Aye," he nodded, "You are officially the newest member of the Heksheim Wyverns." Her grin broadened, and then her stomach sank. She wanted to be ready, wanted to be cool, calm, and collected as she prepared for their first game, but the truth was she was anything but.

"Are you excited?" Fen asked with a smile.

"Of course." She nodded, failing to act more confident than she was. Fen reached across the table and squeezed her hand, quelling her anxiety in a way only he seemed to be able to, like he could read her mind.

"You're going to do great," he whispered, "and you'll have me and Killian there. Win or lose, we're going to be fine. We'll do this the way we do everything else."

"Together?" Ember smiled.

"Together." Killian grinned in agreement.

# CHAPTER 19

# TASTE THE BLOOD

K illian crouched low on his AirWave, racing just inches above the cobblestone. He could've walked, could've strolled leisurely down Waterware Street to his destination, but something in him was itching to feel the wind in his face. He dodged women carrying shopping bags and dryads trimming trees, closing his eyes as he breathed in the salt lingering in the air. He hopped off his board, leaning it against the wall, and walked into Celestial Steel.

Despite the midday sun peeking from behind the clouds, the ceiling of the shop was covered in stars burning brightly against an onyx sky. Killian stuffed his hands in his pockets, naming the constellations in his head as he stared at the ceiling.

"You're early, Mr. Vargr," Cormac said, as he walked in from a back room. "I didn't expect you until Saturday at the earliest."

Killian shrugged with a small grin. "I had some extra time and thought I'd see if they were ready."

Cormac gave a knowing smile and pulled a small box out from behind the counter, twirling it in his hands. "Finished them last night," he said, as he laid it on the counter and pushed it toward Killian, "I must say, I don't think I've ever molded a setting quite like that."

Killian opened the lid and grinned, then quickly snapped it closed and stuffed the small box in his pocket. He handed Cormac a few silver coins and waited as the man counted them.

"Mind if I ask who they're for?" Cormac asked, as he popped open a box and dropped the coins in.

Killian grinned as he stuffed a hand in his pocket. "They're for a friend's birthday," he replied. "It's a bit late, but I thought they would be nice."

"Would it happen to be that girl I see you running around town with? You and Fenrir?"

Killian nodded with a small smile. "Ember." He breathed her name like it was an enchantment. Saying it out loud gave him goosebumps.

"Ah, yes," Cormac nodded, "Ember Lothbrok, the Kitts' girl?"

Killian's grin faded slightly. "She's back with her mum now actually," he replied, "but yes, that's her."

Cormac looked toward the ceiling, like he was thinking very hard about something.

"Well, wish her a happy birthday for me," he said finally, "and tell her I'm sorry I couldn't fix the spell on her ring unfortunately, but I hope it's holding up well."

Killian furrowed his brow and nodded. "Sure," he replied and walked out the door. He thought about turning around to ask *what* spell was on her ring, but the weight in his pocket reminded him that he had things to do.

He patted his pocket one last time, making sure the box was still safe inside, and hopped on his AirWave to head home. He could've taken the Echopoint and saved a ton of time, but there was something freeing about feeling the air high above the island kiss his cheeks as he sped through the low hanging clouds.

222

He landed on the balcony outside of his room, not bothering to go through the front door. He swung the door open, leaning his AirWave against the wall, and pulled the little box from his pocket, placing it gently on the desk beside him. He pulled out the chair, sitting down to get to work, pouring over the book still open on the top of his desk. He opened the box, mumbling spells against the cold metal when his bedroom door swung open. Killian didn't bother to look up as Rafe walked in, leaning against the side of his desk and snatching the small box out of his reach.

"Who's this for, little brother?" He grinned as he tossed it in the air. "Have yourself a *mot* I don't know about?"

Killian made to snatch it from his hand but missed as he yanked it above his head. "She's not my girlfriend," Killian hissed, as he narrowed his eyes, "and even if she was, why would I tell you?" He huffed as he tried to grab the box again, but his brother yanked it further away. "What do you want, Rafe?"

"Da' says Uncle Malcom is coming by tonight." He grinned as he tossed the box into his brother's hands. "He wants you to come to the meeting."

Killian rolled his eyes. "My answer is the same as it has been," he almost growled. "I don't want anything to do with them or their dark dealings."

"You can only run from them for so long you know," Rafe replied, as his face grew serious. "Eventually, they're going to find something that you love so desperately that you would do anything to protect it. They'll latch onto that, dig their claws in, and make you taste the blood. You can't hide from who you are forever." He spoke like he had felt it—like the loss of something he loved rattled around inside of him.

Killian felt the wolf under his skin scratch, clawing against his bones for an escape. He wanted to run, wanted to shed his human skin and sprint deep into the woods, anything to escape this house for just a moment.

When he was little, the change was something he couldn't control. Every time he got upset about dinner or something his father had said or hearing the way his knuckles cracked against his mother's jaw, the wolf would claw its way out, ripping open his skin and shredding him from the inside out. He thought he had died the first time—truly thought he was dead and in Hel—until his mother's soft voice brought him back. The way she rubbed his head and sang him her lullaby rippled in his veins until he was just a little boy again, curled in his mother's lap while she sang blessings against his hair.

He had learned to control the wolf now, learn how to cage it in and only release it when he wanted to, but there were still moments when the control was hard. There were moments when he felt it brush up against his ribs, inside his chest, searching for a weak point to break free.

He took a steady breath as he narrowed his eyes at his brother. "You can tell our uncle and father," he spat, "that I won't be attending." He turned his head and continued his work, not paying his brother any mind as he walked out the bedroom door, closing it quietly behind him. Killian sighed as he ran a hand through his hair. They would not get to him the way they had Rafe, the way they surely would to Lief. Not if he had anything to say about it.

# CHAPTER 20

# PROTECTION BRAIDS

"A spell of safety here I cast, a word of might to hold me fast, a shield before me and behind, to right and left, protection bind. To me may no harm or ill whit come. By power of three, my magic is from. With the sacred light around me, as above, so below, blessed be."

Ember twirled her finger quickly through her hair, spinning small braids throughout with a precision that had become second nature at this point. She wove in small beads carved with runes as she went, and then quickly pulled everything back into a ponytail. She felt the magic woven into her hair, the protection the words provided. Every now and then, she would see small wisps of light float around her fingers, but she did her best to ignore them. After what happened in Elemental Magic, she wasn't eager to toy with them again.

Ember laced up her shoes, gathered her AirWave and gloves, and made her way out of her bedroom and down the stairs, stumbling into the foyer and almost running directly into Aoife.

"Mum." She smiled, slightly out of breath, blowing a stray hair from in front of her eyes.

"Hello, my love." She kissed the top of Ember's head. "Going somewhere?"

Ember's stomach dropped, willing her face not to fall with it as she bit her bottom lip. "My first Rukr game is tonight," she replied, almost a whisper. She looked down at the brief-case in her hands, taking note of the way her hair was pinned back and she had on a nice dress shirt. "You're not coming?" She tried not to look as disappointed as she felt, but she could feel tears pricking the corner of her eye.

"Oh, my love," Aoife replied, "I'm so sorry. I completely forgot. I have a meeting this evening, and I just can't miss it."

"Right, of course." Ember nodded, swallowing the lump in her throat.

"I'll be there next time, Mo Stór." She smiled, kissing her head once again. "I promise."

Ember nodded. "Of course, Mum, have a good evening." She smiled, but it didn't quite reach her eyes.

Aoife blew her a kiss and headed to the Traveling Room, and Ember shook her head, willing herself to focus on the upcoming game and not the hollowness growing in her chest.

"Oh, thank the Gods," Fen breathed, as he shot up from the bench in the changing room.

Ember scrunched her brow as she walked in, leaning her AirWave against one of the lockers, and pulling her gloves onto her shaking hands. "What are you on about?" she asked, as she looked around the room. Everyone was milling about and chatting, no one seemed to be as nervous as she was. No one was pacing the way her feet were begging to. Were they all just really good at hiding it, or was she on her own here?

"You were meant to be here by four," Fen replied, crossing

his arms tightly over his chest, sweat already glistening on his brow.

Ember tilted her head. "Did something happen to Killian this afternoon?"

"Of course not," he said, shaking his head. "Why would you ask that?"

"Because last I checked," she replied, "Killian is my captain, not you. If he has a problem with the time I've arrived, I expect he would tell me himself." She pulled her phone out of her back pocket, quickly glancing at the screen. "Besides, it's barely five past, so I'm not even late."

"On time is late, Ember," he defended.

Ember cut her eyes at him, readying herself to berate him about how often *he* was late, when Killian came up and squeezed his shoulder.

"Cut her a little slack mate," he grinned. "It's five minutes, not five hours." Killian's eyes raked over her, and she suddenly felt very self-conscious in her uniform.

"What?" she asked, twirling a braid nervously in her finger.

Killian grinned with a shrug. "You look nice, Starshine. You ready?"

Ember let out a breath and nodded. "As I'll ever be." She began to tug on her gloves and shoulder pads, strapping the caman to her back when Odette came over with a water bottle and a soothing smile.

"Are you on the team?" Ember asked, as she took a swig of the cold water that did nothing to calm the nerves rolling through her stomach.

"I volunteered to hand out waters." Odette shrugged. "Volunteer work looks good on university applications."

Ember furrowed her brow. She hadn't even considered university, let alone that she might take extracurriculars from a magical school. She shook the thought away as she focused back on the game ahead.

The stadium was packed, every seat filled, a sea of navy with gold and maroon with silver—the Wyverns versus the Griffins, the first official game of the season. Ember's stomach rolled as she stepped onto the pitch, following closely behind Killian and Fen—captain and co-captain. She couldn't help but smile as they whispered to one another, no doubt going over the plays that had already committed to memory. She felt the invisible chord at her sternum thrum—the string that connected them, reminding her she was not alone, not now, not ever.

The crowd roared to life as both teams made their way to the center of the pitch. Ember searched the stands, praying that maybe her mum had left her meeting early and made her way to the game.

Theo waved down to her frantically, a huge smile on his face, Gaelen sitting beside him and trying to keep him from bouncing out of his seat. Otto and Eira were sitting beside them, Maeve grinning brightly as she talked animatedly to Theo.

And looking completely out of place holding a handmade sign that said, *"Go Ember!"* was her mother, decked out in navy and gold, smiling widely as she waved.

Ember grinned, tears pricking her eyes as she waved back. Her mother had skipped her meeting, a meeting she said she couldn't miss, so she could come watch her first Rukr game. Her heart swelled as she looked at her family in the stands, and the utter joy she was feeling could've filled the entire stadium. Ember looked over to Theo, who was smiling and waving, freckled face lit up in the sun.

*"Good luck,"* he signed, and suddenly every bit of the anxiety she felt walking onto the pitch faded.

She strapped into her board and sailed into the air, hovering in the spot she had been assigned as she waited. Sweat trickled down her brow as she eyed Veda across the field, her eyes never leaving her, like she had forgotten the game entirely and was solely focused on Ember. Her heartbeat steadily in her chest as she focused on Killian and Fen. She just had to focus on the game, and everything would be fine.

Get the Brazul through the H-shaped goal post on their end—two points for getting it over the top of the bar, one for underneath. Dodge the Broja if it comes toward her, or hit it as hard as she could with the caman. The rules were simple— it was the lack of rules that made her nervous.

The whistle sounded, ricocheting off the high stands surrounding the pitch and rattling her bones, and the game began. Fen took off to the left, quickly pulling his caman from the strap on his back and got in position. Ember flew higher, one eye on Veda and the other on the Brazul she was desperately searching for. One of the Griffins had it, and she was speeding toward their end of the pitch, one of her teammates guarding her on the other side.

Ember caught the Broja out of the corner of her eye, whipping her body around as she sped toward it. She quickly slipped the caman off her back and wrapped her fingers tightly around the handle, the weight of the wood digging into her hand through her gloves.

She swung—just one swift swing--and sent the Broja hurtling toward the Griffin player, aiming to knock her off course long enough for one of her teammates to grab the Brazul. The buzzing ball of red light narrowly missed the girl's head, and Ember grit her teeth as she sped forward again.

The game went on like that for ages it seemed. Each team scored several points as the game progressed. They were neck-and-neck, no one ever in the lead for very long. The clock hovering above the pitch ticked down, faster than Ember would have liked, and before she knew it, there were only three minutes left in the game, and they were tied—and Ember needed this win like she needed breath.

Her head whipped around to find Fen, who was hanging low, hovering just a dozen feet off the ground. His eyes met hers, and he gave her a nod, a grin creeping up at the corner of his mouth.

That was her cue.

She sped toward the Griffins' side of the pitch, her eyes flashing back and forth between the Brazul and Broja—the · blue and red almost turning purple as it blurred in her vision. She crouched on her board, flying as smooth as possible toward the Griffin holding the Broja, speeding toward their end of the pitch. They were tied, and the next point for either team would win the game.

Ember sucked in a breath as Fen sent the Broja hurtling toward Eve, the Griffin that seemed to not be paying much attention to where Ember now was. The Broja hit her in the ribs, and she let out a yelp, stopping in her tracks and dropping the Brazul as she clutched her side. Ember seized the moment, snatching the fiery ball of bright blue light and speeding toward the other end of the pitch. Fen flanked her on her right, and Killian on her left as she weaved in and out of players swinging camans and the red-hot Broja and made her way to the goal post.

Catriona, the Griffins' captain, came barreling at her from the right. Killian took a defensive position, caman in hand and poised to swing, and used his body to block the force she threw toward Ember. Another player came at her from the left, and it was Fen's turn to guard her, using all his force to knock the boy backwards, rolling through the air with him as he grabbed Fen's collar. Ember was on her own now as she raced toward the end of the pitch, and she was so focused on her speed that she failed to take notice of her surroundings—and who was coming toward her with a speed that rivaled Maia racing the waves by Dranganir.

When she saw Veda hurtling toward her, it was too late. She cried out as the caman made contact with her ribs, doubling over and screeching to a halt mid-air. She made to keep going, and another blow hit the back of her shoulder, and the pop that it made as it dislocated made bile rise in her throat. Tears streamed down her cheeks as she tried to move forward, tried to force her board to keep going, just a few more feet, but the final blow to her stomach made her stop in her tracks. Veda flew in a circle for a moment, laughing, and the entire stadium seemed to fall into a deafening silence.

There weren't many rules in Rukr. It was a very dangerous game, and she knew that when she joined the team. Veda took advantage of the lack of rules as she unstrapped a foot from her board and sent it flying into Ember's jaw as she clutched her ribs. She then sent her fist hurdling to Ember's mouth, sending blood pouring down the front of her jersey.

The only rule was no fatal injuries. And while a cracked rib, bloodied nose, and dislocated shoulder hurt like hell, they weren't fatal.

Ember dropped her hand, choking back tears as she tried to right herself, and Veda quickly snatched the Brazul from her slack fingers.

"I told you you'd regret it," she hissed in Ember's ear, and then sped off toward the goal post on the other end of the pitch.

Fen and Killian were at Ember's side a moment later, holding her upright as she gasped for breath.

"Go get her!" she all but screamed, tears still streaming freely down her face, mixing with the blood dripping from her lip.

"It's over, Em," Fen said calmly. "They won. It's done now."

"Come on, Starshine," Killian whispered, as the two helped Ember down to the grass on the pitch, unstrapping her from her board and doing their best to hold her upright.

"You alright, lass?" Professor Bjorn asked, as he trotted over to them.

"I'll be fine," she replied, trying to smile, but every time she took in a breath, pain shot through her side. Stars began to twinkle at the corner of her vision, her legs began to shake, and she was sure she was going to pass out.

"Take her to the changing room," the professor commanded. "I'll have a healer come down." He sped off in the other direction, mumbling about stupid rules to ancient games, and Fen picked up Ember's board off the ground. Ember stumbled forward, wrapping her arm around her splintered rib, biting into her lip to keep herself from crying. Killian stopped, tossing his board to Fen, and wrapped his arm around Ember's back.

"Grab my neck," he said, as he bent over, readying to lift her into his arms.

"I can walk just fine." She winced as she tried to take another step, sucking a breath as the pain from her ribs and shoulder began to radiate through her entire body.

"It wasn't a request," he replied, jaw set. He hoisted her into his arms, his hands gripping her tightly as he carried her toward the changing room. His smokey eyes raked over her face as he examined her, furrowing his brow in frustration the longer he looked.

"Thank you," she whispered, tears stinging the gashes as they slid down her cheeks, laying her head on his broad shoulder as she tried to ignore the pain in her rib with every step he took.

"Always," he replied through a gentle smile. Gaelen was waiting in the changing room for them, along with Aoife, Otto, Eira, Maeve, and a visibly shaken Theo.

*Theo.*

Ember squeezed her eyes shut, trying not to imagine how terrifying it must have been to watch and how awful she must look now. His eyes widened as Killian sat her on the cot Gaelen had conjured, and she gave him a reassuring smile.

Odette stood in the corner of the room, water bottle in hand and brows scrunched together like she was trying to figure out how to help. Ember's bottom lip wobbled as she sat down.

"Mo Stór," Aoife breathed, as she wrapped Ember in a tight hug. She winced as her shoulder throbbed, and Aoife took a tentative step back. "You cannot scare me like that. What if something worse had happened?" Tears glinted in the corner of her eyes as she squeezed her hand tightly.

"I'm fine," she breathed, wincing as she moved her injured arm.

"Oh, my love," Eira breathed, as she kissed her on top of the head, brow furrowed as she took in her injuries. "You are decidedly *not* fine." She turned to Otto as she shook her head. "I do *not* like them playing this game! And certainly not with the Ellingboe girl." Her eyes were ablaze in a way Ember had only ever seen a mother react, and something about the way she straightened her back and set her jaw loosened the knot in her chest.

"Let them be children, Mo Grá," Otto laughed, as he kissed the top of her head. "You can't protect them from everything forever."

Eira huffed as she crossed her arms. "Well, I can bloody well try."

"Let's take a look, shall we?" Gaelen said, as she floated toward her. She began twirling her hands around her shoulder and ribs, and Ember instinctively held her breath. Glowing lines appeared above her, tracing her injuries, and checking her vitals. Gaelen hummed to herself as she traced compli-cated looking runes in the air, and that was when Ember noticed the wisps.

They hovered in front of her, wrapping themselves around her wrists and up her arms. Ember looked around, but no one seemed to notice the way they wove in and out of the runes floating through the air and around her ribs.

No one, that is, except Gaelen and Odette.

Gaelen's brow rose, and her eyes met Ember's, but she

didn't say a word. Her mouth turned up at the edges, just briefly, before she gave a small nod and continued her work. Small trails of water wrapped themselves around her ribs and shoulder like bandages as Gaelen whispered her incantations, and Ember felt the pain begin to ease. Breathing came easier, and soon, she could move her shoulder again, though it still twinged if she moved it too far.

Odette just stared, brow still furrowed, head cocked to the side like she was studying for a very important quiz.

"You will be sore for the rest of the day," Gaelen stated, as she stepped back, her magic dissipating as she wiped her hands clean. "You will need to rest tonight if you want to use that arm again." She said this more so to the boys flanking her left and right than to Ember. Fen stiffened, almost like he wanted to argue that he would *not*, under any circumstances, be leaving her side, but the stern look Gaelen gave him seemed to make him decide otherwise.

"We'll come check on you this weekend," Killian said. "Someone is going to have to force us to study for exams."

Ember smiled weakly, allowing Gaelen to help her stand, and told both the boys and the Kitts goodbye. She walked back to the Echopoint with the Merrow and her mum, and Theo held her hand the entire way.

# CHAPTER 21

# YOU CAN ALWAYS COME HOME

E mber laid in bed with a book floating in the air in front of her, flipping the pages as she sighed. She had read this particular chapter three times so far, and every time she got to the end, she couldn't remember what had happened. She flicked her wrist, closing the book, and then sent it floating into a pile on the nightstand beside her bed.

It was Friday, and though she had only been in bed for twenty-four hours resting, it already felt like an eternity. Her shoulder ached as she rolled out of bed, and she sucked in a breath as she felt pain shoot through her ribs. She blew out a breath, limping toward her bedroom window as she stared at the ever changing leaves at the back of their property.

It was Samhain, one of the best festivals of the year, and thanks to Veda Ellingboe, she was spending it cooped up at home. There would be no dancing or singing or eating till she was so full she was sure she wouldn't be able to make it home. Considering she missed the festivities last year, she was really hoping she would get to go to this one.

Apparently not.

She jumped when she heard a knock at the door and

turned around to see Aoife smiling at her as she popped her head in. "You have some company, Mo Stór," she said and motioned for her to come downstairs.

Ember crinkled her forehead and followed her down the steps, limping as she went. They walked through the house and to the door that led into the back garden, and Ember winced as she sucked in a breath when they walked out the door.

"We knew you couldn't come to the festival this year," Fen beamed, as he shoved his hands in his pockets, "so we thought we might bring the festival to you."

The garden was bedecked in twinkling lights strung across posts set in a giant circle. Music seemed to play from everywhere and nowhere, and food overflowed from a table set on the side of the garden. Ember's smile grew as Killian grinned at her, Theo standing beside him with Maeve—both practically vibrating out of their skin with excitement. Eira and Otto both came up and gave her a peck on the cheek, and Thea wrapped her in a tight hug. Ember didn't even care that her ribs ached at the pressure. Odette gave her a small wave from where she was swaying to the music, and even Gaelen was enjoying the festivities—though she always seemed to have one eye on the two small children now running through the darkening grass.

Everyone was here, all her friends, and she wasn't at all ashamed about the tears that streaked down her cheeks.

*The blood of the covenant is thicker than the water of the womb.*

"You did all of this for me?" Her voice cracked as she smiled. Killian waltzed up to her and planted a kiss right on her cheek that set her skin on fire.

"Considering what you spent last year doing," he whispered close to her ear, "we thought it best not to leave you alone this time."

Ember swatted his arm, and he laughed as he backed up next to Fen, who looked like he might be sick.

"One night up and about shouldn't hurt your recovery too bad," Otto said, as he walked up with a pair of crutches, charmed to help her stand upright and relieve the growing pressure on her ribs and shoulder. He gave her another kiss on the head and then made his way to grab a drink from Thea, who seemed to be concocting something from the punch and a flask she had pulled from her purse.

"You deserve a night with your friends." Aoife smiled as she gave her shoulder a squeeze, but something akin to pain settled in her eyes. "Now go have fun." She kissed Ember on the top of the head and shooed her away.

Fen was piling food onto a plate while Odette leaned against the table, talking animatedly about something or another. Ember tried not to laugh as his face contorted into confusion, painting on a fake smile as he nodded. He shot Ember a look, and she could hear his voice rattle around in her head.

*Help me.*

Ember let out a laugh as she hobbled over.

"You're all mad," she laughed. "You know that, right? You should be in Sigurvik for the festival. You didn't have to do all of this."

"And go without you?" Killian said, as he slung an arm over her shoulders, making her wince. "Where would the fun be in that?"

"Thank you," she whispered. The love in the air was palpable—so intense it took her breath away. She watched as Theo and Maeve danced in the grass, the latter holding her little brother's hand like she was his lifeline. She listened as Odette continued to talk Killian's and Fen's ears off and laughed as both boys tried desperately to find a way out of the conversation.

She quietly slipped away, making her way to the edge of the twinkling lights, and leaned against one of the posts as she watched her friends and family dance and laugh.

"Enjoying the festivities?" Eira's voice cut through the laughter as she walked up beside her, smiling as she hugged a mug of tea close to her chest.

"It's beautiful," Ember said. "I can't believe you all did this for me."

"Can I tell you a secret?" Eira smiled.

Ember nodded her head.

"I overheard the boys planning to break you out of the house and sneak you to the festival, so I thought maybe this time we would save them the trouble of getting caught." Eira winked, and Ember laughed. She could almost picture the two whispering together as they played chess. Suddenly, her heart ached for a home that wasn't hers anymore—a family that wasn't hers.

"We miss you," Eira continued, as she watched Maeve try to stuff biscuits into the pockets of her dress. "We were hoping we would see you for your birthday dinner. I hope you know you're always welcome at the house, whenever you like."

Ember nodded as she swallowed. "I'm sorry I missed it. I just don't want my mum to think I'm not thankful that she came back for me. I don't want her to think that I've…"

"Replaced her?" Eira asked, voice filled with sadness.

Ember nodded again—she couldn't make any of the words come out.

"I never knew your mum well—not as well as I knew your da'. But I know he would be glad you found your way back to your family." There was no anger in her voice—no jealousy or regret, and something about that made Ember's heart break further. "But I also know he wouldn't want you to forget everyone else that loves you too." She smiled softly. "He wouldn't want you to hide those parts of yourself away or lock up the past like it never happened. You can have more than one home. And no matter where you go or what you do, or how far you have to travel," Eira breathed, as she kissed her on the head, "you can always come home."

## CHAPTER 22
# THE LAND OF FIRE AND ICE

Ember spent the rest of the weekend at home resting, and by Saturday night, she was feeling completely back to normal. After supper, she curled up with a book in front of the crackling fire and had every intention of doing nothing but reading until she had to go back to school on Monday. Theo peeked his head in the room, a small smile painted across his face.

*"What are you up to?"* Ember signed, cocking her brow.

*"Come with me,"* he signed back and disappeared back through the door.

Ember laughed as she set her book down, following Theo through the maze of hallways to the back door in the kitchen. The sun was just beginning to set, and the sky was a beautiful mixture of pinks and blues. She followed Theo through the giant field, past the stables, and through a small, wooded section at the back of the property. He nimbly hopped over a creek and then disappeared on the other side of the tree line. Ember took off after him, and when she exited the trees, the sight took her breath away.

She stepped out of the tree line completely and up to the edge of a cliff that plummeted almost a thousand feet directly into the ocean. She sucked in a breath as she looked below her. Jagged rocks cut through the icy water as waves crashed against the side of the cliff. The sun was setting quickly against the horizon, bathing the sky in magenta and peach. Theo squeezed Ember's hand, nodding toward a small tree-house sitting on the outskirts of the forest. They climbed to the top, hanging their legs off the edge as they watched the sun set over the water.

*"This is my favorite place,"* Theo signed. *"I come here to think."*

Ember smiled with a nod. *"What do you think about out here?"*

*"Dad,"* he signed, flexing his fingers a bit at his side. *"Can you tell me about him?"*

Ember took a shuddering breath as she bit her lip. Did her mum never mention him? The way he had their father's eyes or how their smile was almost identical? Did she not tell him stories? Replay all their best memories as a family?

Ember looked Theo over and thought about the way her dad used to munch on apples as he told her stories or the way he hoisted her onto his shoulders when they went stargazing. She had memories of boat rides and days at the beach, of learning to ride her bike through their neighborhood, and family dinners around a warm table filled with love.

Theo didn't have any of that. To him, an apple was just an apple and not a portal back to another time. He didn't have the memories to anchor him when the waves became too much.

And that realization made her heart shatter.

*"He was funny,"* she signed, trying to come up with the right words to accurately describe the man who had given her life and given her life purpose, *"and he was kind. He loved the stars and fully believed if you connected them in the right way, you could see directly into the heavens, into some magical land beyond ours."*

They talked for the next hour about their dad, and Ember relived every memory she could think of, reaching into the very back of her mind and grabbing onto things she was sure she had forgotten. After the sun had almost fully set, they made their way back to the house, curling up on the couch in front of the crackling fire. Ember reached into her bag that she had haphazardly tossed on the floor and pulled out her dad's journal, rubbing her fingers along the spine and breathing in the smell of weathered paper and old magic. Theo's face lit up when he saw the inscription on the inside and nodded eagerly, a silent plea to continue where they had left off in the woods.

He needed to know everything about who he was, the part that had been missing his entire life, and Ember was all too familiar with that specific brand of aching.

He sat up eagerly as Ember translated the pages, hanging on her every word as they started from the beginning. Soon, his eyes were growing heavy, and before Ember realized what had happened, he was leaning on her shoulder fast asleep. She closed the journal gently, slipping a spare piece of paper in as a bookmark, and tucked it under her arm. She tucked him into the couch, still not sure her shoulder was healed enough to try to carry him to his room, even with a weightless charm.

She made her way up to her room, kicking off her shoes and throwing on her pajamas. She collapsed in bed, content to stay there for the rest of the weekend. She tucked the journal away in the drawer of her nightstand and settled in to go to sleep. Her eyes began to flutter closed when all of a sudden she felt a tug at her sternum, the invisible string that connected her to the boys thrumming ever so slightly. She bolted upright, then heard a faint knocking on the window that led to her balcony. She swung her legs over the edge of her bed, picking up the book on her bedside table, and sneaking over to the window, peeled the curtain back to peer outside. She rolled her eyes as she swung the door open, one hand on her hip and the other still gripping the book.

"Going to defend yourself with a copy of *Magical Moments in Vala History?*" Killian asked with a grin, as he leaned on the door frame. He looked more casual than Ember had ever seen him, wearing jeans and winter coat, gloves on both hands.

"My dagger is in my other pajamas," she replied, as she rolled her eyes, tossing her book on her bed. "What on earth are you doing?"

"I have a surprise for you," he whispered, eyes gleaming with a mischief that drew Ember to him like a magnet, sucking her in like quicksand.

"What sort of a surprise?" she asked, narrowing her eyes at him as she crossed her arms tightly over her chest.

"Now, it wouldn't very well be a surprise if I told you, would it?" he replied, cocking a brow. "Put on something warm and meet me outside." He didn't wait for a reply as he closed the balcony doors and shimmied back down to the yard, leaving Ember in near darkness once again.

She quickly threw on a pair of jeans and a long sleeve shirt, zipping up her jacket and grabbing gloves and a hat. She slipped her phone in her pocket and quietly made her way out her bedroom door and down the steps, deciding that trying to climb down the balcony to the ground didn't seem like a wonderful idea.

Killian was lounging on a patio chair when she walked out the back door and quickly leapt up when he saw her step out. He nodded toward the tree line, and Ember followed him across the yard. They quietly trudged through the small section of woods and to the edge of the cliff, and it took every ounce of courage Ember had to not back away from it.

"I've been planning this for weeks," Killian finally said, a small smile playing at the edge of his mouth.

The moon lit his profile, chiseling his features against the harshness of the night sky, and Ember could've sworn he never looked more god-like than he did in that moment. His eyes sparkled as he grinned, pulling a gold pendant on a chain out of his shirt.

"Isn't she a beauty," he said, swinging it back and forth.

"What exactly is it?" Ember asked, scrunching her nose.

"A Geoport," Killian whispered. "It allows for international travel, sort of like an Echopoint, except further. You typically have to fill out a ton of paperwork and wait like a month or two to be cleared for travel. It's all very annoying, really."

"And I take it you didn't do any of that?" she replied, trying to hide her smile as she crossed her arms.

Killian shrugged. "Nicked it from my da'." He grinned. "Sometimes being the son of a dark artifacts dealer comes in handy." He held out his hand, his alabaster skin almost glowing under the light of the moon.

Ember flexed her fingers at her sides, biting the inside of her cheek.

"Do you trust me?" he almost whispered, reaching his hand out further, barely brushing the edge of her pinky with his fingers.

"With my life," she whispered, as she slipped her hand into his. His fingers wrapped around her small hand, and her breath hitched in her chest. His other hand held the pendant, and he mumbled an incantation into it, gripping her hand just a little tighter. Without any warning, he took a leap off the cliff, yanking her along with him, and she felt herself being sucked through the air as she let out a yelp. Stars glittered around them as they spun faster than she ever imagined possible.

The first thing she noticed when her feet hit the ground was that it wasn't completely solid. It crunched under her shoes as she sank into it.

*Snow.*

Wind whipped her braid, the cold sinking through her jacket and into her bones as she shivered. It was still pitch black, the darkness covering the snow like a shimmering veil.

"Welcome to the land of fire and ice." Killian smiled, still holding her hand. "More specifically, Grundarfjörður."

Ember sucked in a breath as she spun around. White snow blanketed every surface, and a large mountain jutted out of the ground in the distance, almost like it had risen directly out of the inky water surrounding it. "It's beautiful," she breathed, almost like if she spoke too loudly, it would awaken whatever ancient beings slept beneath the glaciers.

"The mountain is called Kirkjufell," Killian continued, taking her hand as they walked past a small waterfall to their left, down a set of stairs, and through drifts of snow. "Grundarfjörður is the fishing village over there," he pointed to a small village hugging the coast, mountains towering behind it.

They made their way to the road, walking toward the sleepy village and toward the docks dotting the coast. Killian shoved his hands in his pockets, shifting nervously back and forth, and Ember almost wanted to laugh. She had *never* seen him nervous, not even a little bit, and the sight suddenly made him look more human than she ever thought possible. "So, you've brought me on a secret, midnight rendezvous to a small fishing village in Iceland?"

"Something like that." Killian shrugged, mischief gleaming in his campfire eyes.

"Come to watch the show?" a voice sounded from beside them.

Ember's head whipped, around and her jaw went slack.

A tall man—at least six foot four—stood in a fishing boat to their left, winding rope around his arms as he grinned. He had shoulder length blond hair littered with braids and beads, and a tattoo that almost looked like a rune covering half of his muscular neck, running down to his left shoulder. His jaw looked like it had been chiseled by the gods themselves, strong and rugged, thick stubble running across the lower half of his face.

And his *arms*.

He was bundled in a thick coat and gloves, but the wind that bit into Ember's cheeks didn't seem to bother him. He stepped off the dock and wiped his hands on his jeans. His blue eyes shined against the moonlight, and there was something vaguely familiar about their particular shade of blue and how they crinkled when he smiled.

"It's particularly clear tonight," he said after receiving no response, "so it should be beautiful."

Killian nudged Ember in the arm, his brow furrowed in annoyance as she quickly snapped her mouth closed.

"You're Irish," was the only thing she could think to say. Not a question. His face darkened as he nodded.

"Aye," he replied, his eyes narrowing, "though I haven't considered myself as much in quite some time."

"Do you have a name?" Killian asked, standing just a little taller and taking one step closer to Ember.

"Aye." The man nodded again, stuffing his hands in his pockets and turning toward the sleepy town. "You folks have a lovely night." And then he left without another word.

Killian watched him walk away; eyes narrowed until he turned a corner out of sight. "What's he doing out so late anyway," Killian grumbled, as he stared at the empty space at the end of the dock.

"I'm sure he's wondering the same thing about us," Ember replied, as she rolled her eyes. "He seemed nice."

"He seemed suspicious," Killian almost sneered. "Maybe I should go put a sleeping jinx on him, just for good measure."

Ember slapped his shoulder. "Killian Vargr, you are sixteen years old. You can*not* use magic off the island!"

Killian quirked a brow as he grinned. "We were just magically transported to Iceland in the middle of the night with an illegal Geoport, and you're worried about a tiny sleeping jinx?"

Ember rolled her eyes as he laughed, a laugh that made her heart leap into her throat. He nudged her arm as he nodded toward the sky, and she tilted her head back in confusion.

"The show's about to start," he whispered, and suddenly the sky was ablaze.

Green and blue mixed with purple against a tapestry of stars, creating a curtain that hung across the heavens. Ember gasped as one hand flew to her mouth, and Killian lightly grabbed the other.

"You know," Killian breathed, "our ancestors thought the Northern Lights were an earthly manifestation of the gods."

"Really?"

"Aye," he nodded, still holding her hand tightly in his, "the winter months were sacred—a time to rest and be one with nature and mingle with the gods when they came down from the heavens. It's still celebrated in some places, just not as heavily anymore."

Ember nodded as she continued to watch the colors dance against the vastness of space.

"I have something for you," he said, turning to her as he pulled a small box out of his pocket and twirled it around in his hands before he placed it gently in hers. "A late birthday gift."

Ember gave him a confused look. It looked like a box you would put jewelry in. Other than her father's ring and her Vegvisir, she wasn't one to wear much jewelry. She opened the lid to the box and gasped when she saw what was inside.

Beautiful jewels in the shape of stars burned brightly against the metal it was placed in, almost like he had plucked the stars himself from the heavens. They twinkled as she ran her fingers across them, and the familiar buzz of magic reverberated through her bones.

"Killian, they're beautiful," she breathed. "Is this Andromeda?" She ran her fingers against the small constellation on each earring, feeling the cold metal tingle against her skin. She traced the birthmark on her neck behind her ear, the one that was the same shape as the pieces of jewelry.

"Aye," he nodded as he grinned, "and they're charmed,

See?" He pulled a glove off, holding it between his teeth as he placed one of the earrings in her ear.

The warmth of his fingertips sent jolts of electricity buzzing through her skin, and each place he touched felt like it had been lit on fire, every nerve ending ablaze. His hand lingered on her neck as she turned toward him, her breath catching as his eyes locked on hers. He cleared his throat as he brushed his fingertip along the jewels adorned to her ears.

"They're charmed to play your favorite books and music," he almost whispered, his voice low, reverberating off the water that lapped against the dock. "I set them up myself, but we can change them whenever you like."

*We.*

He leaned in closer, his breath creating goosebumps in its wake as heat crept up her neck. She sucked in a breath, biting her bottom lip. The pull to him consumed her—an open flame in a room filled with starter. The world melted away around her, even the light playing through the sky seemed dull compared to him—the way his smile seemed to both break and heal something inside of her all at once.

There was nothing left but her, the sea, and the boy with the campfire smoke eyes.

Killian gently wrapped his hand around the back of her neck, pulling her closer as his other finger traced her jaw.

"Happy birthday, Starshine," he whispered.

Ember gasped when her phone buzzed, almost jumping back and falling off the dock completely. She fished it out of her pocket, rolling her eyes as a text lit up the screen.

"It's Fen," she breathed, a little heavier than she expected. In that moment, Killian's phone buzzed too. "He's probably tracking us and plans to tear us apart new one when we get—"

Whatever she was going to say died in her throat, her face dropping as she read the text, her lungs feeling like they had been ripped out of her chest. From the hollow look on

Killian's face, she knew he had gotten the same message. She choked back tears as her bottom lip trembled, her hand shaking as she read the message again, gripping Killian's hand like he was a raft in the middle of a hurricane.

Maeve is missing. Come quick.

# CHAPTER 23

# CHECKMATE

K illian dropped Ember off at home, heading straight to the Kitts'. As badly as she wanted to go with him, she desperately needed to check on Theo. If they had gotten to Maeve, who's to say they hadn't gotten ahold of Theo too? Ember quietly walked in through the back door and made a mad dash for his room upstairs. She felt like she might spontaneously combust as she ran, choking back the tears that she refused to let spill over.

She skidded to a halt in front of his room, suddenly unable to turn the knob. Out in the hall he was okay, no matter what lay beyond the door. She took a shaky breath and swung the door open before she could think about it any further, her bottom lip trembling as she stared at his bed.

He was sound asleep, an open book laying on his chest with his mouth hanging open. She laughed, tears streaming down her face as she crept into his room, lying the book on his nightstand and pulling the blanket up to cover him. Relief washed over her, though it was short lived. Her heart sank when she thought about Fen and Eira and Otto and the aching they must be feeling. She tried not to think about

Maeve and how terrified she must be in that moment. Alone without her family.

She squeezed her eyes shut, rubbing them with the heels of her hands as hard as she could. She kicked off her shoes, climbing into bed with Theo and pulling a blanket over her. She closed her eyes, pulling him as close as possible, almost as if she thought he would slip away if she let go.

She laid there for a few minutes until her heart rate slowed and she felt confident that Theo was safe. She slipped out of Theo's room and into her bathroom, taking a fast shower and changing into clean clothes before making her way downstairs with her bag.

"A bit early, isn't it?" Aoife smiled playfully from her seat in the sitting room, a cup of tea balanced on her knee. Her smile faded as her eyes met Ember's, and she furrowed her brow. "What's wrong?"

Ember's bottom lip trembled; her chest suddenly tight. She took a shaky breath and shook her head. "Maeve is missing," she whispered, tears streaming down her wind-chapped cheeks.

"Oh, my love," Aoife replied, "do they know anything yet?"

Ember shook her head as she wiped her cheek with the back of her hand. "I don't know," she replied. "I haven't talked to Fen."

"Well, do you need me there?" Aoife asked, as she adjusted the sleeve of her blouse. "I can cancel my plans for the day if you need me."

Ember smiled as she sniffed. Something about her mum's readiness to drop everything to help her made her feel safe, even in the wake of this disaster.

"No, I'll be fine," she said, as she shook her head.

Aoife cocked a brow as she looked just over Ember's shoulder. "It seems we're all up a little late—or early—today."

Ember turned around to see Theo behind her, shoes on and still rubbing the sleep out of his eyes.

*"I'm going,"* he signed solemnly.

Ember shook her head.

"No," Aoife said, as she shook her head, "no, I don't think that's a good idea."

*"Not a good idea."* Ember signed.

Theo stomped his foot and crossed his arms tightly over his chest. *"Going,"* was all he could manage to sign in reply.

Aoife sighed as she rubbed the bridge of her nose.

"I'll watch him," Ember promised. "I'll keep him safe." But that was the problem, wasn't it? Suddenly, nowhere felt safe anymore.

Aoife gave a nod. "You will not let him out of your sight," she said sternly, walking across the room to kiss each of them on the head. "You will go straight there and come straight home, and you will stay together. Promise me you will stay together."

"Of course, Mum." Ember nodded. She would feel better if Theo was with her anyway. She couldn't control much, but she could do her best to protect him, even if she couldn't protect Maeve.

They took the Echopoint straight to the Kitts' house, and by the time they arrived, the sun was beginning to peek over the horizon. It took everything in Ember not to run all the way up the long driveway. When she reached the steps, she paused. Did they really need her there? Or would she just be a bother? They needed to be together as a family right now, and Ember couldn't help but feel like she was intruding.

She flexed her hands by her side, unable to bring them up to knock on the door. Theo squeezed her other hand, and for a moment she contemplated just turning around and leaving —until the door swung open. Ember sucked in a breath as Fen appeared on the other side, eyes rimmed red and face blotchy. His bottom lip quivered, like one more thing might send him toppling over the edge of the cliff he was desperately clinging to.

"You came," he whispered, taking a shaky breath.

"Wild draics couldn't keep me away," she said, forcing out the words around the lump forming in her throat.

Fen wrapped her in a hug, squeezing tight for a few moments longer than he normally would've, and Ember made sure she wasn't the first to let go. They made their way inside, and Ember prepared herself to be tackled by Maeve. It felt like a punch to the gut when the realization that that would not be happening washed over her.

The house was quiet, save for the crackling of the fire in the den and what she assumed was Eira at the stove. Ember walked into the kitchen, not entirely sure what she was going to say or how she was going to be any comfort, but she went anyway.

"I'll meet you in the den," Fen said, and Ember gave him a quiet nod before he left, taking Theo with him. She wandered through the foyer and into the kitchen, but she couldn't bring herself to say anything as she watched Eira quietly at the stove. The air was different—thicker. Like all the magic had been sucked out of the home, replaced with a cold fog that seemed to seep into her bones.

"Mu—erm… Eira?" Ember whispered, as she stepped into the kitchen. "Can I help with anything?"

Eira spun around, eyes rimmed red the same way Fen's were, and her bottom lip quivered as she crossed the kitchen toward Ember. "My love," she whispered, "I'm so glad you're here." She kissed Ember on the head, smoothing her hair. "Go sit with the boys, and I'll bring you some tea in a moment."

Ember nodded, leaving the kitchen, and making her way into the den. She took a seat in the chair that had always been considered hers without a second thought, curling up in it and wrapping her arms around her knees. Theo was on the floor playing with Della, who was content to lounge with him in front of the fire, and Fen and Killian were both on the couch.

She could see the gashes along the Cat Sidhe's beautiful fur coat, and suddenly, she felt like she was going to be sick.

"Is she okay?" she asked, as she stared at the creature.

"We found her in Maeve's room knocked unconscious," Fen replied softly. "There was blood everywhere, but it looks like it was mostly from Della—though she and Maevie put up a hell of a fight."

"The kidnapper left blood?"

*Kidnapper.*

The word tasted like bile in her mouth.

Fen nodded, but the grim look on his face told her it must not have amounted to much.

"It wasn't a match for anyone in the system, or any systems that were cross referenced from the mainland. They're a ghost."

A chill went down her spine as she glanced over to Theo, suddenly overwhelmed with the urge to run home and lock him away for the rest of his life. "Do they have any leads at all?" she asked after a few moments. She knew the answer before she said it, but it was the only thing that she could think to ask.

Fen shook his head, running a hand through his hair and adjusting his glasses. "Dad's been out since last night hell bent on searching every corner of the island," he half laughed, as he rolled his eyes. "I think he might've forgotten how big it is."

Ember jumped as she heard the front door slam shut, heavy boot steps sounding through the foyer.

Otto made his way into the den, his eyes softening as they met Ember's. "Mo Chroí," he whispered, wrapping her in a hug, "you're safe?"

Ember nodded, returning the hug, feeling her anxiety ease as she let out a breath.

"Any news, Da'?" Fen asked, as he stood, eyes wide as he bit his lip.

Otto shook his head. "We're not giving up, though. I'm heading out on the boat to check some of the surrounding islands." He looked between the trio, his jaw set. "We will find her. I won't stop until we do."

Otto left the room, and they fell into silence once more. Ember searched for something to say—anything that might comfort him—but everything seemed to fall short. Killian was abnormally quiet as he stared in front of him, the reflection of the flames dancing across the smoke in his eyes. She was about to suggest they play a game of cards to distract them when a knock sounded at the door. Fen furrowed his brow as he looked between Killian and Ember.

"You expecting someone, mate?" Killian asked, the sound of his voice making Ember jump.

"No," Fen almost whispered. "Maybe it's the Guard. Maybe they found something."

Something like hope mixed with fear flashed across his face, and Ember swallowed dryly as her stomach did a flip. She held her breath as she watched Eira walk through the foyer, wiping her hands on her apron, and almost jumped out of her skin as she took a few steps back, her hand flying to her mouth. Ember held her breath as Fen flew around the couch and to the door, Killian and Ember following slowly behind him.

Killian was the first to speak, his eyes narrowed as he took a step in front of Ember. "What the bloody hell are you doing here?" he asked.

It was the man from the dock in Iceland.

The man blinked, jaw dropping as he looked back and forth between Ember and Killian, and then Eira and Fen, who still hadn't said a word. Fen turned to Killian, confusion washing over him. He turned back to the man, still standing on the other side of the door, and shoved his finger in his chest.

"You have no right to be here," he hissed.

"Fenrir Kitt!" Eira scolded, still wringing her hands.

"She's my sister too, mate," the man replied, shoving Fen's hand away from his chest.

*Sister?*

Ember sucked in a breath as she looked between the two, puzzle pieces shifting into place as she realized why his eyes had looked so familiar the night before.

They were the same shade of blue the rest of the Kitts' shared.

"Osiris," Otto breathed, as he walked into the room, stopping behind Eira, who was doing her best to compose herself.

"You're home," Eira added, teary eyed as she stepped closer, wrapping her son in her arms.

"Just go back to whatever hole you crawled out of," Fen spat. "If you can't bother to answer letters for five years, you don't have any right to be here now. We don't need you." Then, he strode out of the room.

"Fenrir!" Eira almost shouted, making to follow him into the den.

Otto gently grabbed her arm and shook his head. "Let him go," he whispered, turning back to Osiris. "Mum has tea in the kitchen, let's go talk."

The adults left the room, leaving Killian and Ember alone in the foyer.

"I didn't even recognize him," Killian mumbled, shoving his hands in his pockets. "He looks so different."

They made their way into the den where Fen was angrily setting up a game of chess, mumbling to himself as he slammed pieces onto the board.

"Whoa, mate," Killian laughed, "what did that rook do to you?"

Fen shook his head as he sighed. "What gives him the right?" he said, as he furrowed his brow. "What makes him think he can just waltz in here after five years and act like he cares about her? You don't walk away from people you care about." He took a shaky breath, wiping away the tears pooling at his bottom lash.

"Why did he move to Iceland?" Ember asked, as she sat beside him, pulling her knees to her chest. "Does he have friends there?"

"I don't know," Fen shrugged. "After he finished school, he just up and left, didn't even say goodbye, just left a note for Mum and Dad." Fen furrowed his brow as he looked back at Ember. "How did you know he was in Iceland?"

Ember's eyes widened as she looked toward Killian, whose face closely resembled a ripe tomato.

"That's irrelevant," she replied, as she shook her head. "What's important now is finding Maeve."

Killian nodded as he sat on the floor on the other side of the chess board, carefully moving a pawn. "So, what's our first move?"

Fen chewed his bottom lip, moving one of his pawns as well. "The Guard isn't getting anywhere with the investigation, and I honestly don't think they can all be trusted."

Killian moved another piece, tapping thoughtfully on his chin. "So, talking to Thornsten is out of the question then?"

Fen rolled his eyes as he moved a knight. "We'd get farther searching the entirety of the Dark Forest by ourselves with nothing more than a flashlight."

"Well, maybe we should." Ember shrugged. Both boys looked at her like she had grown an extra head.

"Ah, yes," Killian nodded, "let's go for a walk in the woods while a mad man is on the loose snatching weans from their beds." He winced as he looked over at Fen. "Sorry, mate."

Fen shrugged as he made his next move, tapping on the table.

"That's not what I mean," Ember replied, as she rolled

her eyes. "I think we should go back to Arcelia. Maybe someone knows something we don't, or maybe we can find some clues. Odette knows the forest better than we do, and I'm sure she would help. Maybe Osiris can come with us too."

"Clues?" Killian all but laughed. "What sort of clues are you looking for, Sherlock? And what is Osiris supposed to do to help?"

Ember furrowed her brow. "He's older, knows more magic than we do." She shrugged as she leaned back against the couch. "I just think we could get further if we ask for help."

"I agree," Fen nodded, "we need to go back and talk to Erevan. But without Siris. I don't need his help."

"This isn't about you," Ember said sternly, as she laid a hand on his arm. "This is about Maeve and getting her back. I don't know what happened with your brother, but we can sort that out later."

Fen chewed on his lip and nodded, making another move on the board as he sighed.

"I guess so." He tried to feign indifference, but Ember could see the ire dancing behind his eyes.

"So, it's settled then," Killian said as he moved a rook. "Tomorrow, we go Arcelia and talk to Lord Erevan."

"If you put so much as a finger outside of the property line, I'll string you up by your toes from a rafter in the barn myself," Osiris said, as he waltzed into the room and ruffled Theo's hair. "What's your name, lad?"

Theo shrunk into himself, clutching his book to his chest as he looked to Ember.

"Um, he's deaf," she said to Osiris, preparing to interpret for him, but the man's eyes almost lit up as he grinned and turned back to Theo.

"*Sorry, mate. I'm Osiris. What's your name?*" he signed to Theo, and Ember's jaw nearly hit the floor.

Theo's face lit up as he grinned. "*I'm Theo,*" he replied before settling back in and continuing with his book.

"Where did you learn sign language?" Ember asked, as she cocked her head.

Osiris shrugged as he stuffed his hands in his pockets. "My best mate was deaf," he replied. "Had to learn if we wanted to talk. Plus, it made getting away with stuff so much easier." Osiris looked down at the chess board as Killian furrowed his brow over his next move. "I see you all made it back in one piece."

Ember felt her cheeks redden as she looked down at her hands, and Fen's eyes bore holes in the side of her head.

"You were in Iceland?" Fen looked at Killian dumbfounded.

"We came back as soon as we heard," Killian replied, and then narrowed his eyes at Osiris. "You got here awful fast as well. How accessible are Geoports in Iceland?"

Osiris grinned as he looked toward the fire. "You'll come to find that the magic you learn at Heksheim isn't the only magic. It doesn't begin and end with us. The world is full of it, and once you learn the rules, you can learn how to break them."

Fen glared at his older brother as he crossed his arms tightly over his chest. Everything the man did seemed to make Fen want to strangle him. Ember grabbed his hand and squeezed it tightly.

"You will not go into the Danann," Osiris continued, walking over to the chess board, "and you will not go to Arcelia, and you will not talk to Erevan. You will stay here and let the adults handle it. This is so much bigger than any of you can fathom." He looked at Fen as if he wanted to say so much more, but instead, he looked back down at the board, moving one small piece that neither of the boys had noticed.

Killian's jaw fell open as Osiris stepped back.

"Checkmate, little brother."

A FEW WEEKS passed by with no word about Maeve and no new leads, and Fen was beginning to grow desperate. And if Ember was being completely honest, she was too. Yule and the Winter Solstice were in just a few weeks, and the trio had concocted a plan to go to Arcelia and talk to the king, despite Osiris's warning.

"So, we go tonight." Fen nodded as they walked to the Echopoint outside of Heksheim. "Siris has to go back to Iceland for a few days, and Mum and Dad won't notice as long as I'm back before sunup." Fen's eyes were hollow, perpetually dark underneath. It didn't look like he had slept in days.

Ember nodded as she adjusted the bag on her shoulder. "I have to make sure Theo is settled, but I'll meet you all back here tonight." She smiled as she traced her fingers along the runes at the Echopoint. "Odette will be here too. I talked to her at lunch."

Fen groaned, and Ember lightly slapped him on the shoulder.

"Want us to walk you home?" Killian offered, waggling his eyebrow.

Ember rolled her eyes as she smiled. "No, I think I can manage," she replied. "See you soon?"

"See you soon, Starshine." Killian smiled, and Ember disappeared through a cloud of smoke and stars. She landed at the closed gate in front of the manor and wiped the dust from her jeans. She made her way through the iron gates and up to the front steps into the warm foyer.

"Mum, I'm home!" she shouted, as she walked toward the kitchen. "Do we have any apples?"

She walked into the kitchen, searching the fruit bowl for a

snack, when Theo barreled into the room, frantic and white as a sheet.

"Slow down," she laughed, as she grabbed a green apple out of the bowl.

Theo grabbed her arm, signing frantically as his breathing quickened.

Ember followed his fingers, furrowing her brow, but she couldn't keep up. *"Slow down,"* she signed. *"Start again."*

A door slammed in the distance, boots thudding across the floor as the sound grew closer.

Theo's eyes widened as he blanched, turning back to Ember, and grabbing her wrist. He signed again, slower this time.

*"Run."*

## CHAPTER 24
# BACK FROM THE DEAD

Ember spun around, her eyes meeting Collum's, and she quickly put herself between Theo and the towering Warden. He made to move closer to her, and Ember instinctually threw the first hex she could think of at him. Her stomach flipped as he deflected it with ease, but she persisted. Annoyance flashed across his face as he winced, blood trickling down his cheek as the next spell grazed her skin.

"What on earth?" Aoife asked, as she walked into the room, coat on and suitcase in hand. "Ember, that is not how we greet our guests."

"Guest?" Ember huffed, still standing firmly in front of Theo. "You know him?"

"I do." Aoife nodded. "We are leaving Sigurvik, and Collum has come to escort us to our new home."

"New home?" Ember asked, choking on the words. "Mum, what are you talking about?"

"She'll explain later," Collum hissed, grabbing Ember's arms while she wasn't looking. She bit her tongue as his dirt-covered nails dug into her skin, but she stood firmly in front of Theo.

"Gaelen has gone ahead of us to prepare your rooms," Aoife continued, either oblivious to or ignoring completely the pain on Ember's face. "All of your things are waiting for you there."

"And Maia?" Ember asked. "Is Maia there already?"

Aoife shook her head as she adjusted her coat. "I'm afraid we can't bring Maia, but Maize will be finding a lovely home for her," Aoife replied, like she was talking about the weather or an old friend she hadn't seen in years.

Ember suddenly felt lightheaded, swaying on her feet as Collum's grip tightened. "I have to say goodbye to my friends," Ember replied hoarsely. "I have to talk to Killian and Fen. I can't leave yet."

"There's no time, I'm afraid," Aoife placated, patting her daughter on the cheek. "We're on a tight schedule and already running behind. I'll have someone send word to Eira soon." She kissed Ember on the top of the head as she smiled. "Everything will be fine, my love."

"Time to go." Collum grinned as he grabbed hold of Theo, and suddenly, she was spinning through mist and starlight. It was almost like traveling by Echopoint, but somehow more fluid, like she was slipping through water, unable to fully catch her breath. The air around her seemed to press into her from all sides, weighing her down like tar. She landed with a thud in the grass, slipping out of Collum's grasp and landing on her back.

She shook her head as she pushed herself up on her hands. She was in a grassy plot, right in front of a large gate that led into the garden of a giant chateau. Ember felt her chest tighten as Collum hauled her off the ground, dragging her through the gate and toward the large double doors. The gate slammed behind them as they walked, and Ember couldn't help but feel like she was being led to a special sort of prison. The air around her was cold and uninviting as they walked through the oak doors and into the foyer, like all of the magic had been sucked out of it.

"Let go of me," she hissed, as she yanked her arm out of Collum's sweaty hands. She moved in front of Theo again, creating a physical barrier between her brother and the man. Aoife had already walked through the foyer and into another room, and Ember grabbed Theo and made to follow her.

"You will stay here," Collum grunted, as he stepped in front of her.

Ember felt her temper rise, the invisible string at her sternum vibrating as her breathing began to quicken. She instinctively threw a hex at him, trying again to make her way past him, but this time, he didn't just block it.

He shot one back.

She gasped as it hit her in the face, throwing her back against a wall. Blood trickled down her cheek, a deep gash now running underneath her eye. Her bottom lip trembled as she sucked in a breath, willing tears not to fall as she stared at Collum.

"You will stay *here,*" he hissed again.

Theo grabbed her hand and gave it a small, gentle squeeze, reminding her so much of Fen in that moment.

*Together.*

He didn't need to say it, or even sign it. She wasn't doing this alone, and somehow, that realization made her breathing slow, her heart rate steadying. Aoife walked into the room again, Gaelen now following behind her, head bowed.

"What on earth," Aoife gasped, as she walked toward them, heels clicking on the tile. "Ember, you're bleeding."

"Just a small mishap." Collum smiled, clearing his throat. "Everything is under control." The way he grinned made Ember's stomach sour, bile rising in her throat. He preened under the weight of Aoife's gaze, and Ember was certain she was going to be sick.

Whether that was the corrupt Warden or a possible concussion, she was unsure.

"Let's get you cleaned up," Gaelen motioned gently, guiding Ember toward what she assumed was the kitchen to clean the blood off her face.

"Nonsense, Gaelen," Aoife said, as she shooed her away. "Let me do it."

Ember's anxiety lessened as Aoife led her into the kitchen, motioning for her to sit on a stool at the bar. Ember furrowed her brow as she watched her rummage through the cabinets, like she had lived there her entire life. She pulled out a piece of gauze from a small box in the cabinet and walked back over to Ember.

"Collum has a bit of a temper on him." She smiled. "It seems you found yourself on the wrong end of it."

"Is there a right end of his temper?" Ember asked, wincing as Aoife dabbed at the cut.

"The one that doesn't land you with a nasty cut on your face," Aoife replied, brow raised. "I don't think it will scar."

"Isn't there a spell for this," Ember winced, "or a tonic or something? Gaelen can heal me like she did at the Rukr game."

Aoife shook her head as she stepped back. "Sometimes we have to learn lessons the hard way." She smiled gently.

Ember furrowed her brow. Lesson? He had attacked her when she was just trying to find her mum. He had damn near kidnapped her. What was she supposed to do? Ember nodded, biting her tongue as she hopped off the barstool. "Mum, what are we doing?" Ember asked. "Why are we here? You're scaring me." She bit her lip as she willed her pulse to slow, but she couldn't seem to get a hold of the anxiety building in her chest.

Aoife let out a sigh as she nodded. "I know you are, Mo Stór," she replied. "I'm sorry for the abruptness of it all, but I promise I will explain it all in time." She kissed Ember on top of the head and smiled. "Don't be afraid, this change will be good for our family."

Ember closed her eyes as she felt her heart break. She was so, so tired of change. Maeve was still missing, and there was nothing she could do to help Eira and Otto. Her heart clenched as she thought about the boys and her friends. Did they even realize she was gone yet? What would they do when they found out she was missing? Would they try to find her? Panic began to rise in her chest. She wasn't even sure if she was still on the island, or in Ireland at all. She could be anywhere in the world. Her panic began to morph into anger as she thought about Collum and the friendship her mother seemed to have with the man. Alarm bells began sounding in her head—this was anything but good.

"Now this way," Aoife continued. "There's someone I want you to meet."

Ember's chest tightened as they walked back into the foyer —she was not keen on meeting anyone else today, thank you very much. As if on cue, the front door swung open, a tall man walking in like he owned the place as she braced herself. His black coat hung almost to his ankles, flowing like a cloak as the door swung shut behind him. He stroked his white beard, adjusting the tie hanging around his neck. He smiled, pearly white teeth and an aristocratic jaw that almost reminded her of Killian, and gave Ember and Theo a nod that was both grace and a warning all in one.

"Mo Chroí." He smiled, wrapping Aoife in a hug, and kissing her on the head.

Ember furrowed brow. *Mo Chroí?*

"Ember, Theo," Aoife said, as she returned the man's hug with a smile, "this is Jarl Ulrik Helvig."

"Jarl?" Ember asked, taking a smaller step in front of the strange man. "You mean like a king?"

"Yes, like a king, you brat," Collum hissed from beside her. "Show some respect."

265

Ember bit her tongue to keep from snapping at him, feeling the gash on her cheek tingle as she did.

"Easy, Collum, the girl doesn't know any better," Helvig placated the young man seething beside her. "More like a chief." He laughed gruffly, turning to Ember. "You'll find we follow the Old Ways here."

"Where exactly is *here?*" she all but demanded. She wasn't some child who could just be yanked about wherever they pleased, not anymore. She would be treated with respect.

"Oh, I apologize. I suppose you don't have your bearings yet," Helvig said with a smile that made Ember's stomach turn. "Welcome to Tórsvik."

Ember's head spun as she tried to think about the maps of Ellesmere she had studied. Were they even still on Ellesmere? In Ireland? Surely, her mother hadn't up and moved them to another country entirely.

"Well, it's a pleasure to meet you, Jarl Helvig," Ember said as politely as possible while giving one of the worst curtseys known to man.

"No need for the formalities," he laughed gruffly. "Some call me Father, but you can call me Granda'."

At this point, Ember was certain she was going to pass out.

"Granda'?" she repeated, squeezing Theo's hand tightly in hers.

"Aye," Aoife nodded with a smile, "Ulrik is your grandfather."

Ember's head spun as she thought back to her first year at Heksheim, to her conversation with Professor Bjorn.

*"Helvig was the family name of the original children of Odin"*—he cleared his throat—*"allegedly."*

*Ember sucked in a quiet breath and silently slid forward in her seat, hanging on to every word he said.*

*"The Helvigs were a powerful family," he continued. "Very power-ful. They controlled most of the lives of the First Families. Some say Odin himself told them about Ellesmere Island and gave them the coordi-*

266

*nates to get here, along with the wards and repelling charms placed around the island to keep undesirables out."*

"If the Helvigs were the ones who decided to settle Ellesmere," Fen asked, as he scrunched his face, "why didn't they make it here with the rest of the families?"

"Now that is the question, isn't it?" The professor smirked. "Their values didn't quite align with the rest of the families, even Freyr, who had some questionable beliefs. They believed that the Vala were the only ones worthy of magic. Clann Helvig believed that they were superior. Their beliefs became dangerous. Some say their ship went down a few hundred miles off the coast and were lost at sea. Others say they never even made it onto their ships."

"And what do you say?" Killian asked through narrowed eyes, lounging in his chair as he sipped his tea, as if this was normal, everyday conversation.

Professor Bjorn let out a gruff laugh and leaned back in his chair, folding his hands over his tweed vest. "There are stories that say the family successfully made it to the island, and instead of settling on the south end here with the rest of the families, they went to the north."

"But that's past the Dark Forest," Fen whispered. "No one goes past the forest."

"Aye," Professor Bjorn nodded. "That would make it the perfect hiding place, wouldn't it?"

"We're o-on the north end of the island," she stuttered, "aren't we?"

Helvig smiled. "You catch on quick." He adjusted the sleeve of his coat, picking off an invisible piece of lint.

Ember's head continued to spin, puzzle pieces slowly falling into place.

Rowan had talked about a Father. Ember originally thought it was her father she was with, until she had run into Rowan's mother in Sigurvik and learned that both her father and brother were dead. Could this be who she was talking about? And if that was the case, then that meant Rowan was...

The front door creaked open, quickly slamming shut, and the light pitter patter of footsteps sounded across the tile floor. Helvig turned around, a smile breaking out across his face.

"Ah, yes, perfect timing," he said, as he greeted the guest. "Ember, I have a surprise for you."

Ember's heart thudded in her throat as she furrowed her brow. She didn't enjoy surprises on a good day, but especially not like this.

"Ember," he continued, "I think you'll remember—"

Ember's stomach leapt into her throat, her heart beating rapidly as their eyes met.

"Rowan?"

# CHAPTER 25
# HOME SWEET HOME

E mber didn't even give herself time to think or form a coherent thought. She just fired the first hex that came to mind, directly at Rowan's chest. Rowan's eyes widened as she ducked, caught off guard, but luckily, Helvig had thrown up a shield, blocking the attack and sending it directly back at Ember. She landed with a thud on the ground, knocking the air out of her lungs.

"Ember!" Aoife hissed. "Honestly, what has gotten into you today?"

"You're supposed to be dead," Ember gaped at Rowan, ignoring her mother entirely.

"You would like that, wouldn't you?" Rowan replied. "Three against one in a rundown house, and then you and that bloody Merrow just left me to die at the edge of the Dark Forest? Might as well have just fed me to the Cu Sidhe yourself." There was fire in her voice, but none in her eyes. They were empty and longing for something Ember couldn't quite place. It almost made her feel bad for the girl.

Almost.

"You used me," Ember whispered. "You used me and just left. I thought we were friends."

Rowan didn't respond, her mouth set in a straight line, arms stiff at her side. Her eyes were hollow, dark circles underneath like she hadn't slept in weeks. Her face was almost grey, lighter than Ember remembered, like she never got out in the sun.

"I know it's a bit of a change," Helvig interjected, "but I hope you will grow to love Tórsvik."

"How will I get to Heksheim every day?" Ember asked.

Rowan snickered, and it took all her energy not to try to hex her again.

"Love," Aoife cooed, as she walked next to Ember, stroking her hair, "you won't be going back to Heksheim."

Ember felt like she had been shot in the chest, all of the air sucked out of her lungs. The thought of never walking to class flanked by Fen and Killian, sitting mesmerized by Professor Bjorn, or studying on the lawn with Odette made her feel like a part of her had died.

"How will I learn magic?" she asked, her bottom lip quivering. "How will I finish my education?"

"I've hired a tutor to come work with you during the day," Aoife replied, "and you'll work with your granda' when the time comes."

*When the time comes.*

The thought of working under him, the man who had turned Rowan against her family and friends, made her stomach sour.

But what choice did she have?

"So, I'll never get to go home then?" she said quietly, thinking about never riding her AirWave through the orchards again with Fen, never seeing Maia, never getting another hug from Eira or hearing Otto's laugh from the den. Never seeing Killian grin at her from across the room. Never going home.

*Home.*

"Mo Stór," Aoife whispered, as she kissed her on the head, "you are home."

GAELEN SILENTLY SHOWED Ember and Theo to their respective bedrooms, a look of pity shadowing her face. Ember closed the door and sucked in a breath.

The room was *huge.*

It resembled a room she imagined a princess would grow up in. Floor to ceiling windows lined the walls, maroon curtains draping them on each side. A king size, four poster bed sat in the middle, a plush rug underneath it and a table on each side. An armoire sat to the right, next to a walk-in closet, and a door leading to her own bathroom sat on the wall to her left. But despite all the lavish comfort, the room felt cold.

Ember threw her bag on the desk underneath one of the windows and tapped lightly on the oak. She pulled her phone out of her back pocket, ready to call Fen and Killian and tell them what had happened, when her world shattered all over again. When her spell bounced off Helvig's shield and knocked her backwards, her phone had been in her back pocket.

It was crushed.

She pushed the button repeatedly, willing it to turn on, but it wouldn't. She felt her last bit of hope slip from her fingers as she dropped it on the desk. She wiped away the silent tears and slipped into her bed when she heard the door creak slowly open. Theo shuffled in the room; eyes rimmed red as he climbed in bed beside her.

*"Together?"* he signed.

*"Together."*

CHAPTER 26

# LIGHT IS COMING

T he Winter Solstice was anything but cheerful that year, but Ember tried to keep her spirits up for Theo's sake. The day after their arrival Gaelen decorated the chateau in greens and reds and silvers and golds, and sparkling tinsel hung in between lit candles on a beautifully decorated tree in the corner of the large sitting room.

As lovely as it was, she felt her heart shatter every time she looked at the posh decorations. There was no popcorn strung haphazardly around the room, no colored paper turned into chains or mismatched ornaments that had been collected over the years. Everything matched—everything had its own special place—and something about that made her feel like she was standing on the moon instead of her sitting room.

*Her sitting room.*

The words still tasted sour in her mouth. She had spent the first week in the chateau looking for a traveling room and finally came upon it on the sixth day. She tapped on the runes carved into the brass handle, waiting for the tree to begin to glow, but nothing happened. She learned later, from one of the other Merrow, that it required a special key to use, and even then, it only took you to the town center in Torsvik.

272

Ember found out quickly that it was the case for all the Echo-points scattered about the city trapped behind the mountains, and the information did nothing but sour her mood. There was no way out, no way back home.

She was trapped.

A little hand wrapped around her own and tugged, and she looked down to see big green eyes looking expectantly up at her. Theo hadn't left Ember's side for more than a few minutes since they had arrived—the only time she could get any time to herself to think was if she slipped away while he was working with Gaelen or in the middle of the night after he had finally fallen asleep.

She gave his hand a gentle squeeze and smiled—or tried to—as they stood in the doorway.

*"Will Odin find me here?"* he signed, as he chewed on his bottom lip.

Ember smiled as she ruffled his hair. *"Of course he will,"* she replied. *"I'll bet he leaves you a pile of presents so big he can barely fit it through the door."*

Theo grinned brightly as he began signing furiously, fingers moving a mile a minute as he rattled off a list of all of the books he was hoping he would get.

There was no Winter Solstice party that year, just an elegant meal served in the posh dining room encased in what felt like a large greenhouse. The table was decorated beautifully, but Ember found it very difficult to make herself care. A fat, roasted pig lay in the middle, surrounded by garland and candles and citrus of all kinds. Bowls of green beans and carrots and mashed potatoes and baskets of rolls were scattered about around it, and Ember's mouth wasn't even watering.

Helvig was there—that was what she had decided to call him. Not the Jarl or King or whatever it is he was. And certainly not Granda'—never Granda'. To his left sat Collum, as stoic as ever, one hand almost always hovering over the dagger hanging from his belt. Every now and then he would shoot her an assessing glare, like he was making sure she wasn't going to bolt from the room and run away.

As if she had anywhere to run to.

Rowan wasn't there—where she was, Ember didn't know or care. She could be locked away in a damp dungeon with little more than soggy bread to eat, and Ember couldn't be bothered to give a damn. She picked at her food, her appetite still not having returned fully, and tried to imagine what the boys were doing.

It was the only thing keeping her sane. Sometimes she would imagine that this was all just an awful nightmare, and she would wake up at the farm with Eira cooking breakfast, Fen stealing her bacon, Maeve chasing the chickens, and Otto kissing them each on the head before he left for work. Sometimes the imagining helped ease the pain.

Today, no amount of imagining or wishing or dreaming took away the ache that was tearing her from the inside out.

After supper, Ember excused herself to the sitting room where she curled up on the couch with a book and tried to drown out the roaring in her head.

"You didn't eat much at supper," Gaelen said, as she sat a cup of tea and some biscuits on the oak table in front of the couch. "Care for a midnight snack?" A smile played at the edge of her lips as she sat in the chair to the left of the fire.

"How would you know what I ate at supper?" Ember asked playfully, as she took one of the biscuits from the plate. "They hardly let you in the room."

Ember had just barely heard her mother whispering something about 'the help eating in the kitchen' to Gaelen before guests arrived, and it did nothing to put out the ever-growing fire in her belly.

"I could try to find your cape," Ember thought out loud, as she sipped her tea. "One of us should be able to leave this hell hole at least."

Gaelen laughed as she leaned back in her chair, more relaxed than Ember ever recalled seeing her.

"Even if you did," she replied, "I wouldn't go. My place is here, with you and your brother. I will not leave you alone."

Ember closed her eyes as she nodded, allowing the words to wash over her.

*I will not leave you alone.*

"The Winter Solstice is the longest night of the year," Gaelen whispered, both to Ember and to herself it seemed, "but it doesn't last forever." She stood up from her chair, kissing Ember on the head as a silent tear rolled down her cheek. "Light is coming, Ember. Hold on for it."

THEO'S FACE lit up as he walked into the sitting room the next morning, seeming to be very happy at the fact that Odin did *not*, in fact, forget him. He tore into presents like they might be snatched out of his hands at any moment, and the way he smiled almost made Ember forget about how miserable she felt.

"How do you like your dress?" Aoife asked from her seat, as she took a sip out of her mug. "I had it made especially for you."

Ember ran her fingers along the velvet dress and tried to smile.

"It's nice, Mum." She nodded, and that was all she could manage. She could barely look at her mother, let alone hold any sort of conversation. Despite her brother's smile as he flipped through his new books, Ember couldn't push away the shadow that crept into her chest. She couldn't stop thinking about her last Yule—her *first* Yule. She tried not to think about the farm and the Kitts and Maeve, tried to focus on Theo and

275

the joy on his face, but the darkness kept inching its way back in, bit by bit.

And that's when she saw them, perched on a tree just outside the sitting room window—a robin and a wren. She smiled as she swallowed the lump steadily building in her throat and hugged her mug of tea to her chest.

Light was coming. It had to be.

# CHAPTER 27
# A PLEA TO THE GODS

K illian tapped his fingers on his knees as he sat in the den at the Kitts' house. The sun was already setting out the window, and dread was very slowly pooling in his stomach. It had been a hard day, Eira had cried more than once and that alone had set Killian on edge. Otto had tried several tracking spells of different variations to find Maeve, and all came back unanswered with nothing to show for them. Even Fen tried to finish his tracking app and use it, but nothing worked. Everyone was exhausted.

It was hard not having Maeve around, especially on a day like Yule. The home felt barren, like all the joy he had come so accustomed to feeling had been sucked out.

Her and Ember's presents lay unopened under the tree, Eira refusing to move them when Otto suggested they put them in the closet for later, and the sight was making Killian's stomach heavy.

"Earth to Killian," Fen said, as he waved his hand in front of his face from the other side of the coffee table, "it's your turn."

Killian snapped his eyes forward to the chess board and

nodded his head, moving a random piece without much thought.

"Okay, what's wrong," Fen said, as he furrowed his brow. "That was an awful move, and you would've known that had you even bothered to glance at the board."

"Have you heard from her?" Killian asked, as he leaned back against the couch.

"From who?" Fen asked.

"From Ember," Killian continued. "Did she ever text you back?"

The boys had sent her a text that morning, asking if she would be by for presents, or Eira's Yule dinner, or just to hang out and enjoy the holiday, but she never responded.

Fen's brow rose as he pulled out his phone. "No, nothing." He shrugged, "Maybe she's just busy? This is her first Yule back with her mum."

"Have you tried tracking her?" Killian asked, agitation building in his chest.

"Have I tried tracking my best friend because she hasn't texted me back in a few days?" Fen asked, as he raised his brow. "Seems a little excessive, don't you think? She'll call when she's not busy."

Killian nodded, but something about it just didn't feel right. He hadn't heard from her since they said their goodbyes on the last day of school. She didn't even show up the evening they were supposed to go to Arcelia. He expected her to be enthralled with Theo during their first Yule together, but he never would've expected her to ice them out like this. Something didn't feel right about it, something he just couldn't get out of his head.

"Something is wrong," he almost whispered, as he clutched his chest, searching for the invisible chord that connected the three of them. "You can't tell me you don't feel it too."

Fen nodded as he leaned back on his hands. "I thought

maybe it was just because she didn't live here anymore, like maybe it had loosened over time and I didn't notice. But since we went on break, I can't feel it at all." His voice was hoarse, like saying it out loud put truth to his thoughts.

"I think we should go check on her," Killian said, as he tapped his foot on the floor. "Just to make sure she's okay."

"Mate, I'm sure she's fine." Fen forced a smiled, but Killian's pointed stare made him pause. "But if it would make you feel better, we can go check."

Killian nodded and pushed off the couch, not waiting to see if his friend was behind him, grabbing his coat as he made his way out the door.

The boys took the Echopoint straight to Lothbrok Manor, and from the moment Killian's feet hit the frozen ground, he knew something was wrong. The wolf under his skin clawed and scratched, begging to be released from its prison as they walked up the quiet drive. Wind whipped around them, and Killian got the distinct feeling they were being watched. They walked up the steps, knocking quickly on the door, and stood back to wait.

Fen knocked several more times, but each time, no answer came, and dread began to pool in Killian's stomach.

"Maybe they're on holiday?" Fen asked, as he bit his bottom lip. "Maybe she's just somewhere without great cell service." He tried to sound sure of himself, but Killian could hear the worry clouding his words.

"She's not here," a voice sounded from the side of the manor. "They've all left."

Killian and Fen whipped around to see a tall dryad—Maize—standing by the trees, Maia at his side. Killian furrowed his brow. Ember would never leave and not take Maia with her.

"When will they be back?" Fen asked, as the boys made their way over to the dryad, rubbing Maia's snout as they spoke.

"From the looks of the house, they won't be," Maize replied, as he shook his head, handing over the reins to Fen. "Mistress Lothbrok asked that I deliver Maia to you. They couldn't take her unfortunately."

Killian narrowed his eyes. "Ember would never leave Maia willingly," he said, "not without talking to us first."

"I know," Maize replied quietly, giving them a solemn nod. "I would have brought her to you directly, but I wanted to wait until the Winter Solstice had come to an end. They left suddenly, and there wasn't much time for planning."

"Suddenly?" Fen asked, as he gripped Maia's lead tighter. "Where did they go?"

"Unfortunately, I'm not sure," Maize said, as he shook his head. "They left no forwarding address or way to contact them. I'm to close the house and move to a new job by the end of the month."

Killian's breath caught in his chest. If Maize was closing the house, then they really wouldn't be back, not for a long while anyway. This wasn't some winter holiday. No... This was something Ember would have told them about if she could've.

"Is she still on the island?" Killian asked, as he flexed his hands by his side.

"I don't know," Maize replied again.

"Do you know anything?" Killian spat, the wolf screaming at him to let him out. Ember was in danger, he knew it, and this bloody creature wasn't doing anything to help her.

"I only know what I've been told, Mr. Vargr," Maize replied. "Perhaps your father would have some more detailed information."

Killian stormed off before he hurt the dryad, anger boiling the blood in his veins as he ground his teeth together. He heard Fen run up behind him, Maia trotting swiftly beside him.

"What the hell was that?" he asked, as he grabbed Killian's wrist.

Killian ripped it out of his grip, making his way toward the iron gate at the end of the drive. "Bloody useless dryad," he mumbled, as he kicked a rock across the ground, "bloody useless."

"It's not his fault," Fen replied, as Maia nuzzled Killian's hand. "He's just doing his job."

Killian ran a hand down his face, pinching the bridge of his nose as he sighed.

"What was that about your dad?" Fen asked.

"I don't know," Killian sighed. "Nothing good, I would imagine."

Fen walked slowly beside Killian, making the trek back to the house on foot instead of through the Echopoint. "Are you going to talk to him?"

"Talk to who?" Killian asked, as he furrowed his brow.

"Your dad," Fen bobbed his head. "Are you going to ask him if he knows where Ember is?"

*Eventually, they're going to find something that you love so desperately that you would do anything to protect it. They'll latch onto that, dig their claws in and make you taste the blood.*

"I don't know," Killian mumbled. "I don't think he would tell me even if I did."

"Do you think she's okay?" Fen finally asked, barely above a whisper.

Killian sighed as he ran a hand through his hair. "She has to be."

Not a statement, but a plea to the gods.

## CHAPTER 28
# GHOSTS FROM THE PAST

Before Ember knew it, it was February, and she had yet to leave the château. Her tutor came every day at seven, right after breakfast, and Ember proceeded to spend her morning practicing spells, creating potions, and learning history in the comfort of her very expensive new home. Helvig came over for dinner once a week, where they sat in that beautiful, enclosed greenhouse attached to the kitchen, filled with exotic plants and a pond that could have comfortably fit a small dolphin. She read books by the fire, sipped tea as she watched rain trickle down the window panes, and talked to the stars each night that hung over the mountains surrounding the city.

And she was miserable.

Because of the strength of the wards surrounding the town, Helios couldn't make it through. She had no way of contacting Fen or Killian, and they had no way to reach her, either. Her phone was still broken, no matter how many times she tried to fix it, and she was certain she would never get to speak to her friends again. What was even worse, the invisible tether that connected the trio didn't feel like it normally did. She could typically feel something connecting them, something that reverberated against her ribs. She had learned to ignore it. It had just become a part of her everyday life. But now that it was gone, she could feel the cavern it left in her ribs.

It felt like she had been cut in half.

She thought about running away, just taking off in the dead of night and searching for a way home. Once, she'd snuck through her window and took off into the night, thinking that if she found a way out, she could make a plan, pack up Theo, and disappear with him forever. Maybe she could find someone to protect her. Maybe they could hide away together or leave the island completely until it all settled down.

Mountains towered over her in every direction, and even from the ground, she could feel the strength of the wards surrounding them. She felt her spirit break a fraction again. Even without the mountains surrounding the town keeping her caged in like a wild animal, her mother would come after her, maybe even sending Collum, and she would be dragged back kicking and screaming. She wouldn't do that to Theo.

And she certainly wasn't going to leave him behind by himself. She would keep searching for a way out—an escape. She would never stop searching.

She put on a fake smile after a few weeks, doing her best to make the most of it all for Theo's sake, trying to put on a brave face, but her strength was waning.

Sun beamed through the window into the kitchen, and the gentle sound of classical music floated through the air.

"Gaelen, I'm losing my mind," she whined, as she leaned over her book, tracing the picture projected off the page of some goddess whose name she couldn't be bothered to remember. Her tutor had given her the day off, save the mountain of homework she had to complete, and the last thing she wanted to do was stay inside on such a beautiful day.

She longed to feel the wind on her face as she flew through the clouds, but a nice walk would do as well.

Before Gaelen could reply, Aoife walked in the kitchen. Ember stiffened, averting her eyes. She was still so angry with her mother, she barely said anything to her on the days she happened to be home. Ember saw less and less of her each day, whatever work she did with Helvig eclipsing her responsibilities as a parent.

But she was going stir crazy, and she was desperate.

"Mum?" she said quietly. "Could I go into town today?"

Aoife furrowed her brow. "What for?"

"Just to explore." Ember shrugged. "Explore my new home."

*Home.*

The word tasted sour in her mouth. But whether she liked it or not, this was home for now—at least until she found a way out.

Aoife smiled, tilting her head. "That sounds like a lovely idea. Should I send for Collum to go with you?"

Ember wrinkled her nose. "No, Mum. I'll be fine," she replied, as she shook her head.

"Just be home for supper, yes? Your granda' will be by tonight," she replied, and then she was gone, just like every day.

Ember ran her book upstairs, grabbing her bag and quickly slipping her father's journal inside. She tore down the steps and out the door, breathing in the smell of the grass after rain. It was February, still chilly enough that she needed a coat, but not so cold that the rain had turned to snow. The sun was shining brightly, warming her cheeks as the wind bit into them, and she couldn't help the smile that took over her face.

She chose to walk into town, instead of using the Echo-point by her house that would take her there instantly, following the curve of the road as it wound around trees and streams. There was something old about these hills—something that felt untouched by the modern world. The houses she passed were simple, wooden exterior and thatched roofs surrounded by gardens that had long died in the brutality of the harsh winter.

She stopped at the edge of the road as she squinted her eyes at what looked like a door in the distance, carved into the side of one of the rolling hills.

"Curious," she mumbled to herself, and she made her way through the grass and to the opening. As she got closer, she realized it was the entrance to what looked like an old mineshaft. She took a quick step back—she knew better than to wander inside. There was no telling how old this mine was—no telling what had made its home inside or how well the walls were holding up. Ember shivered as she turned and made her way back to the road.

She made her way over the top of another hill, seeing a few more mineshafts dotting the hills in the distance, and finally, a city came into view. It resembled Sigurvik, the buildings a rainbow against the bleakness of the grey sky. Seagulls flew overhead, and for just a moment, if Ember closed her eyes tight, it almost felt like she was home.

*Home.*

She made her way down the path further, and the hustle and bustle of the city grew louder. Children shrieked and laughed as they ran down the street, mothers walked among the shops carrying baskets filled with eggs and vegetables and baked goods, and the joy reverberating through the streets was almost palpable.

She walked over a bridge, and out of the corner of her eye, she saw a small cellar door pushed up against the side of one of the buildings. She furrowed her brow as she tilted her head—being this close to the ocean, cellars weren't all that common. The island wasn't very far above sea level, and flooding happened more often than not during the rainy season. She peered closer, and it looked like the door hadn't been opened in ages. The lock was rusted shut, the hinges discolored and coated in salt from the air. That at least meant that nothing was lurking inside. Either that, or something was locked in and forgotten about.

She adjusted the bag on her shoulder and shuddered. She would prefer not to find out if there was anything lurking in the cellar beneath the pristine shop.

Ember wandered along the cobblestone streets, up and down the rows of shops, restaurants and tiny homes tucked in between. She walked past a small flower shop, taking in the smell of daffodils, snowdrops, and magnolias. Most people longed for the flowers of spring—the first bloom of lavender in the open fields—but Ember had always been partial to the flowers that bloomed in the winter. The flowers that grew despite the cold and dark surrounding it, the ones that not only grew, but flourished.

As she walked further, the smell of fish became more prominent. Living in a fishing town, the smell was always present, but she could always tell when she was close to the water. The way it mixed with the salt in the air almost made her homesick.

She wandered into a small apothecary, vials of potions and tonics lined the shelves, along with ingredients she had only ever read about, that seemed plentiful in this hidden village.

"Looking for something in particular?" a voice said from the back of the shop.

Ember turned around to see a woman carefully placing ingredients on the shelves, long auburn hair flowing in waves down her back. Her pale skin almost glistened in the rays of sun beating through the window, her green eyes sparkling as she smiled.

"No, ma'am." Ember smiled. "Just wanted to look around."

The woman furrowed her brow as she studied Ember.

"I've never seen you about the city before." It wasn't a question.

Ember chewed her bottom lip. "I just arrived a couple of months ago. This is my first time coming into town, but it's very lovely."

"Aye," the woman nodded, "we don't get many visitors, let alone people moving here. What's your name?"

"Ember," she said, "Ember Lothbrok."

The woman's eyes lit up knowingly. "Lothbrok?" she whispered. "Are you kin to Torin?"

Ember nodded. "He's my father. Did you know him?"

"I did." She nodded with a small smile. "I knew your da' very well. He worked as a fisherman at the docks, brought me in seaweed and jellyfish at least once a week. He was a good man, your da'. I'm Catriona."

Ember felt her throat bob as she wiped away the tears pooled on her lower lash.

"You were about two when you left, I reckon," Catriona said, as she continued to stock the shelves.

"I lived here?" Ember gasped. "Here in Torsvik?"

"Aye," Catriona nodded, "I reckon you wouldn't remember, but I remember you running up and down these streets very well while your da' visited with William Olsen at the fish shop across the way. Has he not told you about William?"

Ember bit her lip as she shook her head.

"Is he here?" Catriona asked slowly, almost like she already knew the answer.

"No," Ember replied quietly, "no, I'm sorry. He died when I was six."

"Oh dear," she frowned, "I'm so sorry to hear that. He was truly a lovely person."

"He was." Ember nodded, her chest beginning to tighten. She stood awkwardly for a few more moments before she bobbed her head and turned toward the door. "It was nice to meet you." She was eager to get out of the shop, away from talk that made her feel anything.

"Come back soon," Catriona said, as Ember headed toward the door. "I would love to hear more about how you're getting on."

Ember smiled and headed back into the bustling street. She walked past the fishmonger, imagining her dad spending his afternoons outside with the owner while a little Ember toddled around the village. She imagined drinking tea in the cafe down the road, spending warm, summer days on the beach. Torsvik wasn't so different from Sigurvik, she was coming to find. Both towns were filled with ghosts. Ghosts of her childhood. The ghost of her father.

Ghosts of the life she could have lived.

She made it to the beach, wrapping her coat tightly around her chest as she sat in the sand. Grey clouds loomed overhead, waves crashing as she stared at the horizon. The air smelled like rain, and she thought about getting up and walking back home, until someone shuffled through the sand, sitting down beside her.

"Did Helvig send you to watch me?" Ember said, as she kept her eyes on the horizon.

"No," Rowan replied, as she twiddled her thumbs, "I came on my own."

"Give me one reason why I shouldn't hex you all the way to Timbuktu," Ember said, as she flexed her fingers in the sand.

"I wouldn't blame you," Rowan whispered. "I deserve it."

"The pity party won't work on me, Rowan," Ember replied, as she rolled her eyes. "If you expect me to just forget all of the terrible things you did to me, you're going to be very disappointed." Ember ground her teeth. Who did she think she was?

"I'm sorry," Rowan whispered, wrapping her arms around

her knees as she pulled them to her chest, "for everything. I truly am. I don't expect your forgiveness."

Ember's jaw hung slack as she turned to look at the girl— the girl who used to be her best friend. The girl who was more like her than she would care to admit.

"Well, good," she huffed, "because you wouldn't get it anyway." She kept her eyes set in front of her, worried if she looked at the girl, her cool composure would crack. "Then, why are you here?" she asked, shaking her head. "Come to catch up? See how everyone at Heksheim is doing? Ask about Fen?"

"Have you seen my mum?" she asked quietly, bottom lip almost quivering, like she was desperately trying to hold back tears.

The question caught Ember off guard, and her brow raised. "I saw her last year, after you disappeared."

*After you left.*

"Is she… okay?" Rowan hesitated.

"As okay as a grieving mother could be."

Rowan winced, not arguing with her choice in words.

Ember might have felt sorry, had she not remembered the woman's face when she asked if she had seen her daughter.

"And the boys?" Rowan asked. "They're good?"

Ember felt heat bloom in her chest. "I wouldn't know. I haven't talked to them." She fished the broken phone out of her pocket, waving it sarcastically in the air.

"Better not let Helvig see you with that," Rowan chuckled. "He doesn't like anything modern. I had an ink pen when I got here, and he made me throw it away. It's like he's stuck in the 17th century or something."

Ember shook her head, finally cutting her eyes toward the curly-haired girl. "What do you want, Rowan? Really. Why are you pretending like everything is okay?" She needed her to understand that she hadn't forgotten what she did, the way she betrayed her. As far as she was concerned, her best friend was long dead.

"I just wanted to apologize, to try to start over," the girl replied, "to see if we could be friends again."

*Friends.*

She rolled her eyes, gripping the pendant swinging around her neck. "I admire the confidence you had thinking that would work in your favor."

She heard Rowan sigh, standing up from the sand to walk away, but didn't bother to meet her gaze. She hesitated at the edge of the grass and turned around. "You need to be careful, Ember," she almost whispered. "Not everyone here has your best interest at heart."

Ember felt the hairs on her arm raise.

Was that a threat? Or a warning?

# CHAPTER 29

# ELDFJALL CASTLE

S ilver hair whipped back and forth in the wind as a song floated through the trees, not even the raven on her shoulder daring to interrupt. She scrubbed the crimson stained shirt with vigor, her lilac eyes never leaving the cloth as she sang.

Trí STOIRME agus farraige caillimid cé muid féin,
    Ach amháin le fáil ag réalta tar éis titim.
    Snámh i dtreo an chladaigh i bhfad i gcéin,
    óir níl aon áit caillte againn níos mó.

Trí FEAR TAR eis fás agus foraoisí cosc,
    Sin an ait a bhfaighidh tú na daoine óga, goidte agus i bhfolach.
    Thar na gcnoc is na gcloch liath,
    Sin an ait a rachaidh sibh go léir isteach sa chraic.

EMBER TRIED TO SAY SOMETHING, anything to get the woman's attention, but she couldn't get the words out no matter how hard she tried. She walked closer, her legs feeling like they were made of lead, shaky and *unstable as she forced them forward. As she drew nearer, the woman suddenly stopped her scrubbing and her song and looked up at Ember. Her eyes locked with Ember's—wide and wild, her perfectly symmetrical face almost ethereal against the light of the moon.*

*"Their fate is in your hands now," she almost whispered. "We've been waiting for you, Ember Lothbrok."*

EMBER SHOT UP IN BED, sweat clinging to her skin as the cold February air drifted through the open window. A chill ran down her spine as she reached for a jumper at the foot of her bed, yanking it over head and wrapping her arms around one another. She climbed out of bed, quietly latching the window closed as she looked over to Theo, who was sound asleep under the covers.

From the first night in their new home, Theo had taken to sneaking into Ember's room, unable to fall asleep on his own. The first morning, she woke up to him curled up with his pillow in a chair in the far corner, and then the next night, he was on the floor beside her bed. The night after that, he had made his way to the foot of her four-poster bed, until he eventually started sneaking in after Gaelen had tucked him in, climbing in bed beside Ember while they read together.

She quietly snuck out of her bedroom, leaving the door partially ajar as she tiptoed down the large staircase. Even after two months, she still got lost regularly in the large chateau. A labyrinth of hallways and staircases spiraled through the home, a maze that made finding her way through in the middle of the night borderline impossible. But she was thirsty, and she needed to forget about that dream—and that song.

So, she walked.

She made it down to the kitchen, pouring herself a glass of water from a jug in the icebox and sat at one of the stools pushed up under the island in the middle of the room. She tried reading a book Gaelen had left sitting on the counter, tried humming to herself or reciting Sigils and Runes equations, but no matter how hard she tried she couldn't get that damned song out of her head.

She also couldn't shake the feeling that it was less a dream and more a warning.

She washed her cup, placing it quietly on the drying rack and headed out of the kitchen to try and get some more sleep. Somewhere between the kitchen and the stairs, she got lost and found herself wandering down a narrow hall she was certain she hadn't seen yet. Some sort of servant passage, it seemed. The walls were stone, lit by medieval looking sconces every few feet. She suddenly felt transported back in time, like she was in some fairytale, escaping the beast who had her locked in a tower.

A wooden door appeared at the end of the hall, and she quickly slipped out of it and into one of the main halls in the chateau. She was still on the first floor, and now she could hear voices ricocheting off the high ceilings, hushed voices coming from a room at the end of the hall. The stairs were in the opposite direction, but curiosity got the better of her. Though she knew she should've gone up to bed and ignored whatever middle of the night meeting was happening, she brushed away her intuition and crept toward the voices as quietly as possible.

She pressed her ear up against the closed door, that she now realized led into one of the smaller sitting rooms and held her breath as she listened.

"She must go, Aoife," Helvig's gruff voice said from the other side of the door. "It is her birthright—she must."

"I know," Aoife replied, "but she won't go willingly, you will have to—"

A board creaked under Ember's foot, giving away her presence in the hall, and the voices stopped abruptly. Ember sucked in a breath as she backed away, but before she could turn to run back to her room, the door swung open, revealing her mother and Helvig sitting in front of the fire.

"Good evening, Ember," Helvig said, a small smile playing at the corner of his mouth.

"Good evening," she whispered with a nod. Should she bow? Or curtsey? How does one greet their long-lost grandfather, who was the king of a hidden city on a magical island?

She certainly wasn't going to hug him.

"Having trouble sleeping, love?" her mother cooed, as she patted the couch beside her. "Come have some tea."

Ember nodded as she walked into the room, sitting as far away from the burly, bearded Viking as she could possibly get. She sipped her tea, the silence threatening to swallow her whole if it wasn't for the fire crackling in front of her. Helvig seemed to study her, his piercing blue eyes boring holes into the side of her head. She tried not to squirm. What was he looking for? His brow furrowed, and she shrunk under the weight of his gaze—it was intense, like fire waiting to consume her.

"How are you liking Torsvik?" he finally said, taking a sip of what she was certain was whiskey in his glass.

"It's beautiful," Ember replied, forcing a smile.

It wasn't a lie. The town was stunning, all the aged buildings that reminded her of the books she had read about ancient Vikings. The mountains that sat behind it, stretching from one side of the harbor to the other took her breath away, the way it lit up red and orange every evening like the gods had set it on fire themselves.

"How would you like to come see the castle?" he asked next, a question Ember wasn't prepared for in the slightest.

Her brow rose and her mug almost slipped from her hands. "There's a castle?" she asked, tilting her head.

"Well, of course," he chuckled, crossing one leg over his knee. "Where do you think the Jarl lives?"

Aoife let out a breathy laugh.

Ember bit her lip, suddenly feeling very small and out of place, like a pauper being handed a dress made of silk, encrusted with diamonds—she had no idea what to do with it.

"So?" Aoife asked, nodding her head toward Helvig. "Would you like to visit?"

"Sure," Ember nodded, though she felt very far from it, "I'd love a tour of the castle."

"Wonderful!" Helvig said, as he slapped a hand on his knee, making the tea in Ember's mug slosh around as she jumped. "I'm sure you're busy with your tutors this week, so how does Saturday sound?"

"It sounds lovely," she replied quietly. "Saturday sounds lovely." She hated the way her voice sounded now—so small and indecisive, like she had no backbone at all. Where was the girl that took on a Cu Sidhe? Or fought for the life of an enslaved Merrow? Where was the bravery that she had almost died for?

"Perfect," Helvig grinned, pearly white teeth reflecting the fire that flickered in front of him. "I'll send for you after breakfast then."

Ember nodded. "I'll see you then," she whispered, standing up from the couch and setting down her mug. "Thank you for the tea, Mum. I'm going to try to get some sleep." Ember leaned down and kissed her mother on the cheek, then quickly made her way out of the room, trying to keep herself from bolting to the safety of her bedroom.

She climbed into the safety of her bed, huddling close to Theo, and closed her eyes tight. She didn't want to see a castle or explore the town or watch the sun set over the mountains. She wanted to be laughing in the orchard with Fen and Killian or listening to one of Maeve's funny stories. She wanted to curl up in front of the fire and read her book while Fen and Killian argued over a game of chess, Otto laughing in his chair as he read the paper. She held Theo's hand as he slept soundly beside her, squeezing it to steady herself. She didn't want to go to a castle.

She wanted to go home.

SATURDAY CAME FASTER than Ember would've liked, which almost seemed impossible considering how bored she was. After a week of repetitive lessons with a monotonous tutor, she found herself eager to get out of the house, even if it was for a day out with Helvig.

*Granda'.*

The word tasted bitter in her mouth. She shook the thought away as she stared at herself in the mirror. Small braids were scattered through her hair with tiny, silver beads placed throughout, runes carved into them. The dress Gaelen had picked up for her hung around her ankles, forest green speckled with ivory flowers and gold trim around the hem and cuffs of her sleeves. She pulled on her fur lined boots and then donned the woolen caftan that matched her dress. The coat was warm, and she found herself beginning to sweat within minutes. She made her way down the stairs, intent on waiting outside in the cold for whoever Helvig sent for her, when a knock on the door sounded.

Ember groaned when Collum walked inside, gritting her teeth as she gripped the handrail. She stomped—actually stomped—to the door, crossing her arms tightly over her chest.

"Was everyone else too busy with more important things?" she asked lazily.

The young man—he couldn't have been more than twenty —cut his eyes at her, his back still rigid, hands folded in front of him. "The Jarl has sent me to accompany you to the castle," he replied, composure cool and collected. "Right this way, *Princess*." He smirked at the last word, like it was a joke.

She didn't find it very funny. Ember narrowed her eyes, shoving her way past him. "Don't call me that," she hissed, and walked out into the freezing February wind. "Don't you have better things to do than be his little lap dog? Or was the academy too much work so you came running to him the first time he rang?" She pushed him, itching for a fight after being cooped up in this house for so long.

Fire raged behind his eyes as his nostrils flared. "Watch it, brat," he hissed, grabbing her tightly by the bicep. Ember grinned as he lost his cool, and he quickly let her go and smoothed his sleeve.

Collum didn't say another word, Echoing them straight to the courtyard of the most majestic, terrifying castle she had ever seen. The stone was almost black against the bottom of the mountain, something carved from rock that wasn't from Ellesmere—something ancient and dark. It seemed to be almost carved into the side of the mountain, like over the hundreds of years it stood there, it had become one with the bedrock. On the outside of the courtyard, through a massive iron gate, Ember could hear waves crashing against rock at the bottom of a careening cliff.

"This way," was all Collum said, as he led her through the courtyard, up the giant steps, and through the largest set of double doors she had ever seen in her life. Staff milled about, dusting and sweeping and carrying vases of fresh flowers. The front hall was massive, ceilings arched with ornately carved wood beams, runes for protection—and things she didn't quite recognize—carved into each one. Ember spun on the marble floor, taking it all in, when a voice sounded behind her.

"Welcome to Eldfjall Castle." Helvig smiled. "I trust Collum got you here without trouble?"

Collum cut his eyes toward her—a warning.

She put on a pretty smile and turned back to Helvig. "It was uneventful." She shrugged.

Helvig led her through the entrance hall, and she noticed the way he limped, the way he couldn't seem to catch his breath. That he seemed...

Weak. Not the strong king she had imagined he was.

She shook her head and focused in front of her. They wound in and out of more rooms than she could keep track of. Studies and kitchens and the hospital wing, more money invested in each room than she had seen in her entire life. Her eyes lit up when he pushed open the doors to the library, the entire thing had to be twice the size of the Kitts' house alone. It seemed to be never ending, floor-to-ceiling shelves lined the walls, and Ember was certain it would swallow her whole if she allowed it to.

"It's beautiful," she breathed. "How many books are there?" It was a silly question, she knew that before she asked, but she tried anyway.

Helvig chuckled, the way she imagined a grandfather would. "Now that I'm not sure," he replied. "Shall we continue?"

Ember nodded, and he led her down other halls, pointing out rooms and talking about the history of the castle. It was built a few years after a small group of the First Families landed on the banks of Torsvik. The Clan worked together to build the city and the castle, and Ember's ancestors had been at the heart of all of it.

Something about that filled her with both pride and dread.

"I've heard you're quite the talented Vala," he beamed, almost like a proud parent. "I see it runs in the family."

Ember gave a half smile. "Because I'm my father's daughter?" She had heard it time and time again, from every person she encountered that knew her parents.

"No," he replied, shaking his head, "because you're your mother's daughter. You have more than one birthright."

She sucked in a breath and bit her lip.

*Your mother's daughter.*

She shook the thought away as she ran her hand along a door in one of the main halls, electricity pricking at her fingers as she touched the handle. She furrowed her brow, trying to open it without even thinking, but it was locked.

"What's in here?" she asked, as she stopped. More runes were carved in the frame of the door; they seemed to litter the entire castle. What were they protecting? Or hiding?

A shadow of—something—darkened Helvig's face for just a moment before he waved it away with a practiced smile. "It's off limits. There are many ancient relics in the belly of the castle. I try to keep certain doors locked to deter sticky fingers."

Ember nodded, but something told her it was more than that.

"And this is the ballroom," he motioned to the large, ornate room around them, gold trim running along the walls and arched ceilings, and pictures depicting great battles hung throughout the room. People bustled about—Merrow and Vala alike—as they carried things in and out of the room, cleaned the floors and dusted every surface they could reach.

"You'll have to excuse the mess," Helvig said, as they walked toward the throne. It radiated something Ember couldn't quite place, making the hair on the back of her neck stand on end. "We're preparing for the ball in a few weeks, and I'm afraid the castle is a bit chaotic right now."

Ember furrowed her brow. "Ball?"

"Aye," Helvig nodded, "the annual Ostara Ball is on the twentieth of March. We've had a bit of a delay in the planning, but it should all be ready just in time."

A large throne sat at the far end, carved out of ancient looking wood, runes etched with gold. Ember suddenly felt very small.

"Our ancestors held court here hundreds of years ago,"

Helvig continued, motioning to the throne, "though these days this room is mostly used for parties." He chuckled to himself like he had just told a very funny joke.

Ember couldn't wrap her mind around it—the idea that places like this still existed. Kings and courts and grand ball-rooms—it all felt so foreign, so fairytale. The pictures on the wall caught her eye, and Helvig caught her staring.

"Go take a closer look." He nudged her toward the wall. "I have to go check in with Collum for a moment."

Helvig stalked away in search of the lieutenant, and Ember walked over to the paintings, studying them. Merrow warriors under the boots of Vikings, Elves being run through with arrows, a Fae princeling begging for his life at the foot of a decorated general.

Ember's stomach turned. This was her family's history, her legacy. This was who she was by blood, and that thought horrified her.

*The blood of the covenant is thicker than the water of the womb.*

That was what Killian had told her, but was he right? Was it really that simple? How could she be good when she came from a bloodline filled with this much hate? Centuries of it, rippling in her veins and tainting who she was at her core.

*"There is a prophecy that a descendant of the First Families, a Vala born of both dark and light, will rise to power, developing the ability to have dominion over all magical beings. They will be the downfall of the rest of magical civilizations. Should this legend come true in any capacity, it will devastate and destroy entire races."*

Suddenly, the prophecy made so much more sense—maybe this was what she was destined for. Maybe there was nothing she could do to stop it.

*I am destined for darkness.*

The invisible cord at her sternum thrummed, and she sucked in a breath, her heart leaping into her throat. It had been almost three months since she had felt the pull, and she was almost scared to know what it meant.

"Malcom, welcome!" Helvig boomed from across the room. "And I see you brought your nephew with you. It's about time Magnus came to his senses." Laughter echoed through the hall, and Ember narrowed her eyes. Whoever Helvig was talking to was obscured behind the Jarl's burly frame.

*Malcom… Magnus…*

Why did that sound so familiar? She racked her brain, trying to place the names, when the cord at her sternum tightened again, almost pulling Ember forward on its own. Two things happened at the same time, and Ember felt like her heart was going to leap out of her chest. As Helvig stepped to the side, turning to call her over, he revealed the man beside him, and she suddenly remembered where she had heard those names. A burly man in a dark suit stood beside Helvig, and beside him was a boy with platinum hair and smoke in his eyes.

*Killian.*

# CHAPTER 30

# IN THE BELLY OF THE CASTLE

Ember barely registered that she had crossed the room until she was in front of him. His eyes were wide, jaw slack, and all the color had drained from his face, like he was staring at her ghost. In some ways, she felt like he was.

"You're here," she whispered, unable to take her eyes off him. The bags under his eyes were prominent against his alabaster skin, and Ember wondered when the last time he had slept was. He snapped his mouth shut, jaw tensing as his throat bobbed, eyes flashing amber, but he didn't look away.

"Oh, that's right." Helvig smiled. "I forgot you knew Killian. Why don't you two get reacquainted while I have a word with Mr. Vargr?"

Ember nodded, and the two men walked away. She pulled Killian to the opposite end of the room, gripping his wrist like it was a lifeline. He suddenly seemed to snap out of whatever trance he was in and grabbed her shoulder, whirling her around, and wrapped her in the tightest hug she had ever felt.

"Thank the gods," he mumbled into her hair. His chest shook as he took a breath. "We couldn't get any Helios to go through."

Ember pulled away and gave a nod as she bit her lip. "The

wards are too strong, and my phone is broken so I've had no way to get ahold of anyone." Tears pricked at the corners of her eyes as the fire in his swirled. "I never thought I would see you again." She blinked as she took in his finely pressed shirt and dress pants and furrowed her brow. "What are you doing here?"

Killian ran a hand down his face as he blew out a breath. "The day after break, I felt like the bond had been severed, like there was a cavern in my chest." He gripped his shirt, knuckles turning white. "I thought it was just me until I talked to Fen, and he felt it too. We went to look for you at the manor, and Maize told us you had left, and he handed Maia over to Fen."

Ember let out a breath—she had been so worried about Maia and was so relieved that she was safe at the Kitts'.

"I overheard my da' and uncle talking a few nights ago, something about a girl at the castle. It sounded odd, and I thought they were talking about some clients in Scotland, but something just didn't sit right with me."

Ember's heart sank—his dad and uncle had been talking about her? How did they know?

*You are playing a very dangerous game without so much as a glimpse into the rule book.*

That was what Magnus Vargr had spat at her when she had barreled into him in the streets of Sigurvik. It felt like another lifetime.

"My father has made a big deal about trying to get me into the family business," Killian continued, keeping his voice low, "so I started showing interest. Going to meetings, meeting with clients, even sucking up to Veda and Oryn." He made a face like even the idea made him nauseous. "I eventually convinced my uncle I was trustworthy, and he decided to bring me to meet with a very *important* client this weekend. I didn't know if you'd be here, but it was the only lead we had."

Ember choked back tears. "But how?" she whispered.

"How did you convince him? He must know you're my friend."

"It doesn't matter how," Killian replied, his throat bobbing. "Has anything ever stopped me before?" His smile lit up his entire face, seeming to warm every inch of that marble ball room. It was at that moment that she realized just how cold she had been for the last few months.

"You found me," she whispered. Not a question.

Killian smiled lazily, a hand in his pocket and the other tracing the gold trim on the sleeve of her dress. He was so close to her she thought she might stop breathing. "I will *always* find you, Starshine," he replied huskily.

"How long are you here?" she asked, as she looked around, keeping an eye on Helvig, who was still on the other side of the room talking to Malcolm.

"I go back after my uncle is done here, later this evening. What are you doing in a castle? And where's Theo and your mum? What happened?"

Ember bit her lip and took a breath, then explained everything that happened almost three months prior. About how her mother had whisked her and Theo away without any explanation, how she was in a giant chateau on the edge of the city. About the mountains and the wards.

"I don't trust him," she whispered, not knowing who was listening. He seemed to have ears everywhere. "Something is going on, and I intend to find out what it is. I think this is who Rowan was talking about last year. I think this is who sent her to find the Book."

"Rowan?" Killian asked, as he furrowed his brow.

Ember nodded. "She's here," she replied. "Rowan is here. She lives in the castle and has been working with Helvig."

"She's *here?*" he asked, a little louder than Ember would've liked. She shushed him, and he quickly snapped his mouth shut.

"Something is going on, and I think Rowan knows what it

is," she whispered. "That's why I'm here, to try to get a feel for what he's hiding."

"Ember, you don't need to get tangled up with Helvig," Killian warned. "From everything my uncle has said, he's a dangerous man."

"I am forever entangled with him unfortunately," Ember sighed. "He's my grandfather."

The shock on Killian's face made it evident that he didn't know—maybe no one did. "But if the Jarl is your granda'," he whispered, "then that would make you—"

"Don't say princess," she breathed, eyes closed. She couldn't stomach it, couldn't make sense that it was who she was.

"Well," he sighed, "this changes things, now doesn't it?"

"It doesn't," she replied. "He is hiding something, and grandfather or not, I'm going to find out what it is."

As if on cue, Rowan waltzed into the room, and Ember stiffened as she saw Veda and Oryn at her side. The twins' smiles looked almost feral as their eyes locked with hers, and it took everything in her not to recoil as Oryn leaned in and kissed both her cheeks.

"I didn't want to believe it when Father said you were here," he grinned, "told him he had lost his mind. But I stand corrected." His eyes roved over her like she was a mouse caught in a trap, and his grin made her stomach turn sour.

Killian let out a low growl, stepping closer to Ember, and looked like he was ready to slit Oryn's throat clean open. Rowan let out a laugh as she trailed a hand along Killian's shoulder, rounding him to stand between them.

"Simmer down, boys," she said, as she pinned them both with a dark look. "Now is not the time or the place."

Ember bristled, watching as the muscles in Killian's jaw twitched, nostrils flaring as Rowan's hand made contact with his broad shoulder. Oryn seemed to take a step back, holding his head just a hair higher as he kept his eyes on her.

"I was wondering how long it would take you to get here Vargr," Rowan said, as she inspected her nails. "I will say, I expected better timing honestly."

"Our dear cousin has been quite busy." Veda smiled, then turned to Ember, who was looking between the three of them with a furrowed brow. "Has he not told you what he's been up to?"

Against her better judgement, Ember shook her head.

Veda let out a breathy laugh as she grinned. "Killian has finally come around to the family business," she cooed. "It took him a few tries to prove himself, but he's finally got the hang of it."

*Prove himself.*

Ember felt bile rise in her throat as she swallowed dryly. Killian's face was stoic, but she could see the amber flash across his eyes as Oryn inched closer.

"Rafe better watch out," Oryn grinned, "or Uncle will have a new favorite son."

To Ember's surprise, Killian let out a gruff laugh, a small smile barely ghosting his lips. His eyes locked with hers, and she could almost hear what he was thinking.

*Go along with it.*

Veda turned as Malcom called her and Oryn, and she gave Ember another smile. "I'm sure we'll see you very soon, Lothbrok." She grinned and then turned to Killian. "Make it quick, cousin. We have work to do."

"Your family is so charming," Rowan drawled, as she turned her back on the retreating duo. "How on earth do you deal with them at Sunday dinner?"

"Cut the shit," Killian hissed. "What do you want?"

Rowan glared at him, then rolled her eyes. "I wanted to warn you to watch your back."

"Is that a threat?" Killian growled, hackles raised. His eyes flashed gold, and Ember held her breath.

"Not me, you mangy mutt," Rowan replied, as she rolled

her eyes. "Your uncle is a regular here, and he has no prob-lems leaving boots prints on people's backs, if you catch my drift. It seems your cousins might be following in his footsteps."

"I can take care of myself," he grumbled, but it didn't stop him from glancing toward his uncle on the other side of the room.

"Why were you with them?" Ember asked, as she narrowed her eyes.

Rowan shook her head, biting her lip to keep the secret in. "That's on a need-to-know basis." She smiled, but Ember could see the battle being waged behind her eyes. She gave her a nod, then to her surprise the girl looked to her left and right and wrapped her in a tight hug.

Ember stiffened, eyes wide as she looked toward Killian, who seemed ready to hex her if need be.

"Remember what I told you—be careful," she whispered in her ear, then let go and walked toward Helvig.

"What was that all about," Killian asked, as he narrowed his eyes toward the other side of the room.

"I don't know," Ember replied, shaking her head. Killian turned around, just as Malcom motioned for him to leave, and Ember felt her heart sink.

"I have to go," he said, as he stuffed his hands in his pockets, "but I'll be back. I'll figure out a way to get here alone." He began to walk away when he suddenly stopped and turned around. "I forgot to tell you. Cormac from Celes-tial Steel said he was sorry he couldn't fix the spell on your ring."

Ember furrowed her brow.

"What spell?" she asked.

Killian shrugged in reply. Malcom yelled across the room for Killian to leave, his patience apparently growing thin. "I'll come back for you."

Ember nodded, throat suddenly feeling like it was lodged

with cotton as he wrapped her in a hug. "Promise?" she whispered in his ear.

"I swear, Starshine."

EMBER SHOT UP IN BED, desperately trying to suck air into her lungs. It was the third night in a row that she had dreamed of that damn song and that strange woman with the silver hair. Her damp shirt clung to her, drenched with sweat, and she quietly crawled out of bed to change. She rummaged through her pajama drawer when she suddenly stopped, her blood running cold.

The song that was echoing through her dreams didn't stop when she woke up this time.

She whipped her head around, searching for the source of the noise, but it didn't sound like it was coming from any one direction. No, it sounded like it was all around her, reverberating off her bones and rattling around in her skull. Just when she was about to crawl back in bed and try to drown it out, a blue light floated onto the balcony outside of her window. She pulled on her long, woolen coat and her shoes and quietly pushed the glass door open, seeing a little blue wisp bouncing in the air two feet above the balcony floor.

"What are you doing?" Ember whispered, as she closed the door behind her. The wisp started to float away, down into the yard and toward the wall at the edge of the property. Ember sighed, dread pooling in her stomach, but decided to follow it.

What's the worst that could happen?

She followed it over the wall, creeping through the grass and trees surrounding that property of the chateau. The mountains loomed in the distance, towering over her like giants. She pulled her jacket tighter, feeling the midnight breeze from the sea whispering against her skin. She made it to the top of another hill, and all of a sudden, Eldfjall Castle came into view.

"Oh, you've got to be kidding me," she mumbled under her breath.

The wisp stopped, bobbing up and down in front of her as if it could sense her hesitance.

"I am not going in there," Ember said, arms crossed over her chest in defiance.

The wisp bobbed a few feet further toward the castle, and Ember shook her head again.

"No," she said, "I am going home." She groaned as it floated further. Ember rolled her eyes with a sigh, "I'm arguing with a speck of blue light," she mumbled, but she followed it anyway.

She slipped over an outer wall, feeling the ward bend around her as it let her pass. The wisp floated to a door, quickly slipping underneath and inside.

"Feckin' hell," Ember mumbled, pinching the bridge of her nose. She jiggled the knob on the door, but it was locked. Of course it was locked. She sighed as she racked her brain. *"Desellar,"* she whispered under her breath, and the lock opened with a quiet click. She slipped into the kitchen beyond the door, tiptoeing across the stone floor and into a back hallway, the wisp bouncing above the floor, like it was waiting for her. She ran her hands along the stone wall, feeling the years' worth of chips and scratches rub against the pads of her fingers. It was so odd how ancient certain parts of the castle looked, compared to the curated portions Helvig had shown her earlier in the day.

Was that intentional?

She came out into a hall, her feet now touching marble, and realized she was in front of the same door she had seen earlier that day. She ran her hands along the ancient wood, electricity crackling underneath her fingertips. She whispered the unlocking spell once, twice, three times, but nothing happened. She sighed as she chewed on the inside of her cheek.

Why had it brought her here? And better yet, why had she followed a little ball of magical light in the dead of night by herself? The wisp bobbed beside her, like it was waiting on her to figure out some crucial piece of the puzzle.

"What? Are you waiting for an invitation?" Ember whispered to the buzzing ball of light. "What do you want me to do?"

The light hovered, suddenly breaking into multiple more lights, dozens of wisps floating around her arms and hands, and then whirling around the door, setting it aglow like a blue flame. Ember didn't understand why, but she reached out to touch the handle again. It burned against her skin, lighting every nerve on fire as she bit down on her tongue, fighting back tears as she tried not to scream. The fire burned through her veins, up her arm and into her chest, and just as quickly had it started, it was over.

Ember yanked her hand away, cradling it against her chest as the lock popped open with a quiet click. The wisp bobbed through the door, into the darkness, and Ember followed quietly, hearing the door close behind her. Ancient sconces lit blue as the wisps hovered above each one, lighting the path down the treacherous looking stone staircase. It wound down, down, down, and when she was finally convinced she was somewhere under the mountain itself, it leveled out, the hall in front of her widening. Wooden doors lined the walls, each of them locked, and Ember had no desire to try to see what was on the other side.

At the end of the hall, there was a single wooden door, the same runes carved in it as the door in the hallway above her. She winced as she squeezed her hand, the raw feeling of magic still pulsing through her skin. Before she had a chance to reach out and touch it, the wisp began hovering around the handle again, and the lock effortlessly popped open. Ember narrowed her eyes, at no one in particular.

"Are you telling me you could do that the entire time?"

She could've sworn it laughed.

Ember wandered down the damp hall, jumping when she heard a squeak from behind her. She wandered down another set of steps, convinced that this was a pointless endeavor and was just about to turn around and head back home when she heard the song.

The song that had haunted her dreams for months, that had lived in her head and rattled her brain, was coming from the end of the hall.

*TRÍ STOIRME agus farraige caillimid cé muid féin,*
*Ach amháin le fáil ag réalta tar éis titim.*
*Snámh i dtreo an chladaigh i bhfad i gcéin,*
*óir níl aon áit caillte againn níos mó.*


*TRÍ FEAR tar eis fás agus foraoisí cosc,*
*Sin an ait a bhfaighidh tú na daoine óga, goidte agus i bhfolach.*
*Thar na gcnoc is na gcloch liath,*
*Sin an ait a rachaidh sibh go léir isteach sa chraic*


EMBER CREPT to the door the ethereal voice was coming from and leaned against it to listen, laying her ear beside the small window carved in the middle of the wood. The voice sounded ancient and weathered, like someone was sucking the life right from her lungs. Her breath caught in her throat, choking back a sob. Something about the song felt like it was wrong to hear, like she was interfering with some private moment—a

311

moment between this woman and the gods. The singing stopped, and Ember held her breath.

"I didn't know if you would come," the voice said from behind the door. "I was hopeful, but one can never be certain."

Ember felt her entire body turn cold. "Is this yours?" she asked, pointing to the blue wisp floating beside her, like it was a puppy she had found on the side of the road.

"It is as much yours as it is mine," the woman replied, her voice sounding hoarse.

Ember furrowed her brow, choosing to ignore the cryptic message. "Do you know what they are?"

"I do," the woman replied, and Ember could almost hear the smile on her lips. Was she going to make her beg?

Ember sighed, this suddenly felt like a huge waste of time.

"Some people call them Will-o'-the-Wisps," she continued. "They're traces of ancient magic—a magic that hasn't thrived in this world in thousands of years."

Ember felt her breath catch in her chest as she stared at the hovering light floating by the door.

"You can control it—harness it."

"I can't," Ember muttered. "You have me confused with someone else."

"You wouldn't have gotten through that locked door if you couldn't," the woman replied. "Controlling it takes practice, but that just comes with time."

Ember stared at her hand, flexing it a few times.

"Do you have a name?" Ember asked, trying to keep the woman talking. Something wouldn't let her walk away.

"I've had many names," she replied, "many stories told about me around campfires under the stars, but you can call me Aesira."

"Well, Aesira," Ember replied, "it's nice to meet you. My name is—"

"Ember Lothbrok," Aesira replied. "I know. I've known your name for almost as long as I've known mine."

Ember should've been surprised, should've turned around and ran out the door, but she didn't. She stood there, hand still on the door as she peered inside at the strange woman. There was something familiar about her, about the way she spoke, the cadence of her voice, something both comforting and unsettling.

"Everyone seems to know my name," Ember sighed. It was something she still wasn't quite used to.

"There's a reason for that," Aesira replied, "a reason you're different."

"Yes, yes," Ember replied, waving her hand, "the prophecy, the castle, the dark king for a grandfather. I know about it all."

"Knowing and understanding are two vastly different things," Aesira laughed.

"How long have you been down here?" Ember asked, barely above a whisper, ignoring the not-answers the strange woman kept giving her.

"Long enough that I stopped counting," the woman replied.

Ember peeked through the opening carved into the door. The cell was dark, the floor, ceiling, and walls all made of stone. The woman was in the far-left corner, curled into herself, long hair flowing wild past her shoulders. The only light in the cell was the moonlight dancing across the onyx stone, and even that barely lit a sliver of the floor.

"And you were the one calling me? Singing to me?" Ember asked.

"I was," Aesira replied. "There are spells around my cell, around the dungeon that keeps my song out. Seems to be bothersome to the guards, but I knew it would find you eventually."

"Why did you bring me here," Ember asked, brow furrowed.

"My magical core has been severely depleted," Aesira said. "I can't control the wisps without it, can't do anything without it, and someone must know they're here. Someone has to save them."

Ember scrunched her brow. "Who?"

Before Aesira could reply, Ember heard a sniffle, and then a cry, and then a voice in the dark further down the hall.

"Ember?"

Ember's heart stopped as the voice whispered her name. She ran down the hall, blinking her eyes to force them to adjust to the darkness. She stopped in front of a cell door, gripping the rungs as she peered inside. Little fingers wrapped around hers, dirty and cold.

Ember's bottom lip trembled, her chest shaking as she gripped the tiny hand. "Maeve?"

# CHAPTER 31

# A LAMB FOR SLAUGHTER

"**M**aeve?" Ember whispered hoarsely again, tears streaming down her face. The light from the wisp lit Maeve's blue eyes, rimmed red and puffy, and Ember felt her heart leap into her throat.

"You found me," Maeve whispered, bottom lip trembling. "I didn't think anyone would ever find me."

"Of course I did," Ember whispered back, still gripping the little girl's hand. "Are you ok?"

That was a stupid question, the answer evident by the purple and green on her wrists and neck and her almost translucent skin, like she hadn't seen the sun in months.

Ember swallowed dryly. "I will get you out of here and get you home," she said—no, promised.

Maeve gave her a small nod and pointed behind her, then over Ember's shoulder to the cell across the hall. "I can't leave without them," Maeve said, standing taller than Ember remembered she could.

"Maevie, I'll come back for them," Ember replied, "but my only concern right now is you." Ember didn't even know how she would get Maeve home if she *could* break her out of the dungeon, let alone dozens of other children—Vala and Fae alike.

"I know," Maeve smiled, "but they're counting on me, and I won't leave them. I can't."

Ember took a shaky breath—her sense of duty was admirable, something Ember respected and envied. This wasn't the little seven-year-old that was snatched from her bedroom in the dead of night. This was a girl who had chosen to wield her fear like a knife, defending those who couldn't defend themselves.

"Okay, well," she thought out loud, "I'll just get you all out and then we can…"

But she didn't get the chance to finish her thought. Laughter—men's laughter—echoed down the opposite end of the hall. Guards.

Ember's eyes widened as she looked back at Maeve. "I'll be back for you," she whispered, "all of you."

Maeve gave her a silent nod, and Ember tore off down the hall, past Aesira's cell, and up the stone steps. She slipped out the wooden door, hearing it close behind her with a soft click, and snuck through the rest of the palace, out the kitchen door, and into the cold night. She didn't even remember making her way back to the chateau. She just ran as fast as her tired legs would carry her. She burst through the front gate, not bothering to scale the wall back up to her room, and rushed through the front door, probably waking everyone in the large home.

She ran through the halls, throwing doors open and slipping across the marble floor, until she came to the small den in one of the back hallways. She flung the door open, damn near ripping it off its hinges, and barreled into the room where her mother was sitting in front of the fire reading.

Aoife furrowed her brow, closing her book slowly and setting it on the couch beside her. "Ember, what on earth," was all she said.

Despite the chill in the February air, Ember was drenched in sweat. She felt the dirt on her neck, the way it scratched against her skin as she tried to rub it off her face. She probably looked crazy.

She *felt* crazy.

"Mum, you can't trust him," she pleaded, desperately sucking air into her lungs as she closed the door quickly behind her. She rounded the couch to sit beside Aoife. "All of the children that have gone missing this year around the island, they're all here."

"How do you know?" her mother asked, brow still knitted.

"I saw them," she replied. "I snuck back into the castle, and I know I shouldn't have, Mum, but I saw the children all locked up in cells, so many of them chained to the walls with bruises and cuts all over them." Her breath caught as she thought about Maeve and how the life looked like it had drained from those beautiful blue eyes. "Mum, he's been kidnapping them, and he's keeping them locked in the dungeons. We have to help them." She was breathing so hard she thought she might pass out.

Aoife stood up from the couch, walking to the door and quietly locking it. "You weren't supposed to find out like this," she said, as she shook her head, rubbing the bridge of her nose. "I was going to talk to you before the ball, try and explain—"

"Explain?" Ember cut her off. "Mum, what are you talking about?"

Aoife sat back down beside Ember, taking her hand in her own. "Your granda' is sick," she began.

Ember huffed. What did that have to do with anything?

"His magical core is weakened. It's draining slowly, and it has been for years—longer than you've been alive. There are no known standard cures. The healers have tried everything. *We've* tried everything."

317

Ember stared at her mother, and a scared little girl stared back—a scared daughter.

"He found a cure," she continued, "several years back, but it's tricky. There are so many moving parts, so many steps that it's taken a while to acquire what we need."

*We.*

"That's why he wanted the book," Ember filled in the blanks, "and why he needed me to open it. There was something in it he needed."

"He opened the book," she replied.

Ember blinked. "But Rowan said he needed me." The more her mother told her, the more confused she was by the events of the last year.

"He did need you, Mo Stór." Aoife smiled. "Not to open it, but for what was inside."

Ember bit her lip, suddenly feeling very hot, like the fire across the room was licking at the tips of her fingers, singing her hair and nose.

"There is a spell potion in the book," she continued. "It is very complicated with many ingredients that are almost impossible to find, but it would heal his magical core completely."

"What does that have to do with me," Ember asked.

"The key ingredient, the one he has been searching for for years, is Wildling blood."

Ember froze—she couldn't have heard that correctly. "And the children in the dungeon? They're all Wildlings?"

"Oh, no," Aoife almost laughed, "not the ones who have been tested thus far anyway. He's been testing their blood for the last year to see if there were any in hiding. Underaged Vala have notoriously strong magic, it would be easier to detect in a young one. We started with the Fae children, to see if we could get by with it, but it was unsuccessful. That's when we started testing on Vala."

"And then you found me," Ember said. It wasn't a question. Something told her the timing wasn't coincidental.

"You were meant to be his savior the day I found out what you were."

*What...*

Something about the way Aoife looked at her made her sick to her stomach—like she was an animal she had been hunting all season and finally had in her crosshairs.

"That's why we left," Ember whispered, puzzled pieces shifting together. "That's why we left the island, to keep me away from him."

Aoife all but rolled her eyes, nostrils flaring. "Your father didn't agree with my decision to give you to your granda', but I knew you were his only chance. I made a plan when you were six to bring you home, but he found out."

Arguments in the dead of night flitted through her mind —a screaming match against the night sky while waves churned underneath her.

*"This will keep you safe."*

Her father's words rattled around in her head as she twirled the ring on her right hand. Had he put some sort of protection spell on it? Could that have been what Cormac was talking about? A spell to hide her in plain sight, away from her mother?

"You took me on the boat," she whispered. "We were on that boat because of you." Ember felt like the breath had been knocked out her lungs, and she was suddenly filled with a fire in her chest that threatened to consume her entirely.

"The sky was clear that night," Aoife replied, shaking her head. "There were no storms on any radars. It shouldn't have happened like that."

Ember's bottom lip trembled. "You killed him." She felt something in her break, shattering into a million pieces.

Aoife looked like she had been smacked. "I might be a villain," she hissed, "but I am not a monster."

"My entire childhood was ripped away from me because of *you*." Ember suddenly couldn't breathe, her lungs felt like they were slowly filling with water.

"What happened to you made you stronger." Aoife gave her a small, comforting smile that turned Ember's stomach.

"I was a child," Ember whispered, as she took a step back. "I didn't need to be strong, I needed to be safe."

Aoife tried to say something, to argue her point, but Ember cut her off.

Ember shook her head. "So, your plan was to just hand me over? To leave me locked up in a castle and have my core drained? To what end?"

Aoife sighed as she looked at the ceiling. "Our family was promised this island thousands of years ago. It is our birthright. We all must make sacrifices for the greater good."

"And I was the lamb you chose to sacrifice?"

"I wish it could be different," Aoife replied. "We tried so hard to find another Wildling with enough power for what we needed, but you are his last hope. When your brother came along," she continued, "I thought he would solve our problems," she replied, "but he didn't have the same... *mutation* that you did. He couldn't help your granda' the way he needed."

*Mutation.*

Ember suddenly felt sick. This was what her mother thought of her—this is who she was to her, just a means to an end. She furrowed her brow. "Is that why you never bothered to learn sign language?"

"I had other things to worry about," Aoife replied with a wave of her hand. "He was able to communicate with Gaelen, and she could tell me anything important. That's all that mattered."

"And if I say no?" she asked, crossing her arm defiantly over her chest, hoping she looked stronger than she felt.

"The spell requires cooperation—the blood must be given

willingly," Aoife replied looking uneasy. "But I will say, they have ways of *making* you become willing. It would be easier if you just said yes. Don't make this harder than it has to be."

Ember suddenly felt like an animal caught in a snare—the harder she fought, the more stuck she seemed to become.

"What happens to me after?" she whispered.

"Your magical core will be weakened for a while. It's not a one-time thing. It will take a while to have the amount we need, at the potency we need it." Aoife didn't look that least bit sorry, just matter of fact.

Ember knew what that meant, she didn't have to say it. Her magical core was her life blood—without it she would…

No.

"Will I die?" Ember asked quietly, suddenly feeling very afraid.

"Of course not, love," Aoife chided. "If you die, we can't keep him alive now, can we?"

"And the children in the dungeon?" she asked. "If I say yes, what happens to them?" Maeve's face lit up every corner of her mind.

"They will become servants," Aoife said softly, like she didn't have her own young child asleep in the room above her. "Either, in the castle or to noble men and women in town. The ones who are too old to be bent will be disposed of in whatever measure your granda' sees fit. They can't be sent home, as no one can know this place exists—it is our only upper hand."

"Upper hand?" Ember scoffed. "You act like we're on the brink of war."

"In some ways, we are," Aoife replied.

Ember swallowed dryly. "And after he's healed?" she asked, fear gripping her lungs, making it harder and harder for her to breathe. "What happens when he's back to normal?"

"Those are plans we can discuss later," Aoife coddled her,

like a child she was trying to console, "but after his time on the throne is over, you are the heir. This island will be yours."

*I am destined for darkness.*

"Not you?" Ember narrowed her eyes.

"I was never meant to rule. I abdicated," Aoife replied, shaking her head. Something like regret shadowed her face, like maybe that wasn't a decision she made willingly. "I much prefer to work behind the scenes."

Ember's chest shook. She had to get out of there, out of that room and away from the woman in front of her—the woman who felt more like a stranger now than she ever did before. She stalked toward the door of the study, gripping the handle as she struggled to breath. She turned back around, tears streaking down her face.

"Is that the reason you finally came for me?" she whispered, chest shaking.

Aoife's face was a mask—unreadable. "I love you so much, Mo Stór," she replied, "but he is the future of the island. This is our only hope."

It wasn't an answer, but suddenly, Ember wasn't sure if she really wanted to know.

She stormed out the door, running as fast as she could up the steps to her room. She slammed the door behind her and cried—truly cried, unable to fully grasp what was going on. And then something flickered through her mind, a small piece of their conversation.

*We tried so hard to find another Wildling with enough power for what we needed, but you are his last hope.*

*Another* Wildling.

That meant she wasn't the only one.

EMBER DIDN'T LEAVE her room the next day—didn't have any desire to be in the same room as her mother—and by the time the sun was beginning to set outside her bedroom window, she was starving. She read through her father's journal, anything to feel close to him again, and waited for the hours to creep slowly by. A few hours later, Theo tiptoed into the bedroom and laid a sandwich on the desk by one of her windows. She devoured it so quickly, she almost thought she had imagined it. Theo laughed as she ate and laid on the floor with a book and a notebook where he was meticulously practicing his writing. He looked up at her and wrinkled his nose in a grin as she licked the crumbs off the plate.

"Thank you so much." Ember grinned, forgetting to sign. "I was famished."

Theo shrugged his shoulders and smiled, and Ember furrowed her brow.

"Do you know what I said?"

Theo's eyes widened, panicking. He sat straight up, like he was ready to bolt, and then Ember laughed.

"You can read lips, can't you?" She grinned.

Theo nodded sheepishly, crimson staining his cheeks.

*What a cheeky little boy.*

"Why didn't you say anything?" Ember asked.

Theo shrugged as he bit his lip. *"No one ever bothered to learn for me,"* he signed, and Ember frowned.

No one had ever bothered to learn sign language. Gaelen is the one who taught him, and their mother had certainly never put in much effort. He had never been important enough for anyone—never felt important enough for anyone. Ember's heart sank as she climbed off her bed and onto the floor, wrapping him in a hug. She lifted his chin and sat back.

*"I will always bother,"* she promised.

She didn't know what the future had in store for her— didn't know how they were going to escape this nightmare, but she would never regret any of it if she could save him too.

# CHAPTER 32

# AN OMINOUS ROUND OF MIMOSAS AND TINY FINGER SANDWICHES

Theo slept soundly beside her as her lamp lit up the pages of her father's journal. She ran her fingers along the aged paper, tracing the places his pen had been, desperately trying to feel him there, to feel him anywhere. She had spent six years with him, and there were so many things she needed to ask him, so many questions that would likely never be answered—not fully anyway.

"I've missed you more than I knew you," she mumbled, sighing as she flipped the page. She had read this journal cover to cover, had seen every word and picture and indentation from his pen. Her brow furrowed as she carefully peeled two pages apart that seemed to have been stuck together for years, pages she had never noticed before.

There was a list on the left page, a list of names that seemed vaguely familiar. She racked her brain for several minutes, reading them over and over, and then it clicked.

They were shop names from Torsvik, and the people had to be people in the town. But why were they in his journal? Why was that relevant? A drawing of a crow was scratched next to them with a circle around it. It wasn't detailed, not heavily illustrated with any sort of shading, more like an ancient insignia. Her eyes traveled to the next page, and she shot up in bed, eyes wide and jaw slack.

It was a drawing of Eldfjall.

But not just a drawing—it was a rough floor plan. Secret passages and hidden rooms, things only someone very intimate with the inner workings of the palace could know about. There was a detailed plan of the dungeon she had been in just a few nights prior, the locked door and spiral stairs leading to the cells, the hall where Aesira and the kids were locked up, and then it continued, down several more sets of stairs to a…

But there was nothing. Whoever drew this plan, or gave it to her father, either didn't want anyone to know what was past those stairs or never got that far. A chill ran down her spine. She had to find out what this meant.

She looked down at Theo, sleeping soundly, and all she could think about was how both he and Maeve deserve the childhood she never had. They deserved peace and a family that loved them to come find them when they were lost or to learn sign language for them. She bit her lip as she swallowed the lump steadily building in her throat.

*The blood of the covenant is thicker than the water of the womb.*

She felt a fire ignite deep inside her—just a flicker. But she knew if she let it, it would burn this entire city to the ground.

EMBER WANDERED through town with Theo in tow as the little boy desperately searched for an ice cream shop. She had found him rummaging through the kitchen in the chateau looking for something sweet and then promptly begged Ember to take him into town for ice cream. Ember was happy to be out of the house, to stop dodging her mother and looking over her shoulder every moment for a new threat. She stuffed her father's journal into a bag she found in the closet—her bag from the Kitts conveniently left at the manor in Sigurvik—and was content to read through the entries while Theo finished his treat.

Theo got a chocolate cone with sprinkles and quickly ran off to climb on a rickety looking ledge on the other side of the street. Ember laughed—the first time she had laughed in days—and breathed in the fresh air that whipped around her. They walked down the street further, peering into windows and listening to conversations, when Ember noticed they were in front of Monkshood & Wolfsbane, the apothecary she had visited her first time in the city. She lingered at the door, her eye catching something carved into the wooden frame. She squinted, studying it, and then her jaw fell open.

She dug through the bag at her side and pulled her father's journal out, hastily flipping it to the page she had been on the night before. She read through the list of names, Monkshood & Wolfsbane being one of them, as well as Catriona Fitz, the owner of the shop. Her heartbeat quickened as she looked at the picture of the crow next to it, then back to the doorframe, the same roughly drawn bird scratched into the wood, something you wouldn't even notice unless you were looking.

Theo walked over to her, giving her a perplexed look as he tilted his head. She nodded toward the door.

*Do you want to go in?*

An unspoken question. Theo nodded with a grin, chocolate covering his freckled face. They walked through the door, a little bell jingling as they entered, and Ember didn't have to look long for Catriona. She was on a stool, very carefully placing filled vials in a cabinet behind the counter. She smiled with a wave as the two walked in, and Ember headed to the counter as Theo went to explore a vaguely dangerous looking plant by the window.

"Welcome back, Ember." Catriona smiled. "Anything I can help you with today?"

Ember bit her lip. "I'm not sure," she replied, gripping the journal in her hand a little tighter. She didn't have any way of knowing what these names meant—why her father had a list scratched in the back of his journal. They could be people he was watching, people he didn't trust—people who were dangerous. She sucked in a breath to steady herself. Trusting her gut was the only thing she had right now.

"My father had this journal," she continued, voice low, "and a bunch of names were written in it, along with some shops I've noticed around town."

Catriona furrowed her brow as Ember fidgeted.

"I saw this on your door and wondered if you knew what it meant?" She laid the open journal on the counter, and Catriona's face paled when her eyes met the worn page, all the color seeming to drain from her flushed skin. Ember watched as her throat bobbed, quickly looking toward the door and windows and back down to the book.

"Who knows you have this?" she whispered, snapping it closed so fast that Ember thought she might snatch it away.

"No one," Ember replied, as she shook her head. "My dad left it to me."

"I don't know anything about this," Catriona said, as she shook her head, pushing it across the counter toward Ember.

She furrowed her brow, glancing up at the woman. "Are you sure?" she asked. "It seems like you know—"

"I don't," Catriona hissed, making Ember jump. "I think it's time you leave. I have to close up shop early this afternoon."

Ember didn't believe her, even for a moment, but she grabbed Theo and headed for the door, nonetheless. Catriona didn't say another word as she ushered them through the door and quickly closed it behind them. Ember heard the soft click of the lock engaging and sighed as they walked onto the street.

Ember stuffed the journal back in her bag as she went.

She didn't notice the body in front of her until she ran right into it.

"I-I'm so sorry!" Ember stammered. "I didn't see you—" She stopped short as she saw the Warden in front of her, staring at her like she had spit directly in his face. She stiffened under his gaze as she cut her eyes at him. "Actually, never mind."

"Your grandfather sent me to pick you up. You've been summoned to brunch," Collum sneered, like those words were actually painful, and Ember burst out laughing. His mouth didn't so much as twitch.

"Ah, yes, brunch at the castle," she laughed. "That's exactly what I want—an ominous round of mimosas and uncomfortably small finger sandwiches." She laughed some more, wiping away the tears pooling on her lower lash as she took a breath. "Oh, wait, you're serious?" she asked.

Collum nodded, and Ember rolled her eyes.

"Absolutely not," she replied, shoving past him as she made to guide Theo back toward the chateau.

Collum grabbed her wrist, so tight she almost winced. "It wasn't a request, Princess," he hissed. He bared his yellow teeth at her, and Ember stumbled as he moved her out of the way. He made to grab Theo, knocking the ice cream cone out of his hand and onto the cobblestone at his feet. Theo's face paled, his bottom lip trembling as he looked over at her.

Ember was annoyed by Collum's presence, but Theo was scared. She saw red as she stepped between the two, throwing Collum's hand off Theo's shoulder and jamming her finger in his chest.

"Do *not* touch him," she hissed, ire boiling in her veins. She grabbed Theo's hand, squeezing it tight, and followed Collum to the end of the street, a safe point to Echo that wouldn't draw much attention. He grabbed her by the bicep and whisked them away through a cloud of stars. She barely had time to blink, and then they were in the courtyard in front of the castle.

Ember didn't let go of Theo's hand as they walked through the doors.

Brunch was set up in a large dining room, ceilings arched and a long table in the middle. Floor to ceiling windows and two large doors sat on the far end of the room, leading out to what Ember assumed was the gardens. The table was filled with a plethora of different kinds of foods—bacon and sausage, hollandaise eggs on top of English muffins, fruit that Ember didn't even recognize, and of course, tiny finger sandwiches.

Ember sat beside Theo, keeping her eyes anywhere other than the burly man sitting at the end of the table. The thought of eating in the same room as Helvig made her lose her appetite. The door opened and closed, and Ember almost stood up and left as her mother walked in the room, taking a seat in the chair opposite her. Theo grabbed her hand under the table, squeezing it twice, and gave her a small smile—an unspoken promise.

*I'm here.*

"How are you doing, Mo Stór?" Aoife asked, as she placed the napkin in her lap.

Ember stiffened at the pet name. She had no right to call her that, not anymore. She ignored the question, focusing instead on piling her plate full of all the food it would hold. If she kept her mouth full, she wouldn't have to talk. In that moment, Rowan walked into the room and sat on the other side of her. Ember rolled her eyes—was this an ambush?

"Your mother tells me she had a talk with you," Helvig

said from the end of the table—the *head* of the table. "I must say, I'm very pleased that we can all stop walking on eggshells now, no more secrets."

Ember bristled, nostrils flaring. "Oh, yes," she breathed, plastering on a smile that was sickly sweet. "I'm sure keeping secrets was so hard on you all." She laid a hand over her heart and gave them a sympathetic smile. "My sincerest apologies, truly."

Rowan cleared her throat next to her—a warning.

Ember ignored it. She was itching for a fight, all of the sorrow and grief had settled in her core, slowly morphing into fire, burning through her veins and into her fingertips. She felt her magic pulse, heat building against her palms as she gripped the armrest of the chair.

"It's no matter," Helvig replied, as he brushed her off, like her apology had been sincere, "as long as everything is settled."

"Settled?" Ember bristled. "My mother has spent my entire life lying to me, and you think a simple conversation will 'settle' it?"

Helvig cocked a brow, a smile playing at the corner of his mouth, like he was enjoying this—like he was *entertained.*

"Enough, Ember," Aoife shot her a warning glance. "Drink your juice."

Ember barked a laugh, throwing her head back as she grabbed the glass. "Drink the juice?" she asked. "How can I even trust that this is actually juice, hm? Perhaps it's poisoned, and your grand plan is to get rid of me in the middle of brunch." She slammed the glass on the table, orange juice sloshing across the wood. She stood, causing Collum to stiffen, hand against the dagger that sat strapped to his belt. Ember scoffed—some Vala he was, doesn't even trust his own magic enough to not carry a weapon.

Rowan kicked her under the table, but she chose to ignore it.

"Maybe we should go for a walk," Rowan whispered, grabbing her wrist, "to clear your head."

Ember twisted it out of her grasp and slammed her fist on the table.

"No one is trying to poison you, Ember," Aoife replied, a warning dripping in the words. "Sit down."

"Perhaps we should have the Jarl try it first." Ember grinned. "Just to be sure."

"That will be quite enough of that," Aoife hissed— another warning.

Ember grinned, but that grin faltered as Helvig barked a laugh. "Now, now, Aoife," he raised a hand in the air, "it's to be expected that she would be upset, even hurt. I won't hold any baseless accusations against her." He talked about her like she wasn't there—like her temper tantrum hadn't affected him in the slightest. He turned his attention beside her, to Theo, and smiled. "Perhaps we should take young Theo on a tour of the castle." He smiled. "After all, it will be his home soon." His teeth sparkled against the midday sun beating through the windows, and Ember saw red.

"Over my dead bod—" she started to shout, but Rowan quickly stood up beside her, grabbing her arm and smiling at Helvig.

"That is a *lovely* idea," she cooed. "I'll do the honors. Shall we start with the garden?" She dragged Ember away from the table, and Theo followed without missing a beat. Ember stumbled as Rowan pushed her through the glass doors, her sweet smile never faltering as she pulled them into the large garden. A maze of tall hedges sat in the middle; a large fountain lined with benches right in front of it. Rowan gestured toward the maze and walked Ember and Theo into it.

"Let me go!" Ember hissed, yanking her arm free and rubbing the spot Rowan's nail had dug into her skin. "What the hell are you doing?"

"What am *I* doing?" Rowan whispered loudly, checking over her shoulder. "What are *you* doing?"

"Apparently, I'm going for a walk," Ember gestured to the hedges around her, "with my own little watchdog." She was not pulling any punches, and she didn't care who they landed on.

"If I didn't get you out of there," Rowan replied, "Collum was going to hang you from the chandelier by your toes."

Ember rolled her eyes. "I don't need you watching out for me."

"Well, apparently, you do, Em," Rowan replied, as she crossed her arms,

Ember stiffened. "Don't call me that."

"The more you push back, the worse it's going to be," Rowan replied. "They do not tolerate rebellion of any sort. They'll have you locked in that dungeon too before they let you fight."

"The dungeon?" Ember asked, furrowing her brow. "What do you know about the dungeon?"

"More than you think."

"So, what do you want me to do then?" Ember asked, anger rumbling deep in her chest. "Just give up? Give them what they want and forget about Maeve or Theo or all of those kids locked up under our feet?"

"Of course that's not what I want," Rowan replied, as she rolled her eyes. "I'm saying you have to be discreet. If we're going to save them, Helvig and Collum and everyone else have to believe you're on board with the idea—excited about it even. It will be much easier to make plans without nosy lieutenants hovering over your shoulder. If we want to win, you must make them think you've accepted your fate. You have to make them believe you've resigned yourself to lose."

This wasn't the girl she had fought in the crumbling building at the foot of the mountains. This wasn't the hollow faced girl she had first seen in the foyer months ago. No, she was different. There was a new light in her eyes—something had shifted.

"He has other plans," she replied. "He doesn't just want to heal his magical core, not anymore. He wants control." She sighed. "Control over *everything*."

"I'm going to need you to be less vague," Ember replied. "I don't have all day." She shifted her weight—the truth was she would rather be out there with Rowan than inside with everyone else.

"He believes the island is his birthright—that it was promised to his family, specifically by the gods when they settled the island."

Ember remembered her mom saying something about that, but what did that have to do with her?

"He found a page in the Book of Shadows that would heal him, that much is true," Rowan continued, "but he also found another page—not a spell so much as an old legend—instructions of sorts."

"The prophecy," Ember mumbled. She didn't know how she knew; she just did.

Rowan nodded. "He isn't content to just be back to full power anymore. He wants *all* the power, and he needs you to get it."

"What do you mean by *all*?" Ember narrowed her eyes.

"All as in... more than the Vala and Merrow and Fae have combined. A power that would make him immortal."

*Like a god.*

Ember felt a chill run down her spine. "What good am I to him?" she asked, though she wasn't sure she wanted to know the answer.

"I don't know," Rowan replied. "I just know the Wildling he has now doesn't have the power he needs. He's gotten greedy and desperate—and desperate men with power are dangerous."

Ember's throat tightened. That woman in the dungeon—was she the other Wildling?

"Why are you telling me this?" Ember asked. "Why are you suddenly so keen on helping me? You didn't seem to care what happened to me last year."

Rowan averted her eyes. "I regret every decision I made leading up to the day in the ballroom," she whispered, "but I do not, for even a moment, regret becoming your friend."

"Well," Ember replied, "that makes one of us." She tried not to wince as she saw the way Rowan's face fell. The girl was trying, but could she really blame Ember for not trusting her?

"A few months ago, Collum started receiving letters from someone. He was giving them inside information, but something spooked him." Ember held her breath as she listened. "He asked me to take the information he had gathered to the Jarl, but I read them instead. He was going to put so many people's lives in danger, and I couldn't let that happen."

"Who were the letters from?" Ember asked, interest suddenly piqued.

"I don't know," Rowan replied, as she shook her head. "It was all anonymous. I don't even know if they're on the island. But what I do know is that it was that moment I decided to stop being Helvig's puppet. I took over the letters, started writing back to them and feeding them information. I want to help."

Ember wasn't sure if she trusted her—wasn't sure if she would ever trust her again. Her throat tightened as she took a shaky breath. "So, that's all it took?" she asked, as she flexed her hand by her side. "A few measly letters from an anonymous source and the possibility of strangers getting hurt? *That's* what changed your mind? Not the kidnapping of dozens of innocent children?"

"I didn't know he was kidnapping anyone," Rowan bit back. "I'm not the monster you've made me out in your head to be, Ember."

"You tried to *kill me*, Rowan." Ember felt the lick of flames against her palms, magic crackling at her fingertips. "You could've killed Killian or Fen. So, you'll have to forgive me for not giving a damn that you want to do the 'right thing' now."

"I wasn't trying to kill anyone," Rowan replied. "I was trying to survive. By the time I realized what he was, it was too late. I was in too deep, and I had to protect my mum."

Ember bit the inside of her cheek. "You could've told someone," She whispered, resenting the emotion that bobbed in her throat. "Eira or Otto or Professor Bjorn." She swallowed as she silently cursed the tears threatening to spill over. "You could've told me. We could've figured it out together."

"I didn't know who I could trust. I didn't have anyone." Rowan shook her head. "My mum lost herself in grief, my brother and dad were gone. I was alone, and Helvig was there."

"You were never alone, Rowan."

"My dad *died*," Rowan began. "My dad died, and I—"

"So did mine," Ember bit back, "but I didn't decide to grieve him by hurting everyone who loved me. You don't get to play the 'dead dad' card, Rowan, not now, not with me." She could feel the magic rolling under her skin as Rowan hung her head. "We were there," she continued. "We were there, and you were just too blinded by power to see the family you still had. We could've helped you." Her chest ached, the wound she had so carefully stitched close now ripped open again, as raw as the day she received it.

"I can see that now," Rowan nodded, cheeks flushed, "and I'm trying to make amends. I'm trying to fix the damage I caused."

"Some damage can't be undone," Ember replied. She wanted to hurt her, wanted her to feel just an ounce of what she had felt in that ballroom.

"How many times do I have to apologize?"

"I'll let you know." Ember shrugged. She had no intention of forgiving the girl or forgetting all the pain she had caused.

"I'm not asking you to forgive me," Rowan whispered. "I just want to help. I want to make things right."

Theo grabbed Ember's hand and looked up at her, then over to Rowan, tilting his head. She seemed to squirm under the weight of Theo's stare until he looked back up at Ember.

*"Second chance,"* was all he signed before he turned back to Rowan and smiled, and Ember gave him a reluctant nod. She could try—that's the best she could offer at this point.

*"Thank you,"* Rowan signed in reply, and Ember's jaw hung slack.

"You know sign language?"

Rowan nodded her head, a far off look in her eyes. "My brother was deaf. I learned sign language before I could read." She smiled, but it didn't quite reach her eyes, the memory, no doubt, tainted by the grief that surrounded her.

Theo squeezed Ember's hand.

*I'm here.*

"So, if we do this together," Ember replied, steeling herself against the weight of the moment between them, "and that is a *big* if, where do we start? While we try to figure out how to free the children, what are we supposed to do?"

Rowan let out a sigh as she bit her lip. "We pretend that they've won."

# CHAPTER 33
# ONE SHOT

**K**illian pulled his shirt over his head, keeping his eyes from lingering on the bruise blooming on his collar and across his ribs. The cuts from the daggers were healing nicely, but the one on his right pectoral was deep. It would likely scar.

*What's one more?*

Working with his uncle—in any capacity—was not for the faint of heart. He liked to believe he could handle more than most. He had a high threshold for pain, and he healed quickly, but what his uncle was making him do, the people he was pitting him against, he sometimes wondered if it was more than he could handle.

He shook the thought away as he pulled on a coat, sticking the small earring box in his pocket. It was for Ember, all of it. Every cut and bruise, every terrifying job and near-death experience, it was all for her. He would reach his bare hands into a live fire and grab hot coals to swallow them if she needed him to.

Killian strolled out of his house to the Echopoint by the gate, and in another heartbeat, he was walking up the drive to Fen's front door. He let himself in, kicking his shoes off by the door. Osiris was in the den, a map spread across the coffee table as he jotted something in a notebook. He still hadn't gone back to Iceland, and thankfully, he hadn't said anything to Fen about his little trip with Ember. He didn't so much as glance at Killian as he walked through the foyer. Eira popped her head out of the kitchen, likely hearing the door open, and smiled.

"Hello, love," she said sweetly, the smile not quite reaching her eyes, "staying for dinner?"

"Yes, ma'am," Killian replied, walking across the room to give her a hug. His own mother had never been very affectionate, Magnus Vargr wouldn't allow it. He believed that emotion was weakness, and weakness was a cardinal sin in the Vargr household. His heart ached when he allowed himself to think about the childhood he could've had if he had a mum like Eira.

"Fen is in his room, hasn't left all day," she said, as she pointed toward the stairs, and then she slipped back into the kitchen, busying herself with anything to keep her mind off her current reality. Killian tapped his fingers against his thigh —Maeve was still missing, and it was eating the entire family alive.

Killian climbed the stairs to the second floor, each step feeling heavy and forced. He hadn't slept much in weeks, and the way his uncle was working him in his wolf form was not doing good things for his human muscles. Every strained muscle, every broken bone reset, every puncture wound, it all stuck around when it turned human again, and it was wearing on him.

Fen's door was closed, and all he heard on the other side was the furious clicking of his keyboard. Killian didn't bother to knock as he walked in, quickly closing the door behind him.

"Figure it out yet?" he asked Fen, as he flopped on the bed, crossing his legs at his ankles as he put his hands behind his head. Fen was going back and forth between his phone and his computer and barely seemed to register that Killian had even walked in.

"Oi!" Killian called, and Fen startled, turning around and wiping the sweat off his brow.

"Did you bring up a snack?" Fen asked, as he ran his fingers through his hair, mussing it further.

"A snack?" Killian almost laughed. "It's barely half past twelve. Have you not had lunch?"

Fen rolled his eyes. "Of course I ate lunch, but that was an hour ago." He pointed at the computer behind him. "I need brain food."

Killian barked a laugh. "That would actually require a brain to feed." He barely dodged a jinx fired at him—Fen's aim really needed work.

"I think I've just about got it figured out." Fen cleaned his glasses on his shirt and pushed them back up the bridge of his nose. "I just can't get the spell quite right. It won't connect properly. Did you bring the earring?"

Killian nodded, fishing the box out of his pocket, and tossing it to his friend. Most Vala boys had at least one ear pierced by the time they were ten, so he snagged one that Leif had left lying around. Killian didn't wear one anymore, but he could put an earring on in a pinch if he needed to. Fen caught the box, quickly pulling out the small piece of jewelry, and laid it on the table by his phone.

"How did you do this on your own anyway?" Fen asked, as he inspected the earring. It was like the ones he had given Ember, charmed to play music and books that he downloaded on his phone, a spell connecting them. Killian shrugged his shoulders as he grinned.

"I'll carry that secret to my grave," he replied. Fen narrowed his eyes at his friend but ultimately ignored him. Killian stared at the ceiling for a long time while Fen mumbled incantations under his breath, pressing buttons repeatedly on his phone. He tried not to think about her if he didn't have to, tried not to imagine what she was going through in that hidden city—how scared she must be.

No, if he knew anything about Ember, she had surpassed scared a long time ago. He would bet all his inheritance that she was seething mad now, mowing down anyone who stood in her way. Gods help the man who chose to step in front of the meteor that was Ember Lothbrok. She would turn them to dust without thinking.

He tried not to think about her, but he couldn't help it when he was here. She had only lived in this home—been on this island—for a little over a year, but it somehow felt like a lifetime. He half expected to see her curled up in the library, a book in hand and Maia at her feet as the sky burned ruby out the window, warming her hair and skin as it shown in through the room. He hated himself for checking every time he walked up the stairs just in case she had slipped in without anyone knowing, just in case she had escaped. He knew it was foolish —knew she wasn't there.

But he checked anyway.

"I think we're in business!" Fen said, as he clapped his hands, leaning back in his chair with a smug grin on his face.

Killian hopped off the bed, pulling another chair over to Fen's desk. "And you're sure it'll work?" he asked, as he slipped the earring into his piercing. Luckily, it had never healed completely—his father made sure of that.

"It should." Fen nodded. He swiped up on the screen of his phone and pressed the app. It lit up the blue and green. "We should be able to record a message here, and it'll connect with her earrings. If I programmed everything correctly—and I absolutely did—" he waggled his eyebrows, "she'll get the message just like she would a phone call or listening to music."

Killian nodded as he took a breath. "So, let's do this then." He didn't know why he was nervous, but he couldn't shake the tremble in his hands.

"Well, there's a catch," Fen replied.

Killian groaned as he leaned back in the chair.

"She has to actually have the earrings on when we send the message. It won't record for her to listen to later. It sends like a verbal text message and then disappears. She can't answer us. She can only listen."

Killian nodded his head, his chest shaking. "Let's give it a try then."

Fen nodded and then clicked the button on his phone.

"Starshine, can you hear me?" He groaned internally— even if she could, she couldn't answer. "Just hold tight. Fen and I are figuring out a way to come get you." It was a piss-poor message and not half of what he wanted—needed—to say, but it was the best he could do for now.

Fen clicked the 'send' button, but nothing happened. He rubbed the bridge of his nose as he grimaced.

"What happened?" Killian asked.

"It must be the wards," Fen replied. "They're too strong, so the magic can't break past them. She'll probably have to be really close to them, like almost touching them, for it to work."

Killian grit his teeth. Whatever magic Helvig had, it was different than Vala magic—stronger.

"So, we'll try again," Killian replied. "We'll keep trying until it works." He hadn't come this far to just give up now.

"I don't think that will—"

"We'll try again," Killian cut him off, and Fen had the good sense not to argue.

Killian recorded the message again and again, different lengths and different words but all the same message—don't give up. Fen's phone screen didn't so much as flicker. Nothing was getting through those wards, and she was too far for it to work, even if she did have those earrings on. Fen brought their supper upstairs, and they ate in silence, each boy lost in their own thoughts. The sun had already set outside, the moon shining through the window and illumi-nating the walls. Killian was tired, but in a way that sleep could never fix. He was losing hope—and he hated himself for it.

Fen yawned as he stretched his arms over his head. "Maybe we can try again tomorrow?" he asked, rubbing his eyes.

"Yeah." Killian nodded, trying not to let the defeat sink in. "Yeah, we can try again tomorrow."

He saw himself out, making his way home as slowly as possible. Ember was strong, he didn't doubt she would be okay, but he couldn't ignore the way the wolf inside of him clawed at his skin—at his bones.

*"Find her,"* it seemed to say, leaving his chest tight and lungs heavy. He had learned to control the wolf a long time ago, but his grip on its leash seemed to be waning, and he was having a hard time caring if he was in control or not.

KILLIAN LEANED against the vanity in his bathroom, blood dripping from his lip, nose, and brow onto the white marble. He cursed under his breath as he examined himself in the mirror.

"Feckin' hell," he mumbled, wincing as he touched his nose. It was broken—again. And while he wasn't at all surprised, he was incredibly annoyed. He closed his eyes as he took a shuddering breath, his stomach rolling as he thought about the way his uncle's fist had connected with his jaw and then again with his nose and his brow. His eye was already turning purple, but he couldn't find the will to bother trying to cover it.

He bit down on his lip as he felt his nose crack, popping it back into place like he had done dozens of times before. He could've gone to Isra, who would've discreetly made him whole again, but there was something about forcing his parents to see him like this that made him stand a little taller. His mum would see what she was allowing, would not be allowed the excuse of saying she didn't know.

His phone buzzed as he wiped the last of the blood from his brow, a text popping up on the screen.

Supper in ten.

Killian didn't have to be told twice. He quickly changed shirts and made his way out of the manor and toward the Kitts'.

His chest already felt lighter as he walked through the front door, the smell of Eira's scones floating through the foyer.

"What on earth," Eira gasped, as she walked out of the kitchen, her brow furrowed as she cupped Killian's face. She clicked her tongue as she shook her head. "You children will be the death of me. Come in the kitchen. I've got an ointment that should take away the sting."

"I'm fine, Mum, really," Killian said, as he shook his head.

Eira cocked her brow, both hands on her hips as she stared at him. Killian swallowed dryly as he followed her into the kitchen. She was not a woman to argue with. Eira rummaged through the medicine cabinet, pulling out vials and tins as she mumbled to herself.

"Are you going to tell me what happened?" she asked, as she began applying the tincture to his brow.

He winced as the wound pulsed and shook his head. "It was nothing," he replied, "just a stupid mistake." Not even Eira, with all her fire and strong will, could save him from his family, from who he was at his core.

She narrowed her eyes at him but didn't push any further. "Have you heard from Ember lately?"

Killian sucked in a breath. He couldn't tell Eira and Otto

where she was—couldn't drag them into whatever mess was going on over there when they had enough to worry about. And if they found out what they were planning, she would lock them away until they were eighteen years old.

"Not lately," he mumbled in reply.

Eira hummed something as she dabbed the last of the ointment on his face and closed the lid to the jar. "We all miss her," she replied, as she patted his cheek, "both of them. You are not alone in your grief. Don't shut out the ones that love you."

Killian didn't have the energy to argue.

"You made it!" Fen grinned as he walked into the kitchen, but his face fell when he saw his best friend's face. The shock quickly turned to anger as he pursed his lips. Fen knew exactly where the bruises had come from.

"Can we eat upstairs?" he asked, as he turned to Eira. "We have some work to finish."

Eira narrowed her eyes, then bobbed her head as she nodded toward the trays on the counter. "Don't leave your plates upstairs. I don't want bugs," she said, as she put away her tonics and salves. "I'm down here if you need anything." She smiled as she made her way through the back door, no doubt to round up Osiris and Otto before the shepherd's pie grew cold. Killian stood in the kitchen for a beat, her words ringing in his ears.

*I'm here.*

If only she knew how much weight those words carried.

They boys made their way to Fen's room where Fen proceeded to sit back at his desk and resumed scratching away at his notebook while he took bites of his supper.

"Did you ever get it to work?" Killian asked, as he settled himself on the bed. He knew the answer before he asked it, but he tried anyway. Fen shook his head, and they left it at that.

"I played with the code a little," he said, as he picked up

another bite of his food, "to see if maybe I could get the message to reach past the wards, but it didn't work."

Killian nodded—he'd expected as much. Whatever magic Helvig was wielding, it was strong. They wouldn't get through it easily.

Just as they were finishing their supper, not even twenty minutes later, Fen's phone screen flickered on the desk. Just a little. Both boys whipped their heads around, and it flickered again. This time for a little longer.

A connection.

"She's by the wards," Fen mumbled, eyes wide, shoving his plate to the side. His eyes met Killian's and they both nodded—this was their chance. Fen clicked the button to record, and Killian knew he only had a few seconds before she was gone again.

"We're coming, Starshine," he said more clearly than he ever thought he could speak. "Don't give up on me now. We're coming."

He could've sworn he felt the bond at his chest thrum in reply.

# CHAPTER 34

# THE SAME STAR-SOAKED CLOTH

Ember stormed through the doors of the chateau later that afternoon, mind still reeling from her conversation with Rowan. She had told her to fake it, to pretend she was on board with all of Helvig and her mother's sick plans. She had to play the part of a perfect princess, and it made her want to shove each and every one of them off a damn cliff.

She stomped through the house, a righteous anger burning deep in her belly, and found herself in front of her mother's study. She didn't know why, but she reached for the doorknob and pushed her way into the room. Gaelen had already started the fire for the night, making sure the room was warm and comfortable when Aoife came in for the evening. Amber light flickered across the rug, dancing against the setting sun beaming through the window. Tears pricked the corner of her eyes, but she quickly blinked them away as anger built—rage replacing the grief of the life she imagined when her mother walked through the Kitts' door.

She stalked across the room, ripping a pristine looking book from its home on the shelf, and started tearing it apart. One by one, she flung them across the room—tearing at the

346

covers, shredding the prologues, tearing at the words that might've once brought her comfort.

She didn't want comfort now. All she wanted to do was scream.

She moved to her mother's desk, the mahogany gleaming in the orange sun. Anger rolled in her gut as she stared at the paper stacked neatly in the center—itineraries, invoices and plans that had been drawn up, Ember's name speckling several of them. She swung her arm across the top of the desk, letting out a feral scream as everything clattered to the floor. Glass shattered as it hit the wall, and Ember felt herself not caring as tiny shards pelted her cheek and under her eye. Blood trickled down her jaw as she moved to the antique couch in front of the fire, ripping open the pillows and tossing several into the billowing flames. She flipped her wrist and sent a hex toward the wall, sending the pictures careening to the ground.

Her breathing was ragged as she looked around, but the rage in her chest hadn't settled. No, it had only grown—expanded inside her until she felt like she was going to spontaneously combust. She walked to the desk again and rummaged through the drawers. Maybe there was a key to a shed with some AirWaves or brooms or—

There, in the bottom of a drawer, lay an inconspicuous box with a rune carved in the top of it. She felt the lock give as she ran her fingers down the grooves of the carving and flipped the lid open. A satin cape was nestled in the box, starlight woven through the translucent material. She gasped as she clutched it in her fingers, holding it up to the light.

*Gaelen's cape.*

She stuffed it in her pocket for safe keeping. Maybe she would free Gaelen simply to spite her mother.

The sun was creeping further past the mountain out the window, and Ember had the itch to be airborne. She needed to clear her head, to get away from the stuffiness of this house and the fear that had settled in her chest, and the only way she knew to do that was to fly hundreds of feet in the air and forget everything else existed.

She couldn't do that, unfortunately. Her AirWave was back at the manor in Sigurvik, and she didn't know if she would ever see it again. Maia was tucked in a stall beside Arlo, probably going out of her mind with worry, and Ember was stuck on the ground. She sighed as she ran a hand down her face, leaning on the window facing the mountains surrounding Torsvik.

*The mountains.*

She was out the door before she even truly realized what she was doing, heading out of the gate surrounding the chateau and toward the mountains looming in the distance.

The climb to the top felt like it took hours, every muscle in her body screaming with each step. She made it to the top, falling to her knees as she sucked in the air of the thin atmosphere. She ran her hands through the air, feeling the ward ripple as she ran her fingers along it. She could see the edge of the forest in the distance, just a small line of trees so far away it would probably take days to hike to. And though she couldn't see it, she knew just beyond that was home.

*Home.*

Her bottom lip trembled. Would she ever get to go home again? She kept her hand against the ward as she steadied her breathing. It stung, the magic singing the palm of her hand, but at least she was feeling *something.* The air was beginning to warm in Torsvik, but up here, it bit into her skin and chilled her bones. She sat back against the frost-covered ground, wrapping her coat tighter around her body. She ran a hand through her hair, and one of her fingers caught on her earring. She hadn't taken them out since Killian had given them to her, couldn't bring herself to put them away and potentially lose them. She whispered the incantation to turn them on, to listen to some of the books he had downloaded for her. Maybe they would settle her, help her think. Maybe it would douse some of the fire that was rolling through her.

Tears pricked her eyes as the book played. How was she supposed to fake it? How was she supposed to pretend like this was something she wanted? She didn't think she had it in her to even try to pretend.

Maeve and Theo's faces flickered through her mind. She had to do it for them—had to figure out a way to play make believe until she and Rowan figured out how to escape.

Suddenly, the book stopped playing, and static crackled in her ears. She almost took the earring out, thinking maybe she had broken it somehow, when a voice she recognized came from the earrings, rattling in her head and shaking her bones.

"We're coming, Starshine," Killian's voice echoed, sounding a million miles away. "Don't give up on me now. We're coming."

She didn't know why she was going, why the wisp pulled to her the way it did, but before she knew it, she was standing in front of the castle, scaling the wall, and hopping into the courtyard below. She had questions that needed to be answered, and she wasn't going to wait around and see if they manifested on their own. She snuck through the empty kitchens, down the hall and through the door that led to the dungeons. She inched down the spiral staircase, whispering a quiet, "*Lux,*" to light the way, and soon found herself in front of the cell door the wisp had led her too before.

"Do you know what I am?" Ember asked, barely above a whisper. She peered through the small crack in the door and watched as the woman moved closer.

Her silver hair almost glowed in the moonlight, and

Ember had that aching feeling that she knew her from somewhere. She drew closer to the door, and the light from Ember's orb lit up her face. Ember gasped.

She was beautiful, a goddess in the flesh. Even with her sunken cheeks and frail figure, she radiated an otherworldliness that took Ember's breath away. Her hair flowed over her shoulders in wild, silver waves that seemed to have a mind of their own. Her eyes met Ember's, and the lavender flecked with ash cut into her like a hot knife.

"You are what I am," Aesira replied. "We are cut from the same star-soaked cloth."

Ember let out a shaky breath. "You're a Wildling," she said—not a question.

The woman nodded, silhouetted by the moon shining in from the window.

"You're the woman from my dream."

Another nod.

"Why?" Ember asked, every syllable shaking as she spoke. "Why me? I can't do what they all need me to do."

"Your fate was written the day you were born," Aesira replied. "You will save a great many people. You will lead nations to freedom."

"I don't want to lead anyone," Ember said, as she shook her head, tears rolling down her cheeks. "I just want to be sixteen. I want to be a normal kid that goes to parties and stays up too late on Sunday nights. I want my biggest worry to be my final exams or what to wear on my first date." Her chest shook as she bit her lip. "I can't save anyone. I couldn't even save myself when it mattered most. I couldn't save my father. I can't do this by myself."

"You were never meant to," Aesira replied. "This isn't a weight you can carry on your own. You need your family to lift it with you."

Ember scoffed. "What family? In case you haven't noticed,

my family is either dead or offering me up as lamb for slaughter. I don't have a family anymore—it's just me and Theo."

"Your family is so much more than who you were born to," Aesira whispered, "so much more than blood."

*The blood of the covenant is thicker than the water of the womb.*

"I'm just a girl," Ember whispered. "I can't change anything."

"You were not meant to change anything. You were meant to make history," Aesira breathed. "The history of women is in everything we touch."

# CHAPTER 35
# A WAY OUT

E mber sat on the edge of her bed the next morning, tapping her fingers on her mattress as she watched the sun climb higher over the mountain outside her window. She chewed on the edge of her lip, mulling over what she had to do next. She had lost her mind the night before, and she wasn't sure what was in store for her when she finally decided to leave her room. She took a shaky breath as she pushed herself off her bed and headed downstairs to confront her mum.

She had to fake it, had to pretend like she was sorry for the way she acted and that she was ready to fall in line with whatever her duties were to be. The thought turned her stomach, but she kept reminding herself that she was not doing this for herself. She was doing this for *them*—for Maeve and Theo, for Killian and Fen, even for Rowan. She was doing this for her family—her true family.

She steadied herself in front of her mother's office door, going over the apology she had practiced in front of her mirror all night. Just as she was about to open the door, it swung open on its own, her mother standing by the fireplace holding a cup of tea.

"Good morning, love." Aoife smiled as she motioned for Ember to enter the room. It looked like nothing had happened, like she had never even been there. Everything was back in its place—every picture hanging on the wall, every book back on the shelf, even the lamp she had shattered was fixed, sitting peacefully back on the desk. Ember felt heat creep up her neck, scolding herself for feeling embarrassed.

"You know," Aoife continued, as she poured Ember a cup of tea, "I thought maybe someone broke in last night. You wouldn't happen to know what happened, would you?" Her eyes were serious, but a smile played at the corner of her mouth.

It almost made Ember feel bad.

Almost.

Ember sucked on her teeth, putting on her most apologetic face. "I'm sorry, Mum," she said. "I've had a hard time adjusting, and I just sort of... lost it."

Aoife nodded as she sat on the couch, patting the cushion next to her. "Would it have anything to do with what we talked about the other night?"

Ember nodded, not needing to lie about that.

"You don't have to hide your feelings from me," Aoife cooed. "You can talk to me about anything." She held Ember's hand softly, and the way her fingers felt on her skin made her stomach turn.

"I know, Mum." Ember forced a smile. "I'm sorry about how I acted. And for your... office."

Aoife laughed as Ember grimaced. "So, tell me, love," her mum said, "have you had a chance to think about what we talked about yet?"

Ember chewed on the inside of her cheek. "Not much yet."

"Well, I have a proposition for you," Aoife replied, turning her body toward Ember. "If you make the decision to do this

353

willingly, on your own accord with no coercion, your granda' has agreed to train you after his treatments are over."

"Train me?" Ember furrowed her brow.

"Aye." Aoife nodded. "If you agree to be your granda's donor for as long as he needs, after you are back to full power, he will train you to take over the throne."

Ember swallowed as she nodded. Rowan had told her to fake it, go along with whatever they said, but Ember was finding that to be increasingly more difficult with each breath.

"Is it something I can think about?" Ember asked, trying not to squirm. She needed to buy more time.

"Of course, love," Aoife cooed. "I will give you till the end of the week to decide."

*"Is it something I can think about?" She didn't know why she needed to think about it. She should be ecstatic. She should be jumping up and down with excitement at the thought of having a real family again, a permanent family. It was all she had wanted since she was six years old.*

*"Of course, Mo Chroí." Otto smiled as he squeezed his wife's hand. "Take all the time you need."*

The memory of her conversation with Eira and Otto weighed her down. All the time in the world—that's what they were willing to give her when she asked for it. They didn't hesitate or second guess, they didn't give her any ultimatums. They loved her, truly loved her enough to leave the decision up to her.

Ember gritted her teeth as she nodded. "That'll be fine, Mum."

"Perfect," Aoife cooed, taking another sip from her mug. "In the meantime, I've invited Rowan over to go over some etiquette with you before the ball."

"Etiquette?" Ember wrinkled her nose, making Aoife laugh.

"Yes," she nodded, "there are certain things you need to learn, certain customs that you aren't familiar with, and Rowan will be the perfect young Vala to teach you. You are a princess now, and it's high time you learned how to act like one."

Ember groaned. The very last thing she wanted to think about was proper etiquette. She suddenly felt very self-conscious in her jeans and jumper, fidgeting with her sleeve as she bit her lip. "That sounds lovely, Mum." Ember forced another smile. Fake it, she had to fake it.

"Very good." Aoife smiled. "Now run and find your brother, and the two of you wash up, Gaelen should have breakfast ready any moment."

Ember gave a nod and laid down her mug. Aoife kissed her on the cheek, and it took all of her willpower not to physically recoil. The door to the study clicked closed behind her, and Ember let out a long sigh, wiping her cheek with the back of her hand. Faking it was exhausting, on a cellular level. It felt like she was using all her magic to douse the fire inside of her, keeping it to a dull roar. She walked through the hall, her footsteps echoing off the arching ceilings, and made herself think about Maeve, her tiny face, her bruised neck, the way her lip trembled as she stood to protect the other children. She thought about Theo and the fact that the only family he had ever known never truly had the capacity to love him—not fully, not the way he deserved.

She steadied herself against the weight bearing down on her chest. She would figure out how to fake it. She had no other choice.

She had to do this for them.

"YOUR FIRST LESSON," Rowan announced, as she waltzed into the library where Ember was buried in a pile of books, "is to stop slouching." She snapped the book closed under Ember's nose, and then shot a spell at her that made her sit completely straight.

"Cut it out!" Ember snapped, yanking the book back toward her. "Just pretend you taught me something so I can keep reading."

"Are those books telling you how to break the kids out of the dungeon?" Rowan asked, as she pulled out a chair and sat at the table. "Or perhaps how to manipulate your way out of a lifetime sentence with the Jarl if you don't succeed?"

Ember gritted her teeth. "Do you have something useful to say?" She rolled her eyes as she flipped open her father's journal—for the hundredth time. "Or did you just come to annoy me?"

"Oh, I'm so glad you asked." Rowan smiled, flipping her hair over her shoulder.

Ember almost laughed. She was suddenly transported to the library at Heksheim, the two girls giggling behind a pile of books while they studied. What she wouldn't give to go back to last year before everything got complicated, before she knew what betrayal tasted like. She shook her head—wishful thinking never did her any good.

"The ball is in two weeks," Rowan continued, "and everyone will be too busy dancing and drinking and celebrating to notice a couple of teenagers wandering about the castle."

Ember tapped the pages of the journal. "Okay..." She nodded. "Say we sneak down to the dungeons undetected and free the children... what then?" She leaned back in her chair and crossed her arms over her chest. "We can't just walk them out the front door, and we still haven't found a way out of the wards. We're trapped until we do."

Rowan chewed on her lip. "They would have built a way out," she said, as she traced the grains of wood on the table. "When the First Families built the castle, they would've had a secondary escape route—a means to protect the royal family. We're just not looking in the right place."

Ember's brow furrowed as she focused on the page in front of her, on a name she recognized. "I might have an idea." She grinned.

EMBER HAD PASSED Frigg's Spindle dozens of times in the last month, but the walk suddenly felt more harrowing—dangerous. She didn't know where this sudden burst of heroism came from, but they were running out of ideas—and time—and it was one last shot to find information.

The town was bustling with people preparing for the ball, shopping and chatting and encouraging flowers to spring out of the thawing soil. The sun warmed her skin, kissing the freckles on the bridge of her nose, and she breathed in the honeysuckle and thyme. The bridge that straddled the churning river felt unsteady beneath her boots as she hurried across, but Rowan acted like it was any other March afternoon.

"Now," she said, as she plucked a wildflower from the grass and stuck it in her hair, "remind me what we're doing again?"

Ember rolled her eyes as she pulled her father's journal from her bag. "My dad made this list," she said, as she flipped the book open, dodging the children that ran across the cobblestone, "and there's this little symbol right here, almost like a crow. I keep seeing it on a bunch of shops that are on the list, so maybe one of them knows something."

"About…" Rowan furrowed her brow in question.

"The map *next to* the list," Ember replied, a little annoyed that she was having to vocalize this for the fourth time.

"Someone drew it—either my dad or someone he knew—and I am willing to bet someone on this list knows more about it."

"It's just a map, Em," Rowan replied. "He probably drew it while he was wasting time in the library or drinking his tea in the garden. What kind of information do you expect these people to have?"

"I don't know." Ember shrugged, stuffing the book back in her bag. "Maybe there's a secret underground network of magical mapmakers. Or assassins."

"They're just common folk." Rowan shook her head as she kicked a pebble at her foot. "There's nothing inherently special about anyone in this city, other than the fact that they haven't left."

Ember stiffened. "I was pretty common once upon a time too."

The girls stepped into the shop and were immediately greeted with the sight of jewels and silk, fabrics Ember had never even seen before, let alone touched. Several mirrors lined the walls with raised platforms for the wearer to view themselves at all angles. Ember rubbed the fabric of her jacket between her thumb and pointer fingers, suddenly very self-conscious in her own skin.

Ball gowns and diamond encrusted tiaras, fancy lunches and hedges shaped like unicorns. This wasn't who she was, not any of it. What if she couldn't get the children out? What if she failed and was forced to stay here? Her palms began to sweat as she shed her coat and draped it over her arm.

"Is there anything I can help you with?" A woman peeked out from the back room, tall with white hair and skin so bronze that she almost shined in the sunlight coming through the window. There was something eerily familiar about her— the tilt of her head, the cadence of her voice, the way she seemed to stare right through them.

The fact that she only had one eye.

Ember tried not to gape, tried to avert her eyes and look

anywhere else. The woman chuckled as she walked toward them, almost like she was floating.

"It is far more offensive to *try not* to stare, than to actually look, Princess." She smiled.

Ember cringed. "My name is Ember." She tried to sound more confident than she felt.

"I know what your name is." The woman's smile grew.

"Elowyn! We're looking for dresses for the Ostara ball." Rowan smiled, twirling through the shop as she ran her hand down the plethora of fabrics. "Something that will turn heads."

"*Or* just something normal," Ember eyed her friend, "ordinary."

"There is nothing ordinary about you, Princess." Elowyn replied, eyeing her curiously.

"Ember—please call me Ember," she whispered. Not a command—a plea.

"As you wish." Elowyn nodded and made her way to the back of the shop, carrying back handfuls of gorgeous dresses for the girls. They tried them all on, oohing and ahhing and putting on quite the show for anyone passing by the large windows at the front of the shop. Ember was completely out of her element, but she decided it was best to grin and bear it.

To fake it.

"Were you born with only one eye?" Ember asked, plucking up the courage to learn more about the woman. There was a reason she was in the journal, and she was going to figure out what it was.

"My mother always said seers need one eye on each side of the veil." Elowyn smiled. "The gods saw fit to take care of that for me."

"You're a seer?" Ember asked, as Elowyn took some measurements.

The woman nodded. "Among other things. It runs in my family, both a blessing and a curse."

"Do you have children?" Ember asked. Something gnawed at the inside of her brain, right behind her eyes, like she was trying to focus on something that wasn't actually there. Something about the way the woman—

White hair. Bronze skin. Otherworldly features that just didn't quite fit.

"What is your daughter's name?" Ember asked.

Rowan gave her a confused glance—the woman had never mentioned she had a daughter.

But Ember knew.

"Odette," Elowyn whispered, like it was a prayer she said every night, "her name is Odette."

Tears pricked the corner of Ember's eyes. "Why are you here? Why aren't you home with her?"

"Because some things are bigger than us," Elowyn replied. "Change requires sacrifice, and I will carry mine with me to the end of my days."

Elowyn stepped back, and Ember got a look at herself in the mirror, and the sight took her breath away.

A ball gown worthy of a princess—no, a queen. Navy blue fabric trimmed with onyx around the wide sleeves and plunging neckline. Gold was woven into the blue, like stars burning brightly in the heavens. She could almost picture herself walking into the grand ballroom, a pale haired boy on her arm next to her.

"My father..." Ember swallowed, as tears pricked her eyes. "He had a journal he kept. I found a list in it with a picture of a crow drawn next to it. Your name was on that list, and that crow is on your shop." She took a steadying breath as she gently brushed the fabric of the gown. "There is a map next to them, and I was wondering if you could tell me about it, what all of it means."

Rowan had been standing back, giving Ember space. She stepped up beside her and put on her prettiest smile.

"It would really help us out, Elowyn." She smiled.

The woman smiled and nodded toward the back of the shop. Rowan and Ember followed her into an office in the back, and she swiftly locked the door and flipped on the lights.

"Torin was a dear friend," she said. "We worked together during his time here. He's the reason I came to Torsvik." She shuffled through drawers and stacks of paper and pulled out a small, folded parchment, holding it to her chest. "He was a great leader. We thought we could stop them," she continued, "or at least slow them down. He gave me this before he left, asked me to keep it safe until he could come back. It seems he made sure he came back, one way or another." Elowyn handed her the folded piece of paper, and Ember furrowed her brow as she opened it.

"What is it?" she asked. It looked like a roughly drawn maze, just a bunch of lines with no rhyme or reason to the direction they went.

"He never said," Elowyn shook her head, "but I imagine you'll figure it out."

Ember sighed as she nodded, clutching the parchment in her hands. The girls paid for the dresses, and Elowyn assured them that they would be delivered before the night of the ball. Rowan and Ember walked out of the shop with more questions now than answers, and worry was clouding every corner of Ember's mind.

"What are we supposed to do with this," Rowan asked, as she scrunched her nose, snatching the paper from Ember and turning it in the air as she studied it. "What was your father doing?"

Ember shrugged. "Maybe he was going to come back and finish it, whatever *it* is," she replied, anger beginning to heat her cheeks. If he was here, he could fix this. If he was here, she wouldn't feel quite so lost.

EMBER SPRAWLED ON HER BED, books scattered around her as she and Rowan passed the parchment between each other, studying it and looking at references, ultimately becoming so frustrated that they tossed it across the room. Theo was on the floor reading quietly to himself, a history book about Torsvik open in front of him. He giggled as Rowan threw herself back on the mattress, hand on her forehead as she sighed.

Loudly.

"This is pointless," she moaned. "We should be focusing on figuring out how to get the children out of the dungeons, not trying to decipher this chicken scratch." She pointed to the parchment she had haphazardly tossed to the floor.

Ember shot her a glare, and she promptly snapped her mouth shut. Theo gently picked up the paper from the carpet, smoothing the edges as he laid it in front of him, studying it. He ran his fingers over the lines like he was memorizing it.

"We need a plan B." Ember turned to Rowan and popped a grape in her mouth.

Gaelen had brought them a platter of snacks when they had returned home from town, and she was forever thankful for the Merrow and the kindness she continued to show her. She briefly thought about the cape stuffed in her bag—Gaelen was trapped here just as much as she was.

"If we can't get the children out of the castle, we need a plan B."

"We could steal a boat," Rowan shrugged, as she stared at the ceiling, "then find a way to shatter the wards around the beach."

"I don't think these are standard wards." Ember shook her head as she sighed. "I don't think it'll be that easy."

Theo stood up from the floor, carrying the parchment and

the book he was reading with him, and dropped them both onto the bed between the girls.

Ember furrowed her brow. *"What did you find?"*

Theo pointed at the parchment, then at a picture of Torsvik, an old map that labeled every restaurant and butcher, every florist and fishmonger, every street and—

Ember gasped.

She laid the parchment over the page of the book, touching the paper, and began to mumble.

"Sýndu mér leyndarmál þín."

She didn't know what she said—what it even meant—but the words rattled in her bones, echoing through her veins as the fire beneath her skin burned. The page became translucent, all except for the markings her father had drawn. She rotated the page a few times, lining up the marking with the map below it, and gasped.

"What was that?" Rowan asked, eyes wide.

"It's a map," she whispered.

Rowan furrowed her brow. "Not what I meant." But Ember ignored her, eyes glued to the page. Rowan sighed. "Of course it's a map," she replied, talking about the book.

"No, no, no." Ember shook her head as she turned the page and book toward Rowan. "These lines he drew, they all line up with the roads going through Torsvik. And these right here," she pointed to the squares spread across the piece of paper, "these line up with buildings. Look." She pointed to the map again, and each square lined up perfectly over a business or home. "I'm willing to bet that all of those buildings have crows carved into the frame too."

"Okay," Rowan nodded, "so your dad drew a map of the roads in Torsvik And the houses with the crow. How does that help us?"

Ember shook her head, chewing on the edge of her lip. Memories from her first day out in Torsvik flitted through her mind. Empty mineshafts dotting the hills, cellar doors with locks and hinges nearly rusted off. Ember's eyes widened as she looked to her friend.

"What if it's not the roads?" she whispered. "What if there's something under it?"

Rowan's face lit up as she stared down at the map, almost like she could read Ember's thoughts. "It's a tunnel system."

Ember nodded, a grin spreading across her face. "I'm willing to bet each of these buildings has an entrance to the tunnel." She ran her finger across the map, down the streets, up to the castle and the square drawn over it. "There's an entrance in the castle." She continued tracing the lines, past the dungeon, under the mountain past where the wards reached and... "It's our way out."

# CHAPTER 36
# WILD DRAICS COULDN'T KEEP ME AWAY

**E**mber lay in bed that night, flipping through her father's journal, another small book, and studying the map of the tunnels over and over again as she gave Theo a brief synopsis of their plan. He didn't need all of the grand details—didn't need to know how their mother truly felt about him—but he didn't seem heartbroken over the prospect of leaving. If anything, he seemed excited.

So, he studied with her, looking over the maps again and again. They didn't know anything about the tunnels, didn't have time to check them out before they took a gaggle of children into them searching for freedom. They could be caved in for all they knew, or maybe the Jarl found them and blocked off. Maybe it was a plan her father had made, but never carried out for a reason.

She rubbed her forehead, squeezing her eyes shut. They didn't have time to come up with a plan B—this was it. They just had to pray to the gods that it would work. The tether at her sternum tugged lightly, and a lump built in her throat. Theo was sleeping soundly beside her, a book still open on his chest when a knock at the window sounded.

Ember bolted upright in her bed and snapped the book

closed, slipping out of bed toward her balcony door. Another knock, and she gripped the book tighter. She peeked through the closed drapes and let out a gasp at the face smiling at her from the other side.

"You about gave me a heart attack!" she whispered— loudly—as she swung the doors open before she threw herself at the boys on the other side, wrapping her arms tightly around both of their necks. She steadied herself against them, the tether at her chest thrumming as she choked back tears.

"We really have to get you some new weapons." Killian laughed as he looked down at her, snatching the book she had gripped in her hand as she stepped away.

"I have weapons," Ember replied, as she sniffed, crossing her arms over her chest. "I have loads of weapons."

"You," Killian grinned, "Ember Lothbrok, have weapons —plural?"

"I think you'll find that I'm full of surprises, Killian Vargr." She smirked.

"Can we focus on the rescue here?" Fen asked, snapping his finger between them.

"You weren't very focused when you were screaming at every squirrel snapping a twig on our way here." Killian grinned.

Fen's cheeks colored as Ember looked between the two of them.

"Fen's afraid of Sasquatch." He smiled, nodding at his friend.

"Whoa, whoa, whoa," Fen interjected, crossing his arms tightly over his chest. "I'm not *afraid* of Sasquatch. I just think we should all be on alert."

Ember smiled, tears pricking the corners of her eyes as they bickered. Something inside her shook—her magic taking in air, like it had been underwater since she left Sigurvik. She wrapped Fen in a hug, holding him tight, as if she loosened her grip even for a moment, he might slip away.

"You're here." She grinned wildly.

"Wild draic's couldn't keep me away," he whispered in reply.

"How did you get here?" she asked, wiping away the tears that were pooled on her bottom lash.

Fen grinned as he held up his wrist. A braided leather bracelet was wrapped around his arm, metal beads carved with runes scattered about it.

"Where did you get that?" Ember recognized it—it was the same bracelet Collum and that captain wore.

"Nicked it." Fen shrugged with a grin, like it was no big deal.

Ember furrowed her brow at the boys and suddenly felt like she was back in Galdr, desperately trying to keep them out of trouble. "From whom?"

"Siris," Killian replied with a slight grimace.

"You stole it from your brother?" Ember asked.

"The details aren't important," Fen replied, as he shook his head. "What matters now is that we're here to take you home."

Ember's face fell. "I can't leave," she whispered, glancing over at Theo.

Fen seemed to read her mind. "We're taking Theo too," he replied. "Killian told me everything. We can easily Echo, like, five people at a time no problem."

"No, it's not that," Ember said, as she shook her head. "The missing kids are here." She took a breath as she looked at Fen, hope blooming in his eyes. "Maeve is here."

Fen straightened his spine, his face growing dark as he tapped his finger against his leg. "Where?" he breathed, his voice suddenly shaky.

She heard the question he couldn't say out loud.

*Is she okay?*

"She's in the castle," Ember whispered, nodding for them

to walk onto the balcony and quickly closing the doors. "They all are. In the... dungeons underneath."

She didn't mention why they were in the dungeons—what Helvig was doing with them. Fen didn't need to know that, or he might never leave.

"So, what are we waiting for?" He steeled himself as he looked between his friends. "Let's go get them."

"It's not that simple," Ember replied, as she shook her head. "We can't just storm into the dungeons and whisk them away. It's too heavily guarded. But we have a plan and—"

"Who is 'we?'" Killian asked, arms crossed over his chest as he leaned on the railing.

"Oh," Ember replied, gritting her teeth, "um, Rowan has been helping me."

"You're joking," Fen gaped. "Ember, I will not leave my little sister's life in that psycho's claws."

"I'm not saying we should trust her entirely, Fenrir," Ember replied, "but she's not that girl from last year. She could be our only shot at getting Maeve out alive."

*Alive.* The opposite is something she hadn't allowed herself to think about, to even consider.

"And what's the plan?" Killian asked, as he furrowed his brow. "Why can't we just execute it now, see if we can Echo the kids out?"

"We would never get past all of Helvig's guards," Ember replied, as she shook her head. "During the ball, they'll be busy. There will be so many guests, they'll be too focused on keeping an eye on them to heavily guard the dungeons. It should work."

It was a big *should.*

"Oh, great." Fen rolled his eyes. "Rowan has a plan, and I'm sure it's lovely and not riddled with boobytraps."

"She knows the castle like that back of her hand," Ember replied. "She can help us if you will set your stupid pride aside."

"Stupid pride?" Fen bristled. "Shall I remind you *why* she knows the castle so well? She's been working with him for over a year, Ember! Or do you not remember last spring and how she almost killed all three of us? She can't be trusted."

"I'm not asking you to trust her," Ember pleaded. "I'm asking you to trust me."

Fen bit his lip. He didn't say anything else.

"So, what's the plan then?" Killian asked, as he checked over the garden again, shoulders tense. "If the dungeon is crawling with as many guards as Rowan says, how are we supposed to get down there?"

"The castle will be busy during the ball," Ember replied, beginning to pace, "and while that likely means a larger presence of guards, they should be mostly upstairs. Rowan will cause a distraction while we slip away, and she'll meet us downstairs."

"I'm listening." Fen nodded, brows furrowed.

Ember detailed the plan she and Rowan had outlined, down to the abandoned hallway they would be meeting in. She pulled out the map Elowyn gave them, marking the rendezvous points and the tunnel that led under the mountain —to freedom. To home.

"Why can't we just Echo them out of the dungeon?" Fen asked, as he studied the map.

"It would take too long," Killian replied, almost reading Ember's thoughts. "There are so many children, and we would have to take long breaks in between groups to make sure our magic wasn't depleted too much. It leaves too much room for error, too much time to get caught."

"And the castle is warded," Ember added. "Collum has only ever echoed me outside of it, never inside. I don't even know that echoing out would even be possible."

"There are too many variables," Fen said, as he shook his head and handed her the map. "What if it doesn't work?"

Ember folded the parchment and stuffed it in her pocket.

"We will make it work," she replied, "and if something goes wrong, then we pivot. But we will get those kids out." She sucked in a breath as her eye's met Fen's. "We will get Maeve out."

"And what's to stop him from just snatching them back afterward?" Killian asked. "What if this just becomes a game of cat and mouse?"

"We need to tell Eira and Otto," Ember replied, as she fidgeted with the pendant around her neck, "and maybe even Captain Balor. This isn't something we can keep to ourselves anymore. It's too big."

"They're not going to believe us," Fen replied, shaking his head.

"Then, we *make* them believe us," Ember snapped. "I feel like the bruises around Maeve's wrists and neck will be enough proof."

Fen paled, sinking back against the railing as the life seemed to drain from his eyes.

"After we free them," Ember continued, "they won't be as protected as they are now. It might not be forever, but it'll buy us some time."

Killian studied her as she bit the inside of her cheek, averting her eyes as much as possible.

"There's something you aren't saying," he prodded. "Spill, Starshine."

Ember swallowed dryly. "He's looking for a Wildling," she replied, keeping her eyes glued to the balcony floor. "He's been looking for me. He's sick and something about my blood —about Wildling blood—is important to him. It's why he's been kidnapping kids."

"So, then, it's simple." Fen nodded. "We free the children, and we don't let you anywhere near him."

Ember sighed as she blew a stray hair from in front of her eyes. "I don't think it will be that simple unfortunately. I don't think he'll ever simply leave me alone. He needs me for a lot more than healing it seems."

And Ember told them everything, even the parts that ripped her apart to say out loud. The realization of what her mother did, and what she planned to do still, hit her like a freight train, and she found herself struggling to breathe. She looked over toward Theo asleep in his bed and thought about Maeve alone in that cell. They needed her, were depending on her.

So, she would breathe, if not for herself, then for them.

*The blood of the covenant is thicker than the water of the womb.*

"I knew there was something off about her," Killian replied, as he shook his head. "I would love to say I'm surprised, but I know all too well what parents are capable of."

"I'm so sorry, Ember," Fen whispered, and she could tell he meant to with every fiber of his being.

"So, we will be back for the ball," Killian said. "We will make our appearance, sneak away to the dungeons, release the children—"

"And the woman," Ember interrupted.

"Right, and the—" Killian paused, brow furrowed. "The woman?"

Ember nodded. "There's someone else locked up down there, and from what I can tell, she's been there much longer than any of the kids. She needs help too."

"Who is she?" Fen asked, suddenly intrigued.

"A Wildling," Ember breathed. "She's weak. He's drained her magical core to strengthen the wards and give him enough strength to get around, but she isn't strong enough for both. He can't heal himself completely and keep the wards up, so he's been looking for me—waiting for me."

"What if she's been planted by Helvig or Collum?" Fen asked. "What if it's a trap?"

"I don't know how I know, but I do," Ember replied, pinching the bridge of her nose. "I just need you to trust me."

Both the boys stared at her for so long Ember wasn't certain they were still breathing. They finally nodded, and she took a breath.

"And if it doesn't work?" Fen asked, barely above a whisper. "What do we do if it doesn't work?"

"I always have a back-up plan." Ember smiled.

"Right then," Killian continued, as he rubbed his forehead, "we will break out the children *and* the strange woman, then Echo them all home?"

Ember nodded, shrugging her shoulders. "More or less, yes."

"Do we have a plan B?" Killian smirked. "You know, for when this plan inevitably goes to shit?"

Ember cut her eyes at him, fighting the smile that was trying to take over. "It will work," Ember replied. "It has to."

FEN WENT SEARCHING the bedroom for snacks, and Ember and Killian stayed on the balcony, staring up at the stars. She shivered as the wind picked up, and he stepped closer to her, just a step.

"I'm sorry about your mum," he whispered. "I know this isn't the way you were hoping it would play out."

"I dreamed about it for years," Ember replied, as she stared up at the moon. "I thought I had finally gotten my happy ending, my own real-life fairytale."

Killian shook his head as his pinky touched the side of her hand gripping the rail. "That's the thing about fairytales," he breathed. "They very rarely have happy endings. But you can't close yourself off, not from us. Something eventually is going to break."

"What if it's me?"

Killian grinned. "You're unbreakable, Starshine."

She tried to smile, she did, but something about the way he spoke to her, like he actually believed in her, broke her into a million pieces. She thought about the rest of the people on the island—the Vala and Fae and elves and Merrow—how was she supposed to protect them from this? This couldn't be her destiny. She didn't even know if she believed in destiny, not anymore.

"I am destined for darkness," she whispered.

She didn't like to think about the prophecy, but every night for the last two months, it seemed to rattle in her brain, a reminder of who she was—what she was destined to become.

"They have been planning this since the day I was born," she continued. "Maybe this is what the prophecy was talking about. Maybe I truly can't escape my fate."

"You get to decide what your fate is," Killian replied. "You can fight it alone or let us help you."

"I won't put you two in danger," she breathed. "This is so much bigger than we could've imagined. I won't let my destruction become yours."

"Did you know," Killian said, "that for a star to be born, a gaseous nebula has to completely collapse?" He traced her hand with his pinky, goosebumps now covering her arms.

Ember furrowed her brow. "What are you on about?"

"It's okay if you need to collapse." He shrugged. "This is not your destruction, even if it feels like it right now."

EMBER STALKED through the doors of the palace; head held high as Collum trailed closely behind her. She had called for him the next morning, to escort her to the palace. She didn't lie when she told Fen and Killian she had a plan B the night before. She just hadn't told anyone what it was.

She knew in the back of her mind that there was a chance their plan wouldn't work. Fen was right. There were too many variables—too many moving parts—and she had no way of knowing exactly how it would all go down. So, she steeled herself to do what she needed to do. If she wanted to win, she had to play his game. She walked down the corridors and stood in front of the door to Helvig's study, waiting as Collum knocked. Instead of a reply, the door swung open, Helvig sitting at his desk looking more worn out than she had seen him yet. He smiled at her, and she forced a smile back, walking confidently across the floor as her boots clacked against the marble.

"Mo Stór," a voice sounded from the other side of the room, "I didn't know you were coming by today."

Ember almost stumbled as she saw her mother walk in through another door, but she kept her back straight and head high. It was good she was here. She wouldn't have to say this more than once, and she could go ahead and get it out of the way. She gritted her teeth as she forced a smile.

"I wanted to talk to you both," Ember said, as she made it to the desk Helvig was seated at, twirling the gold ring around her finger.

Helvig smiled as he motioned to the chair in front of him. "You've come to a decision then?" he asked, as Aoife walked to stand behind him. The sight of her behind him made Ember's stomach roll—his loyal daughter there to do his bidding in whatever capacity he required.

"I have." Ember nodded, swallowing dryly as she willed her chest not to shake. "I will be your donor for however long you need, and I will be your princess." The words tasted like bile in her mouth, but she smiled prettily, praying they believed it.

"Oh, how wonderful," Aoife cooed, walking around the

desk to kiss Ember on the head. It took every ounce of willpower she had not to physically recoil.

She gave them a small nod and took another breath. "I just have two conditions," Ember said.

Helvig gave her a nod to continue.

"The first is that we wait until after the ball. I'd like one last night to just have fun with my friends, be a normal teenager for a little while longer."

Helvig rubbed his chin, contemplating, and Ember held her breath.

"I think we can manage that," he laughed gruffly. "I remember my first Ostara ball, and you deserve a night to relax."

Ember let out a shaky breath of relief. She steeled herself for her next demand.

"And the second condition?" Helvig asked, eyes narrowing like he knew what was coming.

Ember did her best to control her fidgeting as she looked him in the eyes. "My second condition," she said coolly, "is that after the ball you let Maeve and Theo go home." She looked at her mother next. "You will sign over all parental rights and allow the Kitts to adopt him, and you will never contact any of them again." Ember kept her face as neutral as possible as her mother studied her.

"Very well." Aoife nodded. "That can be handled easily enough. I will have the solicitors draw up the paperwork, and it will be legally and magically binding."

Helvig nodded in agreement. "Nothing a memory loss potion can't handle."

It was the answer she had wanted, but it still felt like she had been kicked in the gut. Her mother had given up Theo so easily, without even thinking. Had it been that easy for her to leave her behind? To just walk away without a second thought? Rage boiled in her veins, her magic sparking against her palms and fingertips. She put on a pretty smile—another lie—as she looked at her mother and Helvig.

"Any more demands?" Helvig asked, as he leaned on the desk, fingers intertwined in front of him.

Demands, not requests—he knew what this was, and the look in his eyes told her he knew she would burn the world down for her family if she had to.

"I think that should do it." Ember smiled sweetly.

Helvig nodded, and Aoife gave her another hug.

"We can talk business later," Aoife waved her hand, "but how are you feeling about your first ball?"

She waved off their discussion like it was a bothersome gnat in her face, like she wasn't about to lose her son.

Ember's stomach flipped as she bit the inside of her cheek. "I'm quite nervous." It wasn't a lie—she wasn't sure that she had ever been more nervous for anything in her life.

"Are you and Rowan going together?" Aoife asked.

"No," Ember shook her head, "I've actually asked Collum to escort me. A sort of peace offering after the way I've acted toward him the last few months." It was the next step in her plan—keep Collum close so he didn't suspect anything. She had asked him over that morning, asking first if he would take her to the castle and next if he would escort her to the ball, after giving her best apology, complete with puppy dog eyes and a trembling bottom lip.

"That sounds lovely, Ember," Aoife cooed. "I'm sure you're going to have a wonderful time.

She excused herself from the study, leaving Helvig and her mother to talk amongst themselves, and let Collum escort her back to the chateau. She ground her teeth as he held her arm, his face still a stone mask as they walked up the long drive.

"Thank you, Collum." She smiled sweetly.

Collum nodded without a word and suddenly disappeared, leaving Ember alone as she walked through the walls into the garden.

She let herself stand there, for just a moment, breathing in the fresh air and feeling the sun warm her face. There was a darkness that was alive in this city, something that lurked in the shadows, hungry and patient. It thrived off the secrets and suffering, living in the deepest corners of the people's souls where they didn't even dare look. It was a weed that infested every crack and crevice. The people of this town were waiting —waiting on the darkness to flee, to die. But Ember knew the truth about darkness like this, the kind that fed off dashed hopes and broken dreams. The truth was that it wouldn't just disappear or die away.

It wouldn't die unless they killed it themselves.

# CHAPTER 37

# APPLES, STARLIGHT, AND IMPULSIVE DECISIONS

Ember smoothed her dress as Gaelen finished her hair, feeling the weight of the metal beads as they clung to her braids. Her waves had been curled, giving them more definition, and Gaelen had given her lipstick and blush with a little mascara and eyeshadow for some color. Ember had never worn make up, but she had to admit she liked the way it looked. Gaelen stepped out of the room, and Ember couldn't help it. She twirled, and the dress swayed and bent like the wind around her. The velvet hugged her skin, and for just a moment, she allowed herself to imagine that tonight was nothing but dancing and food with her friends by her side.

The Ostara ball was a masquerade, and the mask Elowyn had made for her matched her dress perfectly—midnight blue lined with gold and glittering stars. She traced the stars with her fingertips, grief suddenly overwhelming her. She wished more than anything that her father was here. He would know what to do. She slipped the mask over her face, only the emerald of her contacts staring back. She took a breath to steady herself.

Her father wasn't here, so she would have to figure this out herself.

Gaelen came back in the room with a small box and lifted the latch. The prettiest tiara Ember had ever seen sat inside on a velvet pillow. A tiara made of antlers encrusted with onyx and jade, runes carved into the bone. Ember's jaw dropped as Gaelen took it out of the case and set it on her fiery red hair.

"Your mother sent it for you," Gaelen said, as she adjusted the tiara. "She thought it might be nice to wear when you're introduced to your court—your people."

*My people.*

Ember swallowed dryly as she nodded, forcing a smile. She ran her fingers along the jewels and the runes—was she abandoning her people by escaping? She didn't even know she had 'people' until three months ago, and now she was supposed to be responsible for them? For all their lives? She blew a perfectly manicured curl out of her face. She couldn't worry about that. Her concern now was the innocent children in the belly of the castle and getting Theo home.

"Did you want to wear any jewelry?" Gaelen asked, as she pulled out a small box and opened it, necklaces and earrings scattered about in the bottom. Jewels glinted against the light peeking in from behind the clouds. Ember's hands instinctively went to the pendant around her neck and the diamonds in her ears.

"No, I don't think so." She shook her head as she smiled. "I'll just wear mine."

"I'll be back in a moment with the finishing touches." Gaelen smiled, then swiftly left the room.

Ember quickly packed the small bag Elowyn had made for her, stuffing in her books, a few potions she had saved, the map to the tunnels, and anything else she couldn't leave behind. If all went as planned, she wouldn't ever be coming back here again. Fen and Killian had taken the important things—her father's journal, a few of Theo's books, a small assortment of clothes she had grown to love, but nothing else mattered. Nothing here was *hers,* and she couldn't stand what it all represented. She grabbed the cloak she had found in her mother's study, gripping it in her hand as she twirled the ring on her finger. She walked back to the mirror, straightening the tiara on her head as she steadied her breathing.

They were as ready as they would ever be, but somehow that wasn't much of a comfort. She went over the plan in her head again and again, praying that no unexpected roadblocks popped up. They hadn't left much room for error, and they were already going to be cutting it close as it was. She bit her lip as she considered the alternative to success tonight—no, failure wasn't an option, not with Maeve and Theo's lives on the line. If Aoife had no problem sacrificing her daughter, she didn't even want to imagine what she would be willing to do to Theo if it meant the sacrifice was 'for the greater good.'

Gaelen walked back in the room, quickly shutting the door behind her, a small wooden box in hand. Ember furrowed her brow as the Merrow walked up to her, almost like she was afraid of getting caught.

"I don't know what you're planning to do tonight," Gaelen whispered, "but take this with you, just in case." She opened the box, and a beautiful dagger lay inside, a handle made of pearl, adorned with coral and jewels, gold etched throughout. But the blade wasn't made of metal, at least not any metal she had ever seen. It was a deep blue, and waves seemed to pulse inside of it. Ember sucked in a breath as she ran her hand along the blade, the familiar tingle of magic crackling against her skin.

"Galen, this is beautiful," Ember said, as she felt the weight of the knife in her hand. "Is it from your kingdom?"

"Those who aren't taken," Gaelen breathed, "are taught to fight from a very young age, to be able to defend themselves. These knives are handed down by our parents when we are very young. I've had it since I was old enough to understand the consequences of using it."

"I can't take this," Ember said, as she shook her head. "You need to keep it."

Gaelen shook her head as she put her hand on Ember's. "After tonight, I won't have anyone left to protect."

Ember ran her fingers over the handle of the dagger and felt her magic tug, something deep inside her vibrating like it was locked in a cage. Something brushed up against her ribs, up her spine, and it was almost as if a veil had been lifted in her mind, exposing memories that had been buried so deep she could hardly even picture them.

Her eyes welled with tears as memories of her childhood nanny flitted through her mind. Picnics in the park, midnight snacks in front of the fire, cuts and scrapes that never needed to be bandaged. She choked on a sob as her eyes met Gaelen's, and the Merrow was already crying.

"I remember you," Ember whispered, tears rolling freely down her cheeks. "You were my nanny, weren't you?"

Gaelen nodded as her throat bobbed.

"Why couldn't I remember you until now?"

Gaelen led Ember to a pair of chairs sitting in front of a warm fire and motioned for her to sit. "Merrow have special gifts." Gaelen smiled as she brushed a stray hair from in front of Ember's eyes. "Magic that most Vala don't even know about. We have the ability to re-weave memories or hide them completely." She took a shaky breath as she wrung her hands in her lap. "I have been with your family since before you were born." She smiled softly. "Your father rescued me, he gave me a home and always paid me fairly, and for that, I owe him several life debts. The only thing he ever asked of me is that I protect you." She looked at the crackling fire, and something akin to grief seemed to flash through her eyes. "I was supposed to get you away from her, but our plan went awry. I was there the night of the storm."

Ember closed her eyes, chest shaking as she took a breath.

Gaelen didn't have to specify what storm she was talking about.

"It all happened so fast, and I had to make a decision quickly. I knew what your mother was planning, where she wanted to take you, and I knew I couldn't allow it." She stiffened as she flexed her hands in her lap. "So, when the boat splintered and everyone went overboard, I did my best to make the waves push you toward shore. I couldn't stop the storm, but I could do my best to get you out of it."

A tear slid down her cheek as the memory seemed to play out in front of her, like she was reliving it over and over again.

"Your mother was already with child, but I don't think even she knew it yet. I didn't have the power to save all three of you, so I did my best to push her as far away as I could manage. The waves I conjured carried her to the Scotland, and I thought that would be enough. Your father was gone before I could do anything about it."

Her eyes glistened as she held Ember's hand, and Ember was certain she had stopped breathing entirely.

"You were so tiny," she continued, "curled up on the beach completely alone. It destroyed me to leave you there, I need you to understand that." Her grip tightened around Ember's fingers. "But I made a promise to your father—I had to keep you safe. I removed your memories, hiding myself and my magic in them, to keep you safe. I told the authorities that I found you on the beach and that your parents were dead. And then I left for Scotland."

"To find my mother?" Ember asked.

Gaelen nodded. "I found her in the Highlands, and I rewove her memories as well. I couldn't hide you, but I planted false memories—memories of the authorities notifying her of the death of her daughter and husband."

"The body she identified," Ember said, as her chest shook, "none of that was real?"

Gaelen shook her head. "It wasn't," she replied, "but she

believed it was. In all reality, she never left Scotland. We stayed while she was with child, the plan was always to go back to Ellesmere, but we stayed. For what reason, I'm not entirely sure. I think part of her couldn't face the reality of what she had done."

"Why did you come back?" Ember asked, voice shaky as she tried not to fidget with her dress.

"Your granda' got sick," Gaelen sighed, "so she came home to take care of him. After a few months, she got word that you were in Sigurvik, and she was able to track you down."

"And you got my room ready?" Ember asked, as she thought about all the little touches from her childhood nestled in the room. "The books and my dragon? That was you?"

Gaelen nodded. "I saved it all from the cottage in Galway. I hoped one day you would get to have it all back again."

"She never mentioned that you were my nanny," Ember said, as she shook her head. "Why didn't she mention it when I first got there?"

"She didn't remember." Gaelen shrugged. "She thinks I found her in Scotland, so she doesn't remember I was with your family all those years. As far as she is aware, we had never met."

"You protected me." Ember smiled through her tears. "All these years I thought I was alone, but you were protecting me."

Gaelen nodded as she smiled. "I made a promise to your father, and I have done my best to keep it—to protect you both."

*Theo.*

"Now, shall we finish getting ready?" Gaelen said, as she stood up, brushing her hands down her dress as she took a breath. She smiled gently, taking out the strap in the box and handing it to Ember.

Ember hooked it around her thigh, slipping the dagger in and letting the dress float back down over it.

"Watch over your brother," Gaelen said, as a tear rolled down her cheek, "and get him home."

*Home.*

Ember sniffed, tears pooling on her lower lash as she pulled the cape out of her bag. "I don't know what is going to happen tonight," she said, as she handed the silken material to Gaelen, "but after we leave, go home as quickly as possible. Everyone should be distracted at the castle, so you shouldn't have a problem making it to the docks."

Gaelen smiled, more tears rolling down her cheeks as she clutched the cape in her hands, starlight shimmering between her fingers. "You are going to do great things, Ember Lothbrok."

COLLUM PICKED her up at exactly eight o'clock, his dress uniform finely pressed as he stood with his hands firmly behind his back, waiting as she walked down the stairs. He took her arm, and they walked out the door. Right before he Echoed them to the castle, he mumbled, "You look nice, Princess."

Ember cringed, even as the air was sucked from her lungs, flying through stars. People milled about the courtyard in masks of all shapes and sizes, the women wearing some of the most beautiful gowns she had ever seen. She fidgeted with the side of the dress as Collum led her through the door toward the ballroom. Music filled the castle, reverberating off the arched ceilings making the magic thrum steadily in her veins.

"Are we late?" she whispered as they walked toward the ballroom and the grand set of stairs leading into it.

"A princess is never late," he replied, as he shook his head.

Ember gritted her teeth but didn't reply. The crowd below fell into a hush as Collum guided her down the staircase, her dress flowing behind her as everyone watched—every eye on her.

This might be harder than she thought.

The music swelled, and people began dancing again, singing and chanting as whiskey was slung through the air. A boy with pale hair and charcoal eyes walked up to her and Collum, his finely pressed suit rivaling the blackness of the night outside. He had a mask on that resembled a white wolf, and Ember giggled as he bowed.

"I'll take it from here." He winked at Collum and took Ember's arm to walk away. "You look stunning," Killian whispered, leaning close to her ear. The warmth of his breath sent goosebumps down her neck, her cheeks flushing as she smiled.

"You're not so bad yourself, Vargr," she replied with a grin.

They made their way through the dance floor, to the side of the room lined with tables. Food piled every inch of them —roast lamb, duck and rabbit, hot cross buns drenched in honey, bread of all shapes and sizes, bowls filled with seed and fruits and leafy greens, and enough deviled eggs to feed ten armies.

"What the hell is an 'auroch?'" Fen asked, as they approached the table, picking at a slab of meat he had on a plate. He was wearing all black as well and had a blood red mask on in the shape of a draic. Ember laughed as she grabbed a bun and some cheese and stuffed them in her mouth—she was *famished*.

"It's like an ancient cow," Odette hummed, as she popped a few sunflower seeds in her mouth. "Helvig must breed them somewhere."

"Odette!" Ember nearly shouted, wrapping the girl in a hug. Odette hugged her back, the blushed colored dress she was wearing wrinkling between them. "What on earth are you doing here?" Ember asked, as she stepped back, her chest suddenly feeling lighter.

"She *insisted* on coming," Fen replied, as he stuffed a strawberry in his mouth. "Would you believe she even threatened to tell my mum if we didn't bring her?"

Odette's cheeks stained crimson as Ember raised a brow. Suddenly, she remembered the woman whose smile so closely resembled her friend's, and her heart sank.

"Odette, your mum..." she began, but Odette stopped her.

"I know," she whispered. "I can feel her."

"We can go find her," Ember said, as she began to look around the room. "She's bound to be here somewhere."

"Not tonight," Odette said, as she shook her head. "We are here for a reason, and so is she. We will meet again."

Ember tilted her head. She wished she had half the courage the Odette seemed to.

"We have company," Killian whispered, as he nodded his head to the front on the room.

Ember felt the air shift as Helvig and her mother entered the room, gliding down the staircase like it was something that came naturally. She stiffened as she turned away, focusing on her friends, and praying they didn't come up to talk to her. Rowan walked up to the table, her red dress flowing around her ankles, brown curls falling over her shoulders. She smiled at Ember, but her face immediately shifted when she saw the way Fen was looking at her.

"I was really hoping this was some sort of sick joke," he mumbled, as she walked up to the trio, "but I suppose we couldn't get that lucky."

"It's wonderful to see you too, Fenrir," Rowan cooed, as she adjusted the bracelet on her wrist. "Still just as inconspicuous as ever I see."

Fen pulled at his sleeves, the midnight black he and Killian were wearing in stark contrast with the spring colors everyone else seemed to have on. "And you're still a raging bitch I see," he spat.

Ember slapped him in the arm and gave him a look. *Don't start.*

*She started it,* he seemed to say as his eyes narrowed.

"I find your obvious disdain for me so refreshing." Rowan smiled back.

"Obvious?" Fen laughed. "And I was trying so hard to hide it."

"Can we continue this little reunion later?" Ember asked, as she made to step in between them. "We have work to do."

Rowan's eyes widened a hair as she scanned the group. "Quinn?"

"Hello, Rowan." Odette smiled, any surprise at the girl in front of her not evident on her face. "It's so lovely to see you again."

"I'm going to check that everything is ready in the garden." Rowan shook her head, nodding toward the other side of the room. "Meet you in the dungeons in two hours?"

Ember nodded as Rowan left, moving to make sure everything was in place. The distraction would take place in the gardens, hopefully pulling everyone's attention away from the ballroom and outside. Ember wasn't sure exactly *how* Rowan planned to distract everyone, but she knew it would be nothing short of extravagant.

"We will only have a few minutes to get out of the room and to the dungeon after Rowan gives the signal," Ember lowered her voice, as she talked to the boys and Odette. "We have to be focused, clear headed. Whatever you do, stay *away* from the whiskey." She eyed Fen, who carefully set his glass on the table behind him, wiping the amber liquid off his mouth.

"So, what's the signal?" he asked, as he cleared his throat and stuck his hands in his pockets.

"When we get to the dungeons," she ignored his question,

"we will have maybe ten or fifteen minutes before we're missed. We have to let Aesira out, then get the children and make our way through the tunnels."

"Okay," Fen nodded, "but what's the signal?"

"I don't know how long the tunnels are, the map doesn't give specifics," Ember continued, "so we'll need to go quickly and quietly. I don't know what's down there. I'm going to go make an appearance with my mother and Helvig and then find Theo," she said, as she sucked in a breath. "Try to mingle and not act suspicious."

Killian nodded with a grin. "I'll come with you. A princess needs an escort."

Ember scrunched her nose but didn't argue.

"But what's the signal?" Fen whispered hoarsely, as they walked away, but they didn't turn around to answer, leaving Odette to handle him on her own.

"Oh, Ember, love," Aoife cooed, as she and Killian walked toward them. "Don't you look lovely." She brushed a lock of hair over Ember's shoulder, smoothing the sleeves of her dress. "The tiara fits perfectly."

"A gown *and* tiara fit for a princess." Helvig grinned. "How are you enjoying your first Ostara celebration?"

Ember gritted her teeth, forcing a smile. "It's lovely. Thank you, Granda'." She nodded.

Killian squeezed her hand in his—an unspoken promise. *I'm here.*

"Mum," she continued, "you remember Killian Vargr?"

"I do." Aoife smiled. "How lovely to see you Killian. Are your parents here?"

"No," Killian shook his head, putting on his most charming smile, "I'm afraid I just accompanied my uncle tonight. It's a lovely ball." He kissed Ember's hand as he grinned. "If you'll excuse me, I believe I have some clients I must check in with. I'll find you later."

Ember gave him a pointed look as he grinned, but before he could walk away, a slender hand landed on his shoulder.

"Surely, they can wait," Veda Ellingboe tutted, as she walked up beside the group. "Care to dance, cousin?" She turned to Ember and smiled, her emerald dress swaying in the breeze that flowed through the open doors. "I'll bring him back in one piece, Lothbrok."

Ember felt her blood begin to boil as the raven-haired girl grinned, her hand wrapping tightly around Killian's. He winced as he turned to her and gave her a knowing look.

*I'll be back.*

Ember checked her growing temper and smiled, the sickly-sweet smile she had been practicing for weeks now.

"Come find me when you're done." She smiled at Killian, then let go of his hand. The tether at her sternum pulsed as he walked away, like every part of her magic didn't want him out of its sight, either. She took a breath and turned back to her mother, smoothing her dress in mock boredom.

"Is Theo here?" she asked Aoife. "I haven't seen him since I arrived."

"Yes," she nodded her head behind Ember, "he hasn't moved much since we got here."

Ember turned around to see Theo standing in a corner, twiddling his thumbs. Her heart sank. She had been over the plan with him the night before several times, and she knew he was scared. This life, their mother, was the only thing he had ever known. She knew the dread that came with having to leave it all behind and start over, and it broke her heart to see him like this. She walked to the corner and nudged him in the shoulder.

*"Having fun?"* she signed with a small smile.

Theo shrugged. *"Not really,"* he signed. *"Is it time to go home?"*

Ember sucked in a breath.

*Home.*

389

She truly hoped Theo could find a home at the Kitts' with her. She prayed they could find their way out of this together. Ember nodded toward the table where Fen was still standing with a full plate of food, Odette laughing as he tried to balance it. *"Why don't you go hang out with Fen and Odette until we're ready?"* she signed.

Theo nodded with a grin and ran off. Ember made her way around the ballroom, noting the presence of guards and where they were stationed, making a mental note of any exits should things go badly. She was just making another round, going to check on Rowan, when Killian walked up beside her.

"How was your dance?" She grinned, rolling her eyes as he stood stiffly beside her.

"Uneventful." He shrugged. "I have to keep up appearances unfortunately."

"Well, everything seems to be in order, so now we just have to wait." Ember sighed as she looked around the room once more, a smile forming on her face. "I think we deserve to have a little fun before the night delves into complete madness." Ember nodded toward the dance floor, and Killian laughed.

"I am not inclined to dance," he shook his head, "and frankly, you can't make me."

"Please," she giggled, batting her eyelashes as she stuck out her bottom lip.

"I thought we agreed that word was off limits," he whispered, giving her a crooked grin. She stuck out her lip further and he sighed playfully and then pulled her onto the dance floor.

They swayed back and forth to the music, his hand gripping her lower back like it was a lifeline. He spun her around, and she laughed as he drew her back in, her face just inches from his. He was magic, and when she was in his orbit, she felt like magic too. She breathed him in—the smell of spruce and green apples—and steadied herself against his chest. His charcoal eyes bore into hers, the fire from the lamps hovering above them dancing in the smoke.

He grinned as he brushed a stray hair from her face, their movement slowing with the music around them. Her heart beat rapidly in her chest as his grip tightened around her, one hand on the small of her back, the other on the back of her neck. She sucked in a breath—the air around them had her feeling like kindling stepping far too close to an open flame.

"Care if I cut in?" Fen stepped up beside them, and Ember realized how hard she was breathing, stepping back from Killian and smoothing out her dress. Killian shot daggers at Fen, nostrils flaring as the muscles in his jaw twitched.

"Sure, Fen," Ember smiled, clearing her throat.

"I'll go check on Theo," Killian mumbled and then stalked away to the other side of the room.

"Are you scared?" Fen whispered, as they swayed with the music.

Ember shook her head. "I don't think so," she replied. "We've gone through the plan enough times that I think it will be just fine."

"That's not what I meant." He cocked a brow and looked her in the eye. "I mean, are you scared to leave? To leave your mum again?"

Ember averted her eyes. "I don't think scared is the right word," she replied, as she watched Aoife mingle with all the guests, laughing and carrying on like she had done it a thousand times before. Emotions warred inside of her—hurt and anger mingling together to form something akin to…

Grief.

"Do you want to talk about it?" he asked.

"No," Ember shook her head with a polite smile, "not yet."

The song ended, and Ember wrapped Fen in a hug. "You're a good brother," she whispered.

He gave her a nod, tears glistening in his eyes as she pulled away.

"I'm going to go get some air." She turned and walked outside to the terrace overlooking the gardens. Rowan was in there somewhere, preparing the distraction, and all she could do was wait now.

She breathed in the night air, steadying herself against the stars that burned above her. Rage had consumed so much of her in the past weeks that she hadn't given herself a moment to think about the grief that would come with leaving. When she had lost her parents when she was six, they had been taken from her—swept away by Njord and leaving her lost and alone. But this time, she was leaving on her own, making a choice to leave behind the life she had begged the gods for since she was a wean on that rocky beach. Leaving behind a part of her family.

*The blood of the covenant is thicker than the water of the womb.*

Ember smiled to herself—maybe there was more to family than just who you were born to.

"Taking one last look at the sky before we go underground?" Killian grinned as he leaned on the railing next to her. "I promise these stars will still be there when we get out."

"Just taking a breather before it all starts," she laughed. "What are you doing out here? Get tired of Fen's company?"

"I just had something I needed to finish," he whispered.

Ember furrowed her brow, but before she could ask what he meant, he had one hand wrapped around the back of her neck and the other around her waist, pulling her so close to him that she thought they might stay tangled up forever.

And he kissed her.

It was passionate—hungry, like if he let go for even a moment, she might disappear. She wrapped her arms around his neck, and he pulled her closer. Fingers tangled in her curls as he gripped the back of her neck, and she thought she could stand there forever.

She had kissed boys before—one boy, to be exact, when she was twelve years old at the only birthday party she had ever been invited to, for the only friend she had ever had. It had been pleasant enough, if not quick. It had happened during a game of truth or dare on his twelfth birthday, and Ember thought she might spontaneously combust right there on the spot. But kissing Koen Skarsgard when she was twelve was a far cry from this ball with this man on a night where anything could go wrong.

But as Killian pulled away and looked into her eyes and grinned, she realized how many things could go right tonight too.

He tasted like apples, starlight, and impulsive decisions.

He kissed her again, this time slower—deliberate, like he was memorizing the way she tasted, taking his time as he held her against his chest. There was something otherworldly about the way his fingers moved through her hair, twirling around her curls, and trailing down her neck. She wanted this moment to last forever.

Her breathing evened out as he pulled away from her, his smile growing as he brushed his thumb down her cheek, his face turning red.

"Why me?" she whispered. Out of all the girls in the world, why her?

"It was always going to be you, Ember Lothbrok."

He spoke her name like a prayer.

"What are you lot doing out here?" Fen grinned as he ran up beside them, Theo and Odette in tow behind. His eyes narrowed, darting between the two of them, and Ember felt her face flush. Killian's eyes were wide, his lips swollen and red, and he looked like he wanted to be anywhere other than there at the moment.

Fen's eyes widened as his jaw dropped in understanding. "What are you two *doing* out here?" he asked again, but this time it sounded like he would rather not receive an answer.

Before Ember could reply, an explosion sounded in the distance, and screams erupted from the ballroom all the way to the garden. Ember jumped, grabbing Killian's hand as she turned to look toward the maze. A fire burned brightly against the darkness of the night, and Ember shook her head as she laughed. Rowan had caused an explosion in the middle of the maze. It would take them ages to get in and out—it was genius.

"You reckon that was the signal?" Fen said with wide eyes.

Ember nodded, grabbing Theo's hand, and turning toward the door. "We need to go now!"

# CHAPTER 38

# THE PRICE FOR CHANGE

Ember sped through the corridors, the boys and Odette close behind as she ran as fast and as quiet as she could toward the door leading to the dungeon. Everyone in the ballroom had crowded the terrace, running into the gardens to try to get a view of the fire and what had exploded. The group took their chance, sneaking through the crowd and slipping out of the ballroom into the quiet castle.

"Are you sure you know what you're doing?" Fen puffed as they stopped to catch their breath.

Ember spun around to take in her surroundings. "I think so." She nodded. "It should be this wa—"

"There." Odette pointed and, at the end of one of the hall, right next to a wooden door, was a blue ball of light shining brightly—beckoning her.

Ember tore off down the hall toward the dungeon door.

"Starshine, slow down!" Killian whispered, as they ran after her, but she didn't. She came to a screeching halt in front of the door, the runes in the rounded frame glowing blue as the wisp lit them up.

"Is this it?" Fen asked, as he sucked in air.

"Yes," Ember whispered, nodding as she felt the magic pulse off the brass doorknob.

"Thank the gods," Fen breathed, sighing as he leaned against the wall.

"So, let's go," Killian said, as he jiggled the lock, but it didn't budge.

Ember rolled her eyes. "It's locked." She laughed. "Here, let me."

The wisp broke into dozens of tiny pieces, wrapping itself around the locked doorknob and setting it ablaze with blue light. She grabbed the knob, feeling the familiar sting as magic coursed through her palm, molten lava pulsing through her veins. The lock popped open, and she winced as she let go, gripping her wrist and holding her hand at her chest.

"What was that?" Fen asked, wide eyed.

Ember shrugged. "A long story. Let's go."

They sped down the spiral stairs—down, down, down, the light of the wisp leaving a trail of blue light only visible to Ember and Odette.

"Can we light one of these torches?" Fen hissed through the darkness. "Or maybe, I don't know, flip on a damn light switch?"

Ember continued forward. "If we turn on a light, someone could see it from the hallway, and they would be down here before we could do anything. Just stay close. We're almost there."

The stairs leveled out, and they walked down the first dark corridor. They stopped for a moment to catch their breath, leaning against the wall as moonlight from the small windows danced like waves across the floor. The wisp hovered around Ember's hand, wrapping itself around her wrist, tugging her on.

"We need to keep moving," she whispered, shoving open the door to the next set of stairs. "Rowan has probably stalled as long as she can, so they'll know something is up soon."

*They'll see that we're all missing,* she thought.

They sped down the second set of stairs, landing quickly at the bottom.

"Listen," Odette said, as they slowed.

Fen didn't wait another second as he shot in front of her, led only by the light from the moon and the voices coming from the end of the hall. "Maeve!" he cried, as he gripped the rungs of the cell door. "Are you okay?"

Maeve grinned as she looked at her big brother. "I'm okay, but how did you find me?"

Ember got closer and grinned at the girl. "I told you I would be back for you," she whispered, tears pricking at her eyes.

"Get her out," Fen demanded, fire burning in his eyes.

Ember began to fiddle with the lock, waiting for the wisp to wrap around it again, and that was when she heard shuffling behind them. "Rowan?" she whispered into the darkness. She took a few steps into the darkness. "Took you long enough. We could really use some help back here—"

"Not. Another. Word," Collum said, as he grabbed her by the arm, a knife pressed against her neck as the rest of her words died in her throat. "I knew your mum was a bleedin' fool for thinking you'd changed. I saw right through you." He spun her around, pressing her back against his chest, the knife still resting on her pale skin, so close that if she moved if would slice clean through. "The way you pranced about, suddenly the perfect princess. I could see it in your eyes—the plotting, the planning, the scheming. Did you really think you would succeed?"

"Let her go, Collum." Killian's nostrils flared, a flame burning in his palm—ready, waiting.

Collum used his free hand, shooting a spell at the group. Theo's eyes were wide with fear, hiding behind Odette as he clutched her shirt, dodging the hex. Killian tried to fire back, but Collum blocked it with ease.

"I saw the five of you slip out of the ballroom after the explosion," Collum almost bragged. "I decided then and there that your mum's faith in you wasn't enough, so I followed you to see what mischief you had planned."

Killian took a step forward, but that only made Collum press the knife tighter to her neck.

"I have to say," he laughed, almost manically, "I never imagined I would hit such a jackpot. Turning over thieves to the Jarl? Catching you in the act of trying to break out prisoners? He'll reward me greatly for handing you over."

Ember took a shaky break, the knife digging into her skin. She felt blood trickle down her neck as she steadied her breathing and closed her eyes. "You don't have to do this, Collum," she whispered. "Just let us go, and no one will be the wiser. These children are innocent, even you should agree that they don't deserve to be locked up like wild animals."

"The Jarl's word is law," Collum hissed. He removed the knife, running it down the side of her face.

Ember winced as blood trickled down her cheek.

"Maybe," he continued, whispering in her ear, "you will be my prize from Helvig when I turn you over." His breath was hot on her neck, reeking of whiskey. He ran his free hand down her side, grabbing her waist, gripping her dress in his bony fingers.

Ember held her breath, holding back the whimper threatening at her lips.

"You will not touch her," Killian growled, his eyes flashing amber as he clenched his fists.

"I would love to see you try and stop me." Collum grinned.

Fen came at him first. Not with a spell, no. He ran toward him, flying through the air and grabbing Collum's arm to wrestle the knife away. Ember dropped to the floor right as Collum shoved Fen off him into the stone wall. Fen cried out as his head collided with the wall, and Ember moved to crawl away as fast as she could, toward Theo and Odette. He grabbed her ankle, dug in with all his might as he dragged her back to him.

A growl sounded through the dungeons, bouncing off the ceiling and piercing her ears. In less than a second, a great white wolf was standing where Killian stood, tearing toward Collum. He let go of Ember's ankle, swinging the knife with all his might at the wolf, and Killian grabbed his wrist in his mouth, clamping down until Collum screamed. Killian but down harder, bones crunching as he hurtled him harder than Ember had ever seen, straight into the wall. He crumbled as his head made contact with the stone and slumped on the floor where he landed.

Theo ran to Ember, eyes rimmed red as he wrapped his arms around her still halfway behind Odette, Fen breathing rapidly behind her. She squeezed his hand as she wrapped him in a hug.

*I'm here.*

"Bloody hell," a voice sounded from the end of the hall, "you couldn't wait fifteen minutes to begin the bloodshed?" Rowan made her way quickly to the end of the dungeon. "What happened to you?" She looked at Fen on the floor, a bruise blooming on his cheek and blood trickling down his lip.

"I had to try something." Fen shrugged, pushing himself off the floor. "I thought I could get to him before he realized what was happening."

Rowan laughed as she gave him a once over. "Are you implying that you are even remotely capable of stealth?"

Fen huffed as he shoved away from the wall he was leaning against, jamming a finger in her chest, teeth clenched. "The risk I took was calculated."

Rowan smirked as she raised a brow. "Man, are you bad at math."

"I did not come here to be insulted by you, Rowan O'Rourke," he hissed, nostrils flaring.

"Oh?" She grinned as she crossed her arms lazily over her chest. "And where do you usually go?"

"Can we finish this later?" Killian asked. He was back in his finely pressed suit, sporting only a cut on his cheek, no doubt where the knife had nicked him. He walked past the group and over to the cell door, all of the children huddled in the corner whimpering.

All of them, except for Maeve.

She was still standing at the bars, back straight as wisps floated around her hands, like she had been in a dozen battles before, her eyes harder than Ember ever remembered them being. Something burned behind them. Maybe she would've thought it was anger or self-preservation or guilt for not being able to help, except Ember knew that look. She had given herself the same look in the mirror a thousand times before. Her childhood had gone up in flames, and she was watching it burn to ash.

Ember swallowed as she gave her a gentle smile. "Are you ready to go home?"

Maeve gave her a nod, and the wisps suddenly floated out of the dungeon and into the lock. Maeve flicked her eyes to the lock, and then pushed the door open, ushering the smaller children out, and ran to her brother, wrapping him in a hug and whispering something in his ear that he didn't seem to hear.

Ember furrowed her brow as the wisp floated beside her, and then she walked back over to her friends.

"Head for the tunnels," she said. "I'll get Aesira out and meet you down there."

Killian acted like he wanted to argue, but she held up her hand, his charcoal eyes meeting hers.

She leaned into hug him, brushing a kiss against his cheek, and whispered, "Protect them. I'll be right behind you."

"This might be a little easier." Odette smiled as a ball of light appeared in her hand. She cast a quiet spell, and

Ember's gorgeous dress turned into pants and a shirt, the same deep blue and black that she had been wearing before, her knife still strapped to her thigh. She scowled as she thought about the knife, she hadn't even been quick enough to grab it. She tied her hair back in a braid, stuffing the tiara and mask in her bag and made her way to the front of the hall.

"Quite the commotion." Aesira smiled, her eyelids heavy. "I was wondering who would come out on top."

"A warning would have been nice," Ember said, as she rolled her eyes, quickly unlocking the door and swinging it open. The woman sat in the corner, ankles and wrist shackled.

"Tis a blood spell," she said, as she held up the shackles. They clanged as she set them back down, like the weight was too much. "Only his blood can open it."

"Well, it's a good thing I'm his blood then, isn't it?" Ember smiled, grabbing the knife from its holster at her thigh. She winced as the blood pooled on her palm, and then squeezed her hand tight. She walked over to the woman, letting the blood drop on each shackle, and whispered the spell she had committed to memory from the year before. The locks popped open with a quiet click, and Aesira gently shook herself free.

"I owe you a life debt," Aesira said, as she stood. She was shaky on her feet and soon fell back on the stone bed at the wall.

"Well, you can cash that in now," Ember said, as she made to hoist the woman up. "We need to get the kids out."

Aesira shook her head. "I'm too weak," she whispered hoarsely. "I'm afraid all I would do is hold you up."

"If you stay here," Ember replied, "they'll lock you back up again without a second thought. You have to come with us."

"I'll make my way out," Aesira shook her head, "but you must go. There isn't much time."

"I can't leave you here," Ember replied, as she bit her lip, glancing toward the open door behind her. "Maybe we can just—"

"No," Aesira replied, "get the children out. I'll find you when I'm well again."

"I don't think I can do this by myself," Ember whispered, watching as the wisps circled around her wrist and palm.

Aesira grabbed her hand and flipped it over. "Do you see this blueish vein on your wrist?"

Ember nodded.

"The blood flowing through them contains hemoglobin— a protein that has four iron atoms incorporated into it." She ran her cold finger down the vein on Ember's wrist. "Iron is only naturally produced in one place. Do you know where that is?"

Ember shook her head, brow furrowed.

"It can only be forged in the core of dying stars," Aesira whispered. "You are built from, and kept alive by, pieces of stardust—you can do anything."

Ember nodded, anything she wanted to say dying in her throat as she steadied herself. Aesira mumbled something weakly in the palm of her hand and then grabbed Ember's right wrist. The magic flowed over Ember's finger, wrapping her ring in blue light. It pulsed, burning into her skin and through her veins as it spread through her arms and into her chest. She thought she might collapse from the sheer intensity of it all, but then it was gone, only the gold band on her finger remained. Aesira gasped for air, like she had used the very last of her magic in the one enchantment.

"Your father put a protection spell on this ring when you were a child," Aesira whispered. "It's what kept you hidden and safe for so long. This will protect you from him, for the time being anyway. You must never take it off."

*He quickly pulled a small gold ring off his right hand and dug in his pocket, pulling a chain out and slipping it through the ring. He pulled the little girl off his shoulders, setting her gently on the ground, and slipped the chain over her head. "If there ever comes a day that I'm not here," he whispered, as tears pricked the corners of his eyes, "this will keep you close to me. This will keep you safe."*

The memory reverberated in her mind as her chest tightened. Had he known what she would have to face, what she would have to fight? She rubbed the ring, feeling the warmth of the metal against the pad of her thumb. He had sacrificed everything for her, given his life to try to protect her. Even in death, she could feel him there, steadying her.

"You must go now," Aesira said, as she ushered her out of the cell and into the cold corridor.

"Be safe," Ember whispered, and then she ran out the door and down the corridor, meeting up with everyone at the end.

"Your Wildling friend decide to stay behind?" Killian asked, as she walked up beside him.

"She'll be okay," Ember replied, but she wasn't so sure.

They made their way through the tunnels, Rowan, Odette and Fen in the front with Theo, and Killian and Ember bringing up the rear. They walked for what felt like hours, winding through the tunnels, only whispering if they came at a fork and needed to figure out what way to go. The tunnel finally widened, and they found themselves in a large room with walls of stone on all sides, a giant pool of water glistening in the middle. There was no exit, just rock all around and above them, and Ember felt her stomach drop.

"Where's the cave?" Fen asked, as he found a rock to sit on.

"I think we're in it, mate." Killian sighed as he rubbed the back of his neck.

"Let me rephrase," Fen huffed, as he stood up, slinging his arms in the air. "Where is the *exit* to the cave?"

Ember let out a shaky breath, panic building in her chest. This wasn't on the map, not specifically anyway. They expected to find a cave on the other side of the mountain, but instead, they were underwater. Her heart rate quickened as she searched for another exit, but there wasn't one. They were trapped.

"It's an underwater cave," Rowan mumbled, as she shook her head. "We'll have to swim."

"We don't know how far it goes." Fen shook his head. "It could be miles long."

"We've run out of options, Fenrir," Rowan replied.

"I will not send these children to their deaths," he hissed. "Maybe we can... dig our way out."

"Just because it pops into your head," Rowan rolled her eyes, "doesn't mean we need to hear it."

"Enough," Killian hissed, "save your bickering for when we're out of this hell hole."

Theo squeezed Ember's hand. *"Potion,"* he signed.

"What potion?" Rowan asked, as she furrowed her brow.

"Breath of the Deep!" Odette grinned.

"The potion we made in Herbal Magic?" Killian asked, as he cocked his brow.

"If we take some, everyone can get out of the cave without having to hold their breath." Fen nodded, beaming like he had come up with the greatest plan in the world.

"Well, unless the ingredients are air, rock, and water," Rowan replied, "I don't think we have the things necessary to complete it."

Fen's face fell, shoving his hands in his pocket as he nodded. Theo squeezed Ember's hand again and pointed to her bag.

"I don't have enough," she replied, as she shook her head, pulling the vial from the bag. "It won't be enough for everyone, too many people would be left behind."

"So, we're back to square one then," Fen sighed.

Ember sat on a rock at the back of the cave, laying her head in her palms. They hadn't planned for this, hadn't talked about what would happen if they got to the end and had nowhere else to go. They were trapped, their only options to dive into the water and pray or head back into the waiting claws of the devil above them. As a tear slid down Ember's cheek, stinging the gash left by Collum's knife, the water in the pool rippled, something beneath it breaking the surface.

Ember shot up, pulling Theo behind her as she peered below. "Maren!" Ember almost shrieked, as the Merrow smiled up at her. Ember shook her head as she grinned. "I don't understand. How did you—"

Then, another Merrow broke the surface of the glistening pool.

"I owe you a life debt, Ember Lothbrok." Gaelen smiled up at her. "I could not leave my family to fend for themselves."

A tear slid down Ember's cheek as she grinned, squeezing Theo's hand as he squeezed hers.

Family.

*The blood of the covenant is thicker than the water of the womb.*

"Thank you," Ember whispered, chest shaking.

Several more Merrow popped up, and Ember, Killian, Rowan, and Fen began lowering children into the water, handing one to each Merrow. They spoke spells over them, no need for a potion to give them breath under water, and one by one, they swam out of sight, into the belly of the mountain—to freedom.

Gaelen stayed back, the last to leave with a little blond boy clinging to her neck. "I'll come back for you," she said, as she looked at the seven still on the shore, "We'll come back and—"

"No." Ember stopped her as she shook her head. "I have enough potion to get us out. Stay with the children and keep them safe, please."

Gaelen nodded her head. It wasn't a command, but she regarded it as such. "We will be waiting for you on the other side. Swim through the cave, and there is a cavern on the other side. The potion should get you there with enough breath, but swim quickly."

"We will," Ember whispered, and then Gaelen was gone, disappearing before they could blink. Ember pulled the vial out of her bag, handing it to Fen first. "One drop should do the trick," she said, as they each passed it between one another. Maeve, Fen, Odette, and Theo all took theirs, and Theo squeezed Ember's hand.

"Go with Fen and Odette," she said, squeezing his hand back. "Gaelen is waiting on the other side. I'll be right behind you."

Theo wrapped his arms tightly around her waist, and Ember squeezed him like it was going to be the last time she ever saw him. He looked up at Ember, eyes glistening with unshed tears as he nodded and walked over to Fen, Odette, and Maeve.

"Hurry, okay?" Fen said, as he hugged her, whispering in her ear. "Mum will kill me if I show up at home with only one sister."

Ember grinned as she gave him a nod, afraid if she said anything the tears she was holding back would come pouring out.

"See you on the other side." Fen grinned with a mock salute, then the four of them were in the water, swimming down and away.

Ember handed the vial to Killian, who took his drop, and then she held the vial out to Rowan next, but she shook her head, pushing it away.

"I won't be joining you." She smiled. "My work here isn't done."

"I can't leave you alone," Ember said, as she furrowed her brow. "You can't just stay here. What will happen to you?"

"Nothing worse than what already has." Rowan shrugged. "A few beatings, maybe being locked in my room, but nothing worse than I've already endured. My only saving grace is that you won't have to endure it too." She gave a half smile, and Ember's chest felt like it might cave in. "No one knows I was here, and Collum never saw me. I'll go back through the tunnels, act like I found Collum unconscious in the dungeons and the cells empty. Hopefully, it buys you all more time to get home."

"Just come with us," Ember pleaded. "We can get information about the castle some other way. You don't need to risk your life to do it."

"This is my way of atoning for what I've done," Rowan replied. "Someone has to tell the stories that went on in these walls. Either they write our story, or we do."

"I can't let you do this," Ember whispered again. "Sacrificing your life and future isn't worth it."

Rowan smiled faintly. "What if sacrifice is the price we have to pay for change?"

Ember smiled, wrapping her friend in a hug and said her goodbyes.

"Tell my mum I love her, okay?" Rowan asked, tears pooling on her lower lash. "Tell her I'm sorry."

Ember nodded, tilting the vial to her mouth, when a voice rang from the back of the cave.

"Mo Stór," it rang out, "what have you done?"

# CHAPTER 39

# THERE BLOOD OF THE COVENANT

E mber gripped the vial in her hand, backing up into Killian and almost sent them both tumbling into the water. The clock was ticking—he only had so much air to breathe underwater before the potion would stop working all together.

"You have to go." She turned toward him. "Go, and I'll meet you there. I can't leave Rowan."

"I'm not leaving *you*," Killian replied, as he shook his head.

"Killian, the potion!" she almost shouted, but he grabbed her free hand, jaw tense as he stared into her eyes.

"I am not letting you go. Do you hear me?" his voice was desperate, amber flashing against the fear in his eyes. "I lost you once, never again."

She steeled herself, turning to face her mother as she corked the vial and stuffed it in her pocket.

"You've had me worried sick," Aoife said, running her hands down Ember's hair as she reached her.

"How did you find me?" she whispered, tensing every time her mother's hand made contact with her clammy skin.

"The tiara has runes carved into the antlers," she replied.

"A tracking spell is etched into it, among other things, just in case it ever fell into the wrong hands. I saw Collum leave the ball and realized you weren't there either," she replied. "I figured he was going to find you. But when he never came back, I activated the spell. I saw him unconscious, the dungeons empty, and only imagined the worst." She cried as she spoke, but no tears escaped her eyes. "I'm so glad to see you unharmed."

Ember took a step, narrowing her eyes as she clenched her fists. "Unharmed?" she hissed, as she took a shaky breath, taking another step away, "You knew them. You knew what they did to Rowan, what they did to those children, what they would gladly do to me. Do you really think I stand here unharmed?" She looked at her mother, eyes locked as she studied her, cool and calculated.

Looking into her hazel eyes should've felt like home, but it didn't.

"Ember, your fate has been written down since the day you were born," her mother replied. "It is your duty and destiny to stand by your grandfather and take back the island that we were promised, that *you* were promised." She took a breath as she stepped toward Ember. "This would have been much easier had that storm not ripped us apart."

"Maybe it would have," Ember replied, as she took another step back, "but I am not that little girl you left alone to die anymore."

Aoife reached out a hand to grab Ember's, but she yanked it away, running her fingers along the handle of the dagger strapped to her thigh.

"I had no intention of leaving you on the beach," Aoife replied. "I thought you were gone. I knew if for some reason you made it out alive, if they were wrong and that body wasn't yours, I would find you when the time was right."

"When the time was right?" Ember whispered hoarsely. "Every moment spent away from me should have burned a hole through your heart. It should have eaten you alive." Her chest shook as she steadied herself. "You should have torn the world apart to find me."

"I had a duty to your grandfather," Aoife replied. "I couldn't waste precious time while he withered away to nothing. I had to help him. Can you really blame me?"

"I blame you for everything!" Ember whispered, a tear sliding down her cheek. "I was just a prophecy to you, but you were my apocalypse."

"Ember, you need to come back home." Aoife stiffened, voice hardening, "Your grandfather is a reasonable man, but I would hate for something to happen to Theo because of your insolence."

"You will not touch him," Ember hissed.

"He isn't needed anymore, not now that we know you're alive. If you don't come home and do the right thing, I will have to have them hunt him down, and I can't guarantee that Collum will be gentle. Do you really want to be the cause of your brother's death, the way you were the cause of your father's?"

Ember felt warmth burn at her palm, a small flame threatening to envelope her entirely. She gritted her teeth, pulling the knife from the holster and rushing toward her mother. Aoife flipped her wrist and sent Ember careening into the side of the cave wall, knocking the breath from her lungs. She landed with a thud on the floor, and her knife flew out of her hand. Her head throbbed. She could already feel the blood coating her hair, running down her neck. She bit her lip to keep from screaming.

*"Destra!"* Killian shouted from the other side of the cave, but Aoife easily blocked the spell, then forced him to his knees, his hands and ankles bound by invisible rope. Aoife stalked toward Ember, lowering herself to the ground so they were eye to eye.

"You will come back to the palace," she hissed. "You will

kiss your grandfather's boots and beg for forgiveness." She grabbed her chin and yanked it up, forcing her to look into her eyes. "You will do your duty. Either you obey, or Theo dies."

"I would rather die," Ember hissed, yanking her chin from her grasp and spitting in her face. "I would rather die than turn into whatever you've become."

Ember couldn't help the cry that escaped her as her mother slapped her across the face. She yanked her from the ground, digging her fingers into her arm as she dragged her across the cave floor.

"You do not have a choice in the matter." Aoife smiled. "After I have taken care of your friends, you will go home and stay in your room until you've figured out how to behave like a princess." She let go of Ember's arm, binding her wrists. "After that, I'll figure out what to do about Theo and the rest of them."

*Maeve. Fen.*

"No!" Ember shouted—an angry plea.

Aoife laughed. "You cannot escape f—"

Fate. Ember knew that's what she was going to say, but the words died on her lips before she could get them out.

"Get away from her!" Rowan screamed, blood splattering against the stone and across Ember's face. She stood wide eyed as Rowan pulled the knife from the side of her mother's neck, blood running down her pristine ball gown, pooling on the floor beneath her. She dropped within seconds, gasping for air as she reached out a hand for Ember, for help.

Ember's bottom lip trembled as she took a step back. "I hope your final breath is spent thinking about every breath you have taken away," she whispered. "May the gods have mercy on you."

Blood spilled from her neck, and within minutes, she was gone. The spell around her wrists broke the moment her heart stopped beating, but all she could do was stand there, covered in blood, staring at the woman who had given her life. Killian ran to her, wrapping her in his arms as she tried to breathe.

Rowan paled, the knife falling from her hand and clattering against the stone floor as she took a step back. The sound ricocheted off the vaulted ceilings as her eyes met Ember's, and something in her seemed to crack as her friend's eyes fell to the body crumpled on the floor.

"I-I'm sorry…" Rowan's voice broke as her bottom lip trembled. "I'm so sorry. I didn't know what else to do. She looked like she was going to…" Her voice trailed off as she glanced toward the blood pooling around her feet and then squeezed her eyes shut, tears streaming down her cheeks as she took a shuddering breath.

"You did what was necessary," Ember whispered, grabbing her friend's hand and squeezing tightly. Her hand shook, and the only sound that could be heard was a steady dripping of water from the cave ceiling.

"We need to go," Killian said, as he squeezed Ember's shoulder. "They'll come looking for her soon."

Ember took a breath and gave him a nod, and the three of them dragged Aoife's body to the edge of the pool. Ember shoved her in the water, watching as she sank into the bottomless hole. How fitting that her mother would meet her end in the same water that claimed her father ten years ago.

"You don't have much time left," Rowan said, as she grabbed the knife from the ground and handed it to Ember, blood wiped clean. "If I know anything about breathing potions, you've got minutes at best before the effects wear off." Rowan wrapped Ember in a hug, and Ember squeezed her tight.

"Be safe," she whispered.

"I always am," Rowan replied with a half-smile. "I'll see you soon." And then she sped off back into the tunnels.

"Take the rest of the potion," Killian said, as they walked

back to the edge of the water. "We should just barely make it, but someone will come looking for her eventually."

Ember stuck the knife in the holster and fished the vial out of her pocket, feeling her heart shatter as she pulled it out.

"It's broken," she whispered. "It must've shattered when I hit the floor."

Killian bit the side of his lip as he slid off his jacket and kicked off his shoes, leaving only his slacks and white button up. "Then, I suppose we'll have to swim fast," he replied, very matter of fact. "Make sure there's nothing in that bag that you can't leave. We don't need the extra weight while we're in the water."

"Killian, I can't go in there," Ember replied, as she shook her head. "It's too far. I won't make it."

"Do you trust me?" he asked simply.

"It's not about trust it's about—"

"Do you trust me?" he asked again, grabbing her wrist tightly, fire burning behind the smoke in his eyes.

Ember nodded, swallowing dryly. "Of course I do."

"Then, empty your bag."

Ember complied, kicking off her shoes and making sure her holster was secure on her thigh. She dug through her bag, tossing out books and clothes that she didn't need. She stopped when her fingers grazed the tiara, and she plucked it from the bag, running her fingers along the runes carved into the antlers.

She dropped it into the pool and watched as it sank.

The stone was cold under Ember's feet, even with socks on. They had to be far enough underground that they were under the mountain, and Ember didn't even want to think about how cold the water would be when they dove in.

"Do you trust me?" Killian whispered again, gripping her hand.

Ember took a steadying breath as her eyes met his. "With my life."

And then they jumped.

The icy water enveloped her, stinging her skin as she struggled not to gasp. They swam deeper into the depths, kicking harder than she ever imagined possible. Soon, it leveled out into a long tunnel, and they pushed further and further, as fast as they could go. Ember felt her arms grow heavy, and her chest began to burn. She looked at Killian, eyes wide as she grabbed at her chest.

*"Air,"* she signed.

He didn't wait or ask permission, just grabbed the back of her neck and pressed his mouth to hers. He let out a breath, pushing air into her lungs as he held her tightly, lingering only until she was okay to continue swimming. She wished so desperately that they could stay like that just a little while longer.

They pushed ahead, Killian giving her breaths of air when she felt like she was running out, and soon, she could see a pin prick of light in the distance. Her heart beat wildly in her chest as she pushed hard, every muscle in her body aching as she moved the water with her arms. They neared closer, and Ember realized she wouldn't make it—she needed another breath. She looked over at Killian and signed again.

Killian's eyes darkened as he shook his head.

*"It's gone,"* he signed.

Ember's pulse raced as they pushed harder, faster, tacking toward the light, at what she prayed was the surface. Her lungs burned, legs aching as she pushed them through the water. They felt more like weights and less like propellers now. Spots started forming in front of her eyes, and her panic worsened. She was going to pass out. She was going to drown. Killian pulled her, yanking her with him, but she knew she was weighing him down. She yanked her arm away from him and pushed forward, but he began slowing down in front of her, eyes widening as he turned back to her.

He clutched his chest, legs slowing as he tried to push

himself forward, and his eyes locked on Ember's, then they fluttered closed. The invisible chord at her chest rattled, vibrating wildly as she swam for him, grabbing him by the arms and kicking as fast as her body would carry her toward the streams of light breaking through the water far above them.

Ember felt like her chest was on fire, the saltwater burning her eyes as she kicked harder. The light was getting closer, and Killian had gone limp in her arms, making it even harder to haul the both of them through the icy water. Just when she thought she might not make it, another arm grabbed her wrist, then a second took Killian's, and she was speeding for the surface faster than she ever imagined possible.

Her head broke through the surface of the water, and she sucked in breath as quickly as she could, gasping for air as she coughed up the water that had trickled into her lungs. Killian's head broke through the surface a second later, body still limp, and Gaelen carried him to the edge of the lake, hoisting him up on the edge of the rock.

Killian's lips were blue, and he laid on the ground unmoving. Ember's bottom lip trembled as she hovered over him, checking for a pulse she knew she wasn't going to feel. She started pressing on his chest, over and over in the rhythm she had learned in a first aid class at school in Galway.

"What the bloody hell happened?" Fen cried, as he raced toward her, eyes widening as he hit the ground by his best friend's head.

Odette was beside him a moment later, eyes wide as she gripped Fen's hand. Ember felt the back of her head throb where it had hit the stone wall, and she could feel the warmth of blood trickle down her nape. Fen's face turned pale as he looked between the two of them.

"Em, what happened?" he asked again, this time quieter.

Ember didn't answer as she turned to Gaelen. "Help

him!" she cried, tears streaming down her face, mixing with the salt water on her skin. "Please help him."

Gaelen rushed to his side, kneeling as she laid her hand on his chest. "Tilt his head back," she commanded, as she unbuttoned his shirt, exposing the scars littering his unmoving chest, "and open his mouth."

Ember did as she was instructed, tilting his chin up and head back, then gently opened his mouth. He was cold—too cold—and Ember gripped his hand tightly.

Gaelen worked methodically, mumbling a spell over his chest as her hands moved in small circles. Ribbons of magic fell from her palms and sank into his skin, and Ember could see it swimming under the surface toward his lungs. Gaelen shifted her weight to his head and continued the circles over his mouth, until small streams of water swirled past his lips and turned to mist in the air. She continued for several minutes, expelling all the water from his lungs, and Ember held her breath as her hands began to shake.

After what felt like an eternity, Gaelen sat back and took a shuddering breath. Killian still laid there, eyes closed and unbreathing on the stone floor, and Ember felt her chest begin to crack.

"He's not breathing," she whispered. "Why isn't he breathing?"

"I've expelled all of the water," Gaelen breathed, "but I can't put the breath back in his lungs."

Fen let out a strangled sob next to her, burying his face in his hands as bile rose in her throat.

*He can't be dead.*

Light flickered out of the corner of her eye, and little wisps began to circle her wrist and hand. Her magic seemed to vibrate in her veins, and that tether at her chest thrummed wildly as the wisps formed a glove over her skin. She laid one hand on his bare chest, gripping the pendant around her neck with the other as words in the Old Language echoed through her head.

Ember almost jumped out of her skin when fire licked at her palm. Her eyes shot open as she stumbled back and held her hand up. The flame wasn't like anything she had ever seen. It wasn't orange or red—it was so blue it was almost white, a flame so hot it could probably melt steel. The little blue wisps seemed to encircle the flame and her hand, and the fire quickly settled until it was just a bright light burning against her palm.

She laid her hand back on his chest, and the glow seemed to radiate all around his torso and into his arms. The magic pulsed through her fingertips, and she could feel sweat begin to drip from her brow.

"It's not working," Fen whispered, voice hoarse as he hovered by his best friend's head. "It's not working."

Ember ignored him, focusing on the voice that seemed to be chanting inside of her, making her chest rattle as the tether between her and the two boys tightened.

But he was right—it wasn't working. Her magic wasn't strong enough, couldn't carve deep enough within him to make his heart beat again. He was cold—so cold—and her fire wasn't warming him.

A small hand touched her shoulder, and she turned to see Theo smiling behind her.

*Together.* He seemed to say while he gripped her shoulder tightly. Maeve sat on the other side of her, laying a small hand on top of the one that was settled on Killian's chest. The white fire seemed to grow, encompassing both of their hands like—

*A star.*

Suddenly, Killian's eyes shot open, and he let out a gasp, and it was the most beautiful sound Ember had ever heard. Her chest shook as she sobbed, and she threw herself on top of him, wrapping her arms around his neck.

417

"You're alive!" Fen shouted, grinning widely as he wiped the tears from his cheeks, and patted his friend on the back.

"You say that like you're at all surprised." Killian grinned, teeth chattering as the color began to come back to his cheeks.

"It was touch and go there for a moment," Ember breathed, as she took a shuddering breath.

"Are *you* okay?" Killian asked, leaning in close as he touched his forehead to hers. His skin tingled against hers, warmth blooming her chest as he rubbed her cheek with the pad of his thumb.

"I am now." She nodded.

He kissed her forehead, leaving his mouth lingering there for just a moment.

"Don't ever scare me like that again," she whispered.

Fen cleared his throat, and Ember felt her cheeks turn crimson. "We have a lot to talk about when we get home." He frowned, and Ember found herself laughing for the first time in days.

They were in a cavern, the two caves connected by the underwater tunnel. Plush grass lined the floor, stalactites hanging down from the ceiling. The mouth of the cave was at least two stories high, and Ember could see the stars from where she sat. She breathed in the night air, thanking the gods she would get to count the constellations again.

"I told you we'd see them again." Killian smiled.

Ember grinned as they made their way to the fire Fen had going, a pot of tea and some stew boiling over it. They sat around the fire, sipping tea and relishing in the quiet crackling as their eyes grew heavy. The Merrow had brought supplies, and several had taken the Fae children home. Blankets lay across the grass, several of the little ones already asleep, huddled up together around the fire.

"We thought it would be best to spend the night here," Fen whispered, as he tossed them each a blanket. "We can rest and make our way home tomorrow."

*Home.*

Ember smiled, laying her blanket on the ground as her eyes grew heavier. Theo curled up beside her, and soon, he was snoring. Ember couldn't help the smile that took over. They were safe and whole, all in one piece, and they would never have to return to that cold chateau or stuffy castle ever again. A weight settled in her chest as visions of her mother flitted through her mind—blood pouring on the floor, the woman who gave her life taking her last breath at her feet. She held Theo's hand as his eyes grew heavy, and he gave her a very gentle squeeze.

*I'm here.*

Killian laid down beside her, lacing his fingers through hers as he laid on his back, one hand behind his head.

"I'm here," he whispered. "You can talk to me or not talk to me, but I'm here."

Ember stared at the ceiling of the cavern, her eyes beginning to droop, until sleep finally consumed her.

She had no dreams that night.

# CHAPTER 40

# TO BE LOVED IS TO BE KNOWN

"Out of all of the stupid, rash, irresponsible things you have done, this one has to take the cake."

Ember opened her eyes, sunlight pouring in from the mouth of the cavern, and a tall man stood in front of their fire. Ember bolted upright, reaching for the knife still strapped to her thigh.

"Siris!" Maeve squealed, bounding across the cave, and leaping into her brother's arms.

Osiris held her tight, squeezing her as he closed his eyes. "Hi, Maevie," he whispered.

"Do you think if we had any other options," Fen asked, as he kicked out what was left of the fire that they had left burning from the night before, "we wouldn't have used them? This was time sensitive."

"You could've talked to me," Osiris said, as he set Maeve back on the ground, fixing them all with a pointed stare. "Do you have any idea what you've done?"

"I saved my sisters," Fen said, as he pointed at Ember and Maeve, "along with a dozen other children. You've barely said two words to meet since you got home. Why would I ask you for help?"

Osiris rolled his eyes, pinching the bridge of his nose. "You're such a feckin' child," he hissed.

"Well, at least I don't run away from my family just because things get hard."

Osiris looked like Fen might as well have slapped him. He quickly shook away the shock, clenching his jaw as his nostrils flared. "Now is not the time, Fenrir."

"It's never the time, is it?" Fen replied. "How did you find us anyway?"

Osiris fished his phone out of his back pocket and tossed it onto the grass in front of them. Fen picked it up, and a map was on the screen with a blinking dot. Fen's jaw went slack, and he narrowed his eyes at his older brother.

"I've been working on this app for two years," he mumbled. "How did you finish it?"

"You're not the only one in this family with an affinity for technology." Osiris almost grinned. "I finished the code weeks ago, just to give myself something to do, something else to think about. When I woke up last night and saw that you were gone, and that my tracking spell wasn't working, I decided to give it a go." He shrugged as he stuck his hands in his pockets. "It gave me your last known location, and then this morning when I checked again, it had updated. Likely when you were finally through the wards."

"What are you," Fen mumbled, "some sort of secret genius?"

Osiris shot him a grin. "Oh, it's not a secret."

Ember narrowed her eyes at the oldest Kitt. "How did you know there were wards?" she asked, hand grazing the handle of her knife.

Osiris shifted his eyes, the muscles in his jaw tensing.

"You know about the city, don't you?" Ember asked.

Osiris sighed, sitting down in front of the dying fire as he nodded. "There's a group of us who have been working on tearing it down from the inside, brick by brick." He looked at

Fen, concern in his eyes now. "A rebellion of sorts. You don't understand what you've gotten yourselves into."

*"A few months ago, Collum started receiving letters from someone. He was giving them inside information, but something spooked him."*

Her conversation with Rowan played on a loop in her head. Could this be who she was communicating with? Could she have been working with Osiris all this time?

"Maybe not," Fen shrugged, "but at least we're together again. We can handle it."

Osiris sighed as he bobbed his head. "I love the confidence, little brother," he breathed a laugh, "but this is so much bigger than you can fathom."

They cleaned up their makeshift campsite, packing away the blankets and cooking utensils, and set everything on the edge of the lake for the Merrow to come back for. Osiris's words kept ringing in Ember's ears, and the dread about what was to come settled in her stomach, like a stone dragging her to the bottom of the ocean.

Theo wrapped his hand around hers, smiling as he gave it a gentle squeezing.

*I'm here.*

After snatching his bracelet back from Fen, Osiris Echoed everyone to the entrance of Heksheim, then they all took the Echopoint home. There were ten Vala children in total, each of them scared and quiet and looking like they might wither away right in front of them. Ember's stomach did flips as she walked up the drive toward the Kitts' house, and she was very thankful she hadn't eaten anything for breakfast that morning.

Osiris opened the door, and everyone walked in, the small group of children huddled together without saying a word. The house was deathly silent, but mumbling could be heard in the den—two men and a woman. Eira, Otto, and… someone else Ember couldn't quite place. Fen must've heard them too because he suddenly looked like he was going to pass out.

"I am so dead," he mumbled, his face ashen.

Ember took a step behind the boys as Eira stormed in the room, just to be safe.

"Fenrir Kitt, I should skin you alive!" she shouted, a frazzled look in her eyes. "How do you think I felt when I woke up and found you gone?"

"Me?!" Fen exclaimed. "Osiris was gone too!"

"Your brother is not sixteen years old with a curfew!" she replied, pointing a finger at him, nostrils flaring. "Just wait until your father gets ahold of—"

The word got caught in her throat as she sucked in a breath. Maeve peaked out from behind Fen, a giant grin on her face as she ran toward her mother. Eira sank to her knees.

"Mummy!" Maeve shouted, grinning from ear to ear as she wrapped her arms around her mother's neck. "Mummy, I'm back!"

"Maevie," Eira sobbed, her chest shaking as she held her daughter close. The wailing grew louder, and soon, Otto was running into the room. He gasped, tears welling in his eyes as he wrapped Eira and Maeve in a hug, and no one said a word as tears slid down his cheeks as well. Della barreled into the room, like just the sound of Maeve's voice echoing through the house called to her. She leapt onto the little girl, nuzzling her head under Maeve's chin. Maeve wrapped her arms tightly around her neck, and Ember watched as she whispered into the Cat Sidhe's ear—something only for the two of them to hear.

"How did you find her?" Eira whispered, as she looked at Osiris.

"It wasn't me." He shrugged, a smirk playing at the corner of his mouth. "It was those four eejits." He pointed behind him as he rolled his eyes. "I found them in a very precarious cave this morning."

"Cave?" Otto asked, brow raised.

"Ember love," Eira said, as she stood up, furrowing her brow, "what are you doing here?"

Ember squeezed Theo's hand, touching her cheek where Collum's knife had sliced her open with the other. "Um," she stuttered, "it's a long story."

Otto cocked an eyebrow at Fen. "The four of you have some explaining to do."

"And who might you all be?" Eira asked, as she peaked around the corner where the group of children were huddled.

"I would love to know the answer to that as well," a deep voice said from the door leading into the den. Captain Balor's auburn hair was perfectly trimmed, the top swept to the side and his beard neatly groomed. His emerald eyes bore holes into the four of them as he cocked a brow, crossing his arms over his chest.

"We called Captain Balor this morning when we realized both of you were gone," Eira said, noting all of their shocked expressions. "We were just about to send out a search party. You had us worried sick."

Ember sucked in a breath. She didn't know that she would ever trust anyone in the Guard ever again, but especially not a captain.

"Siris, go get your sister and the children something to eat," Eira said, then pointed at Odette, Ember, and the boys. "You four," she commanded, "into the den."

Ember glanced at Osiris—a silent plea.

"You can trust him." He nodded. "He's one of us."

*One of us.*

Ember wasn't sure if anyone could truly help, not anymore.

The sixteen-year-olds walked into the den, Otto and Eira close behind, and Ember made her way to the cozy chair by the fire. She nestled into the plush seat, hugging her knees to her chest, and sank into a comfort she hadn't felt in months. Killian and Fen sat on the couch, Odette in the chair opposite Ember, and Captain Balor stood by the fireplace, leaning on the sturdy mantle as the flame lit his face.

"Start at the beginning," he said.

Ember took a breath and told them everything.

She told Captain Balor about her mother and how she always assumed she had drowned at sea like her father had. She told him about moving into Lothbrok Manor, her father's home. Killian told them about finding Collum and his uncle in town and how they began to suspect that he was involved with the missing children. Captain Balor nodded his head, brow furrowed as he listened, nostrils flaring slightly when they mentioned Collum.

And then Ember told them about Torsvik. Otto's eyes widened as she talked about the chateau, how she and Theo were whisked away without any warning. She told them about the town hidden behind the mountains on the northern coast of Ellesmere and about the Jarl that reigned there. Her throat tightened when she talked about the dungeons and how she found all of the children huddled together in a cell, Fae and Vala alike. She left out the part about Aesira, something told her that was information she needed to keep close to her chest for now.

She glanced at Odette, leaving out the part about the villagers, the crow insignia and Elowyn Quinn being alive. She talked about the ball and their plan to get the children out, then how it all went to shit when they were caught by Collum. She traced the gash on her cheek as she took a shaky breath, then told them about how her mother had found them.

She closed her eyes as her mind reeled—the memory of her mother's lifeless body on the cave floor forever burned behind her eyes.

Tears streamed down Eira's face as Ember recounted it all, but they weren't tears of sadness—not fully. Righteous anger radiated off the woman, rolling off her skin like waves as she clenched her jaw. Anger for Maeve and what she had been through, trapped in a dirty dungeon in the belly of an ancient castle. Anger for Fen at the danger he had been put in. And as their eyes locked, she knew it was anger for her too. Anger at her mother for putting Ember and Theo in danger—risking their lives for the "greater good."

Captain Balor nodded as he blew out a breath.

"Are you going to go get him?" Fen asked, his face set in anger.

"It isn't that easy," Captain Balor replied, as he shook his head. "If Collum had been turned so easily, who's to say there aren't more in my ranks? No, we need to tread carefully."

"The wards there are different," Osiris said, as he stepped into the room. "You can only get past them with a Torc specifically keyed to enter them. The standard issued bands won't work"

Eira furrowed her brow. "And how exactly do you know this?" she asked under her breath. Osiris's cheeks colored red as he looked away from his mother's stare.

"Is your Torc not standard issued?" Fen asked, as he turned to look at his brother.

Eira's eyes went wide as she looked at Osiris.

"I'll explain later, Mum," he whispered, like a little boy caught with his hand in the cookie jar.

"It will take some time to take inventory of his magic," the captain continued, "and of any armies he might have. Even with his magic as weak as you say, I don't know who he might have to help him. But now that he has been caught, I imagine the children will be safe again. He'll just find another avenue."

Ember swallowed dryly. He would come after her again now that he knew where she was and that she was alive. She didn't doubt that for a moment. She would just have to be ready when he got there.

After taking all the kids' statements, as well as Osiris's, Captain Balor took the children back to their homes, escorting Odette as well, letting Osiris know he would be back to talk more in depth with him later. Theo wandered back into the den not long after, curling up on the oversized chair next to

Ember. All of the boys—Killian, Fen and Theo—quickly fell asleep, and Ember took her chance to squeeze out of the chair and slip out the back door.

The moment her feet hit the dirt, she hurtled toward the barn, slinging the doors open and racing down the open corridor. She skidded to a halt in front of the familiar stall and slid open the lock, gently nudging the door open. Maia was curled up in a ball in the back corner, and Ember crept quietly across the layer of hay on the ground.

Maia's head popped up, lavender eyes widening, and Ember could've sworn she grinned. She tackled Ember to the ground, purring and chirping and nuzzling her snout into Ember's hands.

"I'm back now," Ember mumbled. "I won't ever leave you again."

They walked together to the front of the house, and Theo was on the porch waiting. He still looked tired, but the kind of tired that couldn't be reconciled with a good night's sleep. His eyes were dark, but hope flickered somewhere in their depths. Ember sat beside him on the porch, Maia lying quietly at their feet.

*"Now what?"* Theo signed, then rubbed Maia's belly. She purred as he nuzzled the bottom of his leg.

Before Ember could answer, the front door opened, then closed. Ember almost expected Killian or Fen to come out, but instead, Eira stood in front of them, softly smiling as she folded her hands in front of her.

"I'm so sorry about your mother," she whispered. "I can't imagine the pain you both are feeling."

"Thank you," Ember whispered, as she fought the tears threatening to spill over. "It's been... a lot to handle. But I think we'll be okay." She would have to be okay, would have to figure out how to push through this for Theo.

This loss didn't feel like it did before, not like the loss of her dad. It wasn't only the death of a parent that she was

427

grieving, but the death of a dream she had kept locked away in her heart since she was six years old. The death of the idea she had of her mother and who she was. The death of a peaceful childhood. It was a new wound, one carved into the scar tissue of the old ones. A death of the girl she once was.

"We're here," Eira breathed, as she looked at them both, "for whatever you need. We're here." She turned to go back inside, to leave the two to themselves, when Ember stood up quickly, one step toward her.

"I had a mother," Ember choked out, "at one point. I loved her very much." Ember steadied herself as she breathed. She didn't know how to separate Aoife from the mother she knew as a small child and the flawed person she had seen in that cave. "She took care of us because she had to, because it was her duty. She took care of me because of a prophecy she was hoping to fulfill for the greater good." Ember's eyes welled with tears as they meet Eira's. "But you have loved me from the moment I walked into your home, baggage and all, without question. You fed me because you loved me. You gave me a room because you loved me. You bandaged my wounds and scolded me when I did something wrong. You took all my broken pieces and held my hand while I put myself back together again. You never tried to fix me, never acted like I was broken. you never had any ulterior motives. You were more a mother to me in a single year than she was in a lifetime, and you only did it because you loved me."

Eira's chest shook, bottom lip wobbling as she blew out a breath. Tears rolled down Ember's cheek as Theo stood and held her hand.

"Can I come home?" Ember whispered, bottom lip quivering. Theo squeezed her hand as she steadied herself. "Can we come home, Mum?"

Eira wrapped them both in a hug, sobbing into their hair as she kissed Ember on the head. Theo's grip on her hand relaxed until he let go altogether, wrapping both arms around Eira. Ember had never seen her mother hug him. Had he ever been hugged by a mother before?

Eira took a step back, rubbing the sides of their faces as she smiled. "You can *always* come home."

EMBER LOUNGED in the den with Fen and Killian that evening, tucked into her chair with one of her favorite books, the latter two playing a very serious game of cards, when a knock sounded on the door.

"I'm getting very tired of surprise visitors," Fen grumbled, as he laid down a card, taking a swig of his Moon Cider. Ember listened as the front door opened, and she could just barely make out the voice of a man in the other room. A few moments later, Eira poked her head into the room and gave the trio a tight smile.

"Killian love, your father is here."

Killian's face paled, and Ember could feel the tether at her chest tighten. They all made their way into the foyer where Magnus Vargr was impatiently tapping his foot, a sneer painted on his face as he adjusted the long coat hanging down to his calves.

"Come back soon, love," Eira said, as she kissed him on the head and quickly exited the room

"We're going home, Killian," he said, as the trio walked into the room, not even giving Ember or Fen a second glance. "Your uncle is waiting for us."

Ember watched as Killian's throat bobbed, the muscles at his jaw tensing. Magnus's eyes drifted to Fen, then to Ember, and the smile painted across his face made her stomach sour.

"Lovely to see you made it home," he said, his grey eyes

looking so much colder than Killian's as they bore holes into her.

Ember nodded but didn't reply as Killian took a slight step in front of her.

"What does he want?" Killian almost hissed, magic sparking at his fingertips.

"You made quite the mess last night," Magnus replied, too calm for Ember's liking, "embarrassed him terribly. You made him a promise—made this family a promise—and he would like a *word* with you."

Ember's heart sank. What had Killian done?

He stiffened, hands flexing at his sides as he gave his father a nod. He turned to Fen and Ember and gave them both a half smile. "I'll see you at school," he said and then turned to walk out the door.

"I don't like him," Fen huffed, as he stuffed his hands in his pockets, and Ember nodded her head. She was overwhelmed with joy to be home and back with her family, but she couldn't help the guilt that seemed to crawl through her chest, like her freedom had simultaneously sent him to the gallows.

THE FAMILY PACKED around the dining room table that night and feasted on everything Eira could get her hands on. Theo smiled as he signed with Osiris, some conversation about their favorite comic book series that Ember had never heard of, and Fen prattled on about their adventure at the Ostara ball, even when Eira looked at him like she might kill him.

"I ate an ancient cow!" he screamed through bites of potatoes. "And the whiskey was—"

Eira shot him a look, and Fen's face paled.

"I-I'm sure it was very lovely," he continued, as he sank into his seat, "although I'll never know because I did not partake in such an abhorrent drink."

Otto chuckled as he shook his head, patting his wife's hand and mumbling something in her ear that made her blush. He ruffled Theo's hair and signed something, asking how he liked the food, and Theo's grin continued to grow.

Maeve smiled as she ate, joining in on the conversation and laughing at her brothers as they fought over the last scone. But there was a shadow there that only Ember seemed to notice. It flitted across her face when she thought no one was looking, as she rubbed the fading bruises on her neck and wrists. Ember recognized that shadow. She had watched it in the mirror when she was six years old, watched as it burrowed into the cracks in her chest ripped open by grief.

Maeve was suddenly older—something in her had shattered in that dungeon, and Ember wasn't sure if she would ever be the same. She smiled at Ember, and Ember smiled back. The difference between her and Maeve, though, was that Maeve would not be left to navigate this alone.

*I'm here.*

"We're very glad to have you home, Mo Chroí." Otto smiled as he turned to Ember. "I hope you know how much we've missed you." Otto glanced at Theo. "Both of you."

Theo had never had a father—not one that was alive. The idea that he would never know their father felt like a knife to the heart every time she thought about it. But then Otto looked at him—really looked at him—like he hung the moon, and Ember thought maybe Theo would finally have a wonderful father, even if it was different than he had imagined.

Ember had been worried that she would never be close to Otto, that he could never fill the emptiness that was left when her father took his last breath. But the longer she sat at the Kitts' dining room table, the more she watched Theo with

431

Otto and the love he already had for a boy he had only just met, the more she realized that they weren't meant to fill the holes or fix the brokenness. They inhabited places in her heart that she wasn't aware were there, carving out their own spots and repairing the damage life had left her with. Eira and Otto would never replace their parents, but maybe they weren't ever supposed to. Maybe this got to be something new—a fresh start. Maybe this was what love was—to carry grief in one hand and gratitude in another.

She always assumed that there wasn't room in her heart to love another family, not after losing hers. She didn't want anything to take away the love she had for her parents, so she fought against anything that might threaten that.

But this family, her family, didn't take away any of the love she had for her parents. It didn't replace it, it simply added to it. More love. Not different, not less, not divided, just multiplied.

"Mum, are there any peas?" Fen asked, as he finished off the last of his roast.

"Of course not," Eira huffed, as she shook her head. "Ember hates peas."

Ember bit the inside of her cheek as her smile grew.

Maybe to be loved was simply to be known.

## CHAPTER 41
# NEW BEGINNINGS

S everal weeks had passed, and Ember was sitting in the den with Eira and Otto. Theo was lying on the floor with one of his books, and Fen was teaching Maeve how to play some obscure card game he had learned on the internet. It was peaceful—a kind of peace she never imagined she would feel again. She laid down her book and sat up a little straighter.

"I've been doing some thinking," Ember announced.

Eira set down her sewing project, and Otto laid down the paper he was reading, both eyes now on her.

"I was wondering if that offer was still open?" She bit her bottom lip, her stomach coiling into tight knots.

Eira's face lit up, tears pooling on her lower lash as she grinned.

"Of course, Mo Chroí," Otto whispered. "Of course it is."

"Would I have to change my name?" she whispered, instinctively grabbing the pendant that hung around her neck. Her name was the last thing she had of her father, the last thing that tied her to him. It wasn't something she thought she could ever let go of.

"Of course not, love," Eira sniffled. "You can add our name onto yours or discard it entirely and keep your father's name." She stood up and walked across the room, sitting beside Ember and taking her hand in hers. "Either way, you are ours, fully and completely."

"Would the ceremony still work if I'm not a Kitt?" she whispered.

"Mo Chroí," Otto smiled, "you will be ours whether you take our name or not. It won't change anything. Not the adoption or the binding ceremony, and certainly not how much we love you." He looked down at Theo and smiled, adding, "*Both of you.*"

"And if you're worried about your familial rune," Fen grinned, "that's not how that works, either."

Ember furrowed her brow. "How does it work then?"

Otto let out a gruff laugh. "When a magical adoption takes place, there is a special ritual that is done. It's a little more than just a few signatures on a piece of paper. It's the forming of a new bond." Otto pulled a worn out pendant from his pocket and handed it to Ember. "When a magical adoption takes places, your familial rune isn't replaced, you simply just add a new one."

Ember traced the runes, feeling the rough edges rub under the pads of her fingers as Otto continued.

"A new bond is created, a second familial bond. It isn't meant to erase your family. Your family just grows."

Ember was sure she looked insane with the way she was grinning. Tears rolled down her face, and she didn't bother to wipe them away. She looked down at Theo, a hopeful smile on his face.

"*What do you think?*" she signed.

Theo rolled his eyes with a grin. "*What are you waiting for?*"

"We would be honored," she whispered, as she grabbed his hand and squeezed. "We would be honored to be your children."

The room was filled with laughter and joy. Music seemed to play from every inch of the home as Eira flicked her wrist, and Otto scooped Maeve up and began dancing through the halls with her. Eira wrapped Ember and Theo in a hug and soaked both their shoulders with tears as she whispered promises against Ember's tangled hair. Otto threw Theo up on his shoulders, and she listened to her brother laugh like she had never heard him do before. They joked and talked and made plans for the future, and Ember was certain nothing could ever get any better than this. She sank into her chair, watching as her family settled into their nightly routine, a new nightly routine, and an intense wave of peace settled over her like a blanket.

*We're home.*

"THEA!" Maeve squealed, as she swung open the front door. Ember's face lit up as the woman walked into the kitchen. Her coffee-colored hair hung in waves over her shoulders, decorated with several braids, and her emerald eyes twinkled as she smiled at Ember.

"Thea," Ember breathed with a grin. The woman wrapped her in a hug and she choked back the tears that were already brewing.

"I heard you had quite the adventure." She winked. "Are you doing alright?"

"We're getting there." Ember smiled. Every day was a little easier than the last. The longer she spent in the Kitts' warm home, the more the dark cloud hanging over her seemed to dissipate.

"And this must be Theo!" Thea beamed, as the little boy

grabbed Ember's hand with a grin. "It's such a pleasure to meet you."

Theo gave her a shy nod, gripping Ember's hand a little tighter.

"Nervous?" Thea asked with a wink.

Ember blushed as she bit her lip, looking down at Theo. "Maybe a little."

"I have something that should help with that," Eira said, as she poured piping hot tea into a mug and handed one to Ember and another to Theo. In the other hand, she held a potion bottle. She quickly popped the top off and poured the contents into both teas, twirling her finger above the liquid to stir. Ember watched the silver swirl around with the amber like a pool of starlight. "Calming drought," Eira whispered, as she kissed her forehead. "For the nerves."

Ember nodded as she sipped the drink and immediately felt herself relax, every molecule that was vibrating in her body slowing to a leisurely stroll. Theo seemed to feel the effects too because his grin widened, his grip on her hand loosening.

"Shall we?" Thea asked, as she nodded to the other room.

Eira, Ember, and Theo followed her into the dining room and sat at the table. Otto joined them, followed shortly by Maeve and Fen. Fen took the seat beside Ember, squeezing her hand a few times and giving her a reassuring smile.

"Now to clarify for the record," Thea began, as she sat a pen and parchment on the table. "We are here for the finalization of the adoption of Ember Moira Lothbrok and Theodore Avery Lothbrok to Otto and Eira Kitt." She smiled at the family as they nodded enthusiastically, Eira already wiping stray tears from her cheek.

Thea nodded with a smile. "And, Ember, have you two thought about whether or not you will be taking the Kitts' name?"

Ember fidgeted in her seat as bit her lip and looked

around the table. Her eyes met Otto's, and he gave her a small nod with a reassuring smile. She took a deep breath as she tapped her finger on her knee and looked over at Thea.

"You could hyphenate it," Thea offered, as she smirked, "and then you could use whichever name you wish."

"That sounds lovely," Ember replied. Her voice was steady, but nerves still rolled around in her stomach.

"Perfect." Thea nodded with a grin.

Ember met Eira and Otto's eyes, both of whom looked like they couldn't be any happier than they were in that very moment. Her heart rate settled as Theo grabbed one hand, and Fen squeezed the other again, giving her a look of his utmost approval.

"Will she still be my sister?" Maeve asked, as she bounced on her knees in her seat. "Will Ember still be my sister if we don't have the same exact last name?"

Otto scooped her up into his lap and kissed her forehead. "Aye, Mo Chroí," he laughed. "Family is so much more than blood and a last name."

*The blood of the covenant is thicker than the water of the womb.*

"Before we can get to the paperwork," Thea continued, "the bonding ceremony has to be completed. Have you decided where you want to have it?"

All eyes turned to Ember, who didn't realize until that moment that she was supposed to have a place picked out for this elusive ceremony.

"Um…" she stuttered, "I think I would like to have it in the den." The den, in front of the roaring fire, was where she first thought maybe this would all work out. She felt at peace there, surrounded by her family, and she couldn't think of a better place to solidify her place here.

Thea nodded and flicked her wrist, shuffling the pile of papers into a neat stack, and stood quickly from the table. "Shall we?" she asked and motioned for everyone to follow her into the cozy den. Thea stood in front of the fireplace and motioned for the family to join her. They placed themselves in a circle, leaving the middle open.

Ember's heart beat furiously in her chest as she willed her hands to stop shaking. She shifted her weight back and forth, trying to do something with the sudden amount of energy that was suddenly bubbling inside of her.

Apparently, the tea had worn off.

Theo grabbed her hand and squeezed.

*I'm here.*

"Ember, Theo, please come and stand in front of me," Thea said gently, as she touched her arm and moved them to the center of the circle. "Now, Eira, hold Ember's forearm, and, Ember, do the same."

Ember's eyes met Eira's, and it took everything in her to hold back the tears. Eira's eyes were misty as she smiled.

"Otto, please do the same with Theo's arm." And he did, giving them both a gentle squeeze and a soft smile that eased Ember's nerves.

Thea didn't have to tell Ember and Theo to grab hands. He held tight to her, like she was a lifeline, and she did the same. Thea hovered her hand over their arms, and a silver cord spun from her palms, wrapping around Ember's skin, and hugging it like a glove. It felt warm and safe, like crawling into bed the night before Yule and reading till you fell asleep. The cord wrapped around Eira's and Otto's arms as well, and Ember could feel the magic already beginning to thrum through it.

"I will say the incantation, and when I'm finished, the cord will disappear, and the bonding ritual will be complete." Thea smiled. "Are you ready?"

Ember took a shaky breath and nodded. "I'm ready," she whispered. Her eyes met Fen's, and he gave her a teary smile, quickly wiping his eyes with the back of his hands.

Thea closed her eyes and spoke the incantation like she

had known it since birth, and goosebumps ran up and down Ember's arms.

*"Two families, bound together.*
*Strength for storms that they might weather.*
*May the Gods of Asgard guide their steps,*
*Fill their hearts where they have kept*
*An open spot for love to fill,*
*and move mighty mountains so they might be still.*
*Not bone of my bone,*
*Nor flesh of my flesh,*
*But a child of my heart with each dying breath."*

Not just an incantation. It was a prayer to the gods.

Magic swelled around them, the cord wrapping around their arms with an intensity Ember had never felt. Her heart thumped heavily in her chest as the light grew brighter, and just as quickly as it began, it was gone, the chord disappearing and leaving Ember's wrists tingling. Eira wrapped her and Theo in a tight hug, tears soaking the tops of their heads as she sobbed.

"Welcome home, Mo Chroí," Otto whispered, as he hugged the both of them. "Welcome home."

Sometimes it happens that new beginnings don't come at once, but at last.

Life settled back into something akin to a normal rhythm. Ember settled back into her room, all her things already waiting for her from when Fen and Killian had retrieved them

439

from Maize. She put books back on the shelf, unpacked all her clothes, and put her father's journal safely in her bedside table drawer. Looking around the room made her heart ache. It was a glimmer of who she had been before grief had decimated her so thoroughly for the second time in her life.

It would never be like it was, not entirely. The gaping wounds would heal, but the scars would remain—a stark reminder of the pain she had endured, and would endure until her dying breath. She shook away the thought and unpacked the rest of her things, then made her way across the hall.

Theo's new room was right beside Fen's, and he couldn't have been happier. Out of all the things he acquired from their father, the most notable was his love for reading. Books were stacked on every surface he could find, pulled no doubt from the library down the hall. Ember rolled her eyes with a grin as she leaned on the door frame.

Theo was sprawled out on his floor, bags still halfway packed, three books open around him as he laid on his stomach. He jumped when he looked up and saw her, a sheepish grin on his face as his cheeks colored red.

"Three at a time? Really?" she asked with a laugh.

*"How will I ever read them all?"* he signed back, his grin growing.

"Don't forget to eat." Ember laughed, then pushed off the door and made her way downstairs. She walked outside, having had every intention of going to the orchards for a ride, but she stopped short when she saw Maeve sitting on the couch on the sprawling porch, knees pulled up to her chest as she stared at the setting sun. Della laid in front of her, curled into a ball and fast asleep. She hadn't left the girl's side in the week that followed their return, and Ember marveled at the bond between the animal and the little girl.

Maeve didn't seem to notice her walk up. The shadows of grief danced across her face. She was not the same seven-year-old who had been taken from her bed in the middle of the night. Grief had molded her into something no child should ever have to become.

"Mind if I sit?" Ember asked, as she walked over to her. Maeve gave her a quiet nod, and Ember sat down, chewing on the inside of her cheek. They sat like that for a while as Ember tried to think of something to say.

"Can I tell you a secret?" Maeve whispered, her eyes shining with unshed tears.

"Of course," Ember replied. "I won't tell a soul."

Maeve nodded as she took a shaky breath. "I don't think the gods are real," she whispered, "not anymore."

Ember furrowed her brow. "Of course they are," she reassured the little girl. "They gave us our magic, of course they're real."

"Then, where were they?" Maeve asked, as angry tears slid down her cheeks. "When I screamed for them at night, when all the little children cried, when I begged them to save us, where were they? Because they never came. They left me there, rotting in that cell. Loving gods don't abandon their children."

Ember felt her chest crack. She wanted to comfort Maeve, to assure her that the gods were there, that they always would be, but she didn't know if she believed it herself. Maybe they were real once upon a time, and maybe they locked themselves away when they saw what their magic had turned into.

Maybe they died a long time ago.

"I don't know if the gods are there or not," Ember shrugged, "but I know that you have a family who will never leave you. We will always find you."

"Every time I close my eyes, I'm back in that dungeon," Maeve continued. "When it's quiet, all I can hear is crying and screaming. I never knew the silence could be so deafening." She took a shaking breath as she bit her lip. "Sometimes I come outside just so I can hear something else, something happy," she whispered. "Does it ever get any easier?"

Ember stared at the sunset and sighed. She thought about the way she could sometimes still hear her father's screams in the quiet, how she could hear the whispers of the waves beating against their boat. She still had dreams of that night, of the pitch black and the way it wrapped around her like a cloak, sinking through her skin and into her bones.

"I don't know if it gets easier," Ember replied, as she shook her head, "but it does get quieter. You learn to make space to sit with it instead of trying to push it away. It's not fair, but this is a part of who you are now."

"I don't know who I am anymore," Maeve whispered, as she shook her head, tears rolling down her freckled cheeks.

"You are Maeve," Ember said, as she grabbed her hand. "You love to draw and sing and chase the sun. You are an incredible friend and daughter. You have a laugh that can fill up even the largest of rooms." She squeezed her hand gently as tears pricked her eyes. "You fight for those who can't fight for themselves, and you are the greatest sister anyone could ever ask for."

Maeve smiled as she squeezed Ember's hand. "We are so much more than what happens to us, right?" she asked, as she stared at the ground, resting her chin on her knees.

"If we decided to be." Ember nodded. "You might not be able to control what happens to you, but you can control how it shapes you. You can be both strong and soft—the two don't have to fight for space inside of you."

Maeve grinned with a nod, wiping the tears from her face as she dropped her legs over the side of the couch.

"I'm glad you're my sister, Ember," she whispered and wrapped her arms around Ember's neck.

"Me too, Maevie," Ember whispered back.

Maeve pulled away and grinned, and Ember's breath caught in her throat, eyes widening as she gasped. The light from the setting sun lit up her freckled cheeks, and her eyes shined like she had been given new life—a second chance. But they weren't the bright blue Ember had become so used to seeing. They had changed, forged in the fires of that dungeon where she had been forced to rebuild herself from the inside out. They were no longer the beautiful blue that the rest of the Kitts seemed to share.

They were fields of lavender... flecked with ash.


The End

# ACKNOWLEDGMENTS

**Braxton-** We have been through the ringer this year. We lost a child, and friends and family, and there were moments I was sure I wouldn't make it out. This year has been hard, and filled with more grief than I would ever wish on my worst enemy. But we did it, and we did it together, just like we do everything else. There is no one else on this planet I would rather go through hell and back with. Thank you for being my rock while we weathered these storms, and for always supporting my dreams. The Ellesmere Saga, and every future book, would not be possible without you. You are the ultimate "book boyfriend" and the blueprint for every love interest I will ever write. You are my home and greatest adventure; I love you more than the sun, the moon, and all the stars. Forever and Always babe.

**Linsey-** This book, quite frankly, would not have been possible without you. What started as a random meeting on a booktok facebook group, has turned into one of the greatest friendships of my life, even if we are separated by an entire ocean. I am so thankful for our late night brainstorming sessions, the hundred and one voice messages, and the unwavering support you've given me over the last year. The friendship we've formed is a once in a lifetime kind of thing, and I will never take it for granted. Thank you for being my shoulder to cry on and my partner in crime, I truly believe we were cut from the same cloth.

**Rosemary-** You are a force of nature, and someone I am so thankful to have on my side and in my life. It is so rare to find a friendship like we have- something steadfast that evolves over time. We have walked together through grief and joy and celebration and fire, and a hundred different milestones over the last ten years, and I am so beyond thankful or every moment. We have sat in the trenches together and celebrated on the mountaintops. We have had a hard year, but I cannot wait to see what the future has in store for us and our dreams, and I am so excited to chase them with you. I meant what I said before I walked down the aisle- I love you so much, friend.

**Ariel-** I am so thankful for our mini podcasts and brainstorming session, and always annoyed the voice messages on Instagram are only a minute long. Thank you for all of your support and letting me vent at all hours of the day, and for being such an incredible friend. Thank you or reading my first drafts and encouraging me to keep going, and for seeing my heart in everything I write. You are a one-of-a-kind friend, and I am so thankful to God every day that He brought us together. Now go write your book!

**Whitney-** Thank you for helping me bring my characters to life, and for accepting the fact that I will likely send you twenty different word documents because I think of things I need to change at three in the morning. You breathe new life into my stories and seem to always know exactly where I want to go with them, even when I can't think of the right words. I am so grateful for you, and I can't wait to see where the gang ends up because of you.

# ABOUT THE AUTHOR

Appalachian born author with a penchant for adventure. When Brittney isn't writing about magical schools and sarcastic Norse witches and wizards, she can often be found burrowed in her nest on the couch with her emotional support water bottle, reading Dramione Fan Fiction. Brittney lives in the East Tennessee mountains and spends her days chasing dogs, kids, and chickens around their small homestead with her husband. She loves to crochet, explore, and get lost down winding dirt roads. Drawn in Blood is the second novel in The Ellesmere Saga- born of her rich Norse, Honduran, and Irish family history- and she hopes to have the privilege of writing about magical worlds for the rest of her life. If you enjoy reading, writing, and incoherent rants, Brittney can be found on both Instagram and TikTok @bbrewerauthor for your entertainment.

Made in United States
Orlando, FL
03 November 2024

53421682R00274